New York Times and *USA TODAY* bestselling author **Caridad Piñeiro** is a Jersey girl who just wants to write and is the author of nearly fifty novels and novellas. She loves romance novels, superheroes, TV and cooking. For more information on Caridad and her dark, sexy romantic suspense and paranormal romances, please visit www.caridad.com

Debra Webb is the award-winning *USA TODAY* bestselling author of more than one hundred novels, including those in reader-favourite series Faces of Evil, the Colby Agency and Shades of Death. With more than four million books sold in numerous languages and countries, Debra has a love of storytelling that goes back to her childhood on a farm in Alabama. Visit Debra at debrawebb.com

Also by Caridad Piñeiro

Cold Case Reopened

Also by Debra Webb

In Self Defence
The Dark Woods
The Stranger Next Door
The Safest Lies
Witness Protection Widow
Before He Vanished
Finding the Edge
Sin and Bone
Body of Evidence
Dark Whispers
Still Waters

TRAPPING A TERRORIST

CARIDAD PIÑEIRO

THE BONE ROOM

DEBRA WEBB

MILLS & BOON

First Published in Great Britain 2021
by Mills & Boon, an imprint of HarperCollins*Publishers* Ltd
1 London Bridge Street, London, SE1 9GF

www.harpercollins.co.uk

HarperCollins*Publishers*
1st Floor, Watermarque Building,
Ringsend Road, Dublin 4, Ireland

Special thanks and acknowledgement are given to Caridad Piñeiro for her contribution to the *Behavioral Analysis Unit* series.

ISBN: 978-0-263-28352-5

0921

MIX
Paper from responsible sources
FSC™ C007454

This book is produced from independently certified FSC™ paper to ensure responsible forest management.

For more information visit: www.harpercollins.co.uk/green

Printed and Bound in Spain using 100% Renewable Electricity at CPI Blackprint (Barcelona)

TRAPPING A TERRORIST

CARIDAD PIÑEIRO

Thank you to all my friends at Liberty States Fiction Writers for offering your support and insights. A special thanks to Gwen Jones, Linda Parisi and Lois Winston for their hard work to keep Liberty States moving forward. Finally, lots of love to my daughter, Samantha, who is always there for me and is an amazing writer and photojournalist. *Saranghaeyo*, Samantha.

Prologue

King Street Station, Seattle, 10:16 a.m.

I need the perfect hostage.

Tucked behind the protection of the column, he watched the people coming and going in King Street Station, unaware of the danger. Unaware that he intended to grab one of them, and soon.

Peering around the edge of the column, he spied a young boy at a nearby kiosk. The boy, who was maybe six or seven, was focused on the shelves of candy before him, eyes wide in anticipation of a treat. His distracted parents, tourists if he had to guess from the expensive camera dangling around the man's neck and the map tucked into his back pocket, were a few feet away, their attention on a display of postcards, probably to commemorate their visit to Seattle.

He laughed, thinking about how it would be a visit they would never forget if he grabbed their boy. But parents could be overly protective when their kids were involved. If the two of them went crazy when he snatched the boy, it could all go south.

Still, if this was a video game, kids would score high

points for being fast, hard to control and too young to die.

A few yards away a dainty young thing stood chatting to an older man. She was pretty in that girl-next-door kind of way. Brown hair with caramel highlights was tucked up in a feminine braid and as she glanced his way, he noticed her eyes. Blue, but a blue so deep they were almost indigo. A man could get lost in those eyes. Angel Eyes.

He imagined grabbing her, but her body was toned and no matter how angelic she looked, something about her warned that she'd be scrappy.

Again, high points for that feistiness and beauty.

Not so many points for the old man with her.

He looked like an absent-minded professor with his tweed cap, sweater with leather patches on the elbows and silver-rimmed eyeglasses that made his eyes look way too big. The professor didn't seem feeble, but he didn't seem like a problem either.

I could take him, he thought until a tall, muscular man turned to speak to Angel Eyes and the professor. The man was fit and powerful looking but leaning heavily on a cane. He looked like a younger version of the professor. Enough to maybe be a son. This man could be major trouble, but trouble would definitely earn more points in any game.

A second later the man's phone rang. He held up a finger, turned and took a few steps away, probably for privacy during the call.

Perfect. This is my chance.

Chapter One

Seattle, 9:16 a.m.

It was a small step for most people, but a giant leap for Maisy Oliver as she hopped on the Seattle tour bus.

In the year since Maisy had made her mother a promise on her deathbed, she'd been scrimping and saving, planning on how she would leave the nastiness of her past and reach for her dreams of traveling and writing a blog about those travels. Maybe even a book one day.

Granted Seattle wasn't Paris or London or Rome, but her hometown was beautiful and as good a place as any to start on that dream.

And that dream had begun with a great new job that had allowed her to buy what she needed to start her blog and save money for the future.

Armed with a brand-new phone with the supposedly best camera ever and a small journal to take notes, she intended to share the many sights in Seattle on the blog she'd set up earlier in the week. Hopefully she'd be able to grow a following and expand her travels. A ferry across Puget Sound. The Woodinville Wine Country. Victoria in British Columbia.

Who knows where I can go from there! Even Paris,

she thought as she took a seat on the top level of the bus, bouncing her feet anxiously as the bus headed for the next stop on the tour: Pike Place Market. She intended to do the whole loop on the hop-on-hop-off bus before returning to each stop to take photos and notes. She hoped that the tour would give her enough information to line up blog posts for a few weeks while she planned her next adventure.

The bus lumbered to a stop at Pike Place Market, and Maisy snapped off a few photos of the large neon Public Market and Farmers Market signs and the clock above the entrance to the various shops and stalls. As she did so she took note of the people waiting to board the bus, especially the handsome man bracing himself on a cane next to an older gentleman who had to be his father. The two looked too much alike not to be related. In front of them were a man and woman with a young boy, probably tourists if she had to guess.

But then again, she was a tourist today in her hometown.

The people boarded the crowded tour bus and the noisy clamber of someone rushing up the steps drew her attention. The young boy with the family. Barely seconds later, the older man and his son came up the stairs, the younger man wincing with each step he took.

The man was fit, in excellent shape actually, and she wondered if it was some kind of sports injury as they followed the family up the aisle and took the two seats directly opposite her. The young man was on the outside seat, his father on the aisle beside her.

The older man smiled at her and she returned it since he seemed like a nice enough person. His son…too stoic and serious. Tense, especially as his father bumped his arm and jerked his head in her direction.

The man shot her a quick look and rolled his eyes before mumbling something to his father.

Really? she thought, her ego a little stung by what seemed like a rebuff. But not stung enough to avoid the older man when he pleasantly said, "Are you enjoying the tour, young lady?"

"I am, thank you," she said.

"Are you a tourist? I'm a tourist, but my son lives in Seattle," he asked, eyes wide behind the thick lenses of his glasses.

"You might say that," she said as his son murmured, "Dad, please."

EMBARRASSED HEAT FLOODED FBI Agent Miguel Peters's cheeks as his father tried his very obvious matchmaking with the pretty woman sitting across from them on the tour bus.

He'd told his father time and time again that he had no interest in a relationship right now. Or maybe even ever. As the supervisory special agent of the Seattle Behavioral Analysis Unit, his personal time was limited. He'd thought his father would be aware of what that took, considering Miguel's mother had been a renowned BAU profiler. One who'd paid for it with her life, cementing his decision to follow in her footsteps.

But as his father kept up the conversation with the young woman, he had to admit that his father couldn't have chosen better. Not only was the young woman beautiful, with amazing blue eyes and enticing girl-next-door looks, but she seemed bright and interested.

Caring as she patiently answered his father's questions and engaged him with some of her own.

"Are you enjoying your visit, Robert?" she said, and her glance skittered between his father and him.

His father likewise shot a look at him before he said, "I only just arrived a day ago, but I'm enjoying your hometown so far, Maisy."

Hometown? Miguel thought. *Great. More reason to encourage his father to continue with his matchmaking with Maisy. Maisy? What kind of name was that anyway?*

"It is lovely. That's why I decided to share it with people on my blog," the young woman said as the bus lumbered to their next stop at the Chittenden Locks. While some of the tourists on the bus hurried off, Maisy stayed back with the pair.

"Don't feel you have to stay with us," his father said.

She smiled—*She is even prettier when she smiles*, Miguel thought—and waved off Robert's suggestion.

"I'm going to stay on until the last stop at King Street Station and take some photos there before hopping back on for the other stops," Maisy said.

As Maisy stood to snap some photos, his father elbowed him again and murmured, "Perfect."

Like Maisy, his father and he had planned on staying on the tour bus until the station and then heading to the Chihuly Garden and Glass exhibition near the Space Needle.

Determined to avoid his father's meddling and the attractive Maisy, he turned his attention to the locks, which connected the salt water of Puget Sound with the fresh water of Salmon Bay. Boats were lined up to pass through the locks, which also provided safe passage for salmon to spawn.

Barely minutes later, the bus was in motion again and in just over fifteen minutes they were pulling up in front of King Street Station. Slower than usual because of his injury, Miguel hung back, allowing the family who had come on with Maisy at Pike Place Market to rush off. Maisy and his father went next, heading down the stairs with him following, the stitches in his leg pulling with each step. But he was determined to show his father that he was fine during this visit. Especially since his father had rushed out to Seattle when he'd heard Miguel had been shot.

As Maisy and Robert left the bus and strolled toward King Street Station, they started chatting again, Miguel tagging along behind them. When they reached the station, Maisy walked toward one side, probably to take photos for the blog she had mentioned, and his father trailed afterward, leaving Miguel no choice but to go with them unless he wanted to seem antisocial. Truth be told, Maisy probably already thought that, although if she had half a brain, she'd have seen through his father's obvious attempts to get them together.

When Maisy looked in his direction, he forced himself to smile and bear it. As he did so, he noticed one of his BAU members, Lorelai Parker, the assistant to the FBI's director, waiting by the chairs at one side of the station. He was about to go say hello when his phone rang.

His BAU director was calling. Olivia Branson was in Washington, trying to secure additional funding for their office, and probably needed some information from him.

He held up a finger, turned and took a few steps away, certain that he would need privacy during the call, and he wasn't wrong.

"Good morning, Olivia."

"I wish it were. Do you have time to talk?"

Miguel glanced back toward his father and seeing that he was busy chatting with the young woman, he took the call.

Chapter Two

Perfect. This is my chance.

He reached into his pocket, pulled out a black ski mask and yanked it over his face as he hurried around the column. As he moved, he dug into his knapsack and took out a collar bomb and detonator.

The professor looked at him when he approached, eyes blinking like an owl's, but he didn't move, making it way too easy for him to slip the metal collar over the man's head and snap it tightly into place. He wrapped the arm holding the detonator around the man's chest and held up his other hand to display his cell phone, his finger resting over the speed dial number to set off another bomb in the building.

"Miguel," the professor screamed. The old man's body trembled beneath his arm, and his knees seemed to give for a second before he straightened.

The man with the cane turned at the sound of his name. His face paled and fear slipped over his features before he schooled them.

Fear was good. It was just what he needed so they'd do as he asked.

"Don't anyone move or I'll blow his head off! Or blow the second bomb!"

MIGUEL'S BLOOD RAN cold at the sight of his father with the collar bomb around his neck and the wild eyes of the masked man holding the detonator and a cell phone.

He had to stay calm even as pandemonium erupted all around. People had realized what was going on and raced away despite the bomber's threat, screaming and shoving each other to escape the danger. But as others were running from the threat, he raced toward it to save his father and the young woman nearby who hadn't moved an inch.

"You don't want to see him die now, do you?" the bomber screamed out again and waved the cell phone in the air.

Those who remained, a much smaller crowd, froze in place or took shelter behind the banks of chairs scattered around the station. Most would be safe if the collar bomb went off, but who knew where the second bomb was located?

Not to mention that Maisy was just a few feet away from his father and the bomber. Definitely in harm's way if the collar bomb exploded.

And then there was his dad, who was looking at him with wide eyes. Pleading eyes. His face was pale, as white as new snow, ramping up Miguel's fear because his dad's heart was not strong.

Miguel raised his hands, and in a calm and practiced voice, he said, "You don't want to do this. You don't want to hurt anybody."

He inched forward, slowly, deliberately, intent on trying to move Maisy out of harm's way while gauging whether he could rush the bomber and take away the detonator. If he'd been one hundred percent healthy Miguel might have been able to do it, but he wasn't one hundred percent thanks to the bullet he'd taken during an earlier investigation. Plus, he wasn't sure if the detonator had a dead switch. He needed to get closer to see, but as he did so several police officers rushed in, guns drawn.

"Stop or I'll blow you all up. I'll do it, so don't push me," the bomber said and again waved the cell phone in a wild arc above his head.

With that motion and his closer physical distance to the terrorist, the skunky smell of weed wafted over to Miguel, increasing his fear because he was now also possibly dealing with someone who was high and not thinking rationally.

The bomber pointed at him with the cell phone. "You, Mr. Hero. The professor's son, right? Step back and take those pigs with you."

Miguel slowly reached for Maisy, but the bomber called out, "No, not her. I like her. She's really pretty. Makes me calm. You want me calm, right, Angel Eyes?"

Maisy nodded, held out a hand, palm up in pleading, and in a soft voice said, "Right. You need to stay calm. I know you don't want to hurt anybody."

The bomber laughed, a laugh that bordered on unhinged, and Miguel did as he asked. He slowly backed away until he was close to one of the police officers who had raced into the station. In low tones, he said, "I'm FBI. Supervisory Special Agent Miguel Peters."

The officer nodded to confirm he'd heard, and in a whisper, asked, "What do you want us to do?"

"Nothing right now. I'm sure my team will be arriving shortly," Miguel said, trying to process as much as he could about what was happening because something was off. The more typical MO for collar bombs involved a demand for money, whether it was blackmail, a kidnapping or a bank robbery. So far, the bomber hadn't asked for a thing.

"Talk to us, man. What do you want?" he called out, trying to glean as much as he could not only from the man's actions, but from his speech. Was he a local? Level of education? Tattoos or other distinguishing features? Anything that could help in the situation or after…

He tried not to think about the after because that might mean his father was dead. Maybe the young woman as well as any of the people still trapped in the station, depending on where the second bomb was situated. He had to get those people out as soon as he could.

"What do you want?" he repeated because up until now the man hadn't said much.

"What do I want? Where do I start?" He gestured to the officers standing nearby, guns still drawn. "I want them out. All of them or I'll blow the place and kill everyone here."

The officer closest to Miguel peered in his direction, waiting for his instructions.

"How about you let the cops take all those people out of here so we can talk?" Miguel said, and motioned to the people huddled behind plastic chairs for protection.

"And why would I want to talk to you, Mr. Hero?" the bomber said.

Miguel pointed in the direction of his father and the young woman he'd only just met. "I'm FBI and you've got my dad and girlfriend right there. We're worth lots more to you as hostages than a bunch of scared tourists and some beat cops."

The man narrowed unhinged eyes, obviously considering what Miguel had said. Then his gaze bounced around the station, almost as if doing a body count to determine if Miguel, his father and the young woman were a good trade for the people and cops in the station.

But as the bomber did so, the sound of a television intruded from a nearby kiosk, drawing the bomber's attention.

THE BOMBER'S GAZE turned toward the television and Maisy thought, *This is my chance.*

But if she moved, the man might do as he said and blow the bombs in the station and she didn't want to be responsible for that. Too many people might be hurt, including the gentle professor she'd met on the tour bus earlier that morning.

They'd been chatting up a storm on the bus and after, as they'd arrived in the station. He'd been so kind, so friendly. Probably because he'd been trying to matchmake for his stoic son, who might be handsome if he ever smiled.

She couldn't leave the old man. She wouldn't be responsible for any more murder and mayhem like her father had done. Her father, a monster who even now controlled her life.

She had to focus and find a way to get out of this. Get the professor away from the madman.

Focus, she told herself as the bomber's attention was fixated on the television.

THE SITUATION HAD already hit the airwaves and various reporters and news crews had gathered around King Street Station, broadcasting coverage.

Behind the on-scene reporter advising on the hostage

situation, Miguel noticed Lorelai standing nearby. He hoped that she had alerted his team to what was happening so that they would be on their way to the station.

"Good afternoon, this is Drew Anderson reporting for Seattle One News. We're here at King Street Station, where a bomber has taken an older man hostage with the use of what authorities are calling a collar bomb. The suspect also claims to have a second bomb that he will detonate if his demands are not met, but no demands have been forthcoming so far. Authorities estimate that there are still about two hundred people trapped in the station. At this time, all trains coming and going from the station have been locked down while authorities deal with the situation."

The reporter paused and looked off camera and a second later another familiar face came on air.

"We have with us Caitlyn Yang, the Seattle Behavioral Analysis Unit's police liaison. Can you give us a report on what the FBI is doing about this hostage crisis, Caitlyn?"

"Thank you, Drew," she said with a nod to the reporter before facing the camera. "At the request of the local police, the FBI team is coordinating with them on the case. One of our agents is inside with the bomber—"

Before she could finish, Richard Rothwell, a candidate for state senator, pushed his way into camera range. As the reporter turned his attention to him, Rothwell looked directly into the camera and said, "We don't negotiate with terrorists—we outsmart them. I have a plan on my website and never fear, Seattle, I'm here for you because I'm not afraid of the sociopath inside our beloved King Street Station. But please stay home for your safety because I care about *you*." He emphasized the latter by imitating Uncle Sam pointing into the camera.

Miguel gritted his teeth and tried his best not to roll his eyes at the candidate's grandstanding, which would do nothing to help the situation. It might even make things worse with the unstable unsub.

"Listen to him, will ya? Sociopath," the bomber said with a wild laugh. "The Feds, boys in blue and some pompous politician won't stop me." He waved the cell phone around in the air again and said, "If I don't get what I want, I'll blow this place."

"Why don't you tell me what you want," Miguel said.

"What I want? Let's start off by taking down our inept government and judicial systems. How about prison reform? No bail requirements. Free housing and medical insurance for all."

Miguel couldn't really consider them demands because there was little anyone could do to satisfy them in order to defuse the situation. But he had to try.

"I get it, man. Government isn't really there to help us, right? But I'll try to help you. Just tell me one thing you want right now."

For a second the bomber lowered the hand with the cell phone and in a steadier voice he said, "I want a ham sandwich."

"I can do that," Miguel said, but a breath later a powerful explosion took out the balcony above them, raining down bits of concrete, marble and other debris. He was knocked off his feet with the force of the blast.

Stunned, ears ringing, Miguel sluggishly got to his knees. His father, the bomber and the young woman were all lying flat on the floor.

Fear knotted his gut. *Did the collar bomb go off as*

well? he thought and tried to process whether there had been more than one explosion. Whether there had been a second one that he hadn't heard over the force, concussion and confusion from the first blast.

But then the bomber slowly sat up, the detonator still in his hand. He looked dazed, confused. Possibly surprised by the blast.

Did the second bomb go off accidentally? Miguel considered, but then another thought hit him.

This is my chance.

Chapter Three

Miguel shot toward the trio, but his wounded leg gave out beneath him. Frustrated, he pushed on, scrambling, almost crawling to get to the bomber. To get to the detonator before the unsub blew the collar bomb.

To his surprise, the bomber dropped the detonator, struggled to his feet and rushed away.

Miguel went to give chase, but his wounded leg tripped him up again and he knew it was useless. He grabbed his cell phone and called Madeline Striker, the most senior of his agents. She answered, but his ears were still ringing so badly he could barely hear her, and his father was starting to move, propelling fear through his gut again.

"Don't move, Dad. Don't move," he shouted as his father rose to a sitting position and fear ripped through him. *I can't lose him. Not like this. Not like Mami*, he thought, angry with himself that he couldn't do more.

"Miguel. Are you okay?" Madeline said, her voice garbled and indistinct beneath the ringing in his ears.

"Unsub is heading out of the northwest corner of the building. About five foot eight. White. Brown eyes. Wearing blue jeans, black T-shirt, stained gray sweatshirt, black leather gloves and a black ski mask. Copy?"

he asked, and at her affirmative reply, he rushed to kneel beside his father.

"Are you okay, Dad?" he asked, but even as he did that, he kept his head and used his jacket sleeve to secure the detonator without touching it to preserve any fingerprints.

Maisy slipped to their side, but he held his hand up to stop her. "Don't come any closer. Not until we can defuse the bomb."

She nodded and knelt there, smudges of dirt on her face. Bits of debris in her hair and on her clothing. There was an angry abrasion above one eye where she might have been struck by shrapnel from the blast. "Are you okay?" she asked his dad, concern ringing in her tone.

His father nodded and Miguel again admonished, "Please don't move, Dad. We've got to get this off you."

"Please stay still, Robert. It will be okay," Maisy said and took hold of his father's hand.

Miguel crouched beside her and laid a hand on her shoulder. It felt fragile beneath his hand, but he sensed there was steel in her core as she said, "I'm not leaving him, whoever you are."

"FBI. Supervisory Special Agent Miguel Peters," he replied.

She looked at him with those amazing blue eyes the bomber had fixated on and with a nod, she said, "You'd best get to work, then."

He knew she wouldn't relent and leave his father's side.

"Are you feeling all right, Dad?" he said, worried about his father's heart condition.

"I am," his father said without moving a muscle.

"Don't worry about me and do your job. It's what your mother would have done."

Even with the gamut of emotions roiling through him, Miguel knew his father was right and didn't waste any more time arguing with them.

He rose and peered around the station, taking in the destruction. A large chunk of the balcony several yards from them had been blown away and pieces of it were scattered all about the main floor of the station. The force of the blast had overturned chairs in the area and shattered nearby windows. Luckily, the explosion hadn't ignited a fire.

The people who had been trapped in the station had rushed out when they realized the bomber had fled, and there was now an eerie silence inside the space, interrupted only by the continued ringing in his ears.

There were a great deal of police and his team had to get to work, Miguel thought as he limped to get his cane, picked it up and then slowly moved toward the door, the wound in his leg sending shards of pain through him with each step.

Almost as if they'd heard him, his team members walked in together with an officer from the Seattle Arson Bomb Squad. They waited for him by the entrance to the station, not wanting to contaminate the scene.

He walked over, careful not to disturb any evidence. When he reached them, he slipped into his role as the SSA, pushing back his personal fear for his father. His frustration at not being one hundred percent, which had let the bomber escape. He looked at Madeline and said, "The unsub?"

Madeline shook her head. "No sign of him, Miguel.

But the news crews were filming all around the area and we're hoping they might have caught something. We've also asked SPD to get the names of everyone who just left the station so we can interview them."

"Good work, Madeline," he said.

The Seattle ABS officer, Mack Gonzalez, was a friend he'd worked with before. The officer said, "We need to keep the area clear until I defuse that collar bomb. Don't worry, Miguel. I'll take care of your dad."

"Is the perimeter secure? Have you checked for any other secondary devices? Car bombs to take out the first responders?"

"Perimeter is secure and we're checking all vehicles in the area. HAZMAT team detectors haven't picked up anything toxic. Same with radiation detection, so for now, we're good," Mack confirmed.

"Got it, Mack. We'll stay out of your way while you work on my dad, and thank you," Miguel said and clapped the other man on the back of the padded uniform.

He glanced at his team, knowing that they would be itching to move on this case, but there were a number of things they could work on back at the BAU offices. The local ABS and police would collect the evidence and forward them the information they needed to develop their profile and round up additional information to help the locals with their investigation.

"Lorelai, you were here earlier, correct?" he asked.

At that, Liam McDare, their tech guru, went to slip an arm around his ex-fiancée, but she scuttled away from him.

"I was waiting for a friend. I called the team as soon as I saw what was happening. Director Branson as well," she said, always the efficient administrative assistant.

"Excellent. I was on the phone with Olivia so I'm glad you've told her what's occurred. Now I need all of you to get going. Nicholas and Madeline, start interviewing those in the station and get to work on a profile. FYI, no real demands were made before the explosion. Except for a ham sandwich."

"A ham sandwich?" Nicholas asked. As his top serial killer profiler, Miguel relied on Nicholas's expertise in that area and others.

"That's the only real request. The rest weren't realistic demands," Miguel said with a nod and turned his attention to Madeline, who had both personal and professional experience with kidnappers. "Collar bombs like this one are often used in kidnapping or blackmail scenarios. Run those ideas up the flagpole with Nicholas."

He looked at the other agents gathered there. "Liam and Dash. Please round up any video feeds you can from the reporters, CCTV, ATMs, surveillance cameras. Get any images available and run them through facial recognition. Do background checks. You can get David to help you as needed. You know the drill."

"Got it, boss," Dash said with a dip of his head and his team sprang into action, rushing out the door to handle the tasks Miguel had assigned.

Miguel returned his attention to where the ABS officer was kneeling beside his father and the young woman. The officer was in the large, padded suit worn by bomb squad specialists, making him appear gargantuan compared to his father and the woman.

As carefully as he had walked over, Miguel returned,

cautiously picking his way past any possible evidence. He scanned the area for any details that might clue them in to the identity of the bomber and his MO. He picked out small bits of paper that looked like dynamite stick wrappers, as well as pieces of black leather and blue wire, but that didn't make sense. The dynamite and leather pointed toward a briefcase bomb, which was at odds with the box secured around his father's neck. That looked like it contained pipe bombs.

Two different MOs? he thought as he neared the trio.

"You really should leave," Mack said to the young woman as he worked on the collar of the bomb.

"I'm not going to leave Robert alone," Maisy said and vehemently shook her head.

"He's not alone. Mack and I are here," Miguel said, his heart pounding in his chest as the ABS officer fiddled with the hinged collar around his father's neck, trying to unlock the device. The officer muttered something under his breath, but a second later he snapped the collar open and eased the bomb away.

"Something wrong?" Miguel asked, hands jammed on his hips as he watched the officer slowly rise with the bomb and take a few steps back.

Mack shook his head. "I don't think this detonator is connected, but I need to take this somewhere safer to finish defusing it."

Miguel nodded. "You'll give me your full report when you have it?"

"You got it, Miguel," Mack said and walked off, cradling the device as delicately as if it was fragile crystal.

Relief slammed through Miguel that his father was safe, and he stepped closer to him and the young woman. "Let's get you both outside and have the EMTs check you out." He lent his father a hand so he could stand and so did Maisy. Together they helped him to his feet.

As she rose, she looked down and said, "You're bleeding."

Miguel risked a quick glance at his leg where blood had leaked through his khaki pants, probably because he'd torn open the stitches in his leg. "I'm okay. Let's get out of here," he said, and it occurred to him then that he didn't really know who she was.

He held out his hand. "And you are Maisy…?"

She shook his hand. "Oliver. Maisy Oliver," she said, providing him the last name he'd wanted.

Outside, the EMTs quickly got to work, checking all of them for signs of injuries from the blast as well as his dad's heart and Miguel's leg. Luckily, he'd only torn open a couple of stitches. It was easy enough to repair the minor damage.

As the EMT worked on him, his father stood nearby, worry etched onto his features. "Your mother would have been so proud of you today. So proud of the way you handled that situation."

"Thank you, Dad," he said, but braced himself for what he was sure would follow.

"But you risked your life today. Again. It's why I'd hoped you'd choose a safer kind of work. I don't want to lose you too."

Miguel bit his lip and looked away, fighting back an angry retort. His father only wanted the best for him, and he understood his pain. He'd lost the love of his life to the FBI and a terrorist's bullet. But nothing his father said would change his mind about his choice of career. He did it for his mother and for people like Maisy and his father, who didn't deserve to be in harm's way.

"I understand what you want, Dad. But this is my job."

He turned to Maisy and said, "Thank you so much for staying with my father. That was very brave."

"I had to do it," she said and smiled at his father.

He nodded and pressed on. "You're a witness, Dad. I'm going to have to get you settled in a safe house until we catch the bomber. Same with you, Maisy, especially since he's fixated on you for some reason," he said.

Maybe because she's gorgeous, he thought. With the danger over he could fully appreciate the woman standing before him. A beautiful woman with a spine of steel, tons of courage and a truly caring heart based on what he'd seen of her so far.

MAISY KNEW WHAT it was like to be the object of an unhinged person's obsession.

Her father had terrorized Washington State with a series of explosions at various logging and construction sites. During her father's reign of terror, he'd maimed and injured many people and killed one at the site of his last bombing.

He'd been in prison for the last fifteen years and she'd been free of him for most of that time, but then a year ago he'd found her and started a second reign of terror with weekly letters and collect phone calls from the prison. She'd sent the letters back unopened and refused the calls, but that hadn't stopped him.

Much like she worried that the FBI agent was right that the bomber wouldn't stop with her either.

But she refused to let her life be controlled by another terrorist the way her father had dominated her.

"I had to stay with your father, but I'm not going to a safe house," she said and tilted her chin up at a determined angle.

"My dear, it's what makes sense," Robert said and laid a gentle hand on her arm.

"I'm not going, Robert," she reiterated, but his son was having none of it.

"You *are* going. If not into a safe house, we'll provide you with a protective detail," Miguel said.

"And who's going to make me do it? You? Will you protect me?" she challenged, hating how childish it sounded, but determined to be the master of her own fate. It had been her primary goal since her mother's death to finally follow her dreams.

Miguel tapped his chest. "Yes, me, if I have to. You're a material witness and I need to keep you safe," he said, his brown eyes almost black with worry. Bits of dust clung to the thick waves of his dark hair and she unconsciously reached up to brush them away, but then jerked her hand back. The gesture would have been too intimate. One of lovers and not the strangers they were.

"You?" she repeated and blew out a harsh breath. "You'd really agree to be my protective detail?"

With a huff, he jammed his hands on his hips and firmed his jaw. "You got a problem with that?"

She had lots of problems with it, especially now that she had the time to realize what a devastatingly handsome man he was and how hard it would be to ignore that and the gentle and caring way he'd dealt with his father. But a bomber was on the loose and fixated on her, and they were lucky that no one had been hurt today.

They might not be so lucky again if Miguel didn't do his job. And because she knew that they didn't have time to waste, she nodded and said, "I'll go. But only with you. And I have to call my boss and let him know what's happening."

Miguel seemed taken aback by her acquiescence but clearly wasn't going to argue. He held a finger up and said, "I need to make a call to get the safe house ready for my dad."

He limped away for a moment to phone and as he did so, Robert laid a hand on her arm. His touch was soothing, and for a too brief moment, it reminded her of her father's gentle touch before she'd discovered he was a monster. "He means well, Maisy. Don't judge him too harshly. He's just been…determined since his mother was killed."

"And you've been worried for him," she said and covered Robert's hand with her own, once again sensing the earlier tension between the two men.

Robert nodded and his silver-rimmed glasses slipped on his nose before he pushed them up with his index finger. "I have. It was so hard to lose my wife. I don't want to lose him as well. He's all I have left."

She didn't have time to respond since at that moment Miguel returned to their side. "The safe house will be ready shortly. We should go get your things from the hotel, Dad. Same for you, Maisy. We can run by your place so you can pack a bag."

She tipped her chin up, trying to stay strong even though fear was starting to blossom through her now that the adrenaline was wearing off. But she couldn't let the fear take over. After all, that was the purpose of terrorism, wasn't it? To create fear.

"I'm ready," she said, but for what, she didn't rightly know.

Chapter Four

Dashiell West watched over Liam as the man worked on cleaning up the images they had been able to get from the CCTV cameras in King Street Station. In addition to sharpening the images, which were not the best quality, Liam had to address the position of the bomber's body. Once Liam had done that, adjusting the lean, tilt and orientation of the photo, he'd use another program to adjust those variables in order to create an image which could be run against their various databases.

Dashiell walked over to another desk, where David Dyson, their twenty-something intern, was combing through various video feeds and surveillance cameras in the area, trying to locate other images of the bomber which would not only help identify him, but maybe also pinpoint the direction he might have gone after the explosion. "How's it going?" Dash asked.

David looked up at him and smiled, his brown eyes gleaming with intelligence and determination. David had lost a beloved uncle during a convenience store robbery and that had prompted the young man to begin a career in law enforcement instead of going into the private sector with his skills.

"Doing great. I've got one video so far and am using

the location of that camera to look for others in the area," David said.

Dash clapped the young man on the shoulder. "Good job. Keep it up."

"You know I will," David said, his grin broadening with Dash's praise.

Dashiell walked away to his own desk, but as he did so, he noticed Lorelai Parker walk in. Liam's head immediately turned in the direction of his ex-fiancée. When Lorelai had called earlier to advise about the situation, Liam had almost been beside himself with worry that she was in danger. It only confirmed to Dashiell that there were still strong feelings there on both sides despite their canceled nuptials. He also suspected that Lorelai wouldn't still be so angry if she didn't care for Liam.

But their little wedding drama had to take a back seat to finding the bomber, he thought as he walked over to where Lorelai was handing an envelope to Madeline and Nicholas.

His fellow agents had been busy setting up their board at one end of the office space, placing a grainy photo of the bomber at the top of the board along with some preliminary information.

Like the fact that there had been no real demands at King Street Station and nothing else so far, including a claim of responsibility for the bombing.

He didn't need to be a profiling expert like Madeline or Nicholas to know that made no sense.

He approached them, wondering what was in the envelope.

"Seattle ABS sent it over. Agent Gonzalez asked that you give him a call," Lorelai explained and then quickly left the room, but not before shooting a quick glance to where Liam was working.

"What have we got?" Dashiell asked and peered at the photos that Nicholas removed from the envelope and spread out on the surface of the worktable.

"Whoa, bomb collar. Looks like the one from the Pizza Bomber case," Dash said, recalling the incident where a pizza delivery man had been murdered during a bizarre bank robbery several years earlier.

"It does. The second bomb appears to have been concealed in a briefcase," Madeline said and gestured to the photos of the bits and pieces that the local police had gathered at the scene, including a fairly large piece of a briefcase handle.

"Let's get Mack on the line and see what else he's got to say." Dash dialed the ABS officer using the speakerphone and the man answered on the first ring.

"ABS Officer Gonzalez," he said.

Madeline, being the most senior agent between them, took charge. "Special Agent Striker here, Mack. We got your package. What can you tell us?"

"Madeline. Thanks for any assist BAU can give us on this. The bomb around Miguel's dad's neck looks like a copycat of the Pizza Bomber, but it's different in several key elements. For starters there was no timer or secondary way to detonate the device. Also, no dead switch. Plus, the detonator wasn't actually connected to the pipe bombs inside the metal box holding them."

Dashiell, Madeline and Nicholas all shared a look.

"Is it possible that the connection came loose while the bomber was transporting it?" Madeline asked.

"Possible, but unlikely. There were fuses in the bombs, but the detonator wire was too short to reach the battery that would send the charge to the fuses. Either we were lucky he wasn't a good bomb maker or he didn't intend to blow the device."

"But they were real pipe bombs?" Nicholas pressed.

"Definitely. Filled with gunpowder, BBs and nails. If they had gone off, they would have likely killed whoever was wearing it and the shrapnel would have injured anyone within yards of the bomb," Mack noted and plowed on. "We were able to get partial prints off the pipes, detonator and a handle. Also, some DNA that we're already processing."

Madeline pursed her lips and nodded. "What can you tell us about the second device? It looks like a briefcase bomb."

"Confirmed. We have a big piece of the handle as well as bits and pieces of the briefcase and the wire. Initial testing and other evidence indicate he used dynamite in the second bomb. Detonated it with a cell phone."

Nicholas shook his head. "Two different MOs in one bombing. Atypical, isn't it?"

A long sigh came across the line from the ABS officer. "It is atypical. Not to mention that dynamite is highly regulated. Luckily, it was a small blast, and the briefcase was placed in a little-used location. Only superficial damage to the structure and even better, we had only minor injuries and no fatalities."

"Almost as if he didn't want to hurt anyone," Madeline suggested.

"It seems that way. We're sending both devices to the Terrorist Explosive Device Analytical Center at Quantico so they can confirm what was used and provide more information on the devices. ATF is also working on it."

"If TEDAC agrees, we'll have to track down who can supply dynamite in the area and who has access to it," Dashiell said.

"Bingo. In the meantime, we're waiting on BAU to give us a profile or anything else you can dig up to help. We'll keep you posted, as well," Mack said.

"Can you send us the info on the fingerprints and DNA samples? Pictures of the bomb pieces?" Madeline asked.

"Will do, Madeline," Mack confirmed and signed off.

Dash waited as Madeline crossed her arms and glanced at the team, her tall, athletic body in its dark blue suit canted at an angle. She was clearly assessing the information they'd just received, a deep furrow of worry across the brown skin of her forehead. "The object of terrorism is to create terror, so why do we have a bomber who makes no real demands, besides a ham sandwich?" she said with a chuckle and shake of her head. "And who doesn't seem to want to hurt anyone."

"Or is it an amateur?" Miguel Peters said as he walked in, his gait measured, the cane gone, almost as if Miguel thought using it was a sign of weakness. He'd changed into his standard white shirt, rep tie and dark suit. "What do we have here?" the SSA asked.

Madeline filled him in on what the Seattle ABS and PD had so far.

Miguel shook his head. "From the first I got the sense there was something off about the bomber. He didn't make his demands right away and when he did, they were way out there. We haven't received any kind of communication or manifesto, right?" His keen dark gaze skipped over all the members of the team.

"Nothing so far," Nicholas said and looked toward Madeline, who was the BAU expert on kidnappings.

"Nothing, and that type of bomb is one that's been used either in blackmail, kidnappings or bank robberies, all crimes that require precise and timely demands, usually for money," Madeline clarified.

"No real demands. No real detonator. No real injuries since the force of the bomb blast was minor despite the damage it did to the building," Miguel said and began to pace, his gait slightly stilted, as he tossed out the facts they had so far.

"Anything from the videos yet?" he asked Dashiell.

"Liam has images from the station and is working on them so we can process them against various databases. David tracked down video that had views of the bomber from a nearby source. He's searching for other videos in the area so we can possibly narrow where the bomber may have gone," he said.

Miguel nodded and jammed his fists on his hips. "My father and Maisy Oliver, the other key witness to the bombing, are both being safeguarded. I've got some preliminary testimony from them, but let's work with what we've got right now."

Miguel glanced past them as Liam approached, an almost guilty look on his face. "Boss, I've got something weird here," he said.

Liam glanced at Dash, obviously unsure about what he was about to say. "What is it, Liam?" Dash pressed.

Liam nodded and directed his attention to the SSA. "It's about Maisy Oliver."

Miguel's features hardened into stone, his lips in a grim line as he glared at their tech guru.

"What do you have for us?" Miguel said, his voice calm despite his tense body posture.

"I can't find her in the system before age fourteen. Her mother's missing history as well," Liam advised nervously, his gaze darting around the faces of the team to see how they were receiving the information.

Miguel peered at Dashiell. "Can you confirm this, Dash?"

He raised his hands to slow things down. "I was working on a tweak to our facial recognition system because we've got poor images of the bomber, not to mention the ski mask he was wearing."

Miguel dipped his head in acknowledgment. The tension in his body eased, but only somewhat. "I appreciate that. But can you work to confirm what Liam has uncovered? Find out what you can about any possible gap and let me know."

"Will do, Miguel," he said with a nod.

Miguel drew in a breath, nostrils flaring, and released it in a rush. "We've got our work cut out for us. Please get back to it and in the meantime, I'm going to speak to Ms. Oliver and see what she has to say about the bomber and those missing years."

MAISY HAD BEEN pacing back and forth in Miguel's apartment, trying to do what he had asked: recollect any details about what had happened before, during and after the bombing.

She walked to the windows of the skyscraper and looked toward the waters of Elliott Bay and beyond that, Puget Sound. Along the shoreline, assorted boats and ferries moved across the water to Bainbridge Island and other nearby locations while others pushed northward to Victoria in British Columbia.

Even as she stared at the beauty below, her mind replayed all the ugliness of that day. How she'd been standing there, chatting with Miguel's charming father, a retired professor of journalism. She'd been telling him about her new travel blog when the bomber had taken him hostage.

Shutting her eyes, she tried to remember if she'd seen the bomber before that. She vaguely recollected someone moving from behind a column. Slipping something over their face while slinging a knapsack off their shoulders.

The bomber, she realized, eyes snapping wide open.

The snick of the door lock had her whirling around in fear until she remembered that an FBI Agent was stationed at her door for protection.

A second later, Miguel entered and closed the door behind him. His entrance brought immediate peace, surprising her since they'd only known each other a few hours. But in that time, she'd come to know he was caring, honorable and courageous. Add in the fact that he was lethally handsome, and it was a potent, and possibly irresistible, combination.

But as her gaze met his, her earlier fear about being in danger morphed into a different one: he knew she wasn't what she seemed.

He walked over, his dark gaze locked on hers, assessing. Raising his hand, he gestured in the direction of the sofa and said, "Please. We need to talk."

Her gut knotted tightly, dreading what would follow. Dreading the past that she and her mother had tried so hard to outrun but which had chased them for the past fifteen years. Hoping to divert the discussion, she said, "I remembered seeing the bomber before he grabbed your father. He raced around a column without his mask for a hot second."

Miguel nodded and took the seat kitty-corner to the sofa as she sat. "Do you think you could describe what you saw? The shape of his face? Other distinguishing features?"

"Maybe," she said, a little reluctantly. It had been only a fleeting glimpse.

Miguel nodded and hesitated, almost as if searching for how to begin. Calmly, patiently, he briefly explained some of what his team was doing and finished with, "We're running the images through facial recognition. We also ran your image and did a background check. We got back incomplete results. I'm hoping you can fill in some information for me."

"Like?" she asked, well aware of where he was going and yet hoping to avoid it since it could only bring her pain as well as possibly his distrust.

He quirked a brow, seeing through her ruse. Despite that, he was composed as he said, "You know what we found. Or should I say what we didn't find. Care to explain?"

MIGUEL DIDN'T WANT to treat her like a suspect, especially considering how caring and concerned she'd been with his father. How strong to remain behind and calm him as Mack had worked to free his dad from the bomb. But until he heard from her about the gap in her history, she was now a suspect. That was the reason he'd kept out important details when he'd given her the rundown of what the BAU team had been working on.

As her almost violet gaze sheened with tears, she looked away, a sure sign of unease. Her hands were in her lap and laced tightly together. The knuckles white from the pressure.

"Maisy?" he urged, needing to hear the story from her lips. *Kissable lips*, he thought and forced away that realization. Beauty sometimes hid incredible malevolence. Not to mention that a relationship or where it would lead was not in his future.

"My mother and I moved from Woodinville to Seattle about fifteen years ago. When we did so, we changed our names because we wanted to rebuild our lives." A sniffle followed her words and she swiped away a tear.

Miguel leaned closer and laid a hand on her knee, wanting to offer comfort, but also wanting to know more. "Why, Maisy? Why did you have to change your names?"

Slowly, almost as if it pained her, she faced him with shattered eyes. "My name used to be Elizabeth Green. My father was Richard Green, the Forest Conservation Bomber."

Miguel widened his eyes, surprised by the revelation. "I'm well familiar with Green. Your father. My mother worked the case, and her profile was instrumental in helping to catch him."

"I'm glad she did before he could hurt anyone else. What he did…" She drew in a long breath and the words escaped her in a rush. "He was a monster, and we didn't know it, even though people thought we should."

Miguel remembered all the publicity about the bombings and the capture. It had turned into a media circus, almost as much of a big deal as the capture of the Unabomber. The press had hounded Green's family until they'd disappeared and now, he knew why.

"It must have been very difficult for you, Maisy," he said, trying to get her to relax and tell him more about the experience and the very odd coincidence. *A bomber's daughter being almost killed by a different bomber?* Maybe too much coincidence, although his gut was saying she wasn't involved in what had happened.

Maisy nodded and gazed down at her hands. "It was. Neighbors shunned us and our friends… You find out just who your friends are. In our case there weren't many. Almost everyone thought that my mother and I should have known what he was doing, especially my mom since she worked at the landscaping business."

Remembering the case, he said, "That's where your father assembled his bombs."

Maisy did a quick bob of her head. "It was, but my mother was in the office or at the register tending to customers. It was a successful business. She wasn't in the sheds where my father did his evil."

Miguel covered her hands with his and squeezed gently, touched by her pain. "I can't imagine how difficult it must have been for you. You were victims as much as those injured by your father's bombs. Was that when you decided to move from Woodinville?"

HIS HAND WAS warm on hers, the palm rough. He had long elegant fingers, almost those of an artist. His simple touch, one of caring, and his words of understanding, filled her with peace once more.

"It is, and since we were starting over, it only seemed right to change our names. The court was understanding and did it without much trouble. We tried our best to stay out of the public eye, working odd jobs. Barely making it. I managed to finish high school and college," she said, but his sharp investigator's gaze saw past what she was saying.

"But you've been in a prison as much as your father has, haven't you?"

She nodded and fought against the pinching of her throat to say, "He's controlled my life even though he's been behind bars for the past fifteen years. Especially in the last year since my mother passed from cancer. Somehow, he found out my new name and address. He's been writing and calling me almost every week."

Miguel applied gentle pressure to her hand again and as his gaze settled on hers, his eyes were a cocoa brown and filled with compassion. "I'm so sorry about your mom."

"Thank you," she barely eked out, the pain still too fresh.

"Have you responded to your father?"

She shook her head vehemently and the motion made her wince since she was a little sore from the impact of the bomb blast. "No. I want nothing to do with him. Nothing. I just want to get on with my life. With the dreams he stole from me."

Dreams of adventure and writing. The travel blog she had planned on starting with the photos from the bus tour. Which suddenly made her remember. "I was taking photos right before the bomber rushed out. I can send them to you if you'd like."

"I'd appreciate that," he said and spelled out his email address for her.

After she finished sending him the photos, he said,

"It's late. Almost dinner time. I'm not much of a cook as you can probably tell from my kitchen and fridge."

"Pretty empty," she said, much like the apartment in general. It was minimalist with little personality. Totally unlike the man sitting beside her, who radiated power and confidence with his very presence and made her want to learn more about him.

"I don't spend much time here. I'm usually in the BAU office. It's on the top floor of this building," he said and pointed upward.

It struck her as kind of sad. "You live where you work?"

"It's convenient," he shot back quickly, almost defensively.

She recognized the tone. She'd overheard it on the bus before his father had started talking to her and later, when the EMTs had been tending to Miguel's leg. His father had said that he wished Miguel had a safer job and she suspected that his father also wished Miguel would one day have a family. Something that wasn't going to happen to someone who lived to work.

"I didn't mean to be judgmental. You do something very important. You keep people safe," she said, appreciating the sacrifices he made as an FBI agent.

"And I promise to keep you safe and not just from this bomber. From your father as well. You can trust me on that," he said and slowly rose from the chair, grimacing slightly as he did so.

"How's the leg? Were you hurt during a case?" she asked.

"I was shot during a recent investigation and the leg's still a little weak. It's why I was using the cane for some extra support. Thanks to the explosion, the leg's sore again along with other parts of my body. You?"

"Sore," she said and rubbed the shoulder that had hit the ground hard when she'd been knocked off her feet by the blast. She was sure she already had a bruise.

"Then let's get you dinner so you can get some rest. How do you feel about pizza?"

"You can never go wrong with pizza," she said. Her mother and she had eaten it often because they enjoyed it, it was inexpensive and it provided them with left-overs for other meals.

"I'll order and go pick it up. Would you mind setting some places at the breakfast bar?"

"Not at all. I'll be waiting for you."

Chapter Five

Dinner with Maisy was turning out to be more than Miguel had expected.

She was smart. Funny. Passionate. That was obvious from the way she told him about her dreams to travel and start a blog detailing those experiences.

"Is that why you were on the bus tour?" he asked, interested in her and not just as a suspect, which worried him. He had no room in his life for entanglements.

"It is. I've been setting aside money each paycheck in the hopes of visiting other places, but I thought, why not start with Seattle? There are lots of people who haven't been here and it's a beautiful city," she said and finished her second slice of pizza.

"It is a beautiful city. I love the water and mountains all around. It's very different from where I grew up."

She smiled and tapped the tabletop, as if confirming something to herself. "I could hear a slight singsong in your accent and there's your name. Are you Latino?"

He nodded, took a bite of his slice and after he finished, he said, "I was born and raised in Miami. My mother was Cuban and taught me Spanish."

Maisy set down the third slice of pizza she had

grabbed and laid her hand on his arm. "You miss her, don't you?"

Miguel nodded. "I do. She was an amazing FBI agent. Intelligent. Brave."

Maisy shook her head, making him quiet abruptly. "You miss your *mom*. The woman who held your hand when you were sick and made your favorite dish for your birthday."

His throat tightened with emotion and for a moment, he almost couldn't breathe as the memories of his mother flooded back. The little things that mothers did, much as Maisy had so astutely pointed out. Things that his mother had done despite also being a top-notch FBI agent.

Much like you could also do, the little voice in his head said.

"She was an awesome mom," he choked out and set aside his plate, his appetite gone.

"I'm sorry," Maisy said and laid down her slice. "I didn't mean to bring back sad memories."

He shook his head. "Not sad ones at all. Good ones. Sometimes you forget the good because you're all caught up with the bad."

IF ANYONE UNDERSTOOD what it was to let the good memories get lost because of the bad, it was Maisy. "I get it, but sometimes the bad… It's impossible to forget those. To forgive them."

Miguel nodded. "Your dad. Was he a good dad?"

Maisy shrugged, trying to balance the way her dad had been when she was a child against what he'd become. "When I was little, he was always there. Caring. Loving. But as I got older, he became more and more distant. Harder. No matter what my mom tried he kept on pulling away and then we found out why."

"He'd become the Forest Conservation Bomber," Miguel said, voice flat.

His tone made her wonder if he also thought her mother and she should have known or at least suspected. "We didn't know. Didn't suspect. The landscaping business had been doing really well and we both just thought he was busy because there was so much to do."

Miguel hesitated, creating worry in her again, but instead he said, "Speaking of fathers. I should go see how my dad is doing. Would you like to go?"

She nodded. "I'd like that. It would be nice to see that he's okay. Plus, he had mentioned helping me with my blog, him being into journalism and all."

With that, they finished dinner, cleaned up and headed to the safe house, a room in a nearby hotel that was only a few blocks away. With Miguel's apartment being only a studio, there hadn't been room for both Robert and Maisy. Maisy couldn't help but notice that unlike the smaller hotel where his dad had been earlier, this one was bigger and obviously more secure. There were doormen at the front entrance and a security guard patrolled the lobby. Discreet cameras were visible in the lobby, elevators and hallways. Upstairs in Robert's room, they were greeted by another FBI agent, who stepped out to give them some privacy.

Maisy hugged the older man as they entered, and he seemed pleased with their visit.

"How are you, my dear?" he asked and slowly settled into a comfy chair in the suite's living room.

"Sore, as I imagine you are," she said and sat across from him on the sofa.

"A bit. I hope my son is treating you well," Robert said and shot a look at Miguel, who stood off to one side, arms across his chest.

"He is and hopefully this will be over quickly." She didn't want her dreams dashed before they'd even really gotten started.

Robert smiled and nodded. "If anyone can solve this, it's Miguel. He's just like his mother that way."

"Thanks," Miguel said and visibly tensed.

In the short time she'd known both men, Maisy knew the subject of Miguel's mom and Robert's wife was a touchy one and so she changed the topic.

"I would love your advice about my blog," she said, and Robert latched on to that subject with passion, offering many suggestions on what she could post on the blog and how to incorporate social media to grow her following.

After a spirited discussion, Robert said, "I so miss dealing with young minds like yours, but my university had a mandatory retirement age."

Which sparked an idea in Maisy. "Why don't you start your own blog to share that experience? It would be so helpful to people like me."

Robert colored with the praise and nodded. "That sounds like a wonderful idea. I'd be delighted if you could help me."

"I'd love that," she said with a broad smile.

"And I'd love to let you keep brainstorming, but I have to get back to the team. Maybe you and Maisy can coordinate at another time?" Miguel said.

"We can. I understand you have important work to do," Robert said, and Miguel once again tensed, waiting for the shoe to drop, only it didn't. "I will call you tomorrow to continue this discussion."

"I'd like that," she said and rattled off her phone number. Repeated it for him as he wrote it down on a nearby pad of paper.

"Tomorrow, then," Robert said and stood just as the FBI agent guarding them returned with a bag whose smells filled the room.

"Dinner," the agent said and held up the bag.

"Enjoy and thank you for watching my dad," Miguel said as they walked to the door.

"My pleasure. Anything for you, SSA Peters," the agent said and walked toward the dining area in the suite.

Robert joined them at the door, where they exchanged goodbyes, but as they were about to step outside, his father said, *"¡Cuídate!"*

"I will," Miguel said, his voice choked, prompting Maisy to wonder.

Out in the hallway, Miguel turned to her and said, "It means 'Take care.' He used to say it to my mother whenever she left on an assignment."

So much pain, she thought as they walked back to the blue-glass skyscraper overlooking Puget Sound that housed Miguel's home and the BAU offices.

No, not his home, his prison, she thought. He was as much a prisoner of his past as she was, but at least she was trying to break free.

It made her question what it would take for Miguel to escape his past and think that a different future was possible for him. One that didn't end the way his mother's life had.

Maybe you, the little voice in her head said, but as

Miguel dropped her off in his apartment after an FBI agent manned the door, she told herself that was impossible. She had dreams of an independent, adventurous life. One where she stood on her own and didn't need the protection of a man like Miguel.

But he could protect her from her father. From her past, and maybe that was part of the reason he intrigued her so. However, she wasn't ready to sacrifice all that she dreamed of. The sooner they could finish this investigation, the better it would be for both of them.

Which had her going back to the photos on her phone and her memories of the bomber in the hope of aiding in the investigation.

MIGUEL ENTERED THE BAU offices where Dash, Liam, and David were hard at work on their computers, digging up the information he had requested earlier.

Nicholas and Madeline were inside the large conference room, sitting kitty-corner to each other and poring over assorted papers. He wondered if they included information on Maisy and her father. He'd taken a moment away from her to text his team about what he'd discovered. Hopefully, whatever they had would confirm his gut reaction that Maisy had nothing to do with the bomber's actions.

He knocked on the door to the conference room and at Madeline's nod, he entered and sat. "What can you tell me?" He liked hearing what his team had to say before interjecting his own ideas into the investigation. He interrogated people much the same, letting them do the talking. It was amazing how much some criminals were willing to say voluntarily.

Madeline handed over a folder and as he opened it

the face of an older white man stared back at him. Richard Green. Maisy's father.

He tried to find anything of her in him physically but decided she must take after her mother. As he read through the details, Madeline gave him a quick rundown.

"Richard Green, aka the Forest Conservation Bomber. Green had a successful landscaping business in Woodinville and was quite involved with local environmental groups, most of them legit. Somehow, he connected with the Forest Conservation League. Several of their members had been arrested for spiking trees, monkeywrenching and arson. Green escalated their tactics to include over a dozen bombings at various logging locations and at a new construction site."

"Hug a tree, kill a human," Nicholas said with disdain.

"Extremism of any type can turn deadly," Miguel added, thinking of the many radical groups he'd handled during his counterterrorism activities.

"Maisy and her mom—" he began, but Nicholas beat him to it as Madeline handed him another folder, this one with photos of Maisy and her mother.

"Maisy was formerly Elizabeth Green. Her mother's maiden name was Patricia Kelly. Both her parents were only children, like Maisy. Maisy really has no other family except her father. Maisy and her mother have lived in Seattle since Green's imprisonment. Patricia was sickly for the last three years of her life before she passed from uterine cancer. From what we can see, Maisy was a dutiful daughter and took care of her mother."

Miguel nodded and peered at the photos of Patricia Oliver that his team had gathered from the DMV and news articles published during Richard Green's trial. She'd been a beautiful woman and it was obvious where Maisy got her looks. But the last photo of her from the DMV showed the ravages of illness and the difficult times she and Maisy must have suffered after escaping to Seattle.

The photos of a young Maisy were as telling. The teen had clearly been overwhelmed by all that had happened during the trial. She'd been sad and fearful based on her face and body language in the photos.

"What do you read from all this?" he asked his team.

"Your mother's profile and physical evidence gathered at various locations led to his capture at the landscaping business. Green didn't put up a fight when the agents showed up to arrest him, maybe because he was clearly guilty. No doubt about that, but he refused to cooperate about whether anyone else in the Forest Conservation League had assisted in any way," Madeline said.

"I doubt he acted alone, although he could have. Being in the landscaping business, he had access to everything he needed to build his bombs. Fertilizer. Fuel. That was his MO and that's nothing like what we have here," Nicholas said.

"If you're wondering about Maisy and her mother, they seem to have been terrorized by the press, neighbors and possibly even Green," Madeline added.

Miguel quirked a brow and closed the folders. "If I'm hearing you right, you don't think Maisy had any role in the bombing. Is that correct, Madeline?"

Madeline tipped her head and glanced at Nicholas, who likewise nodded and said, "I concur. If anything, Maisy and her mother were suffering from a form of PTSD based on what I see in the file. They've been doing all they can to avoid anything to do with the trauma. They changed their names and basically hid from the world. Now Maisy has suffered another trauma very reminiscent of the crimes her father committed. I wouldn't be surprised if she has nightmares or hypervigilance after that event."

Relief slammed into Miguel that his two profilers felt Maisy wasn't involved with the bomber, but he worried about the possible trauma that both his father and Maisy had suffered that day. And he also worried that the bomber wasn't done, which meant they had to work quickly to assist the local PD with a profile and anything that might help identify the bomber. Hopefully TEDAC could provide additional details once they'd examined the bomb remnants.

"Have you got anything on the profile for the bomber?" he asked.

Madeline and Nicholas shared an uneasy look before Nicholas quipped, "Besides that he likes ham sandwiches?"

Miguel had to chuckle. "Besides that. Although looking on the bright side, that likely eliminates Islamic extremists."

"It likely does. Plus, they would have claimed the attack already," Madeline said.

Miguel nodded and gingerly rose from his chair. His leg was throbbing, and other parts of his body were starting to chirp with pain from the bomb blast. "Excellent work on Green and Maisy. Keep digging to see if Green has any connection to this. Also, Maisy mentioned to me that she hadn't heard from her father for some time, but in the year since her mother passed, he's been terrorizing her with almost weekly letters and calls. Let's find out how he got Maisy's new name and info and see where that leads."

"Got it, boss," Nicholas confirmed.

"We've got this," Madeline added.

Satisfied that Nicholas and Madeline would glean additional information, he headed to the office area and over to Liam to see if he'd made any progress. As he neared, he noticed that Liam's attention was distracted for a moment as Lorelai offered a good-night to the group, almost glaring at Liam as she did so.

It had been a touchy situation in the office ever since the couple had called off their engagement, but Miguel couldn't let that interfere with this investigation.

"Liam, could I see you for a moment?" he said and tilted his head in the direction of his office.

Liam frowned, but nodded and hopped to his feet. As he entered the office, Miguel closed the door behind the young man, who took a seat in a chair in front of Miguel's desk. Miguel settled himself in his executive leather chair and stretched out his leg to ease the low throbbing there.

"You okay, boss?" Liam asked.

"Fine, and you, Liam? I imagine today must have been tough for you," he said, hoping to get the young man to open up.

"Not as tough a day as yours," Liam said, but then looked away and plowed on. "I nearly lost it when we heard from Lorelai that she was at the station. All I could think about was whether she was safe. Whether I'd see her again."

"Seems to me you still have feelings for her," Miguel said, leaning his elbows on the arms of the chair and steepling his hands before his mouth. He gazed at

Liam intently, trying to gauge what the young man was thinking.

"I do, but you know my family has a bad track record. I got cold feet and now… I promise I won't let this interfere with the investigation. If anything, I have lots more reason to find the bastard so that we can shut down any danger to the public or the team."

Miguel hesitated, carefully weighing Liam's words and tone. Satisfied that he was serious, he said, "Do you have anything for me?"

Liam nodded. "We constructed an image of his face that we're running against DMV and other agencies. David was able to pull a photo of him from a video, but also masked. Dash is working with those images using the facial recognition software he tweaked."

A knock came at the door and Miguel spied Dash there. As the top tech person, he oversaw Liam and David and so Miguel waved him in.

Dash's eyebrows issued a question he didn't ask, and Liam quickly said, "I just filled the SSA in on what we had so far. May I go back to work?"

Miguel nodded and Liam hurried back to his desk. Dash took Liam's spot and arched a brow. "Should my nose get out of joint that you went to Liam for a report?"

Miguel held his hands up in surrender. "No offense meant. I needed to make sure the Lorelai situation isn't out of control. I don't think it is, do you?"

Seemingly accepting the unspoken apology, Dash said, "It isn't. If anything, I'm betting we'll still be attending a wedding. How much did Liam tell you about our progress?"

With a heavy sigh, Miguel said, "That you have images you're running against various resources. I've sent you some photos that Maisy took. Don't know how helpful those will be."

"Quite. One of them contained a partial facial view. Part of the chin," Dash explained and used his hands to pinpoint the area that had been revealed by Maisy's photo.

"That's good news. When do you think we'll have a sketch to send to local PD, ABS and the other agents in our office?" Miguel asked.

"We should have a 3D rendering of the suspect's face as well as general physical characteristics by the morning. In the meantime, we're running what we have for now just in case we get a hit."

"Good work. Send me everything as soon as you can. I'm going back to my apartment to review everything Nicholas and Madeline dug up, plus the surveillance videos of the bombing. Something's off and I need to put my finger on what," he said and stood.

"Will do, Miguel," Dash said.

Miguel took only a moment to make sure his team had loaded all their work to their network and, satisfied he had everything he needed, he headed to his apartment a few floors down from the BAU offices. As the elevator opened, he caught sight of the FBI agent guarding the door.

When he neared, he said, "We're good for the night. Get some rest and I'll see you in the morning."

The agent nodded and walked off, leaving Miguel staring at the door to his home.

Not that it felt much like a home, as Maisy had clearly seen. It was just a place to lay his head for some rest. A place to work when he needed the solitude he couldn't get in the BAU offices.

Not a home, but he had to admit that with Maisy there it felt different. It felt more domestic, especially as he entered and she was curled up on the couch, watching a television program.

"Hi," she said, her voice slightly husky. Eyes half-closed, sleepy, until she saw him and beamed him a smile.

"Watching anything interesting?" he asked and walked over. He couldn't fail to notice it was a show about counterterrorism.

"It is. Scary as well when you think about how many plots you've stopped," she said and patted the space beside her.

He slipped off his suit jacket, folded it and laid it on a nearby chair. He sat down beside her, loosened his tie and undid his top two buttons of his shirt. Staring at the screen, he recognized the case that the show was highlighting—a German operation where it had seemed like a lone-wolf attack until additional ties to Al-Qaeda had been revealed. He explained to her and she listened intently, asking questions and shutting off the program to focus on him.

As he finished, she said, "That's fascinating. So what the FBI, NSA and CIA communicated to the Germans was able to stop a bigger attack?"

"It was. Much like we've gotten critical information from others, like the British police advising us about a possible transatlantic aircraft plot. It created a number of immediate security measures regarding liquids on flights and eventually we caught the terrorists before they could hurt anyone."

"It's why you're so married to what you do," Maisy said.

He'd never thought of it that way, but it was very similar to being married. To being committed to that one thing and not anything else. Not even a family.

"It's why my focus is on that and nothing else," he confirmed.

A long pause followed before Maisy cupped his jaw and gently urged him to face her. "It must be lonely. Being married to the job. Your mother wasn't that way."

"No, she wasn't. She was gone a lot, but she was also always there for me," he admitted.

Maisy stroked her thumb across his cheek, her touch soothing. Comforting. "I want to thank you for being here for me. I don't know what I would have done today after the bombing."

But he knew, because she'd shown him her true colors today and not just during the hostage situation. She'd shown him later with his dad and now, when she'd finally made his apartment feel like a home. When he'd shared his work with her, something he'd never done before with anyone.

"But *I* know. You'd have been strong the way you were today. The way you were when you and your mom built new lives for yourselves. You're a strong woman. A caring woman," he said and covered her hand with his. Stroked it to reciprocate the soothing and comfort she'd given him.

"Thank you. I only wish I was as strong as you, but promise me one thing," she said and paused until he nodded. "Promise me you'll stay safe. *¡Cuídate!*"

Somehow the promise took on new meaning with her. A challenging meaning because he could already imagine hearing that from her every morning. Could imagine coming home to Maisy.

And that was possibly more risky than the bomber who was on the loose.

"I promise," he said and rose from the sofa carefully, mindful of the stitches in his leg. He had stopped using the cane because the pain had lessened and the doctor had said to only use it when he felt he needed support. "Time for rest. I'll take the couch."

She shook her head and said, "You take the bed." She paused then and stared around the spacious studio apartment. "There is a bed, right?"

He gestured to the wall at one side of the room, opposite a small dining room table and chairs. "Murphy bed. Are you sure?"

"You're a big man," she said and bright color flooded her cheeks. She hid it, rather unsuccessfully, by covering them with her delicate hands.

"You're cute when you're flustered," he said, smiled and playfully tapped her nose.

She mimicked the gesture. "And you're kind of handsome when you smile."

Heat filled his cheeks and he stopped himself from taking the flirting—*whoa, flirting*—to another level. "Good night, Maisy. Feel free to use the bathroom to change."

"Thanks," she said, grabbed her bag and hurried to the bathroom, but even as she did so, he couldn't stop smiling.

Armed with that smile, he rounded up a pillow, sheets and a blanket for Maisy. Yanked down the Murphy bed for himself. As he did so, he calculated the distance from the bed to the couch. Barely a few feet away. Too close and yet not close enough because it was too easy to picture her slipping into bed with him.

He suddenly wished that he had opted for a one bedroom instead of the studio because even those few feet would have lessened the temptation of having Maisy close by. In just a day she had touched his heart in ways no one had in a long time. He had to guard against that because he couldn't afford any distractions during this investigation.

The only damage the bomber had done so far had been to a building. Miguel intended to keep it that way. When Maisy came out, looking fresh-faced in her cotton pajamas, he bid her a terse good-night and escaped to the bathroom, determined to get his guard up.

When he exited, she was tucked beneath the blanket on the couch, all the lights off except for one under-cabinet light in the kitchen she'd thoughtfully snapped on.

He rushed to the bed and eased beneath the covers. Grabbing his laptop from a nearby table, he pulled up the files for the information they had so far. But his mind was only half on the work. The other half was on Maisy's gentle breathing until it lengthened and grew more regular, confirming that she had finally fallen asleep.

It was only then that he could focus on the investigation. His one hope was that they would catch the bomber quickly to avoid any more damage to the people and city of Seattle. No, make that two hopes: the second was that Maisy would be out of his life before he got any more attached to her.

Chapter Six

Maisy had lingered on the couch, feigning sleep, when Miguel had risen from bed with the first rays of the sun coloring the dawn. She'd heard him padding around in bare feet, opening drawers and a closet before heading to the bathroom, where the hiss of water in the pipes said he was showering. She told herself not to think about what he might look like dripping wet in the shower because this time together was limited and could go nowhere. They each had their own path to take and they would never meet again.

Determined to avoid those thoughts, she dressed, folded the sheet and blanket, and made a pot of coffee. The first drips of earthy brown java were filling the carafe when Miguel's phone started chirping angrily. It stopped for a second, but then started up again, warning her that something important was up.

Her instincts were confirmed when Miguel raced out of the bathroom, hair wet, dress shirt and pants unbuttoned, displaying the lean and toned muscles of his chest and midsection.

She looked away and busied herself with pouring a cup of coffee as he snatched up his phone and answered.

"SSA Peters," he said as he dragged a hand through

his wet hair to smooth the longer strands at the top of his head.

The muffled words coming across the phone dragged a muttered curse from him and he grabbed the remote for the television and snapped it on. A "Breaking News" chyron in bright red and white scrolled across the screen.

"An explosion rocked a vacant apartment building in West Seattle this morning. Firefighters are at the location tending to a small blaze ignited by the blast. We're waiting for additional information as to the cause of the explosion and whether it has any connection to yesterday's terrorist bombing in King Street Station," the female newscaster reported as video of the firefighters tackling the fire flashed across the screen along with police officers securing the location.

"You're saying that the bomber sent a communication to us at the same time as the blast?" Miguel asked, his gaze focused on the news report as he listened to what one of his team members was reporting. He nodded at whatever they said and advised, "I'll be there in five. Start tracing who sent the email and get on social media. I have no doubt he'll be rubbing our faces in it on there as well."

He swiped to end the call and glanced at her as she said, "Is it him? The bomber from yesterday?"

He nodded again and said, "He's calling himself the Seattle Crusader. He says government isn't doing enough for the people of Seattle and so he's decided to help move things along. His first demand is that the minimum wage be increased to twenty dollars per hour. If we don't meet that demand, he'll keep blowing up parts of the city."

Maisy shook her head in disbelief. “But that’s not even something that anyone can do right away.”

“It isn’t, but at least it’s something. Not like what we had yesterday. Hopefully the team can trace the email so we can pinpoint where he might be. I need to get to work,” he said and snapped off the television. “I’ll send an agent down—”

“I’m going with you,” she said and set aside the cup of coffee she had just poured.

“No way, Maisy. We’ll be way too busy—”

“But you promised you’d be the one to safeguard me. And maybe I can help out somehow. Maybe I can remember something more about the bomber or what I remember of my dad, his trial and stuff,” she said and tilted her chin up, almost daring him to refuse her request again.

A half smile slipped onto his lips. “Stuff, huh? I guess I’ll be able to focus better if you’re with me, even if I know any of my agents could protect you capably.”

“For sure. I guess you should finish dressing,” she said and gestured to his unbuttoned clothing, ignoring the rush of heat to her face and throughout her body as she looked at him again.

He coughed uncomfortably, slipped his smartphone into his pocket and immediately buttoned his shirt and pants, a stain of color on his cheeks as well. As he stuffed the shirt into his pants, he said, “There are to-go mugs in the middle cabinet.” Apologetically, he added, “Please. Light and lots of sugar.”

“No problem,” she said and prepped two coffees as he finished dressing, made the bed and eased it back into the wall.

MIGUEL IGNORED THE questioning glances as he walked into the BAU offices with Maisy in tow and introduced her to the team sitting around the table in front of their board.

"Maisy Oliver. Please meet my BAU Team. Special Agent Madeline Striker. Her specialty is kidnapping cases. Special Agent Nicholas James is our go-to guy for serial killers. Special Agent Dashiell West is our cybercrimes and tech hotshot." He paused and gestured to the two younger men sitting off to the far side of the office, diligently working on their computers. "You'll get to meet Liam McDare and David Dyson later. They're our tech gurus."

A slight cough interrupted him, and he glanced toward the door leading to his director's private offices. "So sorry, Lorelai. How could I forget you? Lorelai Parker, the administrative assistant to Director Branson, who is in D.C. right now."

"And who is on the phone with Caitlyn Yang about this morning's bombing," Lorelai said, walked over and handed Miguel some message slips. "Caitlyn is coordinating with Seattle PD, ATF and Mack at ABS. They should have more info for you shortly."

Miguel nodded and at Maisy's questioning gaze, he said, "Caitlyn is our liaison with local law enforcement. Thank you, Lorelai."

As Lorelai walked out of the room, Liam's head swiveled to watch her walk to her office and Miguel once again worried about whether their personal drama would interfere with the BAU's efficiency. Which reminded him they had to get working on the latest bombing. Turning to Maisy, he said, "Please have a seat."

Then he glanced toward his team and added, "What have we got so far?"

"A demand, finally. There's a new Twitter account for someone calling themselves the Seattle Crusader." Madeline hit a button to turn on an overhead monitor that projected an image of the Crusader's profile with its Twitter thread about the bombing. The first tweet said:

Shaking up Rat City until the politicians listen to our demands.

"'Rat City...our demands.' What's that telling us?" Miguel tossed out for consideration.

Dash's fingers flew across the keyboard and seconds later, he said, "Rat City is possibly a giveaway that he's local. It's a reference to the White Center. Used to be a dump there with lots of rats, and also a hangout for sailors. Water rats was slang at one time for sailors."

Miguel went to the whiteboard and wrote down the word "local" under the grainy picture of the bomber tacked to the board.

Madeline added, "'*Our* demands.' It hints at the fact that the bomber is not working alone."

"So we may be dealing with a terrorist cell and not just an individual bomber," Miguel said and wrote that down on the board. "What else?"

Nicholas gestured to the second tweet in the thread and read it aloud. "No peace until the minimum wage is twenty dollars per hour."

"'No peace.' He's co-opting part of the call for social justice," Madeline noted and continued. "It could mean he's been involved with other groups using that phrase."

Miguel nodded, added the language beneath the

photo and glanced at Dash. "Can you get us a list of anyone arrested during the riots after the bombing yesterday? By the way, how are we doing on the footage from the bombing at the station?"

MAISY LISTENED INTENTLY as Dash reported on the progress they'd made with the images from the CCTV in and around the station, Maisy's photos and the news crew videos. With a few strokes of his keyboard, he added a map to the image already being projected against the screen and as he spoke, he added pins to the map.

"We have the first bombing in the station and now this morning's blast near the White Center. The feeds we were able to access helped us track the unsub as he passed Century Link and T-Mobile fields and entered the SoDo area. We lost him there but are now working on getting video feeds from the area around the latest bombing location."

Miguel nodded, jotted down some notes on the board while Dash continued with his report. "As for the images, we've got a composite thanks to Maisy's photo. It let us add more detail to the bomber's face and we're running that composite against various databases and hope to have something shortly."

"Good work. Nicholas, what can you add now that we've got a serial bomber happening?" Miguel prompted.

"Two early-morning bombings, although I'm still bothered by the second bomb that exploded at King Street Station. It's off, Miguel. Totally off. Can you run that video for us, Dash?"

Dash did as Nicholas asked, putting up the CCTV feed. As it ran, Nicholas said, "We all thought the bomber looked surprised when that second bomb went off. Now we have 'our demands.' Maybe the reason he's surprised is that he wasn't the one who set off that second bomb. Maybe his partner tripped it before the bomber expected."

"Or maybe the bomber didn't expect for any bomb to go off," Madeline proposed. "We had no real demands despite that being the typical MO for the kind of collar bomb that was used. This morning we have another bombing, but I've done some digging and it turns out that the building that was blown up this morning was vacant and slated for destruction."

"We have another situation where the bomber chose a location that would do little collateral damage," Miguel said.

Unlike my father, Maisy thought. Her father had picked his targets to cause damage, both to the locations and any innocent passersby. "He doesn't want to hurt anyone," she said aloud, drawing the attention of the team members. "Or he's just been lucky. Even if the building was supposedly vacant, there could have been someone homeless there. Or one of the firefighters could be injured."

"But he didn't choose locations which would definitely cause injury like the Forest Conservation Bomber," Madeline said and eyed Maisy intently. "It's the eight-hundred-pound elephant in the room and I'm sorry to bring it up, Maisy. But it had to be said."

"It does, but I want you all to understand that my mother and I knew nothing about what he was doing," she pleaded, disheartened that she had to defend herself yet again after so many years.

To her surprise, Miguel walked over and laid a hand

on her shoulder in reassurance. “We believe you, Maisy. And we get that you’ve been living in a prison much as your father has been, thanks to his actions.”

Every member of the team peered at his hand on her shoulder, but no one said a thing about it.

“You’re suffering every bit as much as one of his victims,” Nicholas said. Then he quickly added, “And you’re right that even if this bomber doesn’t intend harm, there’s no guarantee that no one will be injured or worse.”

The phone in the center of the table chirped and Miguel leaned over to answer the call. “SSA Peters here.”

“Miguel, it’s Mack. I’ve got some info for you.”

“You’re on speaker with the team and Maisy Oliver, the young woman from the station yesterday,” Miguel said.

“I wish I could say ‘Good morning’, but it isn’t. Another bombing without a doubt. Initial review of the bomb fragments by ATF and me lead us to believe it was constructed much like yesterday’s briefcase bomb. Tripped by a cell phone. The dynamite appears to be the same make as well. Blue wires again. We’re in the process of trying to locate DNA samples and fingerprints. We’ll keep you posted.”

“Thanks, Mack. We’re working on a profile as we speak and will fill you in as soon as we have anything,” Miguel said and disconnected the call.

“A serial bomber, but again, a different MO between the collar bomb and the use of the dynamite. That’s unusual, but it could confirm that we have two or more people working together,” Nicholas said.

“And we have two very different locations. The very

public and crowded King Street Station and now an apartment building that's abandoned and soon to be destroyed," Madeline tossed out for consideration.

"Not really, Madeline," Nicholas interjected. "The second bomb in the station was in a little-used area. You might even say an abandoned area. Again, no harm intended."

"Terror was intended and now it's our job to trap this terrorist before he strikes again," Miguel pointed out.

And creates even more psychological harm, Maisy thought.

"Let's get to work on the building. Dash, can you find out who owns it? Why that might have made it the bomber's target. Also, to the best of my knowledge blue wire is mostly used in commercial buildings. Let's find suppliers in the area," Miguel said.

"On it," Dashiell confirmed, grabbed his laptop and headed to a desk near the two techies.

Miguel looked at Madeline and Nicholas. "The demand. Unreasonable. Nothing we can really do to fulfill it. Why? Does he really want those demands fulfilled or is it just a smoke screen for something else?"

Madeline nodded and glanced at her teammate. "Nicholas and I will work on it. I think we all agree something is very off about this bomber and hopefully we can work up a profile that gets us closer to understanding his motivation so we can prevent another bombing."

"Great. I look forward to hearing anything you can put together," Miguel said and looked at Maisy. "Would you mind joining me in my office?"

Chapter Seven

Maisy shook her head. “Not at all.”

She rose and he held his hand out in invitation. She slipped her hand into his and followed him to his office. Unlike his very sterile apartment just a few floors down, this room was filled with bits of his life. As she sat, she tried to piece all those bits together to get a better picture of the man who was intriguing her on too many levels.

A bookcase behind the desk held an assortment of subjects. History. Psychology. Forensics. Crime. Some literature. Propping up the books, knickknacks from all over the world. A replica Aztec sun stone in gleaming black obsidian. Well-handled maracas painted with an age-muted floral design and the word “Cuba.” A few different crystal beer steins that brightened the heavier objects on the shelves.

The walls were not as eclectic, more formal. Pictures of the BAU team with assorted politicians. Miguel shaking the hand of the President as he accepted an award. But the picture on his desk was purely personal. One of him with his father and a woman she assumed was his mother.

The desk was otherwise scrupulously neat and organized, like his apartment.

"Maisy?" he said, and she realized he had asked her something that she hadn't heard because she was so lost in her thoughts.

"I'm sorry. I didn't mean to ignore you," she said and leaned forward in her chair to make sure he knew that he had her complete attention.

He arched a brow. "I asked if you wanted some more coffee."

"No, thanks. I'm already jumping out of my skin, trying to process everything that's happening," she said and clasped her hands in her lap to tame her nervousness.

MIGUEL UNDERSTOOD. HE was always like that during the course of an investigation, his mind racing with all the facts they had and searching for all the ones they didn't.

"I get it. You feel like you're on a knife-sharp edge, barely keeping your balance. Waiting for what's coming next while hoping you can stop it," he said.

"You don't think he's done," she said and wrung her hands.

He shook his head. "Sadly, I think he's just getting started. And it is a he. Most serial bombers are men, like the Unabomber and Eric Rudolph, the Olympic Park Bomber. Your father."

"You mean the Forest Conservation Bomber. My father died the day that killer was born," she said, her voice alive with pain.

He nodded, in sync with her emotions, especially considering how Richard Green had terrorized Maisy in addition to the residents of Washington State. "In some ways, you're not wrong. With a bomber like your…like Green, they become consumed with what they're doing. With the building of the bombs and placing them. With the justification of what they're doing, whether it's protecting the environment or railing against technology."

"And this bomber. What do you think is his justification?" Maisy asked.

Miguel frowned and leaned back in his chair. Jammed his elbows on the arms of his chair and steepled his hands in front of him for a long moment. "That's what's bothering me about this bomber. The demands so far are unrealistic. Is that because he really doesn't want to stop bombing? Or is it for some other reason, especially since the locations of the bombs suggest an intent not to harm anyone?"

Maisy was likewise silent for a moment. "Unlike the Forest Conservation Bomber. He wanted to hurt people."

"Maybe as revenge for what he saw as damage to the environment. Revenge is often a motivation as well," Miguel said, but a second later his phone rang, snagging his attention as he saw the call was from his team in the conference room.

He picked it up, scowled and opened his desk drawer to remove a remote control for the television on one wall of his office. As he flipped on the television, he said, "I got it. Putting you on speakerphone."

Maisy swiveled in her seat and they watched the television, where the reporter was breaking news about another bombing at a construction site in the SoDo section, almost halfway between the original bombing site in King Street Station and that morning's blast near the White Center.

"He's already claiming this one," Madeline said.

Nicholas chimed in, "The Seattle Crusader just tweeted that he'll stop once the city council sets up a permanent homeless encampment on the grounds of the Seattle Japanese Garden. In the second tweet in the thread, he warns that next time people will feel the wrath of his bombs. Maybe even Angel Eyes."

Fear ripped through his gut at the mention of Maisy. If the bomber was still fixated on her like that, she was in even greater danger. "Dash, do you have anything yet on the account?" Miguel said.

Dash immediately replied, "We're still trying to get Twitter to give us info. Subpoena has been served on them so we're hoping to have it soon."

"But not soon enough," Nicholas said, concern ringing in his tone. "He's escalating. One bombing yesterday. Two today, just hours apart, and now he's threatening harm."

To Maisy, Miguel thought, and glanced her way. Her face had gone chalk white at the bomber's mention of her. His gut clenched again at the thought that the bomber's threats were possibly no longer empty ones.

"And we still don't have demands that anyone can really meet," he tossed out, hoping to hear what his team would think about those requests.

"Not a one," Madeline said. "That's not typical of an extortion-type bomber. And the foul-up on the detonator at the station makes me wonder just how mission oriented he is."

"Still no one hurt and I'm not sure he will go through with that threat," Nicholas said, but that only partially relieved some of Miguel's worry.

"Any info on the first construction site? Owner? Other info?" he said.

"We have an owner, but it appears to be a shell company. Trying to track the real owner," Dashiell said.

"Good job. Let's get info on the second construction site. Reach out to ATF, Mack and Seattle PD for anything they might have. It's too soon for TEDAC, but let's push them. Let them know we've got two more explosions."

As his team confirmed his orders, Miguel snapped off the speakerphone and glanced at Maisy, who had barely regained some pink to her cheeks. "He won't hurt you, Maisy."

She shook her head and clenched and unclenched her hands. "It's not me I'm worried about."

He acknowledged that with a slow nod and chastised himself. Even in the short time he'd known her, he should have recognized her worry would have been for others. Much like her worry the day before had been for his father and not herself.

"You're a brave woman, Maisy Oliver." The sort of woman who could handle the kind of life he led. If he wanted a woman, which he didn't.

She shook her head and a harsh laugh escaped her. "Not by choice. Sometimes I wish…" She looked away, but it was impossible for him not to see the shimmer of tears in her eyes.

He rose and walked over. Cupped her cheek and gently urged her to face him. "You wish for a normal life. One untouched by violence, but sadly, that's not the kind of life the two of us have been forced to live. It's how we handle it that defines us."

As a tear escaped, she swiped it away and said, "I

want *my* life, Miguel. The life I dreamed of before my father stole it. I won't let this bomber steal it again."

He wanted to say, "That's my girl," only she wasn't and never would be. Much as Maisy had chosen what she wanted to do with her life, so had he and it didn't include a woman like Maisy. Or any woman for that matter.

"I won't either. Believe me. You're safe with me," he said and motioned to his desk. "I have to get to work."

"Don't let me stop you."

WHILE MIGUEL WORKED at his desk, presumably reviewing a variety of reports and information on what they had so far, Maisy slipped in earbuds and turned her attention to various news reports, both written and televised.

Over and over the reporters repeated the Seattle Crusader's tweets and showed photos of the damage done at the three different locations. Many of them also made note of the references to Angel Eyes, but luckily the BAU team had kept her name and photos of her from the press in order to safeguard her.

As it had occurred to Miguel and his team, it struck her that the spot destroyed at King Street Station, as well as today's two locations, had been fairly isolated. This was much different from the places her father had chosen. He had injured someone at almost every bombing site while, this time, thankfully no one had been hurt so far.

But for how long? she thought. Would this bomber escalate when his unreasonable demands could not be met?

The phone rang again, and Miguel picked it up and

tucked the receiver between his ear and shoulder as he listened while continuing to work. He turned to face her and said, “Seattle ABS confirmed dynamite was used at this morning’s location. The same kind as he used at the station. They’re working at the second spot now, but initial inspections lead them to believe it was also dynamite. Blue wires again, which must be his signature.”

She nodded, processing the info, but before she could say anything, Miguel rose and gestured for them to leave his office and join the team outside. The BAU members were gathered around the table and in front of their whiteboard with all the information they had gathered so far.

On the television, a newscaster was just finishing up with details of the bombing and had reached out to an on-location reporter stationed just outside the construction site that had been damaged.

“We’re here with state senate candidate Richard Rothwell. Senator Rothwell—”

“Not Senator yet, Jessica,” Rothwell said with a smarmy smile, hands held up to stop the young female reporter.

The reporter nodded and said, “You’ve just tweeted that politicians and the FBI are failing Seattle.”

“They are totally failing the city and its people. It’s been close to twenty-four hours since the first bombing and we’ve heard nothing from the BAU team. Now we have two more bombings without any progress, but I can work with them to move the investigation along.”

“Over my dead body,” Miguel said, and all the team members nodded in agreement.

“What do you think about the bomber’s demands?

Is that something local politicians should consider?" the reporter asked.

"Well, that's a little more complicated and my team and I are reviewing it. As you can imagine, it's a fine line to walk when you're dealing with a terrorist, but we'll have something for you later today," Rothwell postured.

The young woman turned back toward the camera and said, "Well, there you have it. That was state senate candidate Richard Rothwell and as he said, we'll be hearing more from him later."

"Hopefully not," Nicholas said as Madeline snapped off the television.

MIGUEL COULDN'T AGREE MORE. He was about to address the team when Lorelai came into the room to advise that he had a call from Director Branson.

It was impossible to miss that tech guy Liam perked up when his ex-fiancée entered, and as she walked out, he said, "How are you doing?"

"Fine," Lorelai replied with a diffident shrug and walked out with Miguel following her to take the call privately.

Lorelai motioned for him to use the director's office and as he closed the door, the phone rang and he picked up.

"Good afternoon, Olivia. I'm assuming you've seen the initial reports we've sent you via email," he said, hoping to head off any discussion of Rothwell's appearance.

"I've done a preliminary review in between budget sessions, but as you can imagine, the news is non-stop reports on the bombings and Rothwell. Do you have anything new to report?" she asked. In the background he heard other voices, which said she was in between meetings.

"We just got confirmation from Seattle ABS that dynamite appears to have been used at all three locations and we're working on tracking the source, as well as the wire used. The demands so far are unrealistic, but luckily all the locations seem to be chosen so as to not injure anyone," he reported.

"But he's escalating and so is Rothwell," she said.

Which he hadn't failed to notice. "He is and we're going to have to handle Rothwell."

"Sooner rather than later, Miguel. I know you're working hard on this, but it's time you let the public know what you can and counter Rothwell's insinuations that you're not doing anything."

"But every second he takes away—"

"Is a second you could be using to solve this case, yes. But it's getting noticed in D.C. If we're going to get the funding we need to continue to help others, you're going to have to take the time to handle Rothwell." Her voice grew muffled toward the end and he heard her say, "In a minute," to someone else.

Miguel inhaled deeply and blew out a harsh breath. Dragging a hand through his hair in frustration, he said, "Understood, Olivia. I'll schedule a press conference for later today."

"Thank you, Miguel. I know you will get it done."

She disconnected before he could say another thing, clearly juggling multiple tasks on behalf of their BAU team.

Just as he had to handle Rothwell, no matter how much he might not like it.

Replacing the receiver, he exited Olivia's office. "Lorelai, would you please contact Caitlyn and ask her to set up a press conference at four. I'll let her choose the location. I just need lead time to get there."

"Will do, SSA Peters," Lorelai said with a nod.

But before he left, he said, "You doing okay? That bombing yesterday must have been scary for you."

She hesitated and sucked in a breath. Held it before blurting out, "It was. It makes you think about what's important."

"It does. If you need to talk, we're all here. Some more than others if you know what I mean," he said, and she offered him a stilted smile but nodded.

"I know. Same here, Miguel."

He returned to where the team and Maisy were gathered, discussing the information they had so far. Instead of interrupting, he took a seat next to Maisy and sat back to listen, absorbing their details while formulating what to say to the press later.

In no time he had worked out what he would report, but before that, he intended to call Mack at ABS, the police chief and the mayor to give them a heads-up to what he would be saying at the press conference. Besides, it was time that BAU provide them with the information that they had so far.

Beside him Maisy sat patiently, but he worried that with something so personal because of her background, she might be suffering emotionally during the investigation. He laid a hand on her shoulder and gave a reassuring squeeze as he stood.

"You're all doing a great job so far. I want you to focus on finding out more about the ownership on today's locations. Likewise, the origin of the wire. My gut tells me we're going to find something there."

"On it," Dash confirmed.

"And we're finalizing our profile of the serial bomber, but I have to tell you that it's a tough one. We're still struggling with the motivation because those demands are so unreasonable," Madeline said.

"Almost as if he doesn't care if we satisfy them," Nicholas added.

"I agree. There's something else motivating him. Making *them* do this, because I don't believe he's working alone. See what the DNA and fingerprints we have so far can confirm about that," Miguel said.

"Got it, Miguel. Nicholas and I will work on that while Dash and his techs deal with the rest," Madeline advised.

"Great. Maisy and I are going to take a short break and prepare for the press conference," he said and with another gentle squeeze on Maisy's shoulder, he urged her to rise and head to his office for the preparation he had mentioned.

But as soon as they were inside the office, Maisy said, "Will I be at the press conference?"

It was something he'd been thinking about in addition to his statement to the reporters who would be there. In truth, he had been silently waffling about it.

"I know that you and your mother worked hard to avoid the public eye, so I have to ask, do you want to be there?"

Chapter Eight

Do I want to be there? she asked herself, but the answer came to her almost immediately.

"If you think it will help the investigation, I will be there."

His answer was not as immediate. After a long hesitation, he said, "I'm not sure it will help other than to let the bomber know we're protecting you. That could draw him out—"

"Then I will be there. I'm not afraid of him. I'm tired of being afraid," she said, thinking of how much time she and her mother had lost hiding out from her father. All for naught since her father had tracked her down anyway.

He stepped closer and cradled her cheek. "You're a unique woman. Don't ever change."

His touch sent comfort and need through her. It had been way too long, maybe never, since a man had looked at her like this. Touched her like this, and it was worrisome because it could upend her plans for what she'd wanted for so long.

She took a step back from him and wrung her hands together because she was way too tempted to touch him back. To avoid it getting personal again, she said, "Do you think we could get some lunch? I'm kinda hungry."

In sympathy, his stomach rumbled, and he laid a hand over his lean midsection to quiet the noise. "Me, too."

Happy laughter and Liam's shout of "You rock, Lorelai," filtered into Miguel's office. They looked back toward the common space where the rest of the team was working and where it appeared that the ever-efficient administrative assistant had arranged for lunch to be brought in.

Miguel held his hand out in invitation. "I guess we should join them."

Maisy normally had trepidation about being with people, having avoided them for so long. But in just two short days, she'd grown comfortable with Miguel and his dad. Even with this group of FBI agents who had accepted her into their midst. Not an easy thing to do considering her family's history. In the back of her mind there was still doubt about their acceptance, but she wasn't going to let that keep her from helping them end the bomber's reign of terror.

They joined the team at lunch, but Maisy kept silent so she could listen and watch Miguel and the team members interact. It was clear Miguel was the person in charge and yet there wasn't any hint of competition or tension, except for possibly the whole Lorelai-Liam situation. The tension there was obvious to everyone.

But the rest of the team seemed fluid and assured in their positions. It made her wish that she was as sure of her position in life. After all, she'd only just really begun her life by stepping on that bus yesterday, and then it had all come to a crashing halt. Or maybe it was more accurate to say it all blew up in her face.

Since she was surrounded by Miguel's team, however, hope filled her that this was only a bump in the road because she trusted that they would soon solve this investigation so she could get on with her life.

Lunch passed amiably, but as they were cleaning up and getting back to work, tension built inside her as the time neared for the press conference. With barely half an hour to go, Miguel got a call from Caitlyn with the location for the gathering.

"I'm not sure that's a good idea," Miguel said and shot a quick look at her.

She couldn't hear what the team's liaison said, but Miguel was clearly unhappy with whatever plan was in place. Despite that, he said, "I hope you're right."

He swiped to end the call and peered at her intently. "The press conference is going to be at the site of this morning's bombing. We'll be taking along other agents to secure the area, so you'll be safe."

She peered at him, trying to read him since he was clearly not happy with Caitlyn's choice. "But you're not in favor of the location, are you?"

He scowled and shook his head. "Not one hundred percent. There are too many variables in such a public place, but as I said, we'll have other agents there for security. That's my main concern."

She appreciated that, but more importantly, she had total confidence in him and his team.

She laid a hand on his arm and said, "I trust you. I guess we should get going."

As he had before, he cradled her cheek, offering reassurance with that simple touch. "Thank you for that trust. I just need a few minutes to get a team together to secure the area and then we'll head over."

Instead of stepping away, she cupped her hand with his and said, "Whenever you're ready, I'm ready."

MIGUEL'S TEAM OF agents had gone ahead to secure the space and at their signal, he and Maisy drove to where a number of news teams were gathered in front of the vacant apartment building that had been slated for destruction even before the actions of the Seattle Crusader.

As their car pulled up, Miguel noticed that besides the news crews, there were also quite a few of what appeared to be demonstrators gathered at the location. Using the headset he was wearing, he instructed his team. "Get photos of everyone in the crowd. It's possible the bomber has come back to check out his handiwork."

A second later, a knock on the glass had him looking into Caitlyn's worried features. He opened the door, stepped out and then helped Maisy from the car. "I guess someone leaked the location of the press conference," he said to the BAU liaison.

"I'm so sorry, SSA. You were right that this area would be hard to keep quiet," Caitlyn said.

"It's okay. We can handle this," he said, took hold of Maisy's hand and guided her to a spot to the side of where various microphones had been placed before a sea of videographers and photographers from the local papers and television news. An agent stood there, hands folded in front of him and at his nod, Miguel guided her to the agent.

"You'll be okay here," he said and at her nod, he and Caitlyn walked up to the microphones.

Shutters clicked and reporters jockeyed for positions as Caitlyn began the press conference.

"Good afternoon. I'm Caitlyn Yang, the BAU liaison. I have with me Supervisory Special Agent Miguel Peters, who is leading the team investigating the bombings that have taken place at King Street Station, the location behind us and the construction site in SoDo."

"You mean the Seattle Crusader, don't you?" someone shouted.

Miguel decided it was as good a time as any to take control of the press conference. "The individual we are investigating has named himself the Seattle Crusader. My team has received information from local authorities and is working on our profile of the bomber, as well as interacting with other agencies."

"But are you any closer to catching him?" a too-familiar voice called out from the crowd as Richard Rothwell moved to the front of the gathering and all cameras shifted in his direction.

Before anyone could stop him, Rothwell took a spot beside Caitlyn and continued. "As I said earlier, I am more than prepared to work with the FBI in order to capture this individual. But in the meantime, why aren't we considering some of his demands? For example, since the suspect is demanding the government up the minimum wage to twenty dollars per hour, let's meet him in the middle and give the good people of Seattle seventeen dollars! You all deserve more, don't you?"

While the press conference was happening, the number of people had grown and after Rothwell finished, a crowd of supporters, probably paid to be there, cheered and held up campaign signs with his name.

Miguel waited for the cheering to die down somewhat and said, "Thank you, *Mr.* Rothwell. While we appreciate the offer of assistance, my team has this under control."

"But do you?" Rothwell challenged, pompously puffing out a chest covered with the vest of a pin-striped suit. "I have a number of connections in government who could assist—"

"And I appreciate the offer, but as I said, we have this under control. We're interfacing with various agencies both here and in D.C. We'll have more information from them shortly and will be offering our complete profile to ATF, Seattle PD and ABS within hours. Additional investigations are ongoing to pinpoint the origin of the materials used in the bombings. Finally, we believe the bomber is not acting alone and will provide additional information on this conspiracy within twenty-four hours."

Miguel didn't fail to notice Rothwell's reaction to that statement. The man did a little jump, and his face paled. It sent up a red flag and as wild as it might be, his gut told him that Rothwell's involvement in this might be about more than the campaign.

Replacing his obvious discomfit with bluster, Rothwell said, "I can assure you that we're all looking forward to your report, Agent Peters."

Tired of the man and his interruptions, he said, "That's Supervisory Special Agent Peters, *Mr.* Rothwell. Now if you'll excuse me, we have bombers to catch."

He didn't wait for any questions, leaving Caitlyn to wind up the press conference and forward any pertinent questions to him at his office. To the side of the space, he joined Maisy and the agent guarding her, who walked them to the car waiting to return them to the BAU offices.

As soon as they were seated and on the way, Maisy said, “You said ‘bombers.’ I know your team was tossing that out, but are you sure?”

He thought about it for a hot second and nodded. “The team put it out there for discussion after the Crusader’s tweets. My gut tells me we’re not wrong going that route. This bomber isn’t acting alone. Which reminds me…”

He took out his phone and dialed Caitlyn. “Sorry for leaving you to the wolves.”

“No, I deserve that. You were right about the location,” the young woman said again.

“And as I said, no problem. But I need something from you and your connections,” he said.

A resigned sigh came over the line before Caitlyn said, “Anything. What can I do?”

“Anything and everything you can get me on Rothwell. The man. His businesses. Who’s feeding him information.” He kept to himself that he felt that Rothwell always seemed to be one step ahead of them, but maybe that was because Rothwell knew more about what was happening than he let on. That maybe he was somehow involved with the bombings.

“You got it, Miguel. I’ll try to round up what I can by later tonight and will send it to you,” Caitlyn said and hung up.

“You think Rothwell is part of this, don’t you?” Maisy asked.

“I have no proof, but I think it’s worth exploring. How about you?” he asked and stared at her, trying to gauge her reaction.

She wrinkled her nose and pursed her lips—full lips he had trouble ignoring—and said, "I agree. He just rubs me the wrong way. And how come he's always there like a Johnny-on-the-spot."

"And stinks like one, too," he teased, prompting a smile from her.

"For sure. What do we do now?" she said.

He liked that she said "we" because it was a team effort, including her. "We go back to work."

MAISY SAT AND listened as the BAU team reviewed what they had gathered in the short time they were gone to do the press conference. Unfortunately, it appeared that they had hit a dead end at getting any information about who had opened up the Twitter account.

"The email used to open the account is fake and was created just an hour before at a computer at the local library. No CCTV inside the library and we've had Seattle PD dust for fingerprints, but the computer was used by multiple people since then. Liam is searching for any CCTV feeds in the area of the library," Dashiell noted.

"And there was no sign-up for the computers. They could be used by anyone at any time. No one remembers anything out of the ordinary. We've sent agents to the homes of the librarians on that floor, as well as the security guard, with the initial photo that Dash and his team created. Still waiting to hear from them," Madeline indicated.

"Good. Hopefully, it might trigger a memory. Do we have anything else from ABS on the explosives or other evidence?" Miguel asked.

"Dynamite again. Looks like the same batch that was used at the station. The blue wires again. TEDAC is analyzing the bomb materials and in the meantime, David is working on getting a list of any licensed blasters in the area who might have access to that kind of explosive as well as the wire," Nicholas offered.

"And the DNA casework unit is analyzing the touch DNA samples taken from the briefcase handle and collar bomb. They should have something by tomorrow and run those results against CODIS," Dashiell added to the team's report.

It seemed as if they were covering all the bases so far, but what did she know? She was only a civilian drawn into this investigation. The crime was too painfully similar to what her father had done so many years earlier. Which made her wonder if there were other bombers like her father who were no longer imprisoned. Or maybe protesters who had used explosives. To her surprise Miguel, who had been mostly leaning back in his chair, listening to his team report, must have been thinking the same thing.

"I'd like to make a list of any possible unsubs who fit this profile. White. Above-average intelligence, but usually underachievers. Socially inept. Let's start with any known bombers or people on our terrorist watch list. Add to that any protesters arrested for using fireworks or other explosives. As for the DNA, when we get the results, let's check them against whatever genealogy databases we can access."

Madeline peered around the table at the team members and said, "We'll tackle that ASAP."

"I will as well," Miguel said and shot a quick glance in her direction. "In the meantime, I think we all could use a break. Go get something to eat. Take a walk. Clear your minds. I'm going to take Maisy for dinner and then head home to work. If anything pops up in the meantime, call."

"Got it, Miguel. I am ready for some food and a walk to clear my brain. Anyone want to join me?" Nicholas said and rose from the table.

"I'm game," Madeline said and likewise stood and stretched.

Dashiell glanced over his shoulder at where Liam and David were at their desks, still at work. "We have just a few things to finish up and then we'll meet you."

Miguel slowly unfolded from the chair, clearly favoring his one leg, reminding her that he was still recovering from an earlier wound. He winced as he took a step away from the table, but then schooled his features and forced a smile in her direction. Holding out his hand, he said, "Ready?"

"Yes," she said and slipped her hand into his. He squeezed her hand gently, offering comfort with his touch. Comfort that filled her and said that she could count on him, and his team, to end this threat to her and to the city of Seattle.

Together they walked out of the BAU offices and to the elevator, but once inside, he said, "There's a good fish place a block or so away if you'd like."

"Are you good to do the walk?" she asked, well aware of how gingerly he'd been moving.

"A walk will do me good. My leg stiffened up from sitting for so long, but it's almost healed," he admitted and pressed the elevator button for the lobby.

She wanted to ask how he'd been hurt but worried it would go down a road like that which his father had taken. That it was time for him to change his career, but Miguel intrigued her, and she needed to know what made him tick.

As the elevator moved toward the lobby, she said, "How were you hurt? If you can tell me, that is."

With a slight shrug, he said, "I can if you really want to know."

"I do. Before you my interactions with the FBI were…let's say not as pleasant," she said, recalling what had happened in the days and weeks after her father had been identified as the Forest Conservation Bomber.

"Apologies for that, but I hope you understand that we have a job to do to protect people," he said.

The elevator doors slid open noiselessly, spilling them into the pristine lobby of the building. Still hand in hand they stepped out and across the lobby filled with workers leaving for either dinner or the night after a long day. Outside the weather was unseasonably warm for an October night, making for a pleasant walk to the restaurant just a couple of blocks from the skyscraper where Miguel worked and lived.

After they were seated, she returned to their earlier conversation, which they'd set aside to enjoy the beauty of the fall night.

"Do you mind sharing how you were hurt? What the case was about?"

She needed to know what made him give up any kind of personal life to protect people like her. Maybe by knowing that, she could battle her growing attraction to the handsome FBI agent. Sitting back in her chair, she waited for him to answer.

Chapter Nine

Miguel delayed, unsure of where the discussion would go if he told her. Hopefully not to where such discussions usually went with his father.

"We had identified the unsub…" He stopped at the puzzled look that slipped across her face at his use of the term.

"I've heard that used, but what does it really mean?" she asked.

"Unknown subject. It's the person or persons who are unidentified and the focus of our investigations. Just easier to say unsub," he replied with a smile and shot a quick glance at the menu. Well familiar with it since the restaurant was a favorite, he immediately knew what he would order.

"Totally easier. So you had identified the unsub," she prompted and also took a look at the menu.

He nodded. "We had cornered him when he opened fire. I was shot during the confrontation, but we were able to capture him. My team and I got the job done."

"That's important to you, isn't it? That it's the team that accomplished it," she said, acutely in tune with him, which pleased him.

"It's a team effort. Everyone on the team contributes

to the end result. If one person is off, it could impact the efficiency of the team."

"Which is why you're worried about Lorelai and Liam," she said just as the waitress came over to take their orders.

"The salmon, please," Maisy said.

"The same and a bottle of the sauvignon blanc," Miguel said and immediately returned to the conversation. "It worries me because of the effect on the team, but also because I think they'd be very happy together."

"I can't argue with you. They seem to still care for one another despite the obvious tension," Maisy said and added, "Tell me about the rest of the team."

Miguel didn't hesitate to offer up his observations of the other team members and each of their respective specialties.

Several minutes later, the waitress returned with a bottle of wine to uncork and pour it for them. When she stepped away, Maisy held up the glass and said, "To your team."

"To the team," he replied and sipped the wine. The taste was crisp in his mouth, fresh with overtones of grass and a slight fruitiness.

"You care about your team being happy," Maisy said as she peered at him over the rim of the wineglass.

With a slight shrug, he said, "I do. In the last several months, many of the team members have found their significant others. It worried me at first since it happened during our investigations, but I see how much more centered they are and that's a good thing."

"But not you."

And there they were at that spot he hadn't wanted to reach like he did with his dad. "Not me. Not ever. When my mother and her partner were killed, I saw the pain that was left behind. My father. Her partner's wife and baby. A baby who will never know its father."

It had been painful for him as well to deal with those deaths. With the loss of his mother at the hands of a terrorist and its aftermath. It had only intensified his desire to follow in his mother's footsteps.

"That makes for a lonely life."

It was impossible to miss how she avoided his gaze by fixing it on the wineglass. It was likewise impossible to miss that the comment was also about her. About her life, and it made him sad.

"It was tough for you. You were so young, and people were cruel. And in a different way, you lost the father you knew and gained a monster. One who is tormenting you again," he said, but at that moment the waitress and another server came over with their meals. With almost artistic efficiency, the cedar-plank-cooked salmon was plated before them, along with an assortment of grilled vegetables.

Once they'd left, Maisy said, "I won't let him stop me from living. You shouldn't let your mother's death stop you either."

"It hasn't," he said, jabbed at a piece of salmon and shoved it into his mouth. Emotion made it tasteless since he hated to admit that Maisy might have a point.

MAISY COULDN'T MISS Miguel's upset, but she also couldn't say what was on her mind. For too long she'd held back because of the need to stay hidden to avoid the press and her father. Watching her mother slowly die before her eyes had only confirmed that it was time for her to reach for her dreams. To live. But happily, and to avoid any more unhappiness during the meal, she changed the topic.

"What was it like to grow up in Miami? It's probably very different from here."

He stopped shoveling food and met her gaze. The tension fled before her eyes, and a small smile quirked one side of his mouth. "Very. Tropical for starters. More diverse since there are so many different Latinos and other cultures."

"But your mom was Cuban?" she asked and forked up some asparagus from her plate.

He nodded. "She was born in Cuba and her family escaped Castro's regime in the early '60s. She loved this country. I think that's what made her join the FBI. She'd do anything to protect this nation."

"She sounds amazing," Maisy said with a sigh and sipped the last of her wine.

Miguel immediately refilled her glass. "Your mom must have been amazing as well to deal with everything that happened."

Maisy smiled. "She was. As difficult as it might have been, she tried so hard to give us a good life. It wasn't easy, but we had some happy times despite everything."

Nodding, Miguel finished the last bite of his salmon. "Once we're done with this investigation, you'll be able to go on with your life."

She didn't know why, but the prospect of that didn't make her as happy as she'd been only yesterday, when she'd set foot on the bus to start the rest of her life. Maybe because of Miguel. He had so many layers and so much pain, and something inside of her responded to that. Maybe too much.

When the waitress came by to ask about coffee and

dessert, she demurred, aware that Miguel needed to get to work. Aware that she needed a little distance from him to deal with what she was unexpectedly feeling about him.

After they finished the bottle of wine and chatted some more about Miami, Miguel paid and they strolled back to the BAU office and his apartment, but even though it was a leisurely pace, she sensed that Miguel was on high alert. He swiveled his head slowly around to keep an eye out, making her wonder if he was taking the Seattle Crusader's threats toward her seriously.

"Do you think he'll come after me? Attack others?" she asked as they neared the door to his building.

"I won't let him hurt you. Or others," he said, laid a hand on her shoulder and gently squeezed.

To her surprise, she felt herself drifting toward him, stepping against him. He eased his arm around her shoulders to keep her there. Dropped the barest hint of a kiss on her temple.

She slipped an arm around him beneath his jacket, but as she did so, she brushed against the holster tucked beneath his suit. It jolted her, that reminder that they weren't ordinary people. That fate had thrown them together unexpectedly and would tear them apart much the same.

Because of that, she stepped back. "I guess it's time for you to get to work."

As HARD AS Miguel tried, his full attention kept on drifting away from his laptop to Maisy as she huddled beneath the covers on her makeshift bed.

It had been tense when they'd first gotten back from the restaurant, and he'd changed while Maisy showered. After, in silence, they'd slipped into their respective beds. Maisy had pulled out her tablet and slipped on headphones to watch something in deference to his need to work. Not that she'd needed to do that since he was used to working in utter bedlam and could usually focus without fail.

But not tonight. The more time he spent around her, the harder she was to ignore. And the harder it was not to imagine having her in his life more regularly. If she would have it, that was. She had her own plans for life, and he was sure they didn't include a relationship.

Like mine doesn't include one, he thought and returned to reviewing the initial list of terrorist suspects his team had identified. Satisfied with their choices, he went through those they hadn't chosen, but didn't find any to add at the moment. Except for one—Richard Rothwell.

Some might say it was his hubris driving him to dislike the politician, but he'd long ago learned to not let pride interfere with an investigation. He'd also learned to follow his gut and his gut was telling him that there was something off with Rothwell.

Because of that, he turned his attention to learning what he could about the politician and his background. And as he read, more and more pieces fell into place, convincing him that he wasn't barking up the wrong tree. The Seattle Crusader was parroting many of Rothwell's political stands, although taken to an extreme. That only made Rothwell's less progressive positions more palatable.

And Rothwell was heavily into real estate and construction. That meant someone at one of his active builds might have access to dynamite and wire.

But so far, they only had shell companies owning the two bombing sites. His team was going to have to bust through those shells and see if they led to the blow-hard politician.

He shut his laptop and sank down beneath his comforter, but as he did, a sharp cry of alarm drew his attention to Maisy.

She was restless, kicking away her blanket and sheets. The muscles in her arms twitched a second before one arm flailed out, as if pushing someone away.

Nicholas's comments about Maisy and her mother suffering from some kind of PTSD flashed through his brain. PTSD and nightmares like the one Maisy was clearly having.

He eased from his bed and approached her slowly, not wanting to scare her. As she swept her arm out again, almost tumbling herself from the sofa, she blasted awake and screamed at the sight of him. But as she realized it was him, she calmed, sat up and wrapped her arms around herself.

Her teeth were chattering as she said, "I'm sorry. I didn't mean to wake you."

He sat across from her and cradled her cheek. "I wasn't sleeping. Are you okay?"

Am I okay? Maisy asked herself and shook her head.

"It was a dream, but it was so real. My father…he was there, and bombs were exploding everywhere. My mom was with me and I was trying to protect her, but…" She couldn't finish because the vision in her mind was too extreme. Too scary.

Too alone, which made her lean toward Miguel, seeking his comfort.

Comfort he didn't fail to give.

He wrapped his arms around her and drew her into his lap. Held her against him as he murmured, "Your dad can't hurt you anymore. I'll make sure of that."

"I know," she said, hating how childlike she sounded. Much like she had sounded over a decade earlier, when the reality of her father's actions had come to light.

He surprised her then by exploding to his feet, cradling her in his arms and walking with her to his bed.

"Miguel?"

"It's big enough for both of us," he said and laid her on the comforter.

She nodded and as he released her, she slipped beneath the sheets. He joined her a second later and as he had before, drew her into his arms, belying his comment that the bed was big enough.

It felt way too small with his hard body pressed to hers, but it wasn't just desire that filled her, but comfort. Safety. He was a rock. Her rock and she believed him when he said she would be safe.

Armed with that, the nightmare faded into the dark, replaced by a lightness in her soul created by his touch.

MAISY WAS STIFF in his arms at first, but the tension fled her body little by little and her breathing lengthened, confirming that she had fallen asleep.

But sleep didn't come as quickly to him, lying there beside her. Her lithe but strong body pressed to his, forcing him to tamp down unwanted desire. Desire that would only complicate even more the confusing thoughts he was having about her.

To keep those thoughts at bay, he turned his attention to what he'd been working on before Maisy's nightmare.

The list of suspects. The dynamite. Wire. Locations. Rothwell. Rothwell. Rothwell.

Annoyance at the politician flared through him, which was good. It would keep him from thinking about Maisy's body. Her warm breath, toothpaste fresh, spilling across the skin of his chest. Her skin, smooth, so smooth along his.

He muttered a curse as desire flared to life again, but luckily, Maisy peacefully turned in his arms and shifted away from him.

Safe. He was safe, at least for tonight. And she was safe and that had to be what he focused on: keeping Maisy and Seattle safe.

He couldn't let anything else distract him.

Chapter Ten

Breath, hot against his neck. The brush of hair, silky smooth, along his chin. Her body, soft beside his hard, slowly awakening need from the night before.

He sucked in a slow breath and held it just as she did the same, and her softness tensed with awareness. Awareness of arms wrapped around each other and tangled legs as they undid their pretzelness and shifted toward the edges of the bed.

"Good morning," he said first, his voice morning rough. Or at least that's what he told himself.

"Good morning," she said and looked at her watch. "It's early. Not even six."

To which his phone alarm responded by blaring like a trumpet on steroids, warning that it was time to rise. From the bed, that was.

"I need to get going. You can use the shower first if you want."

She blinked twice, almost a crime because it hid her amazing blue eyes for those brief moments. With a quick lick of her lips, she said, "I showered last night. Remember?"

How could he have forgotten? Maisy coming out from the bathroom, steam chasing her. The smell of her lavender bath gel perfuming the air. Her face rosy cheeked from the heat of the water as she settled into bed with the tablet.

Get a grip, Peters! You're an FBI agent not a love-sick teenager, he told himself.

"Sure. Yes, I remember now. Sorry. I'll hit the shower and then we'll go to the office."

MIGUEL VIRTUALLY JUMPED *out of bed*, Maisy thought, recalling a rabbit she had scared out of a small vegetable garden her mother and she had planted at one of their rented homes.

With him gone and the susurrus of water running through the pipes, she likewise rushed from the bed, straightened it and then raised the Murphy bed back into the wall.

Grabbing some clothes from her suitcase, she quickly dressed and went to the kitchen to make some coffee. Feeling almost at home, she took the to-go cups from a cabinet. Grabbed half-and-half from the fridge and placed it beside the sugar canister on the counter.

Maisy had just finished making her coffee and was pouring his—light and lots of sugar—when he came out of the bathroom half-dressed.

And suddenly the heat she felt wasn't from the sip of hot coffee she'd taken. Dragging her gaze away from his unbuttoned shirt and the sculpted chest beneath, she turned her attention to prepping his coffee. Slowly scooping, pouring and stirring until he stood next to her, fully dressed.

"Ready?" he asked.

More than ready, she thought and nodded. "All set."

As he had yesterday, he laid a hand on her shoulder

as if to guide her out of the apartment. He was a toucher, she'd learned in just the short two days since fate had tossed them together. And she kind of liked it because it was a comforting touch. A protective one.

In no time they were out and up in the BAU offices where his team was already at work. If it wasn't for the different clothes they were wearing, she might have thought that they had been there all night. But even if they had gone home, like Miguel they had probably spent the better part of the night reviewing the information for the case.

That was clear as Miguel stepped over to the board, greeted them and said, "What do we have today?"

Madeline popped up from her chair and handed out a sheet of paper to each team member. "Nicholas and I reviewed our watch list and have selected these terrorists as candidates for our possible unsub. We've also added our top candidates from those recently arrested in the riots."

Madeline sat and with a half glance at Nicholas, she tagged her team member to continue. "Each of these men fits our profile. They've all been either engaged in incidents involving explosives or violent political attacks. Our top candidate calls himself the Freedom Fascist. Real name Bob Smith. He's suspected of planting several IEDs at local police stations and the federal courthouse. Local PD had him in custody, but he was released thanks to new no-bail policies. Now he's gone to ground."

When Nicholas paused to hand out additional papers with the unsub's rap sheet and history, Miguel wrote his name on the board. But after, he said, "I'm not sold on Bob being our unsub."

Miguel's comment had the team all sitting higher in their chairs and glancing around at each other, making Maisy wonder if his challenge was sitting well with the team.

MIGUEL TOOK NOTE of his team's faces. Madeline's had paled slightly beneath her flawless brown skin. Nicholas's cheeks were ruddy, as if with embarrassment. Dash's face was hard, immobile. Only the drum of his fingers gave any hint to what he was feeling. Possibly nervousness.

"We ran through the lists over and over, Miguel," Madeline said.

"He fits the profile," Nicholas said.

"Almost too perfectly," Miguel replied and then gestured toward Maisy. "And don't let Maisy throw you from our usual routine. No one hits it out of the park the first time every time."

"Why do men always use sports metaphors?" Madeline mumbled, but with a smile.

"Because sports rock," Dash said with a laugh.

"They do and so does the work you did on this list. But like I said, I'm just not feeling Bob as our first choice. For starters, he's using M-80s and our unsub is primarily relying on dynamite. By the way, any luck on that front?" Miguel said and looked at Dash for an answer.

"Liam and David are running down lists of active construction sites and licensed master blasters at those sites. Also working hard on breaking past the shell on those shell companies. Trying to find the real owners."

"What about Rothwell and his companies?" Miguel pressed.

"Working on it. He's part owner of quite a few corporations and as you might guess, a lot of companies under them. Liam is compiling the list and I guess you're hoping we'll find a link."

"Or that we can completely eliminate him as a suspect. It's what we need to do. Examine every possible clue, and his turning up all the time is just too much coincidence for me. But let's get back to the list of candidates you worked up," Miguel said and went into listening mode like in his normal routine. Trying not to let Maisy change things up, just as he had asked his team to not let her presence change things.

But it was hard to do as she sat there silently but clearly engaged. It was obvious from the way her face reflected her thoughts. She had an expressive face. Eyes widening when she took in new information. Narrowing, as if in doubt, while they discussed another two of their suspects. A slight nod, later toward lunch, as despite his misgivings, they settled on Bob Smith, aka Freedom Fascist, as their primary unsub.

Like she had the day before, the ever-efficient Lorelai had arranged for lunch to be brought in, but as the food was laid out in the center of the table, Miguel excused himself and headed to his office.

They needed to find the Freedom Fascist and interview him. First thing was to reach out to Seattle PD and put out a BOLO on the man as a person of interest. Second was to contact some of his local informants and see if they were familiar with the man and if so, what information they could provide to either capture him, confirm he was the unsub or eliminate him as a suspect.

To his surprise, he hit gold with the second call. One of his informants, Joseph Michaels, was a former drug dealer turned pub owner with connections to the local antifascist movement. Miguel suspected that despite his claim to not be dealing, he was likely providing drugs to some in that movement.

"You know this guy?" Miguel asked.

"Not only know him, he was here in the pub having lunch just a few minutes ago. Had a few buddies with him and I overheard him talking about the bombings," Joseph said.

"I imagine he supports the bombings," Miguel said, thinking about the demands and how they fit the narrative some of the protesters were spouting.

"More than that. He was telling his buddies that he's the bomber and they were all congratulating him."

Miguel considered it for a second and with a shake of his head, he said, "Did you believe him?"

A choked laugh greeted his statement. "Dude, who knows. I mean, if you really did it, would you be bragging about it in public? But he sounded pretty convincing. Claimed he had a master blaster giving him the dynamite. That he was getting another bomb ready for tomorrow."

And if he was the unsub, that meant they needed to get him into custody. One of the points in their profile was that the bomber would strike again soon, and Joseph had just confirmed that was the Freedom Fascist's plan.

"Do you know where he and his friends were going?"

"They were headed over to the courthouse for another protest. If you're looking for him, he had a pig face mask in his pocket. Black hoodie, blue jeans and a bright red T-shirt."

"Thanks, Joseph," he said, and another laugh drifted over the phone line.

"No thanks necessary. Just make sure there are some extra dead presidents in my paycheck."

Before Miguel could say anything else, his informant disconnected the call. Normally he'd consult with his team, but time was of the essence since their possible unsub was on the move. With another call to his Seattle PD contact, he passed on the information and asked them to provide backup.

If luck was on their side, the Freedom Fascist would be in custody in no time and they'd be able to interview him. He hung up and headed out to update his team, including eating some crow that his team's top choice might actually be their unsub despite his earlier hesitation.

His people, including Liam and David, were sitting around the table, sharing a story about one of their assignments with Maisy, who sat rapt next to his empty chair. As he walked in, laughter erupted as Nicholas described his role in the capture of the unsub.

"The unsub went up and over the fence and I followed, only I didn't count on the slope on the other side of the fence. One second I was on my feet and the next I was heading down that hill," he said and gestured with his hands to show his roll. "But it was like bowling for unsubs since I knocked him off his feet as I tumbled down the hill."

"And Madeline was there to finish the collar, high heels and all," Dash teased.

"After clearing the fence and not rolling down the hill," Madeline said.

"Girl power," Maisy added.

Madeline beamed her a smile and said, "Totally."

Which was the perfect time for Miguel to step into

the conversation. "You guys nailed it with your choice of unsub. I just spoke to a confidential informant who says Bob was bragging about the bombings. The CI gave me some info on where Bob might be. Seattle PD is on their way to provide backup. We need to make the collar."

The team leaped into action, rushing to get their bulletproof vests and weapons and as he went to do the same, Maisy laid a hand on the sleeve of his suit jacket. *"¡Cuídate!"*

He smiled, took hold of her hand and gave a reassuring squeeze. "I will. Liam and David will be here for anything you need."

"I just need for you to come back in one piece."

Warmth filled him with her touch and her concern. "Count on it," he said and for the first time ever, he was able to imagine the fear that his father must have felt every time his mother walked out the door. Maybe because for the first time ever, he was the one who had someone waiting for him to get home safe.

It was a humbling revelation, but he tried not to think on it too long because that would be too much of a distraction. Instead, with another squeeze of her hand, he slipped away to get ready.

THE CROWD MILLING in front of the courthouse was luckily not that big and for the most part, not that violent, unlike some earlier activities. Many of the protesters were masked in one way or another. There was a sea of black bandannas, balaclavas and hoodies, but brightly colored Halloween masks broke up the darkness of the throng. In that darkness there was only one person in a pig mask wearing the clothing his CI had detailed.

There were about a dozen uniformed police officers along the edges of the crowd as he and his team arrived. Silently he directed Madeline and Nicholas to approach their unsub from one side while he and Dash would close the cage from the other.

They walked quickly toward the man, but as some in the crowd noticed them, they began to be jostled and pushed around and a murmur of warning started. It caused their unsub to look back toward the growing commotion and as he spotted their jackets and bulletproof vests with the bold yellow FBI markings, he bolted.

Madeline and Nicholas gave chase, driving the unsub toward Dash and Miguel. Dash took off first and Miguel followed more slowly, mindful of his limitations because of his leg. But as the unsub ducked and weaved through the crowd and the protesters made it difficult for his team, Miguel made a direct path toward the edge of the crowd and corralled a few officers for assistance.

As the unsub neared the hoped-for freedom of open sidewalk, with his team fighting to give chase, Miguel and his assembled officers flanked the unsub, cutting off his escape. The unsub stopped short at the sight of them waiting for him, but then dodged to one side, as if he would be able to squeeze by the small opening between one police officer and the wall of the courthouse.

The crowd, seeing what was happening, pushed toward that spot as if to open the space up for the unsub, but Miguel rushed around and blocked that last little avenue of escape. Seconds later, their unsub was wrapped in a cocoon of police officers while his team held off the few crowd members brave enough to go after them in the hopes of freeing their comrade.

At their car they wasted little time removing the unsub's mask to confirm his identity and handcuffing him while reading him his Miranda rights. Once he was bundled in the car, they raced back to the BAU offices and hauled him up to their interrogation room. For safety's sake, two FBI agents from their office and two Seattle PD officers stood guard outside the room.

As he entered the room, he caught sight of Maisy from the corner of his eye as she sat at their worktable. She offered him a smile filled with comfort and he returned it, but then all his focus was directed at the unsub as he sat down.

Madeline and he sat to conduct the interview while Nicholas and Dashiell watched from the room next door through the one-way mirror.

Madeline began, using the good-cop voice and demeanor that she had perfected in the many years they'd done this dance with other unsubs. "For the record, this is an interrogation with Special Agent Madeline Striker and Supervisory Special Agent Miguel Peters interviewing Robert Smith. Bob, you've been read your Miranda rights. Do you understand that anything you say or do can be held against you in a court of law and that you're entitled to counsel? If you can't afford counsel, we can provide one for you. Do you wish to continue with this interview at this time?"

Bob negligently tossed his handcuffed hands in the air and shrugged. "I've got nothing to hide. Mind telling me why you're violating my civil right to protest by bringing me here?"

"I assume you're aware that there have been several bombings in the Seattle area," Madeline said.

"Who isn't? It's been all over the news," Bob said with another, almost insolent, shrug.

"But you have more intimate knowledge of the bombings, don't you, Bob?" Miguel said, leaning forward slightly to be in the unsub's face a little more.

Bob was unfazed. If anything, he grew more belligerent, likewise leaning forward until he was almost nose-to-nose with Miguel. "As if you guys have something on me. You're incompetent. Stupid. That's all over the news too."

Miguel didn't back away, determined to play hardball, while Madeline said, "Bob, you know better than that. We have someone who heard you claiming responsibility for the bombings. Your past manifestos are in line with the Seattle Crusader's demands. We're just waiting for DNA results from the bombs and I'm sure they're going to point to you."

Bob laughed and fell back against his chair, shaking his head. "Just shows how stupid you are. Do you think *I'd* be stupid enough to leave DNA behind?"

"You were stupid enough to get caught planting a box filled with M-80s at the courthouse. You know M-80s are illegal unless you're licensed, right? Just like dynamite and I doubt you have a license," Miguel said.

"But almost any idiot can buy a gun, right?" Bob countered, a derisive smile on his face.

"I understand you did a beautiful job of wiring those M-80s. If they hadn't caught you, it would have made quite a big bang," Miguel said.

Another shrug greeted him and then Bob turned his attention to Madeline. "You'd think you would understand why we do this. Why we're trying to break the system."

Madeline didn't allow him to faze her. "Why bombs? And where did you get the dynamite?"

"Easy, Madeline. I can call you Madeline, right?" Bob said, slipping on a smarmy smile.

"Yes, of course. Please tell me. How did you get the dynamite and wire? How did you choose the kinds of bombs to build?" she said.

"Friends in the right places. As for building them, I like to tinker."

"Tinker? How do you tinker?" Miguel said, his gut telling him that something wasn't right about Bob Smith. So not right that he was beginning to think, as he had at first, that this was not their unsub.

"I play around—"

"With dynamite. Amazing that you're still alive," Miguel shot back.

That smarmy smile returned, and Bob held his hands up and wiggled his fingers. "Magic hands."

"Please tell us how those magic hands built the collar bomb," Madeline cajoled, her voice as sweet as Vermont syrup.

"Sure," he said and with those hands, he detailed what he had done as he spoke. "I'd seen that show on Netflix about the Pizza Bomber. And you guys offer such good information on your website. Amazing stuff really. Made it real easy."

"So why didn't it go off? Why did you seem surprised when the second bomb exploded at King Street Station?" Madeline pressed.

Bob seemed a little put off by her questions, maybe even taken aback. Again, or for the first time? The CCTV footage of the bomber had not been released to the public although there had been a number of videos posted by witnesses. However, none of the witness videos had shown that moment of surprise when the second bomb went off.

"It was a bigger blast than I expected," Bob said, but Miguel could see the beads of sweat collecting on Bob's upper lip.

"But no blast from the collar bomb. Why do you think that is?" he said.

Another careless shrug was the only answer as Bob looked down at his hands.

"Magic hands fail you, Bob? Did you trip the second bomb by accident? Not build the collar bomb right?" he pressed, leaning forward again, so far across the table and in Bob's face that it was impossible for their unsub not to see him.

He reacted like Miguel had wanted. "Get out of my face, dude. That won't work on me."

"You're lying. You don't know anything about these bombings that isn't in the news," Miguel said.

"That's not true," Bob almost shouted.

"A liar. And what you were telling those people… all lies. You're just grandstanding. Trying to make a name for yourself because you're nothing," Miguel challenged.

"I am the Seattle Crusader," he shouted back.

"Tell us more, then. If you do, we can make it easier for you," Madeline said, almost cajoling.

"You guys can't do spit," Bob parried.

"Why are you wasting our time? You don't know anything. That's obvious. Are you trying to score brownie points with your masked buddies? Will taking credit for the bombings make you feel big, little man?"

Their unsub slammed his hands on the table, the

sound as loud as a gunshot in the small room. "You think you can stop us, but you can't. We're winning this war and we'll use any means necessary to do that."

"Including wasting our time," Miguel said calmly and sat back, more convinced than ever that this unsub was lying.

"If that's what it takes to show how incompetent you are. To show your Gestapo tactics to silence us, but that's not going to happen. And I'm not going to cooperate anymore. I want an attorney."

"Come on, Bob. We can't help you if you don't help us," Madeline said, her tone pleading.

"I. Want. A. Lawyer," Bob said, enunciating each and every word as slowly as molasses in winter.

Miguel rose from his chair and Madeline did the same. Looking down at the unsub, he said, "Fine. Seattle PD will escort you to their station house and you can call an attorney from there. This interview is concluded."

A second later, two Seattle police officers walked into the room to guide the unsub out, but as Bob stepped into the space, he looked around.

Their whiteboard had been removed in anticipation of the interview, but Maisy was still at the table and as the unsub saw her, he peered at Miguel. With an evil glint in his eyes and a tight smile, he said, "Angel Eyes is real pretty. Are you screwing her like the government screws all of us?"

Maisy paled, but Miguel ignored the question, which only riled Bob even more. To his surprise, Bob broke free of the police officers and chest bumped him as he screamed, "Can't perform, Peters? Is that it? Can't screw her?"

The two officers grabbed him and got him under control. "Well, Bob, you just bought yourself a charge of assaulting a Federal officer and in front of several witnesses and CCTV," Miguel said and pointed to the camera in the interview room which would have captured the attack.

"Please take him away and charge him," Miguel said, and the two officers complied, hauling off a screaming Bob, who continued to curse Miguel, the other agents and the government.

As the team reconvened around the table, Miguel said, "He's not our guy."

Chapter Eleven

Maisy couldn't believe what had just happened and what followed as each of the team members nodded at Miguel's assessment.

"He didn't seem to know anything about the collar bomb," Nicholas said.

"And those 'magic hands'? There's something off about his height, the size of his hands and those of the bomber. Is there any way to get a better approximation of the hand size?" Madeline said.

Miguel concurred with a nod. "Is that possible, Dash?"

"We can try to get more info on his physical attributes. Pupil distance, et cetera," Dashiell said and stared at Nicholas, who shifted uneasily, rocking from one side to the next on his feet. Something about the quick look he shot her had her insides twisting into a knot.

"What is it, Nicholas?" Miguel asked and likewise peered at her.

"We got a call while you were interviewing the unsub," Nicholas said and once again looked her way, making her blood run cold in anticipation of what he would say.

"Spill, Nicholas," Madeline said, clearly aware of how the delay was affecting her.

"Maisy's father reached out to us. He's seen the news and is worried about Maisy. He wants to help us any way he can to catch this bomber," Nicholas said.

Despite his words, Maisy heard the "but" behind them, as did Miguel.

"What else, Nicholas?" Miguel said.

"He'll only talk to us about the bomber if Maisy is with us. He wants to talk to her tomorrow."

For a moment the world dimmed around her and her ears went deaf. She knew the team members were discussing the request because she could see their lips moving, but she couldn't hear them. Couldn't even really do anything since her body had gone numb.

But then Miguel came to her side and touched her hand. Slowly warmth and feeling returned, spreading out from the gentle pressure of his hand on hers. "Are you okay?"

Her gaze was unfocused, shimmering with incipient tears. Her chest was heavy, almost so heavy that it was hard to breathe, but somehow she dragged in a breath and said, "I'm not sure."

THERE WAS NO doubt Maisy was upset. Her face had paled to a sickly green and tears clung to her thick lashes until the first one escaped and slipped down her cheek. He cradled her jaw and swiped the tear away. "Let's get some air."

A quick nod and she was on her feet, moving away from the table and toward Miguel's office, but he thought she needed more than that.

He slipped his arm around her waist and guided her

toward the elevator. At her surprised look, he said, "We both need a break. How about a coffee?"

She nodded again and eked out, "Coffee would be nice."

As the elevator arrived, they stepped on and rode down to the lobby. They did a slow stroll across the gleaming marble tiles, out onto the street and down the block to a local coffee shop. He continued to keep her close since her body still trembled and only the faintest hint of color had returned to her features. She stumbled a bit when she ordered, obviously still discomfited.

After he'd ordered and they had their coffees, he guided her toward a table against an inside wall and far enough away from the windows to offer some privacy but allow him to keep an eye out for anything untoward. The table was also close to an emergency exit in case of trouble.

Maisy wrapped shaky hands around the coffee mug and after a few sips, he asked, "Feeling better?"

"A little."

He took a sip of his own coffee and narrowed his eyes to examine her reaction as he said, "I know you've had a surprise."

Her mug hit the tabletop hard. "An understatement. But I guess nothing about my father should surprise me anymore."

"You don't have to do it. I have no doubt—"

"But you do have doubts. I haven't known you long, but even I can see you're frustrated," she said and laid her hand over his, returning the comfort he had offered earlier.

With a shrug he said, "Not so much frustrated as

concerned and puzzled. Like I have a lot of pieces, but there's one missing to complete the picture."

She squeezed his hand. "You will figure it out."

He arched a brow. "But will it be quick enough?" Shaking his head, he looked away and said, "I wish I could channel my mother. I have no doubt she'd be seeing all the pieces of that puzzle."

Maisy hesitated and peered at him over the rim of her mug. She took a sip and said, "Don't sell yourself short. You will solve this."

Much like she had just done, he delayed, unsure of himself. Unsure of the request he would have to put to her as much as he might not like it. With a deep breath, he exhaled and pushed forward.

"You don't have to talk to your dad tomorrow. I won't put you through that." She'd already suffered thanks to his actions and his recent contacts which had terrorized her.

"But could it help you?" Maisy asked, her deep blue gaze locked on his, assessing his response.

Would it? he asked himself. Although his gut and some of the evidence so far indicated that the bomber was not acting alone, could it possibly be her father directing the attacks from prison? But if he was, would the Forest Conservation Bomber attack a location where his daughter would be? Although how could he know that?

Miguel met her gaze straight on. "I won't ask you to talk to your father. I know how much he's already hurt you."

"Would it help?" she pressed, her hands clenching the mug so tightly her fingers were white from the pressure.

He reached out and covered her hands, urged her to release the mug, and he twined his fingers with hers.

Despite his misgivings about not having all the pieces of the puzzle, he had faith in his team and himself.

"We will solve this."

THE WARMTH OF his calloused hands reached deep within her, offering comfort...and more. After all, he was a handsome man, but his caring and understanding were what made him truly impossible to ignore.

But she had to ignore him because she had plans for her life and Miguel wasn't a part of those plans. Much like having her father in her life again wasn't part of what she had envisioned for herself.

But she knew how troubled he was about the investigation and she was too. She'd overheard the team's concerns about their profile for the unsub and Miguel had been open with her about his feelings. Much the way she had been open about her fears.

Despite that, she was a strong woman, and she would not let her father control her again. Or scare her again.

"Like I said before, I know you will find the bomber. But I don't want anyone else to be hurt because of something I did. Or didn't have the courage to do."

Miguel squeezed her hands and offered her a smile filled with understanding. "Nothing you do or don't do will hurt anyone, Maisy."

"I want to help. Whatever it takes, I'm ready to do it, even if it means talking to my father. I'm only going to ask one thing. I want you to go with me tomorrow to see him."

DASHIELL PEERED AT Madeline, Nicholas, David and Liam as they gathered around the table.

"I'm not sure Maisy will go along with speaking to her father. She seemed very upset," he said.

"Not unexpected. As Nicholas mentioned, she and her mother are probably suffering from a form of PTSD so anything connected with her father is bound to cause great distress," Madeline said.

"Definitely," Nicholas chimed in. "Still, I think we all agree there may be more than one person behind this terrorism. Maybe even the Forest Conservation Bomber."

"What about Bob Smith? Is he off our lists of unsubs?" David asked.

"We did the analysis you asked on body parts, comparing the unsub's height, width, hands to the photos and videos we have, and he doesn't fit," Liam said.

Dashiell walked to the whiteboard, picked up the eraser and held it over the Freedom Fascist's name on the board. When Madeline and Nicholas nodded, he erased his name.

"Where does that leave us? Liam? David? Do you have anything else for us?" Dashiell asked.

David nodded and handed a report to everyone at the table. "We ran the photo we created against several databases and this is a list of possible suspects, complete with their pictures."

The phone in the middle of the conference table rang, rattling against the wood. Madeline reached over and hit the speakerphone button. "Yes, Lorelai. Madeline here. What can we do for you?"

"Director Branson just called. The TEDAC director called her to say they had an initial report they'd be sending to her. We should have it in less than half an hour," Lorelai said.

"Any idea what they've found?" Liam asked his ex.

"From what the director said, they've identified the dynamite and wire makers, have a couple of fingerprints and DNA. They'll be sending the profile over so you can run it through CODIS and the genealogy services."

"Great. That's wonderful, Lorelai. As soon as you have it, please send it over," Madeline said just as Miguel and Maisy walked down the hall.

Miguel immediately read their mood. "I guess we have good news?"

Dashiell nodded and said, "TEDAC report is on the way with lots of information."

"Good to hear," Miguel said and shot a half glance at Maisy. "We have news as well."

Holding his breath, Dashiell waited for what their witness—and a woman Miguel obviously cared about—would say. While he waited, he corralled his concern about how Miguel's attraction to Maisy might affect the investigation. He also once again inspected the team members gathered around the table to see how they would react to Maisy's news.

"Maisy?" Miguel prompted.

Maisy risked a glance at Miguel and after looked toward them. "Miguel and I discussed it and… I will meet with my father, but I've asked Miguel to be there."

Nicholas nodded and said, "I don't think that will be an issue. His one request was to speak to Maisy, and he has to expect that the FBI will be there as well."

Miguel clapped his hands and said, "Great. Make the call. As soon as we have the TEDAC report, let's jump on running anything they have for us. In the meantime, what else do we have?"

MAISY SAT IN a chair and watched as Miguel assumed control of the meeting. Easygoing control, she noticed again. He waited and digested what his team had gathered. Prompted their ideas and then offered his own, leading the investigation in his laid-back way. But despite that, there was no doubt who was in charge.

Power radiated from him, drawing her in while at the same time, she couldn't miss his concern that so far, they were missing key pieces of the puzzle.

The phone rang barely half an hour later, signaling that the TEDAC report had arrived. The team immediately reviewed the results together and divided up what to do with the report.

"Liam, David and I will work on running the DNA and fingerprints against the databases," Dashiell advised.

Madeline held up the list of possible suspects. "I'll do a deeper review of this list."

"I'll make arrangements for a visit tomorrow to Maisy's dad," Nicholas said.

"Good. Please forward me the TEDAC report, your lists and anything else you dig up. If Maisy doesn't mind, we'll visit my father and go over what he remembers about the bombing," Miguel stated.

Maisy dipped her head and said, "I don't mind at all. You know I love your dad."

Miguel smiled. "Thank you. Please excuse me while I step aside to call ahead and let him know we're coming."

He waited a beat for any feedback, then headed out, leaving Maisy sitting with the team. She normally wasn't comfortable about strangers, a side effect of having virtually been in hiding for the past fifteen years.

Not to mention the fear still roiling her gut about seeing her father once again. But the team had made her feel comfortable and she knew they were working hard at keeping her and others safe from the Seattle Crusader.

"I want to thank you for all that you're doing," Maisy said, her comment heartfelt.

Madeline nodded and offered her a brilliant smile. "We couldn't do anything else."

A few minutes later, Miguel walked back in and laid a hand on her shoulder. "Ready?"

"Yes, thanks," she said, rose and walked beside Miguel down the hall to the elevator lobby. While they waited, Miguel glanced at her, eyes narrowed, a worried look on his features.

"Are you really ready?"

Maisy didn't know if she'd ever be "really ready" for what might happen tomorrow. She hadn't ever contemplated seeing her father again. If anything, she'd hoped she'd never have to see him again, but the Seattle Crusader had made that impossible. Regardless, she was strong enough to handle this, especially with Miguel and his team at her side.

"I'm as ready as I'll ever be."

With a slow nod, he said, "I know you will be."

The ding of the elevator shattered the moment.

Together they boarded the elevator and as they'd done earlier, traveled through the lobby and down the few blocks to the hotel where Miguel's dad was living. As he'd done earlier, he wrapped an arm around her waist and drew her close, the action one of comfort and protection. But as had happened before, it was impossible to ignore that he was a vital and attractive man.

Every now and then she'd peer up at him, take in

the strong line of his jaw, slightly shaded with the start of an evening beard. Full lips, more relaxed now than in the office.

He did a quick glance down at her and their gazes locked, his brown eyes sharp, but warm as he perused her features. He smiled and a dimple emerged at the right side of his mouth, making him look more boyish. Less formidable.

But then suddenly Miguel was searching the area, back in FBI mode. She tracked his gaze, looking around, but saw nothing.

"Everything okay?" she asked.

"Just thought I saw something, but I must have imagined it," he said, gently squeezed her waist, and they continued their walk in peace.

THE SEATTLE CRUSADER CURSED and clung to the trunk of the tree he'd hidden behind. Counting to ten, he sucked in a deep breath and peeked past the trunk.

Seeing Angel Eyes and the FBI agent walking away, he blew out a relieved exhale and did another count of ten before following them again.

If it was up to him, he'd be back home in the tent he'd set up in the homeless encampment under the highway and smoking some weed. But he had his instructions and if he was going to help his brothers, not to mention himself, he had to do as he was told.

That meant finding out where the two witnesses were being held, as well as the location of the BAU office. The latter was easy enough. He'd only had to search the web to get the address of the building.

But learning where the witnesses were had been harder. It had forced him to surveil the FBI offices since yesterday in addition to planting the two bombs last night.

He laughed as he thought of how well those bombings had gone off and the attention that his tweets had gotten. It was going just as planned, which reminded him that he had another tweet to share tonight.

Yanking out the burner phone he'd been provided, he stopped and tweeted.

Time for criminal reform. No bail. Shorter jail terms. Fairer parole policies. It's time to decriminalize before it's too late.

His phone made a little whoosh sound as he touched Send and the tweet hit the outside world.

But as he looked up, he realized that he had lost sight of Angel Eyes and the FBI agent.

Luckily, he knew they'd be returning to the FBI offices at some point.

Unluckily for them, he'd be waiting for them and would be ready to act.

Smiling, he reached into his pocket and took out the cash he'd been paid. More than enough for a nice dinner tonight. And once he finished his tasks, he'd have enough for daily meals and a place to stay. A place big enough for him and his brothers once they were released, as he'd been promised.

With a whistle, he shoved the money back into his pocket, turned and headed for his favorite pub, dreaming of the biggest burger they made.

The first of many, he thought. Just a few more tweets and bombs, and he'd be set for life.

Chapter Twelve

This is what a family should be like, Maisy thought as she sat at the small hotel table with Miguel and his dad.

They'd been chatting amiably about Maisy's blog, but also about her suggestion that his father, Robert, help other budding bloggers and journalists with the knowledge he'd gleaned over the years as a professor. Sadly, the discussion soon turned to the investigation and how Maisy was supposed to speak to her father in the morning as well as trying to glean what they could about what Robert remembered from the day of the bombing. Unfortunately his father remembered very little.

"It's okay, Dad," Miguel said, but his general frustration about the investigation was painfully obvious.

"I know I'm missing something, Dad. And I know that if *Mami* was alive she'd see what I'm missing," Miguel said.

Robert reached out and laid his hand on Miguel's shoulder. "Trust in yourself. You are your mother's son, but more importantly, you are brilliant in your own special way."

A half smile relieved Miguel's too serious features, making him look younger. "Thanks, Dad."

"I agree, Robert. Miguel and his team are making

progress. I have no doubt they'll catch the Seattle Crusader in no time."

Much like Robert had done before, he reached out and laid a comforting hand on her shoulder. Funny thing, she had thought Miguel's touchiness had come from his Cuban mother, but Robert was also as demonstrative.

"I understand you have to face your own challenge, Maisy. Am I right?"

With a sideways glance at Miguel, Maisy said, "I have to see my father tomorrow."

A little hum escaped Robert before he said, "And how does that make you feel?"

She inhaled a breath, trapped it inside her. Slowly she let it escape and said, "Scared—no, make that terrified. What he did and after, it terrorized my mom and me for so long. I never wanted to see him again and now..." Her voice trailed off, her throat choked with emotion. Tears were once again threatening, making her sniffle as she battled them.

"It's okay to be scared. Terrified," Miguel said and covered her hand with his.

Comfort filled her as it did so often with his touch. Peace, something which had been sorely lacking in her life during the past fifteen years.

"But you'll be there, right? To help me?" she said, not sure she could face her father without his support.

"I'll be there. Always," he said and as her gaze locked with his, it was too easy to imagine an always with him.

"Thank you," she said.

The chirp of Miguel's phone shattered the moment. "Please excuse me," he said, rose from the table and walked a few feet away to take the call in more privacy. Still, the room was small, making it impossible not to eavesdrop.

"Okay. 9:00 a.m. tomorrow. Sea Tac. We'll meet you in the lobby at eight fifteen."

He ended the call and from across the short distance, his gaze met hers as if seeking her confirmation.

With a nod, she said, "I'll be ready."

SHE SAYS IT, but is she really ready? Miguel wondered. He didn't know if he would be, recalling how he'd suffered after his mother's murder and how it still affected him at times. How it hung over him, keeping him from moving on, he realized with surprise.

Much like Maisy had been a prisoner of her past, so had he and maybe it was time to change that.

"We should get going. We have an early morning."

He walked back to the table. Maisy and his father had risen, and he took a moment to hug his father. Hard. "Goodnight, Dad."

Maisy drifted over to likewise embrace his father. "Thank you for everything, Robert. Miguel is so very lucky to have you."

"And now you have me too. I'm here for you."

Maisy smiled, an enchanting smile. Her gaze glittered joyfully, devoid of the pain that had clouded her beautiful blue eyes earlier.

The sight of her, so much happier, lightened the pain and anxiety in his heart, prompting him to take her into his arms. "You're not alone anymore."

She hugged him, her head tucked against his chest. Her slender arms wrapped around him. "I know."

They ended the embrace, and his father offered his routine but heartfelt send-off. *"¡Cuídate!"*

Miguel smiled and said, "Love you."

After his father opened the door so they could leave, he kept his arm around Maisy's waist as they walked out of the hotel room, bid goodnight to the FBI agent stationed at the door and strolled the few short blocks back to the BAU offices.

Back to my home, only it isn't much of a home, is it? he thought.

But as Maisy and he stepped into his apartment, it felt different. It felt not as…lonely.

He stopped and faced her. Cradled her cheek and applied gentle pressure to tilt her face upward. "It's my turn to thank you," he said.

She narrowed her gaze and skipped it over his features, puzzled. "Why?"

"Because you've helped me more than you can imagine," he said and stroked his thumb across the creamy skin of her cheek.

Her lips quirked up in a smile and she shook her head. "That's hard to believe."

"Believe it. Your strength in dealing with your past… It's made me think about my past. My mom. That pain I still carry with me every day."

She smoothed a hand across his chest and then laid it over his heart. "But we have to find a way to put it away, don't we? It's the only way we can build a future."

A future? he thought. Suddenly he wasn't as closed off to a future that was about more than just work. *A future that includes this amazing woman*, he thought and bent his head, covered her half smile with his lips.

Her lips were warm against his. So soft and mobile as she returned his kiss, rising on tiptoes to meet him more fully. Pressing her lush body to his, her curves flattening against him, rousing passion.

He tightened his hold on her, relishing the feel of her. The way the warmth of her body seeped into his, kindling heat within him. But not just the heat of passion. Kindling fire and life in his heart.

As the kiss deepened, so did the need to touch her. He inched his hand between them to cup her breast, and her nipple beaded beneath his palm. She moaned and he hesitated, but then she covered his hand with hers, urging him on.

He tugged at the hard nub, dragging another moan from her. The moan ripped through the haze of passion, jerking him back to the reality of their situation.

It must have done the same for her as in unison, they uneasily eased apart, gazes locked. Arms still wrapped around one another.

"I'm sorry. I shouldn't have done that," he said, but took no other motion to break apart from her.

"Don't apologize. I'm as responsible," she replied and reached up to wipe her thumb across his lips. The touch sent another zing of need through him, but she offered him a wry smile and said, "Lip gloss."

He chuckled and nodded. "Not quite what the other agents expect me to be wearing."

"No, but it looks good on you," she said and as her gaze settled on his face again, it was hot. Possessive.

"But it looks way better on you." He couldn't resist slipping his thumb across her mouth, the touch possibly more intimate than their kiss.

His phone chirped and he reached between their bodies to pull it out, glance at the face of it and swipe to take the call. "Dashiell. Do you have something new?"

"Another tweet from the Crusader. This one calls for no bail and shorter prison terms for drug possession. Another threat that a bomb is on its way unless we do as he asks."

"I'll check it out. In the meantime, ask Madeline to see if anyone on that list or a relative has been jailed."

"On it. We'll keep you posted if anything else hits tonight."

Dashiell ended the call and Miguel finally took the step back from Maisy. He had to refocus his attention on the case to keep her and others safe.

"I need to review the new information," he said, and Maisy nodded.

Maisy gestured toward the bathroom. "I think I'll take a shower and get ready for bed."

"Great. I'm going to see what we have so far and shower in the morning," he said.

"Great," she parroted, obviously growing uneasier by the second despite their earlier closeness.

"Great," he said and wanted to kick himself for how stupid it sounded. Luckily, she bolted to her bag to grab some clothes and then to the shower.

He blew out a harsh breath and dragged a hand through his hair in frustration. He was used to cases not going the way he wanted, but this case was getting way too complicated.

First there was the bomber himself and their inability to stop him. He seemed to have no interest in harming anyone yet, but for how long? Eventually he would escalate the situation and possibly hurt someone.

The sound of flowing water in the shower intruded and reminded him that it was best he get ready for bed before Maisy emerged from the bathroom, shower fresh. Skin flushed from the hot water.

He muttered a curse as passion rose again and he leaped into action.

Quickly changing into sweats and a T-shirt, which would let him rush up to the office in case he needed to, he tugged down the Murphy bed and settled there with his laptop.

He pulled up his notes and, in his brain, worked through the bomber's assorted requests, which were starting to add to his profile of the typical serial bomber.

White male. In it for either revenge or justification. The demands were continuing to be unrealistic, but he ran through them anyway.

A higher minimum wage. *Maybe someone stuck in assorted low-paying jobs?*

The homeless encampment in the Japanese Gardens. *Possibly someone who has experienced homelessness?*

The demand for bail and prison reform added a dimension that actually narrowed the list of possible suspects to someone directly touched by that system. It was why he'd asked his people to see if anyone on their list had relatives in prison.

Which directed his thoughts toward Maisy's father. He had tossed around the idea in his brain of the Forest Conservation Bomber being involved with the bombings, but the motivations were too disparate. Protecting the environment versus the assorted social issues raised by the Crusader.

The methods of the bombings were also too different. Fertilizer-based bombs versus ones made with dynamite.

Finally, Maisy's dad had intended to do harm. *Had*

done harm and so far, the Crusader's targets were clearly in areas where no one would be hurt, especially since the detonator on the collar bomb had not been connected.

"So far" being the operative words, which propelled him to continue working, trying to get closer to the persons behind the bombings. He was sure of that one thing: the bomber wasn't acting alone. There was language in the demands that pointed to that and his gut told him the bomber was a puppet and someone else was pulling the strings.

Maybe even Rothwell. There was something about the politician and his too-convenient appearance whenever something happened that bothered him. And it had nothing to do with the politician's insults.

He'd been insulted before and by better than Richard Rothwell.

Armed with that thought, he pushed on, determined to have more to the Crusader's profile by the time they met with Maisy's dad in the morning.

MAISY LINGERED IN the shower even though she knew that no matter how long she took, Miguel would be awake and working hard on catching the bomber.

A bomber just like my dad, she thought as she shut off the water and toweled down.

A bomber who she feared would one day hurt or kill someone just like her father had done.

No, not my father, she reminded herself. As she'd told Miguel, her father had died the day that the Forest Conservation Bomber had been born.

She had died that day as well. Elizabeth Green, the young girl who had dreamed of traveling and writing, had disappeared and been replaced by Maisy Oliver, a woman who had been afraid and in hiding for the past fifteen years.

But she'd made her mother and herself a promise as she'd watched her mother slowly die from cancer: that she'd start to live again. That she'd dream again, the dreams she'd had as a child.

She was not going to let this bomber, or her dad, defeat her.

Slipping into her pajamas, she tiptoed from the bathroom to not distract Miguel, but as she caught sight of him, she suspected his attention was totally focused on his work.

Until he spotted her, and slowly lifted his gaze. "Good night, Maisy."

"Good night, Miguel."

Even though it had grown late what with their visiting his dad, the dinner they'd picked up and shared after that visit, and a pleasantly long hot shower, she was too wired to sleep.

She made up the couch with the sheets, comforter and pillow, and settled in, making sure that she was nestled deep in the comfortable cushions and unable to see Miguel because he was way too distracting.

She grabbed her tablet, plugged in earphones and went to a streaming service to try to catch up on a series that she had been watching about unique buildings. It wasn't just the architecture that captured her interest, but the equally fascinating settings for many of the structures.

She had pictured herself visiting such different locales and writing about them. It was why she'd worked so hard after her mom had died to find a better-paying job. A job she had unfortunately had to put on hold with this investigation. Luckily, her new boss understood why she was absent, but she was eager to go back to work. Back to her normal life and her dreams.

And nothing, not her father, this bomber or even Miguel, was going to keep her from that.

Chapter Thirteen

The Forest Conservation bomber was being held at the federal detention center, a multipurpose prison that held various types of detainees. It wasn't far from the airport so the ride to get there wasn't that long. Unbeknownst to Maisy and her mother, their flight from their Woodinville hometown to escape her father's crimes had actually put them closer to where he was being imprisoned.

And although the ride wasn't long, it was silent and tense.

Miguel sat beside Maisy in the back seat while Nicholas drove, with Madeline in the passenger seat.

Maisy was pale and as Miguel laid his hand on hers, her skin was ice-cold even with the heat in the car.

"It'll be fine," Miguel urged, trying to calm her.

She nodded and forced a smile, but her distress was plain to see. Her amazing blue eyes were dead, almost cold. Every muscle in her body tense except for a nervous tic at her jaw.

He twined his fingers with hers, trying to offer what comfort he could through the rest of the drive and the process for being cleared for entry into the detention center.

As this was a special visit, the warden met them as

soon as they went through security and walked them to a room normally used for visits by attorneys. "I hope you get what you want from Green. He's a tough nut," the warden said.

"Has he given you problems?" Miguel asked the older man.

With a shrug, the warden said, "He's not violent despite his criminal record. Just a know-it-all, trying to challenge every rule or regulation. He thinks he's smarter than everyone."

Which just confirms part of our profile, Miguel thought. Serial bombers, much like serial killers, thought they were more intelligent than everyone around them.

"We appreciate that heads-up as well as allowing this visit on such short notice," Miguel said and shook the other man's hand.

"Not a problem, SSA Peters. We understand the urgency of the situation. Whenever you're ready," the older man said and gestured toward the door to the visiting room.

Miguel peered at Maisy. "Are you ready?"

HER THROAT WAS so tight, her heart pounding hard enough to split her chest open, that Maisy couldn't speak. She could only nod and brace herself for her first look at her father in fifteen years.

As she walked in, she thought, *He's aged.*

His once caramel brown hair had gone gray and the lines around his mouth and eyes had deepened. Despite that, his skin was tanned and his body whipcord lean, as if he'd been exercising. It almost wasn't fair that he looked that good when she thought about how her mother had suffered and deteriorated thanks to the cancer that had claimed her life.

"Elizabeth. Or should I call you Maisy now?" Richard Green said and before she could reply, he added, "You've grown into such a lovely young woman. You look so much like your mother."

"Mr. Green. Supervisory Special Agent Peters," Miguel said and then gestured to his team members. "Special Agent Striker and Special Agent James are also attending this interview."

At his words, her father almost seemed to preen, as if having that many FBI agents was testament to his importance. "Thank you for coming, especially you, Maisy. I hope you understand that I never meant to hurt you and your mother. And I never meant to hurt anyone. I was just trying to defend something that couldn't defend itself."

Which was what he'd said throughout his trial although the investigators had provided numerous proofs of his intent to maim and kill loggers and other people the Forest Conservation League had seen as enemies. Clearly her father still didn't believe he deserved to be in jail for what he'd done.

"But you did hurt and kill," she shot back, not buying his apology.

Her father's face hardened, growing tense. "I had hoped you could forgive me. That's why I've been trying to reach you. The calls and letters were my way of trying to make peace with you because even though I'm in prison, I'm still your father. And I love you, Maisy. You have to believe that."

Miguel laid a hand on her shoulder and applied gentle pressure, urging her to sit across from her father.

She hated to do it, almost felt like it was accepting his apology, something she wasn't prepared to do. But she knew she had to keep the lines of communication open to hopefully get some useful information for the Seattle Crusader investigation. But there was something she needed to know first.

"How did you find out my new name and address?" she asked.

Her father smiled, but it held no warmth or happiness. "I have my ways, Maisy. Friends who still appreciate what I did and help me."

It made her wonder if those friends were behind what was happening, and Miguel must have felt the same way.

"I guess that means you may have insights for us," Miguel said.

Her father nodded and skipped his gaze over the stern faces of the three FBI agents. "I do. This bomber is a novice. He doesn't know what he's doing, almost like he's shooting off big M-80s to get attention."

"Why do you say that?" Maisy asked, taking the lead.

"If I had made the bomb, it would have taken out more of the buildings and the old man in the station. This bomber doesn't really know how to use dynamite to its full potential."

"You mean how to hurt someone, don't you? Like the people you hurt. Like you hurt Mom and me. Do you even care that you did that?" she shot back, unable to stay silent.

Her father reached for her hand, but she pulled it back, dreading his touch.

With a shake of his head and a harsh laugh, he said,

"You're so cold, just like your mother. But despite that, I did care for her and you. I still care. That's why I asked you to visit. I want to help."

"If you want to help, tell us what else you know," Nicholas said, jumping into the conversation.

"Like I said, he's a novice, not like me. He doesn't understand the power he has and how to use it. If he did, he would make reasonable demands," her father said.

"Like asking for money like you did?" Maisy countered.

Her father glared at her. "Money that I intended to use to buy wilderness areas in danger of being destroyed."

"Do you think he's working alone?" Miguel asked.

Her father's answer was immediate. "No, I don't. Someone is directing him because he's a novice. Stupid almost. Someone much more intelligent is pulling the puppet's strings," he said and mimicked someone playing a marionette.

"Someone like you?" Madeline asked, arching a dark brow in emphasis.

"Me? You think I'm involved?" her father said, clearly incredulous at the question.

"Do you even care that he's targeting me, Dad? Angel Eyes? Does that matter to you?" Maisy pressed.

"Of course it does. Why do you think you're here?" he said, his gaze almost pleading as it traveled across her face and then over the FBI agents.

Miguel answered, "I think we're here to satisfy your ego. Your need to be better than the Crusader. To prove how much smarter you are than him and us. That's why I think we're here because so far, you haven't told us a thing we don't know."

"I *am* better than the Crusader. And to tell you something you don't know, he's going to strike again and this time, he's going to hurt someone," her father parried.

Maisy risked a glance at Miguel, and it was obvious that he was done, especially considering that nothing her father had said, not even his last outburst, had provided any useful information.

Pushing to her feet, she said, "I'd like to go, but before I do." She faced her father. "Do not contact me again, *Richard.* You're not my father. The father I had was kind and gentle and not a monster like you."

WHEN RICHARD GREEN lunged at Maisy, Miguel blocked his arm and pushed him back into his seat. "You heard the lady. I'm going to make sure the warden knows of your harassment and blocks your mail and phone access."

"You can't do that!" Richard shouted, but Maisy was already in motion, rushing toward the door, flanked by Madeline and Nicholas. Miguel followed, tuning out the Forest Conservation Bomber's shouts that chased them as they exited.

When his team members shifted to walk in front of Maisy for protection, Miguel slipped to her side and wrapped an arm around her waist. She was trembling, but her head was held high. "You are amazing," he whispered in her ear.

"I'm my mother's daughter," she replied, meeting his eyes, her cerulean gaze direct and blazing with anger and determination.

"She must have been an incredible woman," he said and hugged her close, but that action drew raised eyebrows from both Madeline and Nicholas.

Despite that, he didn't pull away from Maisy, walking with his arm around her until they were out of the detention center and at their car. Once they were settled in the back seat, he said, "I appreciate you doing this. I know how hard it must have been for you to see your father."

Maisy shook her head. "Like I told him, he's not my father. My father is dead."

Miguel nodded. "I understand. I just wish that we would have gotten some useful information, given the pain you suffered by coming here."

Madeline twisted slightly in the passenger seat to look back at them. "In a way we did. Green confirmed much of our profile."

"You're right about that, Madeline. He has confirmed our profile, but that also has me worrying about when the Crusader will strike again and who he might harm," Nicholas said with a quick glance at them as he drove.

"Which means we need to keep on pushing to get more info. Hopefully Dash's team has more info on the list of licensed blasters as well as the DNA profile." Miguel whipped out his smartphone to call the team back at the BAU offices.

Dashiell answered, an upbeat tone in his voice. "Good morning."

"From the sound of your voice I guess it is a good morning," Miguel said and fixed his gaze on Maisy's face while he listened to Dash's report. Her eyes locked with his, expectant.

"We have a list of blasters and we've been able to limit it to those who have access to the type of dynamite used."

"How many blasters do we have to chase down?" he asked.

"Six, and at least two of them are working at sites owned by guess who," Dash said, excitement filtering into his tone.

"Let me guess. Rothwell," Miguel responded, pleased that his gut instinct was possibly not too far off.

"Bingo. Rothwell. Plus, we've also refined the list we gave Madeline to focus on anyone with family members who might have criminal backgrounds. Unfortunately, that list is still fairly long," Dash said, some of the enthusiasm leaving his voice.

"That's still progress. What about the DNA profile?" he pressed.

A heavy sigh filtered across the line. "No match in CODIS. Whoever he is, he's managed not to be in trouble with the law."

"A novice much like our profile said," Miguel said and shifted his gaze to meet Madeline's and Nicholas's for the barest moment.

"I'm just the tech guy, but if I had to guess, the Crusader hasn't been at this long and is probably being directed by someone else," Dash said, and in the background, someone called out to him, clearly needing his attention.

"I have to go."

Miguel peered out the window to see where they were. "We'll be there in about five minutes."

Five minutes to jump back into the investigation, but that also meant they might be running off to speak to the blasters and the most promising leads on their list of suspects identified by their facial recognition software.

Which would leave Maisy sitting by herself in either their offices or his apartment for long hours.

"We may need to leave you alone to continue with the investigation," he said.

"I'll be fine. Don't worry about me. Maybe I could even go visit your father," she said and patted his hand.

But he did worry about her, cared about her, maybe more than he should. And even though it would be nice for her to visit his father, and his father would likely appreciate the company, it was an iffy thing. "I may not be able to protect you if you go to visit him."

"I understand you have other responsibilities, and I don't want to be a bother," she said, but he could see she was a little disappointed. A visit to his dad would let her work on her travel blog and it would do his father good as well.

Despite his better judgment, he found himself saying, "I could have another agent take you over and back if that's okay with you."

Her smile was the only answer he needed.

Chapter Fourteen

Maisy loved spending time with Miguel's dad. He was so kind and caring and in love with sharing his knowledge. But she also loved sharing what she knew, and they spent the better part of the afternoon making a website for Robert so that he could post articles about writing and journalism. They also set up a way for people to contact him in case they wished for him to do a speaking engagement.

"Thank you so much for helping me with that," Robert said and sat back, a broad smile on his face.

"It was my pleasure. You've given me so much useful information," Maisy said and hit a button to save the contact page on the site.

"Together we are formidable pair," Robert declared with a laugh, but his mood dimmed quickly, and Maisy understood why.

"We will stay in touch. I promise," she said.

"I know, my dear. It's just that...you'd be so good for Miguel. He needs someone like you in his life," Robert said, but then busied himself with gathering the papers where he'd been jotting down notes on using the website and ideas for articles and workshops.

"Your son and me… It's complicated," she said, snapped her laptop shut and slipped it into her knapsack.

"I may be old, but I understand what that means. It was complicated for my Gloria and me, but we found a way to be together. To have a happy life until… It was worth the pain," Robert said and sniffled as he pulled off his glasses, closed his eyes and pressed his fingers at the bridge of his nose to hold back his tears.

Maisy rose from her chair and embraced Robert, held him tight until he sucked in a rough breath and said, "I'm fine, my dear. Just fine."

Maisy was sure he would be because he had people in his life who cared about him—his son for starters. She'd seen how Miguel treated his dad, no matter how exasperated his father made him.

Robert was a lucky man to have people who cared.

She had no one.

You have Miguel, the little voice in her head said, but Maisy wagged her head to shake loose that thought.

A knock came at the door and at Robert's "Come in," the FBI agent who had escorted her over walked into the room.

"Sorry to interrupt, but we should be heading back," the agent suggested.

"Not a problem. We just finished," Maisy said, slipped on her jacket and grabbed her knapsack.

She returned to Robert's side, hugged him hard and said, "I'll come back again soon."

Robert returned the embrace and said, "Take care."

She smiled and nodded. "I will."

The agent and she exited Robert's hotel room and made the return trip to the BAU offices, the agent alert to what was happening around them. He constantly scanned the area and stayed close to her, making her feel both safe and worried at the same time. Despite the Seattle Crusader's threat to harm someone and his mention of her, Maisy didn't think he'd actually go through with it.

But as they reached the building housing the BAU offices, a blur of black and gray snagged her attention and also that of the agent. He shoved her behind him and turned in the direction of the motion and as she peered past his arm, she saw the man with the ski mask standing less than twenty feet away. He wore the same hoodie and jeans as the Seattle Crusader.

The FBI agent held his hand up, whipped out his pistol, and said, "FBI. Put your hands up!"

At that the man turned and started to run. The agent was about to give chase when the world exploded beside them. The force of the blast knocked them down and bits and pieces of glass and concrete rained down on them. After the noise of the explosion faded, the blare of car alarms from nearby automobiles sounded, triggered by the force of the blast.

Maisy's ears were ringing, and her elbow ached from where she had been thrown to the ground by the force of the blast. She examined her injury and noticed that her jacket was torn, her elbow skinned and bleeding.

She started to stand, but the FBI agent with her laid a gentle hand on her shoulder and said, "Hold on, miss. Let's get that bleeding stopped."

She wanted to say it was just a skinned elbow, but then she tracked his gaze to her other arm. A sharp tear ran across her jacket and blood flowed freely from beneath it. The agent helped her ease the jacket sleeve off to reveal the gash across her upper arm. Then he quickly whipped off his tie and wrapped it around the wound, making it tight enough to stop the bleeding.

He had barely finished when Miguel rushed up to them, followed by Madeline and Nicholas. He knelt by her and placed an arm across her back to offer support.

"How bad?" he asked the agent who had been guarding her.

"Not too deep, I think. I haven't had a chance to check out anything else," the agent explained.

"We'll get on it," Madeline said and quickly directed Nicholas, the agent guarding her and the other agents who'd streamed out of the building to safeguard the area and any evidence.

The blast had taken out part of a pillar on the building housing the BAU offices and the force of the blast had shattered all the glass along the one side of the building as well as a few stories above the pillar.

The sound of an ambulance pulling up drew Miguel's attention. "Let's get you over to the EMT," he said and helped her to her feet. Her knees were wobbly, and she needed his support to walk over to the ambulance. But seconds later she was seated in the ambulance and an EMT was working on her arm.

"Not very deep. She won't need stitches," he said as he tenderly cleaned the wound.

She winced at the bite of the antiseptic and he apologized. "Sorry."

"No worries," she answered, but at Miguel's muttered curse, she met his worried gaze. "I'm okay. Really," she said to reassure him.

"You could have been killed," he said and dragged a hand through his hair in frustration.

"I'm okay, but the Crusader was here. We saw him right before the blast."

I SHOULD HAVE been here, Miguel thought, concern for her overriding all his thoughts.

This is what it's like to care for someone. To think of nothing but them even when the world around you is on fire, he thought.

But he didn't have the luxury of that in his life. He couldn't care for someone as deeply as he cared for Maisy because his focus had to be on the bigger picture. On his responsibilities for others.

"We'll find him. Right now, I need to get you safely inside the BAU office, but I have to oversee my team. Are you up for it?" he asked as he glanced at the EMT, who signaled he was done with Maisy.

"I am. You go. I know you have responsibilities."

He was about to respond when Dashiell raced over, Liam and David tagging behind him, which was perfect.

"Dashiell, I need you to take Maisy back up to the office and get her interview while her memories are fresh. She also indicated that they'd seen the Crusader right before the blast, so please check CCTV cameras and find out what you can."

"Got it, Miguel," Dashiell said and held his hand out to Maisy. She slipped her hand into his and Miguel's gut tightened.

With jealousy? Over Dash, who had no interest in her, especially since he'd found his own special someone just a short time ago? Miguel thought and once again had to tell himself to focus on what was important at the moment, namely finding the bomber who was terrorizing Seattle.

"I'll be up as soon as I can," he said and ran his hand down her back in a gesture meant to reassure.

"I know you will," she said with such trust, his heart constricted.

He'd already failed her, but he wouldn't do it again. As they headed toward the door to the BAU's office building, he marched over to the side of the structure where the explosion had taken out part of one of the support pillars for the building. Luckily, it seemed like minor damage at the blast site. An ATF agent and Mack from Seattle ABS were already there, examining the pillar. Police tape had already been set up around the perimeter of their crime scene, and he eased under it and headed toward the men, mindful of not stepping on any possible evidence.

Like before, he noticed bits of paper and hints of blue wire. At the blast site, Mack and the ATF agent were examining the damage.

As he approached, Mack rose, shook his hand and introduced the ATF agent. "Special Agent Cummings."

"SSA Peters. Good to work with you. What have we got?" he asked the two bomb experts.

"Dynamite again. Enough to make a substantial blast, but not do major damage," ATF Agent Cummings said.

"The blast created a lot of shrapnel from the glass of the building and the concrete of the pillar, but it's surface damage," Mack added in explanation.

"Maybe because he was here and didn't want to get hurt himself," Miguel said.

"The Crusader was here? In the area?" Mack asked

and searched the surrounding area, not that the Crusader would be stupid enough to hang around.

"Maisy said she and the agent guarding her saw him right before the blast. I have Dash and his team checking out the CCTV footage to see what we have."

"Keep us posted," Special Agent Cummings said and sank back down onto his haunches to review the blast site again.

With a nod, Miguel left the two men to their investigation and headed upstairs, eager to hear what his team might have found and to see Maisy and make sure she was okay.

Maisy, Maisy, Maisy. She'd been on his brain the entire morning as they'd run down their prospective leads, speaking to two of the licensed blasters. Neither had raised alarms with him and they still had another four to go, but that would have to wait now while they processed any new evidence from this blast.

It was another explosion that would have likely not injured anyone, although there were never any guarantees. People could have heart attacks from the shock, like in the Olympic Park Bomber case. The shrapnel that had cut Maisy's arm could have easily slashed her neck and a vital artery.

His heart sunk to somewhere in the middle of his gut as he imagined Maisy gone from his life. Taken by a terrorist the way his mother had been, way too soon.

Way, way too soon because he hadn't really had a chance to get to know her.

Which is how it has to stay, he reminded himself.

Rushing into the building, he hurried to the elevator, hands jammed into his pants pockets, feet tapping as he waited for it to arrive. As the ding announced the elevator had arrived, he barely contained himself to allow the sole passenger to exit and marched on, impatient to reach the BAU offices.

As soon as the door opened on the floor, he dashed out and into their offices. A quick look confirmed that Dashiell had likely taken Maisy to the interrogation room and he pushed on to that space. Inside, his team was sitting with Maisy as she told them what she had seen before the blast.

All heads turned in his direction as he entered. He forced a smile and went straight to Maisy's side, passing a hand across her back to offer support.

"How's it going?" he asked.

Maisy glanced up at him and said, "The bomber was there with us when the bomb went off."

He nodded. "How close was he?"

"Maybe twenty feet away. By the edges of the park next to the building," she said.

He faced Dash. "Would our cameras capture that area?"

Dash shook his head. "Probably not, but we might have caught him when he placed the bomb by the pillar. I have Liam and David reviewing the CCTV tapes to confirm that."

He nodded. "Good. Mack and ATF Special Agent Cummings will send what they have, but after an initial examination, it looks like our man again. Dynamite and blue wires. The bomb was placed and constructed in a way to make a statement."

"But possibly not hurt anyone again?" Nicholas said.

Anger surged through him. "Maisy and our agent were hurt. Maisy could have been killed if that shrapnel had been a few inches higher."

Beneath his hand, Maisy shook, and he smoothed his hand across her back again to gentle her.

"We need to push. Harder. Faster before his next bomb kills someone," Miguel said, but before he could continue, a knock came at the door.

"Come in," he called out sharply, irritated at the interruption.

Liam opened the door cautiously, obviously sensing Miguel's impatience.

"We have something. I've cued it up on the computer for you to see," Liam said and gestured outside to their work area.

Miguel squashed his irritation and nodded. "Good work, Liam. We'll be there in a second." He turned to his team and said, "I'm sorry if I was abrupt, but leaving a bomb at our door is a challenge. He thinks he's smarter than us. That he can keep on terrorizing the city, but we will stop him."

"No doubt about that, Miguel. We will stop him," Madeline said, rose from the table and was followed by Nicholas and Dash, leaving Miguel alone with Maisy.

He leaned against the table so he could examine her better. A few bits of debris were tangled in the thick strands of her caramel hair and he brushed them away as he asked, "Are you okay? Really okay?"

Her gaze shimmered with unshed tears, but she stiffened her lips and nodded. "A little sore. Arm hurts like crazy, but okay. Alive," she said with a rough breath.

"He won't get to you again. I promise you that. I won't let you out of my sight again," he said, but her smile turned rueful and she shook your head.

"You will because you have to get to work. Like

now," she said and jerked her head in the direction of the door.

He hated that she was right. The job had to come first before anything else, including Maisy.

"Let's go," he said and quickly added, "please."

HE WAS RATTLED and Maisy understood why. Hell, she was absolutely terrified, but she knew that for the good of the investigation and for them—if there was a "them"—she had to stay calm.

They walked to the workspace where Madeline, Dashiell and Nicholas were already seated at the table. Liam stood off to the side at one of the computers and as Miguel and Maisy settled themselves at the table, he said, "About an hour before the blast, a group of what looks like homeless people walked by the building. Watch the man in the center of the group."

The projection monitor snapped to life and a video played showing a group of about half a dozen people approaching the building. They were coming from a nearby highway area and Maisy supposed that like at many other underpasses on the edges of the city, the homeless group had set up an encampment.

The video jumped to another angle, probably from another camera, Maisy thought.

This angle showed the same group, who strolled toward the column, surrounding one man as Liam had mentioned. His hood was up and there was something familiar about him. She pointed to him and said, "The one in the middle. That's his hoodie."

No sooner had she said that than the man slipped to the edge of the group with a black knapsack and placed it next to the pillar. As he did so, the hood fell back to reveal his face before he quickly jerked it back up.

"That's him! I know that's him!" she shouted and pointed to the picture as Liam froze the video.

"That's our man and quite young. Early twenties," Miguel said.

"Like the Austin Serial and Smiley Face Bombers," Nicholas said.

"We're already working on cleaning up the video and will start running it against the various databases," Liam said just as David walked over, a smile on his face.

Dash glanced at his intern and said, "I hope there's a reason for that smile."

Chapter Fifteen

“We didn’t get a hit on CODIS, but we got a hit at the DNA testing service we can access. Not an exact match, but the individual in the database is likely a cousin,” David said.

Miguel dipped his head and said, “Excellent work. Please get us whatever information you can on that individual so we can interview them.”

“Will do,” David said and headed back to his computer to work.

Miguel turned his attention to the team. “Nicholas, I need you to get back on the street to interview the other licensed blasters on our list. Madeline, please work with Dash and Liam on that list of possible suspects. Hopefully with the new photos of the unsub, we’ll be able to at least limit the list. In the meantime, I’m going to take Maisy home so she can rest. I’ll be back later.”

“That’s not necessary, Miguel,” Maisy said, a stain of color on her cheeks, as if she was embarrassed by his concern.

“But it is. I want to make sure that you’re safe, not like before,” he said and skipped his gaze across his team members to see if anyone disagreed.

“This latest bomb could have been specifically set

because the Crusader knew that Maisy would be here," Nicholas said.

Miguel appreciated his support. "Anything happens, call, text or email. I'll be working at my place."

He glanced at Maisy, almost daring her to contradict him in front of his team again, but she remained silent. Slowly she rose, wincing as she did so, making him slip his arm around her waist to offer support.

She shrugged off his assistance, obviously upset with him.

He got it, but that wasn't going to make him change his mind. Together they walked out of the BAU offices, to the elevator and down to his condo. No words were exchanged. In fact, she avoided his gaze, clearly still annoyed with him.

They had no sooner stepped inside his condo when she whirled on him. "I appreciate your concern, but you have a job to do."

He blew out an exasperated sigh and dragged a hand through his hair. "My job is to protect you."

She jabbed him in the chest with a very pointy index finger. "Your job is to catch the Seattle Crusader. That's how you'll keep me and tons of others safe."

He couldn't argue with her, but he did. "And do you think I can keep my mind on this investigation if I don't know that you're safe? The entire time I was with Nicholas earlier, all I could think about was whether you were okay."

His revelation obviously surprised her. "You were thinking about me?"

With a heavy sigh, he looked away and said, "I was."

She cradled his cheek and gently urged him back

to face her. "I was thinking about you, too, but I don't think that's a good thing for either of us, is it?"

"No, it isn't. We both want different things from life," he admitted.

"We do, but if we want to get on with our lives, you need to trap this terrorist. You can't do that holed up with me here."

He hated that she was right. Worse, he hated that even though she was right, he was still worried about the prospect of leaving her here alone. After all, the Crusader had struck right on their doorstep, almost as if to taunt them that both Maisy and the FBI weren't safe.

But he had to leave her, as much as he might not like it.

"Why don't you take a shower to relax? You're probably sore from being tossed around."

"I am. Again," she said with a wry smile and a short chuff of a laugh.

"I'll have another agent at the door until I come back," he said and before he could stop himself, he dropped a quick kiss on her lips.

MAISY WAS SURPRISED by his show of affection, and worse, she wanted more than just that brief touch. But that would only complicate things even more as they had both said.

They wanted different things from life and yet…

She wouldn't think about how tempting it was to imagine having a life with Miguel. To share it and bring him the peace he was missing. The life he was missing by living here at work.

"*¡Cuídate!*" she said and rushed off to shower and

ease some of the pains in her body from being thrown by the blast.

The heat of the water helped ease some of the soreness and the waterproof bandage protected the gash on her arm. But as she swept her soapy hands across her body, she noted the assorted bruises from the first blast that were only just turning purplish and yellow as well as a few newer bruises.

She finished showering, wrapped a towel around her body and used another to create a makeshift turban around her hair. But when she exited the bathroom, she discovered that Miguel was still in the apartment. He sat at the kitchen table in front of his laptop, tapping away at the keys.

He raised his head as she walked in and explained. "I can't get an agent here for another hour or more and the rest of the team is working on their assignments. If you feel up to it, would you mind going back up to the BAU offices with me?"

She was physically up to it, but emotionally… Every minute spent with Miguel made keeping her emotional distance from him harder. But she also didn't want to keep him from doing his job because the safety of others was at risk.

"I'm up to it. Just give me a few minutes to get ready," she said, rushed to her suitcase and pulled out clothes to wear. She hurried to the bathroom, where she dressed and with a few quick strokes through her hair, brushed out any tangles. It would air dry, curlier than normal but otherwise fine.

When she exited the bathroom, Miguel glanced in her direction again, but his look went from all business to something else. Something dangerous that ignited heat throughout her body.

"You're so beautiful," he said.

Heart beating heavily, she told herself to deflect, deflect, deflect. "Why, Supervisory Special Agent Peters, I bet you say that to all the girls."

He laughed as she intended and shook his head. "You are truly something. Seriously," he said and shot to his feet. "Let's go. Please."

She nodded and rushed to his side, and he laid a hand at her back to guide her toward the door. The touch was comforting. Possessive.

At the door, he said, "Please let me."

She paused as he wanted and he went to the door, opened it and looked around the hallway before extending a hand to confirm it was okay to exit.

Slipping her hand into his, she walked with him out the door and to the elevator but didn't release his hand, the touch uniting them in more than one way.

When they reached the offices, Dashiell was sharing high fives with Liam and David. Liam turned to face them as they walked to where Nicholas and Madeline were adding information to their whiteboard.

Miguel smiled as the enlargement of a Washington State driver's license went up next to the earlier, grainy photos they had created from the various CCTV feeds and Maisy's photo of the unsub.

"Good news, I guess," he said and pulled out a chair for Maisy to sit at the table.

"Good news," Dashiell confirmed and explained. "Using the program I tweaked, we were able to splice in more of the unsub's features from the CCTV footage and recreate his face. As soon as we did that, we got a hit. Chris Adams. Twenty-six. No priors. Last employer was none other than the city of Seattle. He worked in the parks department but was let go about six months ago."

Miguel peered around the room at his team. "Do we have anything else on Adams?"

Madeline shook her head. "Still working on it. We're reaching out to the cousin whose DNA hit earlier, but since his last name is Adams as well, we're confident we're on the right track. We've also identified two siblings who are currently serving time for armed robbery and drug dealing."

Miguel nodded. "Which would explain the Crusader's demands about bail reform and sentencing. What about his last known address?"

Nicholas held up a piece of paper. "Got it. I was just about to go visit the location and see what I can find."

"I'll go with you. In the meantime, see what else you can dig up and also, let's get his last place of employment, address, et cetera up on the map and see if that gets us anywhere," he said and started to go, but then he laid a hand on Maisy's shoulder and gently squeezed it.

"You'll be okay here," he said, but it was part question, part statement.

"I will be. I just wish there was more I could do to help," she said, glancing up at him with those amazing eyes, trusting eyes. He hoped he didn't disappoint her again the way he had earlier when she'd been hurt.

"Okay. And team…good job. Reach out to Seattle PD, Mack at ABS and ATF Special Agent Cummings and fill them in on what we have. See if they have anything to add. Also ask for a BOLO on Chris Adams."

"I've got that," Madeline said, and Miguel had no doubt she'd have everything in line within minutes. It was why she was one of his best agents and working on his team.

"Thanks, Madeline." When they left the elevator bank and then headed out of the building, Miguel checked to make sure the area was safe. The Crusader had attacked on their home turf, reminded them that no one was safe anywhere.

That was doubly evident at the sight of the various first responder vehicles and news vans parked in front of the office building as well as the assorted officers working just past the yellow barricade tape at the blast scene.

As one of the reporters noticed them, she came running in their direction, and with a quick look at Nicholas, Miguel urged his team member to move a little faster. They beat the reporter to the car and were safely inside and pulling away from the reporter as she reached them.

"Vultures," Miguel mumbled beneath his breath.

"I don't blame you for not liking the press all that much," Nicholas said.

Miguel shrugged. "They can really have a negative impact on an investigation between revealing information and creating unnecessary pressure."

"Like in the Olympic Park Bomber case," Nicholas said, trying to understand how he felt.

He nodded. "Definitely. We can't risk naming an unsub unless we're one hundred percent sure about it."

"Which is why you haven't named Rothwell as an unsub?" Nicholas said, well aware of Miguel's suspicions about the annoying, and potentially dangerous, senate candidate.

"Especially Rothwell. If I say anything without having the proof to back it up, it's not fair to him or to my team," he said and shot a quick glance at the other man before returning his attention to the road.

NICHOLAS PEERED AT his boss as Miguel grew silent. He admired Miguel's restraint, even to someone as obnoxious as Rothwell. It was a testament to his character and his inherent sense of fairness, reinforcing the kind of man he was. A good man. An honorable man.

Nicholas wasn't sure he could be as restrained if someone he loved was at risk. Earlier that summer when he'd been trying to solve a serial killer case and fallen for the victim's older sister, he'd nearly lost his mind when Aubrey had been taken hostage by their unsub.

Although Miguel had been business as usual during this investigation, it was impossible to miss that there was a connection between him and Maisy, which worried him. Any distractions could prove fatal and today's bombing right on their doorstep was ample warning that they all needed to double their focus on this case.

Which was why he took the lead as they rang the bell for the superintendent when they reached the apartment building where Chris Adams had lived. The older Latino man immediately answered the door but narrowed his gaze warily as he spotted them. "Can I help you?"

They both held up their badges and identified themselves. "FBI. Special Agent Nicholas James and Supervisory Special Agent Miguel Peters. Are you Gonzalo Garcia, the building superintendent?"

The man's eyes widened in surprise. "*Sí*, I am. FBI? I don't understand."

Nicholas whipped out a copy of Chris Adams's driver's license photo. "We understand this man used to live here."

The superintendent peered at the photo, nodded and then opened the door wide for them. "Please come in. It's better if we talk inside."

Nicholas and Miguel did as he asked and watched as the older man inspected the street before he closed the door.

"Is there a problem, Mr. Garcia?" Nicholas asked since the man was clearly spooked.

"Chris lived here about six months ago, but after he lost his job and fell behind on his rent, the landlord had me evict him," the superintendent said.

"Was he violent when he was evicted?" Miguel asked.

The man shook his head. "Not at first. But then Chris got involved with some of the homeless people down beneath the highway. They started coming around and causing problems. Turning over garbage cans or setting them on fire. Hassling tenants for money as they come and go to their cars. That's why I didn't want anyone to see us talking. I don't want no problems."

"Did you call the police about the incidents?" Nicholas asked even though he knew what the answer would be.

"I did, but their hands are tied. As long as no one gets hurt, we're on our own," Mr. Garcia said with a resigned shrug.

"You said Chris lost his job," Nicholas said, leaving it open-ended so the super could add anything he knew.

"Chris wasn't bad at first, but he partied a lot. I think he was high at work and someone got hurt so they fired him."

Nicholas and Miguel shared a look. "He was with the parks department, right?"

The super nodded. "He was. Worked mainly at Riverview, but also Denny Park. Some others, I think."

"Has Chris been around lately?" Nicholas pressed.

Mr. Garcia shook his head and frowned. "Not in the last couple of weeks. He had been staying down at the encampment beneath the highway overpass. I figured he either got himself another place or maybe overdosed or something. Shame, really."

"It is. If you think of anything else, or if you see Chris around, would you mind giving us a call?" Nicholas said and handed the man his business card.

The man tapped the card against his hand and nodded. "*Sí.* I will."

They left the superintendent's apartment and walked away from the building, perusing the area as they moved toward the highway overpass. It was several blocks away, but quite a number of homeless could be seen through the area and a few tents had been pitched here and there along the edges of the public sidewalks. The closer they got, the denser the appearance of tents and makeshift lodgings.

As they passed, people stared at them and Nicholas suspected that even if Chris was still hanging around the encampment, they wouldn't get any help in finding him. That was confirmed as they walked over to one person after another. They either hurried away, avoiding them, or refused to answer. Another, smaller group of more aggressive people moved as if to surround them, but Nicholas held his hands up in surrender and he and Miguel turned around and walked back to their car.

"We'll need to set up surveillance around the encampment," Miguel said as he slipped behind the wheel.

"I can do that with David. He wants to be a field agent and it'll be good experience for him," Nicholas said.

Miguel nodded. "Sounds good. Maybe after we get back you can both change into something less law enforcement and see if that helps at all."

Nicholas replayed in his head what the superintendent had told them, one fact sticking out. "He mentioned Denny Park. Isn't that close to the federal courthouse?"

"And some parts of Riverview are not all that far from some of the bombing sites. Same for this encampment and his old apartment," Miguel said, but instead of driving directly to the BAU offices, he detoured by Riverview and then up to the area by the courthouse and the park.

"Do you see what I see?" Miguel asked as they drove past a corporate park and one headquarters stood out: Rothwell Industries.

"I do," Nicholas said and didn't fail to notice his boss's smile. With every bit of information they uncovered, they were getting closer and closer to finding out who was the real Seattle Crusader, and he suspected that it wasn't going to be just Chris Adams.

Chapter Sixteen

Maisy nursed the tea that she had prepped for herself while Madeline added even more information to the team's whiteboard.

"Do you think you're getting closer to catching the Crusader?" she asked and sipped her tea.

Madeline leaned her hands on her hips as she peered at the board. The action drew the jacket away from her athletic physique and revealed the weapon tucked into a black leather holster. She tilted her head as she considered the evidence she had just written onto the whiteboard and nodded.

"I think we have one of the Crusader's minions," she said and turned to face Maisy. "I'm sure someone else is directing him and making the bombs."

Maisy considered the information and nodded. "Adams doesn't seem like the mastermind type to me."

"Your father… Sorry, the Forest Conservation Bomber said our unsub is a novice and I totally agree. I also think that there's another reason for these bombings. Not the demands for bail reform and homeless encampments."

"You think that it's a smoke screen?" Maisy wondered aloud.

"Definitely a smoke screen," Miguel said as he hurried in with Dashiell and walked straight to the whiteboard. He placed several red magnets on their map and gestured to them. "Adams's apartment, a homeless encampment where he's been seen and the location of a couple of the parks where he worked before being fired."

Miguel grabbed two other magnets and snapped them onto the whiteboard decisively. He pointed to the first one. "Federal courthouse where several riots have taken place, but more importantly," he said and gestured to the second spot, "the corporate offices of Rothwell Industries. Right near the park and courthouse."

Liam rose from his computer and walked over at the same time that Lorelai entered their work area. They nearly bumped into each other but jumped back, staring at each other uneasily as they both mumbled, "Sorry."

"You first," Liam said and held his hand out to cede the floor to her.

"No, you first. I was just coming to see if you wanted dinner brought in," Lorelai said.

"What do you have, Liam?" Miguel asked as Lorelai and Liam continued to do their awkward little dance.

Liam dipped his head in apology to Lorelai, walked over to Miguel and handed him some papers. A broad smile came to Miguel's lips and he shot a quick glance at Nicholas as he said, "The cousin has confirmed that he's related to Chris Adams, so we've got him thanks to the DNA evidence off the bombs."

Miguel's phone chirped to warn of an incoming text. He pulled it from his pocket, read the text and then jerked his head in Liam's direction. "Please put the TV feed up on the monitor."

Liam raced back to his computer, careful to avoid Lorelai, and with a few keystrokes, put up the feed of a press conference with none other than state senate candidate Richard Rothwell.

"It's a disgrace that the FBI continues to refuse my help. Especially considering that the latest bombing was right at their door," Rothwell said, his too-serious expression and tone almost comical.

"Smug bastard," Nicholas murmured.

"While I don't believe in caving to terrorists, we must consider that the Crusader's demands are intended to help so many. Issues like bail reform and the plight of the homeless are ones I intend to address once I'm elected to the Senate," he said, and a small cheer rose in the background.

The camera panned away from Rothwell to the crowd.

"You getting this, Liam?" Miguel asked.

"I am," their tech confirmed, but instead of returning to Rothwell, the reporter took over the broadcast.

"This is Allie Smith reporting from Rothwell Industries. Back to you, Ernie."

"And back to our investigation. Nicholas and David are going to the homeless encampment near Adams's old apartment. BOLO is out for him. In the meantime, let's keep working on busting past the shell companies. I'm convinced they're going to lead to Rothwell," Miguel said and as everyone rushed off to continue work and Lorelai went to order dinner, he came over, sat beside Maisy and brushed back a lock of hair that had fallen onto the side of her face.

"You holding up?" he asked, his gaze skimming over her features, searching out what she was feeling.

"I am. Tired. Sore. Hungry," she admitted with a laugh and a wag of her head.

"We'll go down to my apartment as soon as we finish dinner, unless you'd rather get something to eat on our own," he said.

Dinner alone with Miguel. Dangerous, she thought. "We can eat with the team. I'm sure you're anxious to be here if something happens so you can wind this up now that you have an unsub."

Miguel nodded and once again brushed his hand across his hair. "We have Adams, but I want whoever is directing this and whoever made those bombs."

She understood his determination while she was also sad that their time together would be coming to a close.

"You'll get them. I have no doubt about that," she said and laid her hand over his. Squeezed it gently. "Your mother would be really proud of the work you're doing."

A sad smile flitted across his lips. "She would. She's the voice in my head, pressing me to do my best."

The moment was shattered as Lorelai returned to the work area with two FBI agents carrying bags from one of the nearby restaurants. The aroma of yeasty bread and sweet cream wafted into the air as Lorelai laid out assorted plastic food containers and bread bowls on the surface of their work area.

"I figured you were tired of sandwiches, and something warm would be nice. There are four different soups for you to choose from. If you don't need anything else, I'm going to head out," Lorelai said.

Liam piped up immediately, "Are you sure you don't want to stay and eat with us?"

Lorelai fidgeted, leaning side to side on her four-inch heels, but then she said, "No, thanks. I have a date."

Liam's face fell and Lorelai rushed from the room, obviously uncomfortable.

Miguel clearly got the tension between the two since he jumped to his feet, clapped his hands and said, "Let's eat."

MIGUEL'S BELLY WAS full of tasty seafood chowder and bread, but there was an emptiness inside that even the best gourmet food couldn't fill.

As Maisy sat back in her seat and rubbed her stomach, a contented sigh escaped her and slipped into him, filling some of that void inside him. Warning him that maybe, just maybe, Maisy was what would fill the emptiness. An emptiness that he hadn't really acknowledged until she had come into his life.

Peering around the table, he noticed that the meal had relaxed his team members, which was a good thing. Sometimes too much tension blocked the flow of ideas, but so far, he was pleased with what his team had accomplished. But they still had a long way to go to resolve the investigation.

Despite that, it was time to get Maisy home and to enter his own zone because sometimes he worked better alone.

He slowly rose to his feet, wincing a bit as the stitches in his leg pulled with the motion. "I think it's time we went home. Keep me posted on any developments. I'm going to dig into Rothwell and see what I can find."

He held his hand out to help Maisy up and she slipped her hand into his. Inside him, another bit of the emptiness filled with the warmth of her skin and her tender squeeze.

But as aware as he was of every nuance of Maisy

beside him, he didn't fail to notice how Madeline's eyebrows rose as she saw their held hands. How Dashiell likewise fixated on that while Liam crossed his arms, his gaze puzzled.

Miguel understood their concerns because he'd had similar ones as his team members had found their significant others during the course of their last few investigations. Nicholas and Aubrey. Madeline and Jackson. Dashiell and Raina. And of course, the ongoing drama between Liam and Lorelai, his ex.

He gazed at Maisy and thought, *Now it's my turn.*

With a light tug on Maisy's hand, he urged her from their work area, and they walked out of the offices, to the elevator and down to his apartment.

As soon as they were through the door, he released her hand and they stepped apart, gazing at each other, obviously uncomfortable. He broke the tension with a flip of his hand in the direction of the Murphy bed.

"I'm going to be working and you're probably sore. Maybe you should take the bed tonight so you're more comfortable."

She opened her mouth, as if to object, but then just nodded. Clasping her hands before her, she said, "Thanks. But there's room for you as well."

And there was the eight-hundred-pound gorilla in the room again, and he might as well address it. Walking up to her, he cradled her cheek and stroked his thumb across her creamy skin. So smooth. So soft. His gut tightened at the thought of all that skin against his and she was more than he could resist.

Bending closer, he brought his lips to hers until only the space of a breath was between them. "This," he said, whispered his lips across hers and shifted back barely an inch. "This is why that's not a good idea."

In answer, Maisy reached up and cupped the back of his head, keeping him close. "This," she said, repeating his earlier action, her lips a butterfly kiss against his. "This is why we have to share that bed. Whatever happens, I don't want to say that I ran from this. From us."

A low groan escaped him, and he couldn't fight it anymore. He wrapped his arms around her and hugged her close, her softness crushed to his hardness. Every inch of her fitting to him as if they were two pieces of a puzzle.

Over and over they kissed, until their breaths became one and almost ceased to exist as they strained toward each other.

But then something registered. Sound. Vibration.

"Damn," he said and fumbled with the phone in his jacket pocket, dropping it with a thud.

That sound killed the desire as effectively as a cold bucket of water.

"SSA Peters," he said, and mouthed an apology to her.

"We've broken through one of the shell companies and like you thought, it's part of Rothwell Industries," Dashiell advised.

"That's great, Dash. We're one step closer to Rothwell. I'm sure he's the mastermind behind this," Miguel said.

"I agree, Miguel. We'll keep on working to break past the other shell. Hopefully it'll lead to Rothwell also."

"I don't doubt that it will and if we can get Adams into custody, maybe he will flip on Rothwell. As for the licensed blaster, I think there's one on our list that's at Rothwell's current construction site. If you can get an address for him, I'll go with Madeline to interview him."

"We'll try to get it ASAP," Dashiell said and ended the call.

Miguel tossed the phone onto a nearby tabletop and it clattered noisily, making Maisy jump and take a step away from him.

"You need to get to work," she said and smoothed her hand across his chest.

"I do. Why don't you—"

The phone rang and vibrated noisily on the tabletop.

"Again?" Miguel muttered in frustration, swept up the phone and answered, "SSA Peters."

"We've got the address for the blaster from his license application and his photo from his driver's license," Madeline said.

"Great. Meet me in the lobby. We'll speak to him and see what he has to say," Miguel directed.

Facing Maisy, he said, "I have to go."

"I understand. I'll be waiting up for you."

The last bit of emptiness inside him disappeared at the thought of Maisy waiting for him at home. A home and not just a place to lay his head between investigations.

"That'll be nice. I'll make sure an agent is at the door while I'm gone," he stated and rushed to the door, Maisy following.

At the door he faced her, bent and kissed her, a long, slow kiss filled with promise.

After they broke apart, Maisy smiled, cupped his cheek and swiped her thumb across his lips. *"¡Cuídate!"*

"You take care as well. Do not open this door for anyone."

"I won't," she said and when he stepped out, he heard the snap of the locks falling into place.

He immediately called up to the offices and arranged for an agent to come down. He didn't leave until he saw the agent come off the elevator and only then did he hurry to meet Madeline in the lobby.

She was scrolling through her phone, a happy smile on her face when he met her.

"How's Jackson?" he said, certain that was who had put the smile on Madeline's face.

Madeline laughed and flipped her phone so he could see the photo of Jackson and his six-year-old daughter, Emmy, happy faces streaked with flour as they showed off the batch of cookies they had apparently just baked. Just a month earlier, Madeline had been the lead agent when Emmy had been kidnapped during a Take Your Child to Work Day event at Jackson's office.

"Looks like things are back to normal after the kidnapping," he said and they walked together to Miguel's car, chatting.

"As normal as anyone can be after something like that," she said, some of her earlier happiness gone.

"I know it was a rough case for you, being so similar to when your sister was taken," he said, well aware that Madeline's case had not had such a happy ending.

"It was, but there was a silver lining. Meeting Jackson and his daughter…it's changed my life. I have a life," she said with a rough laugh, and then peered at him intently as they paused by his car.

"I think things are also changing for you. Or am I wrong to think that?" Madeline asked.

Miguel shrugged. "It's complicated and I know you can understand that," he said and slipped into the car.

Madeline joined him, in the passenger seat, and provided an address for the blaster's home in the Central District, an area which was one of the oldest residential neighborhoods in the city and which had seen quite a number of changes over the years. The neighborhood had a mix of homes and small businesses and had at one time been a predominantly African American neighborhood. Gentrification had changed that and led to a number of new construction sites as well as many resident-driven projects to improve the area's parks and schools.

"I understand that you're attracted to Maisy and I get it. She's a beautiful woman, but more importantly, she's brave and kind and caring," Madeline said as if she was arguing the case for Maisy.

"She is and I am. Attracted. But you more than most understand just how hard a job we have. The long and erratic hours. The cases that take their toll on your soul," he admitted.

"The cases can break you. The pain and suffering of the victims. The frustration that you can't solve the case fast enough to keep someone else from suffering," she said, totally in sync with him. But before he could say anything else, she continued, "Being with Jackson and Emmy…it's lightened that load. It's made it easier to deal with all that pain and suffering because I'm not alone anymore."

Just like I don't feel alone anymore, Miguel thought, but kept it to himself since they were nearing the edges of Central District and he had to focus on finding the address for the licensed blaster they were going to interview.

After a few turns, he pulled up in front of a small brick house on a block of mixed homes. Some had been renovated and sparkled brightly beside others that needed care, just like this home. One of the steps had cracked and fallen off to the side and the paint on the white trim around the windows was peeling. The downspout had pulled loose from the gutter, allowing water to pour down and stain the brick along that side of the home. A white wrought iron fence surrounded the property, rusting in spots and with a front gate that was slightly askew.

There was a light on, but curtains hid their view past the older jalousie windows across the front of the house.

Miguel parked in front and killed the engine. They exited the car, but as they pushed the gate open, it squeaked loudly. Someone drew the curtain aside, as if to see who had come onto the property, and then let it fall back in place again. He shared a look with Madeline, who peeled off from him to walk to the edge of the fenced-in property so she could keep an eye on the backyard.

He walked up to the door and knocked. The muffled sound of voices came from behind the wooden door and then it opened just a crack. A woman stood on the other side. Mid-thirties and very pregnant from what little he could see past the small sliver of the opening.

Holding up his ID, he said, "FBI. Supervisory Special Agent Miguel Peters. I'd like to speak to Randy Davis. Is he available?"

"He's not home," she said, but at the same time, the thud of booted feet carried from behind her, followed by the slam of another door.

"He's running," Miguel shouted at Madeline, who rushed across one side of the yard while he raced down the stairs and to the other side.

He caught sight of a man sprinting across the yard in his direction and ran to cut him off. Before he could reach him, the man vaulted over the low wrought iron fence and raced across the neighboring yard. Miguel followed, grabbing hold of the fence to hurdle over it, but as he landed, his leg buckled a bit, still weak after the shooting. It sent him sprawling to the ground in a heap, but he pushed back onto his feet, giving chase in an awkward run, every other step filled with pain.

But Davis, their unsub, was fast and quickly disappeared from view.

He stopped, fists on his hips in frustration as Madeline caught up to him.

"I lost him. I couldn't keep up," he said with a rough breath.

"We'll get him," Madeline said and patted him on the back. The gesture was meant to console, but it only frustrated him even more.

"We will," he said and jerked out his phone to call Seattle PD. In no time he had arranged for a BOLO to be put out on Davis and police surveillance of the premises. Then he reached out to fill in Mack at ABS and the ATF special agent. With another call back to the BAU offices, he had Dashiell working on getting a search warrant so they could see what evidence would turn up at the blaster's home.

"Let's head back. Hopefully we'll have the warrant shortly and see if Rothwell is more than just Davis's employer," Miguel said and brushed some dirt off his suit as they returned to his sedan.

Once they were inside and heading back to the BAU offices, Madeline said, "I have to admit I thought you were a little off base when you pegged Rothwell as being involved, but there are just too many connections to him."

Miguel took a quick look at her as he drove. "So now you agree that he's part of this?"

With a shrug that barely shifted the fine wool of her suit jacket, she said, "I think it's way more probable than not."

Miguel quickly ran down what they had so far, intending to convince her that it was more than just probable. "Two shell companies owned by him, since I have no doubt the second one will be a Rothwell property. The licensed blaster works at one of his construction sites. Adams worked barely a block or so from Rothwell's business office."

"All circumstantial," Madeline reminded him.

"For now. In time we'll get what we need to nail him," Miguel said, more convinced than ever that Rothwell was the mastermind behind the Seattle Crusader.

With another shrug, Madeline said, "I hope you're right and that we'll be able to get him before another bombing hurts someone."

"I know we will."

Chapter Seventeen

Maisy couldn't sleep. She couldn't even get comfortable knowing that Miguel was out there, possibly in danger. That his team was out there, likewise risking their lives to keep others safe.

It made her wonder how the wives and husbands of the police, FBI and other first responders did this every day.

Could I do this every day? she wondered, but then forced her thoughts away from that.

Miguel and she had been thrown together by this investigation and it was unlikely that their relationship would become more after this terrorist had been caught.

So she had to grab whatever joy she could with both hands.

When Miguel walked in, limping slightly as he entered, she shot to her feet and hurried to his side. Seeing that his suit and shirt were smudged with dirt and grass stains, she ran her hands across his arms and chest, as if searching for any injuries.

"Are you okay?" she asked.

He cupped her cheek and strummed his thumb there. "I am. The licensed blaster ran off when we tried to question him, and I fell going over a fence to chase him."

"Your leg," she said, glancing down to see if he'd ripped his stitches again.

He mimicked her action, peering down at his leg, but there was no sign of any damage.

"It's fine and you're up late." He slipped his hand into hers and with a playful tug, drew her toward the bed.

"I couldn't sleep. Had too much on my mind. I was worried," she admitted and faced him as they stood by the edge of the bed.

"I wasn't in any danger, unlike you. It kills me that you were hurt today. That I failed you," he said and tenderly ran his hand along the bandage on her arm.

She smiled and cradled his jaw. "You didn't fail me or anyone else. I see how hard you and your team are working to catch the Crusader."

"And yet they are still free, because with the blaster running away, I'm totally sure that it's someone higher up directing Adams and the blaster."

"Rothwell?" she said.

He nodded, but then shook his head. "It's late. You should try and get some sleep."

"I don't know if I could, but what about you? Aren't you tired?" she said and urged him to sit on the edge of the bed with her.

"A little," he admitted, and she sensed his reluctance with the admission.

"Why don't you take a moment and rest?"

MIGUEL WAS BONE-TIRED and his leg was throbbing from the earlier pressure he had placed on it. But more than anything, he was tired in his soul at the prospect of coming home to an empty house. A house without Maisy.

He'd never felt that way before. The thought of being alone like that had never bothered him. Until now.

So even a few minutes of respite beside her would be an unexpected blessing before she was gone.

"Just a short break," he said, eased off his suit jacket and holster and laid them beside the bed. Then he removed his soiled shirt and toed off his shoes.

Maisy was resting against some pillows in the center of the bed and he scooted over and joined her there. Tucking her against his side, he leaned back and closed his eyes, savoring the moment.

She swept her hand across his T-shirt, her touch soothing, but he needed more than her comfort. He needed her in every way a man could need a woman.

"Maisy," he said and half turned toward her, meeting her gaze. Her blue eyes had darkened to almost violet and he had no doubt of her desire. It was there in her gaze and the trembling of her body beside him.

But he wouldn't push her if she wasn't ready. "Are you sure?"

"I am," she said, and as if to prove it, she pressed him down into the pillows and rose over him. Grabbed the hem of his T-shirt and drew it slowly up and over his head to bare him to her gaze.

"You are so handsome," she said and ran her hand across his chest again.

"And you're stunning." He cradled her breast and beneath his palm and the thin fabric of her pajama top, her nipple beaded into an even tighter nub.

He caressed her and she ran her hand across the length of him, yanking a needy moan from him. That sound shattered the last of their restraint.

She jerked at his pants, wanting him free of them as much as he needed to see her bare and beneath him.

He got his wish a second later as she lay back and took him with her, inviting him to join her. To be one with her.

But he didn't want to rush. Didn't want to miss a second of being with her, this precious gift that he'd been given by fate.

He took his time, showing her with his hands and lips how much he treasured her, kissing and caressing her body until she was quivering beneath him. Clutching at him as her body rose ever higher toward a release.

When he eased his hand between her body to find her center, pleasure her, her climax ripped through her.

She called out his name and gripped his shoulders. Shifted her hips along his erection and he couldn't hold back any longer. He fumbled for only a moment to slip on a condom, and then he drove into her, pausing to savor the feel of her warmth and tightness. So tight.

"Maisy, *mi amor*—" he began, but she covered his mouth with her hand and murmured, "Love me, Miguel. Love me."

He did, driving into her. Kissing her as he moved, drawing her higher and higher. Climbing with her until it was impossible to hold back and he fell over, losing himself in her. Accepting her loving cry of satisfaction as she joined him.

Falling down onto her, he eased to her side slightly and at her protest, he said, "I'm too heavy."

She wrapped her arms around him and smiled. "You're just right."

And for the first time since his mother's murder, he felt right. Felt at peace with her beside him.

But then the muffled sound of his phone came from his suit jacket and he knew.

This moment of peace was over.

NICHOLAS AND DAVID kept their distance as they spotted someone who matched Chris Adams's description slipping out of a tent and heading away from the highway.

They'd been on their feet most of the day, trying rather unsuccessfully to get help from the legion of homeless in various encampments.

They had started at the one closest to Adams's last known location, striking out time and time again since no one wanted to help them. After stopping for a quick bite for dinner, they'd actually found one helpful soul who had directed them to the Riverview Playfield and the nearby highway area.

"My sister was in King Street Station when that bomb went off. We were lucky she wasn't hurt," the man had told them after providing the information.

"We appreciate the help," Nicholas had said and headed to Riverview.

It was dark by the time they reached the park, and the ball fields and playground were empty. A number of trails ran from the playfields to some wooded areas and while they'd thought it was possible that Adams might have pitched a tent there, their informant had pointed them in the direction of the highway area.

Armed with that, they'd started a search of some of the homeless camps in and around the roadway, but with little success and cooperation.

Near midnight, they'd spotted their possible suspect, but hung back, unable to positively identify him in the dark. But as he passed beneath one streetlight and the smallest sliver of his face was visible, Nicholas had no doubt it was Chris Adams.

He laid a hand on David's arm to instruct him to hold up and pulled out his cell phone to call Miguel.

It took a few rings for his SSA to answer, not a usual occurrence.

"Yes, Nicholas," Miguel prompted.

"We have eyes on our unsub. He's just left a tent near the intersection of the 509 and West Marginal Way South and now he's heading south on First Avenue South."

"Great. Text us a link to track you and we'll meet you there," he said.

"Will do." He sent Miguel a text with a link to their location so he could follow where they were going.

Shoulders hunched, face hidden beneath a black hoodie, their unsub continued on the street, passing by a number of industrial buildings and a site where multicolored steel barrels were piled high behind a chain-link fence. Their unsub pushed on until he reached a break between properties and a fenced-in yard holding a number of forklifts, pallet trucks, scaffolding and other construction supplies.

"Rothwell's?" David asked as they hurried their pace to not lose track of Adams because the area between the two buildings was relatively dark.

"Possibly," he said since there was no identifying signage on the property.

When they neared the end of one building, they caught sight of Adams approaching a dark-colored, pricey sedan parked just beyond the edge of the fenced-in yard. The nose of the car faced forward, making it impossible for them to see who was behind the wheel or if anyone was even in the car.

As Adams hurried toward the passenger's side of the car, they likewise sped up, hoping to get a better look.

They were close enough to snap off a photo when the car shot off in the direction of the Duwamish Waterway.

"Damn," Nicholas cursed as he and David gave chase on foot. The car quickly moved away from them, but not before Nicholas confirmed the license plate he had seen earlier.

MIGUEL RACED TOWARD the location the tracker had provided, Maisy at his side. Madeline and Dashiell were in a second vehicle just moments behind them.

The phone rang and seeing Nicholas's number in the caller ID, he immediately picked up.

"Adams just got into a dark, late-model sedan. Jaguar, I think. The license plate read Vote Roth. They were headed east toward the Duwamish."

"We're almost there," he said and shot a glance toward the GPS. "I think we can head him off on South Holden. Meet us there."

"Roger that," Nicholas said, and Miguel immediately called Madeline and Dashiell to provide an update and instructions.

"We're headed to South Holden, but if we miss him there, he could try to make a run for it by South Donavan," he said, and Madeline completely understood.

"We'll try to cut him off, but keep us posted," Madeline advised.

"Do you think we'll get him?" Maisy asked, but as he took a turn sharply, she braced her hands on the door and seat beside her.

"You okay?" he asked, worried for her safety even though Maisy had insisted on coming with him, determined to see the investigation through to the very end.

"Yes. Is it him? Is it Rothwell?" she asked, anger sharp in her tones.

"It seems that way," he said and took another rough turn that led them down the highway toward Nicholas's location. As they reached the street, Nicholas and David were waving them down on the highway.

He jerked the car to a stop and his team members hopped in. "No sign of them here, so he must be headed to South Park," David said, leaning forward to speak to Miguel.

"Please call Madeline and let her know," he said, intent on focusing on the drive and keeping an eye out for their unsub's car. He headed toward the waterway, hoping to pick up their trail as Madeline and Dashiell shot past them, staying on the road to try to head them off at the next entrance to the maze of industrial and factory sites in the area.

MADELINE PRESSED THE pedal to the metal and streaked by Miguel and the rest of the team to try to reach the next exit for the industrial area.

"If the unsub headed toward the waterway, we may be able to head straight at them," she said and executed a harsh turn, wheels squealing to push them in the direction of the water.

They had barely gone two blocks when twin beams of light erupted from a side street.

Almost colliding with the car as it jumped into the intersection, Madeline screeched to a halt. A second later, the driver of the sedan, seeing that escape was blocked off in that direction, whipped back toward the water, likely trying to double back to freedom.

Madeline gave chase while Dashiell called the rest of the team, hoping that they'd be able to box him in.

"We're headed toward the marina," Dashiell said, his attention half on the road and the map on the GPS system.

"On it," Miguel said, but as they neared the water and the sight of masts and boats by the marina, the unsub's sedan veered wildly to the left and right and a sudden blast of light erupted inside the car. The sedan jerked to a halt, and the passenger's side door shot open. A man stumbled out, clutching his midsection.

The sedan peeled away while the man crumpled to the ground, clearly injured.

Dashiell was immediately on it as Madeline drove to the man and stopped the car.

A second later, Miguel pulled up, but Madeline waved him in the direction of the sedan, which was clearly disappearing down the street again. "He's heading toward the highway. I think he shot Adams."

Miguel nodded. "Call it in and keep us posted," he said and took off after the sedan.

Madeline rushed over to where Dashiell was tending to the injured man—Chris Adams without a doubt. She called for an ambulance and then knelt beside Adams, trying to offer comfort and get information while Dashiell tried to stem the flow of blood from the abdominal wound.

Too much blood, she thought.

Chapter Eighteen

The red taillights of the car were only a couple of blocks ahead of him but shooting straight for the exit to the highway.

Maisy was holding tight to the dash and front seat as they fishtailed from the side street onto the highway. In the dark of night, there was luckily little traffic, allowing him to keep an eye on the unsub's car.

From the back seat he heard Nicholas calling in to Seattle PD for backup and pinpointing their location as they sped onto the 99. There was more traffic there, forcing the unsub to weave in and out of slower-moving cars to make his escape. Miguel was worried that they could cause an accident, especially as a duo of Seattle PD cars swept onto the highway and joined them in the pursuit.

Miguel actually fell back, letting the police cruisers take the lead and also have the freedom to thread the needle and stay on the unsub's tail. Barely a mile later, another police cruiser jumped onto the highway and worked its way in front of the unsub's car in an attempt to box him in between the three cruisers giving chase.

Suddenly, the dark sedan stopped short, forcing two of the cruisers to peel away to avoid rear-ending it. In another surprise move, it shot almost directly across the highway to an exit and rushed off, leaving Miguel as the only vehicle that could follow.

"Hold on," he said, their sedan nearly flying over a bump on the exit and back onto one of the side streets.

Luckily, the police had called it in and no sooner had the unsub's sedan hit the access road for the highway than a cruiser was there, blocking the road.

With another sharp, almost two-wheeled turn, the sedan whipped onto a side street.

Miguel followed, his gaze locked on the unsub's taillights and on the nav system which showed that the sedan was headed into a dead end close to the Duwamish River. A quick look in the rearview mirror revealed the flashing lights of a police vehicle and the wail of sirens just ahead of them said they were closing the noose around their unsub.

Barely fifty yards ahead, the moonlight gleamed over the waters of the river. As the driver realized there was nowhere else to go, the car slammed to a stop at an awkward angle. The driver's side door flew open, but a cruiser was already there.

Two policemen threw their doors open and drew their weapons as Miguel pulled up. Not seconds later, a second police car drove up, followed by a television news crew who must have been listening to the police radio.

The reporter and cameraman were already filming as Miguel and Nicholas approached, guns drawn, David and Maisy trailing behind them.

"FBI. He's armed," Miguel called out and flashed his badge at the police officers, who had their weapons trained on the sedan.

"Toss your weapon and come out with your hands up," he instructed, but hung back, aware that the unsub may have already killed someone just minutes earlier.

The gun rattled against the pavement as the driver tossed it out. A second later, a familiar voice said, "I'm not armed."

"Step out with your hands on your head," Miguel said, expectant. Sure of who would exit the sedan.

A second later, Rothwell's salt-and-pepper head of hair popped out, squashed by his interlaced hands as Miguel had requested. The senate candidate stumbled a bit to exit the low-slung sedan, but then he stood, fully visible to one and all, especially the news team.

Justice, Miguel thought as he silently instructed Nicholas to keep his weapon trained on Rothwell while he walked over and handcuffed him. By then a second news team had hit the scene and Miguel schooled his features as he read Rothwell his Miranda rights.

Rothwell said nothing, just nodded, but it would be enough, especially with all the cameras rolling to capture the moment.

Miguel escorted Rothwell to the police cruiser and turned him over to the custody of Seattle PD. "Lock him up. No one is to interview him without us. If he asks for a lawyer, give him his mandatory call, but let us know."

"We understand. We just got word that Adams is at Harborview. Your agents are with him," the one officer said as they took custody of Rothwell.

"We'll head there now," Miguel said and walked toward where Maisy, Nicholas and David waited by his vehicle.

As he did so, he was besieged by the reporters who

had arrived on the scene. A reporter shoved a microphone almost into his face and he patiently eased it back.

"Can you confirm that state senate candidate Rothwell is the Seattle Crusader?" the reporter asked.

"Our investigation is still pending. We have no comment at this time," he said and pressed past the news crews to Maisy and his team.

When he got to her side, she said in tones only loud enough for him to hear, "Is it over?"

Sadly, he had no doubt it was. What was left was for them to pull together all that they already had plus whatever Adams and the blaster could provide to make their case bulletproof.

Which meant he and Maisy would go their separate ways as well.

"It is," he said and forced himself to look away from her crestfallen expression since she also seemed to understand what that meant.

He opened her door and helped her into the car and as he passed by Nicholas, his team member shot him a questioning look.

Miguel ignored it, focusing on what he would need to do at the hospital in order to get the evidence to not only charge Rothwell, but eventually secure a conviction.

Once they were in the car, he sped toward Harborview Medical Center, and thanks to the late hour, they were entering the ER area barely fifteen minutes later. Madeline and Dashiell were walking down the hall with a doctor, heads bent toward each other as they apparently discussed the status of their suspect.

Madeline noticed him immediately as they entered the waiting area and strode to him, a deep frown marring the perfection of her skin.

"Not good, I gather," he said when Dashiell joined them a second later.

"The bullet nicked an abdominal artery, and he lost a lot of blood. He's in surgery to repair the damage and it's touch and go," she said.

"Hopefully he'll pull through," Miguel said and had to ask the hard question. "Were you able to get anything out of him?"

"We did," Dashiell said. "Apparently Adams approached Rothwell a few weeks ago near his offices since he knew Rothwell was a candidate. They chatted about prison reform on account of the troubles that Adams's brothers had had."

Almost like a tag team, Madeline continued with the report. "A couple of weeks after that, Rothwell approached Adams and offered him some money and to help Adams with his brothers' sentences. Adams took the bait, but that's all we were able to get out of him before he passed out from blood loss."

Miguel dragged a hand through his hair in frustration, but there was little they could do about Adams except pray that he made it through the surgery. If he did, they might be able to get more information from him to close the book on Rothwell.

And thinking about Rothwell… "We'll pray that Adams survives the surgery. In the meantime, we need to go interview our erstwhile state senate candidate to see what he has to say."

Maisy's hand slipped into his and drew his attention. "Adams will make it. We have to believe that so you can put Rothwell away."

He forced a smile and nodded. "Hopefully."

Dashiell held up a small laboratory vial. "This may

help. It's the bullet the ER doctor removed. Hopefully its ballistics will match any gun Rothwell handled."

Miguel took the vial and held it up to the light to examine it. "He tossed out a 9 mm Glock and this definitely looks like the same caliber."

He pulled an evidence bag out of his pocket and tucked the vial into the bag. "Let's go speak to Rothwell."

BY THE TIME they reached the police station barely fifteen minutes later, Rothwell had already lawyered up and wasn't talking.

You could almost touch the tension in the interrogation room as Miguel and Nicholas sat across the table from Rothwell and his counsel. David and Maisy were waiting outside for them while a trio of Seattle detectives was in the space behind the one-way mirror, watching the interview.

"Richard, I can call you Richard, can't I?" Miguel said, determined to try to convince the politician to speak despite his having lawyered up.

"SSA Peters, Mr. Rothwell has already indicated that he has no interest in chatting with you," the lawyer said, his tone as smarmy as Rothwell's had been during his various television interviews.

"You understand that Mr. Adams has already admitted that your client hired him to take part in the Seattle Crusader bombings. Mr. Rothwell owns two of the locations where the bombings occurred. We have a gun that was fired by Mr. Rothwell—"

"My client advised me that it was Mr. Adams who pulled the gun on my client and he was only trying to defend himself when the gun went off."

"Which begs the question of why Mr. Adams was even in the car with your client," Nicholas pressed.

"Mr. Adams approached my client and offered to stop the bombings in exchange for the payment of one hundred thousand dollars. As a concerned citizen, my client agreed to meet with him to see if he couldn't convince Mr. Adams to turn himself in," the lawyer said and shot a quick look at his client, who was still sitting there silently. His arms were across his chest, an almost bored look on his face, infuriating Miguel.

He glared at Rothwell, ignoring his counsel as he said, "We know you hired Adams. We know you shot him to shut him up. The licensed blaster at your current construction project is on the run, but I bet that when we get him, and we will get him, he'll confirm that you were the one directing this terrorist campaign."

"As we've already said, my client was trying to stop Mr. Adams from committing any additional crimes," the lawyer insisted.

"And we'll prove otherwise and when we do, we're going to press for the maximum penalty of life imprisonment under the Patriot Act unless we get some cooperation from your client," Miguel said and at that, Rothwell's lawyer finally showed some concern.

"If you'll give us a moment," the lawyer said.

"Of course," Miguel said, rose and left the room, Nicholas following him out into the hallway.

A second later, the detectives came out of the nearby viewing room, and another police officer approached.

"What is it, Sergeant Lewis?" the one detective asked the uniformed officer.

"A Randy Davis turned himself in to custody a few minutes ago. He wants to speak to the FBI."

Miguel smiled and peered at Nicholas. "Rothwell's blaster. The net is closing on that arrogant bastard."

"It is. Time to let him and his counsel stew in there while we chat with Davis," Nicholas said.

Miguel nodded, but then peered toward Maisy and David, who were still sitting on the bench outside the interrogation room, patiently waiting. But if they were going to interview Davis and then Rothwell again, it might be hours before they were done.

He held up a finger and walked over to Maisy and David, knelt before them. She held a hand out to him and he took it, tenderly squeezed. "We are going to be here for some time. Maybe you should go back to my apartment."

"I can drive her back," David offered.

Miguel nodded, dug into his pants pocket and handed over his car keys to the young tech intern.

"Thank you, and David, you can head home afterward. I don't think we'll need you until the morning when we can hopefully tie up all the loose ends," Miguel said.

"Are you sure? I don't mind waiting," Maisy said and tightened her hold on his hand, as if fearful that once she let go…

He didn't want to think about letting her go, but come morning, or the morning of the following day, that's what he would have to do. He'd have to let her go.

"I'm sure. Don't wait up for me," he said and despite his better judgment, he leaned close and brushed a kiss across her cheek.

"Thanks for taking her home, David," he said and meant it. She was going home. His home, and he didn't want to think any more about how that might change in just a short time.

He needed to think about what to do next in regard to Davis, the licensed blaster, and Rothwell. Adams as well, which prompted him to dial Madeline as David and Maisy walked away.

Maisy cast him one last forlorn look as they turned a corner to exit the police station, but then she was gone.

"Miguel. You there?" Madeline asked.

"Yes, yes, I am," he said, turning back to the moment at hand.

"Any news on Adams?"

"He's pulled through surgery. They have him in surgical ICU but are hopeful that they'll be able to move him to a regular room by the morning," Madeline said.

"That's good news. Maybe once he's stable, we can get more information from him."

"We'll be here, waiting to interview him," Madeline said.

He had no doubt that Madeline and Dashiell would stay until they had what they needed to get Rothwell.

"Thank you and try to get some rest," he said and ended the call.

Turning toward Nicholas and the detectives, he announced, "Time to interview Davis."

Chapter Nineteen

Maisy had changed and slipped into bed once she got back to Miguel's apartment, but she couldn't sleep.

She turned on the television and almost every station had breaking news reports about Rothwell's arrest. The news crews that had tracked them to the marina were running video of the politician's capture and her heart leaped in her chest at the sight of Miguel, gun drawn until Rothwell had tossed out his weapon.

He risked his life for her and for others. A true hero.

A lonely one, she thought, taking what might be a last look around the sterile apartment. Only there was something not as solitary about it in the days she'd been there. On the counter there were two mugs, waiting for their morning dose of coffee. Her computer, journal and some pens rested on the coffee table, calling for her attention, only she didn't feel like writing at the moment. Her heart was too heavy with what would happen now that the investigation was almost over.

She surfed through the channels, avoiding those running reports on the Seattle Crusader. Finally, she found a channel with a travel show and snuggled down to watch, imagining herself visiting the locations, cruising down the Danube from Budapest to Belgrade while lounging on a chaise on the deck of the boat.

Maybe one day, she thought as her eyes grew heavy lidded, but when the door opened and Miguel walked in, all other thoughts fled her brain.

He came straight away and sat on the bed, smudges as dark as charcoal beneath his brown eyes. He settled his gaze on her and said, "You're still awake."

She shrugged. "I couldn't sleep so I turned on the TV. All the news channels were running stories on Rothwell."

He nodded and undid his tie. "It'll only get worse in the next few days. There's blood in the water and the sharks will be circling."

Maisy sat up, clutching the bed covers to her, almost defensively. She didn't know why since Miguel had seen all of her anyway earlier that night.

He noticed the gesture and said, "I still need to do some work. I'll just take a nap on the couch."

"You need to rest. You look like you could drop," she said and cradled his cheek. His skin was rough with a thick evening beard and she ran her thumb across it. The rasp seemed overly loud in the quiet of late night. Even louder than the television on across the room.

Miguel seemed to sense the tension in her. He covered her hand with his. "It's going to be okay, Maisy. We offered the licensed blaster immunity and he testified that Rothwell pressured him to provide the dynamite and wire."

"What kind of pressure would make someone do that?" she wondered aloud.

With a dip of his head, Miguel said, "Davis's wife is pregnant and on bed rest. It hit them hard financially and Rothwell said he'd fire him if he didn't cooperate. Once he did, however, Rothwell threatened to tell police he was the Crusader."

"Davis and Adams. They were just pawns in Rothwell's little game, just like my mother and me," she said, anger rising up at Rothwell and the many lives he had ruined with his actions.

"Not like you at all. I think you would have been strong enough to stand up to Rothwell," he said and drew her close, offering comfort with his embrace, but she wanted more than comfort from him tonight.

She wanted to be with him one last time because she knew that come morning, the clock would be ticking on their relationship.

Sweeping her hand beneath his suit jacket, she helped him ease it off, her hands trembling as she restrained herself. But then he jerked off his holster, seemingly as impatient as she was. Suddenly in a rush, they tossed off clothes and sank beneath the bedcovers together, everything else forgotten except being together before the morning came.

She urged him on with the gentle caress of her hands, bringing him close. Straining toward him because she wanted every inch of her body tight to his, as if to imprint that memory on her brain and skin.

THE WEARINESS THAT Miguel had felt as he'd walked in had vanished the moment she'd laid her trembling hands on him.

He moved in her, joined with her emotionally and physically. Wishing to hold on to that connection even as he pushed them ever closer to a release. Taking her breath into his, the scent of her as the musk of their lovemaking perfumed the air.

She arched beneath him and dug her fingers into his shoulders as she came, the bite of her nails a reminder of the pain he'd feel when she was out of his life.

"I love you," she cried out, her body quivering against his, and he lost it.

"I love you, too," he said and buried himself deep, his body shuddering as his release slammed into him.

He eased to her side and took her into his arms, not wanting to miss a minute of being with her. His breath still choppy as hers was, until little by little it lengthened, the trauma and labors of the day stealing him away to rest.

To dream of what it might be like if every night could be spent in the love and comfort of her arms.

IT SEEMED TO Maisy that she had barely fallen asleep when the noise of the shower dragged her awake.

Her body was still slightly sore, especially the area around the gash on her arm where the shrapnel had injured her.

But that pain was nothing compared to the ache in her chest at what might happen today. However, the pain was balanced by the possibility that Seattle and its people would be safe from the terror created by the Seattle Crusader.

She slipped out of bed and grabbed some clothes just as Miguel came out of the shower, a towel wrapped around his lean hips, droplets of water glistening on his skin. He rubbed another towel against his head to dry his hair and when he was done, the short strands stood in a disarray of spikes.

"Good morning," he said, his voice rough.

"Good morning. I'm just going to take a shower," she said and rushed away, afraid that if she said anything more, she would fall apart.

MIGUEL WATCHED MAISY rush off and he understood.

Whatever had happened yesterday between them had been amazing. But today he had to deal with the reality that they might close the Seattle Crusader case and once they did that…

He rushed and dressed, needing to get up to the BAU offices to assemble all the evidence that they had and anything else that Liam might have found while the rest of the team had been chasing after Adams and Davis.

Which reminded him that he needed an update on Adams's condition. It had been a few hours since the last message Madeline had sent him.

"Good morning, Miguel," she said, the tone of her voice a weird mix of cheery and exhausted.

"Is it a good morning?" he asked.

"Adams was moved to a private room about half an hour ago. Seattle PD is guarding him, and we were just heading there to see if he was able to talk to us."

"Keep me posted," he said and busied himself with making coffee while Maisy showered and dressed.

He had just finished prepping to-go cups for them when she came out of the bathroom, the wet strands of her hair framing her gorgeous face and those unforgettable blue eyes.

"Are you ready?" he asked, the simple question loaded with so much meaning.

"Ready as I'll ever be," she responded and together they headed up to the BAU offices.

When they entered, Nicholas was at their whiteboard, filling in the information they had gotten the night before from their unsubs.

As he shot a quick look at the board, he thought they had enough evidence to support charges against Rothwell and Adams, especially with the licensed blaster agreeing to testify in exchange for immunity. But he wanted the case to be bulletproof and with Davis getting immunity, a good attorney would try to downplay his testimony by arguing that Davis would say anything to avoid prison time.

Which meant they needed every bit of evidence they could get.

He guided Maisy to the table and noticed that Liam was at his computer, wearing the same clothes that he'd had on the day before.

He walked over and clapped Liam on the back. "Have you been here all night?"

Liam glanced up at him, eyes bleary with exhaustion. "I have, but I think you'll be happy with what I've found out."

"Why don't you come and fill us in and then head home," he said, but a second later, Lorelai walked in and shot a worried glance at Liam.

"You don't look too good," she said and went to his side. She brushed her hand across the short strands of his light brown hair, the gesture loving and dragging a smile from Liam.

"I'll be okay," he said and lovingly laid a hand on Lorelai's slender waist, but she jerked back, the earlier tenderness gone.

She was all business as she said, "Director Branson

has seen the news and has asked that you call her and provide a report on where you stand with the investigation."

Miguel eyed Liam. "Are you ready to add your input to the report?"

Liam nodded. "Totally ready."

"I'll set up the video call," Lorelai said and marched away, her stilettos snapping against the tiled floor.

Liam tracked her departure and smiled sadly. "I'm a fool," he muttered.

As Miguel glanced toward their work area, his gaze fixed on Maisy and he muttered, "You're not the only one."

He didn't wait for Liam's reply, although the tech guru followed him to the main work area so he could provide his report as part of the update to Director Branson.

The ever efficient Lorelai pressed several buttons and a second later the video feed from his boss jumped onto the projection monitor at the front of the room.

"Good morning, Olivia," Miguel said.

Olivia nodded. "Good morning. I see from the news reports that we have several suspects in custody. Do you have anything to add?"

"Rothwell is being held by Seattle PD along with a licensed blaster who worked for him. We've given Davis, the blaster, immunity in exchange for his testimony. Chris Adams, the individual who actually placed the bombs at the various locations, is in the hospital. Special Agents Striker and West are waiting to conduct an additional interview with him, but Adams has confirmed that Rothwell hired him to do the bombings. It appears Rothwell himself made the bombs, but we're going to need additional physical evidence to prove that," Miguel advised and then looked toward Liam.

He gestured to him and said, "Agent McDare has some information for us."

Liam stepped forward. "We had tracked one shell company to Rothwell, but I was able to also connect the second shell company to him. More importantly, it appears that Rothwell has placed insurance claims for both of the properties which were damaged."

Olivia nodded. "So in addition to using the bombings to possibly improve his public perception during his campaign, he's benefitting financially as well."

"It seems that way. We'll work on getting a search warrant of his various properties to see if we can turn up any other evidence. In the meantime, we're preparing our report so that the U.S. attorney can review the cases against the various individuals and proceed with action as is appropriate," he said.

"Wonderful news, Miguel, and thank you to all the team members. I'll report to the FBI director. If there are any other developments, please keep me posted," she said, a broad smile on her features before she ended the video call.

Miguel faced his team and Maisy, likewise smiling. "You've all done a great job, but now we have to tie up any loose ends so that the case the government presents is airtight."

"I'll keep on digging," Liam said, but Miguel shook his head.

"You need to take a break to make sure you don't miss a thing. Nicholas and I will head out as soon as we have the search warrant, and also check on Adams."

Liam started to argue, but Lorelai jumped into the fray. "Liam, please. Miguel is right and none of us wants to see you fall flat on your face."

"Really? Not even you?" he said, eyes narrowed as he gazed at his ex.

With a roll of her eyes, she said, "Not even me," and hurried from the room.

"I guess I'll go," Liam said and walked away, leaving Miguel, Nicholas, David and Maisy behind.

Miguel glanced at Nicholas. "Can you please follow up on the search warrant?"

"Will do," Nicholas said and headed to his office to check.

"We could use your skills later, David. I know you had a late night so why don't you go get some rest as well and come back in a few hours."

Unlike Liam, David didn't argue. "I'll be back after lunch," he said and left.

Miguel sat beside Maisy and took her hand into his. "You didn't get much rest last night either," he said and loved the bright splash of color that erupted across her cheeks.

"No thanks to you, only..." She paused, uneasy, and peered around the room. Seemingly satisfied that anything they said would be private, she said, "Where do we go from here? Back to our old lives?"

"Isn't that what you want? Travel. Adventure."

She barked out a rough laugh and shook her head. "I think I've had my share of adventure for a little while. Home is looking good and with the Crusader in custody, there are lots of places in Seattle that I can feature on my blog."

"And maybe you could even share your experience with the Crusader and the FBI, private parts omitted of course," he said and chuckled.

He had a wry smile on his face and Maisy wasn't quite sure what to make of his slightly less serious demeanor this morning. Especially about a subject as serious as what the future would hold for them. But she didn't want to weigh down the discussion quite so soon.

"I don't know, Miguel. I bet some people would be interested in how the FBI works undercovers," she teased and got a kick out of how a stain of color worked across his cheeks.

"I think the only person I want interested is you, Maisy. It's not what I expected when this investigation started, believe me," he admitted with a wag of his head.

"Me either, but here we are, and I can't imagine not having you in my life, as hard as it might be," she said and cupped his cheek.

"It is hard. Dangerous. And I can't ask you to live with that fear. With the possibility that one day—"

She didn't let him finish, laying her thumb across his lips to silence him. "I know you've seen that first-hand with your mom."

"And with her partner, who was killed with her. He left behind his wife and a newborn. I saw her pain and the loss."

"Pain and loss are part of life sometimes, but do you know what's sadder? Never having loved at all. Never experiencing what we've experienced in the last few days. That comfort and peace. The joy that I found in your arms," she said, leaned forward and kissed him.

The feel of her lips, the warmth of them, broke through the chill in his heart at the thought of not having her in his life. He answered her kiss, meeting her mouth with his over and over until they were breathless.

Only then did he break apart from her, but he leaned his forehead on hers and skimmed his hand through the caramel locks of her hair. "You are a determined woman. A strong woman."

"A woman who can handle a life like yours," she said, trying to convince him, only that wasn't necessary.

"You can handle anything, I think, including a life with me. It's why I want you in my life. Today. Tomorrow. Forever. That is if you'll have me," he said.

A smile slowly erupted across her features, brightening the blue of her gaze to the color of a summer sky. "If that's a proposal, the answer is yes."

"Then there's only one thing that would make me happier—how soon can you marry me?" he said and dropped a playful kiss on her lips.

She chuckled and shook her head. "I think I like this new impulsive side of you."

In truth, she made him feel lighter, as if the weight of the world that had descended on him with the deaths of his mom and her partner was no longer holding him down. "It's thanks to you. You've set me free of the past."

She leaned her forehead against his again and said, "Just like you've set me free. Together we can do this."

"We can. If you don't mind, I'd like to go see my dad. Tell him the good news. Let him know that he's free to move around now that we've caught the Crusader."

"I'd like that as well," she said, rose, and held out her hand to him. "I'd like to go now, if you can, that is."

Miguel looked toward Nicholas's office. "Let me just check with Nicholas about the search warrant."

"Sounds good," she said, and he hurried off to his team member, who was on the phone with someone.

As Nicholas hung up, Miguel said, "How are we doing?"

Nicholas leaned back in his chair and laced his hands together behind his head in a casual pose. "They're getting the judge out of bed to sign the warrant. May be another hour before we have it so I may go get a shower and change if that's okay with you."

"It is. Maisy and I are just going to see my dad. We have some good news for him," Miguel said with a smile.

Nicholas's gaze skipped from him to where Maisy waited in their work area. "Let me guess. You and Maisy—"

"I proposed," Miguel jumped in, surprised by his own excitement at the prospect.

Nicholas did a quick wag of his head. "I have to admit, I never thought I'd see this day, but I'm happy for you. I think Maisy will be good for you and that you'll be good for her."

Miguel looked back toward her and smiled. "I think so. Now, if only Liam would see what a mistake he made."

Nicholas nodded. "I think he may have. I overheard him saying something to David just before he left."

"Let's hope so. I'm not sure I can take more of the Lorelai-Liam drama in the office," he said and gestured to Maisy. "We're going to visit with my father, but I'll be back within the hour. Hopefully we'll have the search warrant by then."

"Hopefully. I'll see you later and… I'm happy for you, Miguel."

"And I'm happy for you, Nicholas. When you first met Aubrey during that serial killer investigation, I have to confess I was worried, but I see how happy she's made you," Miguel said.

"I am happy. More than I ever thought possible so if you'll excuse me, I'm heading home," Nicholas said and shot out of his chair.

"I'll see you later," Miguel said and followed Nicholas out the door to where his team member paused to congratulate Maisy.

She hugged the other agent and after, walked to his side and twined her fingers with his. "Ready to go?"

Ready? he asked himself, but didn't hesitate to say, "More ready than I ever thought."

Chapter Twenty

Liam juggled the flowers as he rode the elevator up to the BAU offices, which he'd left just a little over two hours earlier.

He'd gone home as instructed and as soon as his head hit the pillow, he'd fallen asleep. But the moment he'd opened his eyes, he'd known what he had to do without delay.

The elevator door had barely opened when he rushed out, pushed through the doors of the BAU offices and hurried to the director's anteroom, where Lorelai was seated at her desk.

She looked up as he approached and seemed surprised that he was there. Surprised but pleased, he told himself.

"Good morning, Lorelai," he said and held out the bouquet of flowers to her, but she didn't take them or return the greeting.

Fear gripped his gut, but he pushed on. "I know I've hurt you and I'm sorry. But when I called off the wedding, it wasn't because of you—it was because of me. Because I was afraid that I would mess things up the way my family messed things up."

Lorelai wagged her head and blew out a rough sigh.

"You are not your father or your mother, Liam. You don't have to make their mistakes again," she stressed.

"I should have known that, but when I realized you were at the station with the bomber, it hit me. Hard. I didn't want to lose you," he said and held out the flowers to her again, holding his breath that this time she wouldn't refuse them. Refuse him. "Please marry me, Lorelai. This week, like we had originally planned."

"It's not that easy," Lorelai said, but took the flowers from him and smiled. "Carnations. My favorites."

"It is that easy. I called the restaurant. They haven't rebooked our room yet. The minister's still available also. Please forgive me and say yes. Make me a very happy man."

She dipped her head to the bouquet and inhaled the spicy fragrance of the carnations. As she lifted her gaze to meet his, she smiled and said, "Yes."

THE HOTEL ROOM door flew open as soon as Miguel knocked. "Thank God you're both okay. I just saw the news on TV," his father said and invited them into the room. "We're fine, Dad," Miguel said and his father narrowed his gaze as they walked into the room hand-in-hand.

"I'm so glad, Miguel. You know how I worry about you," his father said and followed them into the room.

Miguel shared a quick glance with Maisy, but then smiled. "I know you worry, but I think you'll be happy to hear that Maisy agreed to marry me."

Robert smiled and his gaze sheened with tears. He walked over and hugged Maisy and then Miguel. "I am so happy. I think I worried as much, maybe more, about you being so alone."

Maisy hugged Robert and said, "Well, you don't have to worry about that anymore. I think Miguel and I will be very happy together."

His father's teary gaze skipped from Maisy to him. "I know you will be. You've made this old man very happy."

"And we're very happy, Dad. I hope that you'll think about spending more time in Seattle," Miguel said.

This time the tears, of joy and not sorrow, slipped down his father's cheeks. "I think I will. Maybe even move here, that is if you don't think I'll be intruding."

Maisy laid a hand on his jacket sleeve and smiled. "I know this is all so sudden, but I think it would be wonderful to have you here."

"I agree, Dad. You can even help us plan the wedding," Miguel said.

"A wedding. You and Maisy! How wonderful," he said and hugged them once again.

It is wonderful, Miguel thought and savored the peace of the embrace with his father and Maisy. It was a peace he'd never expected, but he welcomed it.

In their arms, he was finally free of the pain of the past. Free to forge a future and a family with this amazing woman.

MIGUEL HUGGED MAISY to him as they moved to the languid beats of the slow dance. He brushed a kiss across her temple and said, "This is nice."

She skimmed a kiss along his jaw and said, "It is. Everyone seems so happy."

Miguel looked around at his team members as they danced with their significant others. Madeline and Jackson. Dashiell and Raina. Nicholas and Aubrey. Liam and Lorelai, dressed in their wedding best.

They all looked so happy and he hoped they were as happy as Maisy and him.

Caitlyn Yang stood off to one side of the room with her boyfriend, David beside them with his girlfriend.

My team, he thought with pride at what they'd been able to accomplish in the past few months. Catching a serial killer. Freeing a young child from a kidnapper. Proving Dashiell's sister was not an embezzler. Stopping Richard Rothwell and his rampage as the Seattle Crusader.

It had taken them the past week to tie up all the loose ends. Adams, who had planted the bombs, had luckily survived his wounds and together with Davis, the licensed blaster, had provided them the last bits of evidence needed to create an airtight case against Rothwell. If there was one thing that bothered him it was that the U.S. attorney had agreed to accept Rothwell's guilty plea in exchange for a reduced sentence. Miguel had thought Rothwell should serve the maximum sentence considering all the harm he'd done in order to win the state senate seat and make some cash from the insurance payouts on the bombed buildings he owned. Still, thirty years in jail might be the equivalent of a life sentence given Rothwell's age.

And I've been freed from my life sentence of loneliness by meeting Maisy, he thought and bent his head to kiss her.

She kissed him back and he could feel her smile against his lips. It dragged a smile to his lips as they kissed again and again.

But then a sound and vibration crept into his awareness, pulling him away from the joyful moment.

He yanked his smartphone from his jacket pocket. *Director Branson.*

"Good evening, Olivia," he said and as his team members heard her name, they looked his way and stopped dancing.

"Good evening, Miguel. I'm so, so sorry to interrupt your celebration and please wish Liam and Lorelai my best," she said, her tone contrite.

"I will and I know you wouldn't be calling unless it was important," he said and little by little his team members drifted over to hear the discussion.

"It is. We have a new case and I'm sending all the information to you. I need the team to review it and be ready to discuss it in an hour," she said.

Miguel glanced at his team members' faces and had no doubt. They were the FBI Seattle BAU team and could tackle any case that came their way.

"We'll be ready."

*****

THE BONE ROOM

DEBRA WEBB

This book is dedicated to my readers! I adore you!
Thank you for following the journey of my
characters through nearly eighty novels!

Chapter One

Winchester, Tennessee
Tuesday, October 19, 8:30 a.m.

Thirty.

Thirty.

It sounded old.

She looked old.

Naomi Honea stared at her reflection and grimaced at the beginnings of crow's-feet around her eyes.

"Too much time in the sun without a hat," she muttered. She knew better. It was the curse of pale skin.

It was true. But there was nothing she could do to prevent spending time outdoors. She was a farmer now, after all. Just like her dad. At least she had been for the past year. She reached up and bundled her wild red hair into a sleek ponytail, then looped a band around it. Had the calluses on her hands like he'd had, as well. She searched the blue eyes she had gotten from her mom—the eyes, the hair and the freckled pale skin she'd inherited from the woman who had taught her about being strong and stubborn and utterly independent.

Naomi sighed and turned away from the mirror.

It was her birthday. The first one she'd spent entirely alone.

That was the thing about being an only child. When the parents were gone, there was no one else.

Well, there was her mother's brother, Donnie, but he wasn't exactly known for keeping in touch. At seventy, he still considered himself a sort of playboy. She could count on seeing him at funerals and the occasional holiday. But hearing from him on her birthday? Highly unlikely.

It wasn't entirely his fault. She'd been gone for all of a decade. He and everyone else she'd once known around town had gone on with their lives. Her reappearance was scarcely a blip on their radar.

She walked into the kitchen in search of her boots. Found them by the back door. The neighbors and a few of her old school friends made an effort in the beginning when she first moved back. But everyone was busy these days. Besides, she really didn't *know* anyone her age around town anymore. Plenty of acquaintances but no true friends. Too much time and distance. No fault but her own. Her mother had warned her about scurrying off to California to follow her dreams.

You'll be all alone, Naomi. You won't know a soul.

Until her nineteenth birthday she'd never been farther out of the state of Tennessee than LA—lower Alabama. Growing up her family had taken vacations to Gulf Shores, Alabama. At the ripe old age of eleven she'd met a boy on their annual trip to the beach who turned her world upside down. He wasn't just any boy, mind you. A boy from the *real* LA. His mother was the lead in a movie being filmed in Fair Hope. Naomi had soaked up his every word about living in California and having an actress for a mom. She'd even been allowed to visit the set and watch a scene filmed—four different times. Who knew that acting was such difficult work? The actors carried out a scene over and over until the director was happy. Her new friend's mother said that some directors simply could not be pleased. Many years later, Naomi learned this firsthand. The hard way. The acting gig was not the romanticized life she'd grown up believing it would be. It turned out to be terrifying and frustrating and unforgiving. But when things occasionally went right, there was immense joy and fierce satisfaction. Like the high of an intensely addictive drug, the wannabes struggled over and over to find and hang on to that moment again.

For several months after that sultry couple of weeks on the sand when she was eleven, this incredibly interesting boy and she wrote to each other. Eventually he'd lost interest and the emails had stopped coming. Or maybe he had moved. Who knew? Regardless, she had been smitten with the life he had described so vividly. The life she had witnessed ever so briefly that one summer. She could hardly wait for the years to pass. Living in Winchester was the most boring thing in the world, and she wished the time away.

She was going to be an actress and live in LA and maybe find her old pen pal and live happily ever after.

Well, she had lived in LA rightly enough. After a brief attempt to be a good daughter and go to college first, she'd dropped out—to her parents' dismay—and driven away from home in her ancient convertible (the one she'd inherited from her daddy's sister after she passed). She'd found a room to rent over a garage and snagged a job as a stand-in dog walker and part-time waitress. Her story was cliché at best, but it was hers and she was determined to live it to the fullest. She'd spent the next ten years struggling to find her big break in the world of television and movies. There had been a good many commercials, even a few appearances on a reasonably popular sitcom and one dramedy. Enough to keep her hopes alive.

Six years into her adventure her mom had died suddenly. She'd come home for a month to help her dad. Not only had she learned that he'd been keeping her mom's terminal illness from her, he also begged her to stay, but she couldn't. At twenty-five she still believed that her dream could come true, and on some level she felt betrayed by him and her mom—both of whom had made the decision to hide the truth from her. It had taken some time, but she'd forgiven her dad. A brief visit here and there had mended the hurt and Naomi had thrown herself fully back into the struggling actor role. The rejections continued to far outweigh the callbacks. She was too Southern-sounding (despite having worked so hard to lose her Tennessee drawl). She was a redhead who refused to go blond. Too thin. Too this. Too that.

Then only four years later her dad had died. This time it was truly unexpected. No one had known his heart was failing him. By that time her dream had dimmed, and the loss of her dad had finished breaking her heart. She'd come home to prepare her parents' beloved organic farm to be sold, but somehow, she hadn't been able to bring herself to follow through.

This was the home where she'd grown up. The house where she'd been born, since her mom had waited too late to say she thought the baby was coming. Naomi had gone to school in Winchester, had her first taste of acting in a middle school play and lost her virginity in the back seat of the class president's car during a high school football game.

For all its ordinariness, this *was* home.

Her parents had poured their lives into this farm and she owed it to them to carry on that legacy. Owed it to herself, too. After ten years of struggle it was fairly clear that she wasn't actress material. She simply didn't have that special something the casting directors were looking for.

But she had no regrets for trying.

As her grandmother once told her: if she hadn't gone after her dream, she would still be wanting to.

Maybe this was her way of hiding from failure. That wasn't true. But she hadn't exactly come home with her tail between her legs. She'd survived in Hollywood. Paid the rent and other necessities. So she hadn't exactly failed, she just hadn't soared as she had hoped.

Not the end of the world, just the end of that goal. Now she had a new goal. Take this organic farm to the next level.

She pulled on her boots and walked out the back door to start her morning chores. Now she was more popular than she'd ever been back in high school or in Hollywood, for that matter. With the help of Arlene Beck, the agronomist, who had begun working with her parents before Naomi was born, the two of them had turned the struggling farm into a thriving enterprise. The CSA—community supported agriculture—deliveries had boomed. They made deliveries all over the county and many more folks had signed up for next year. Watching the growth was exhilarating. It wasn't like the high of acting but it was amazing in its own way.

If the growth continued Naomi would need to hire more full-time hands. The two full-time employees along with the part-timers she employed now would never be enough at this rate of expansion. Her parents would be thrilled. She certainly was. It was the oddest thing. She'd wanted so badly to be far away from Winchester and now she was so grateful to be back and to carry on with the dream her parents had worked so hard to do.

It was far more satisfying than she'd expected. Her only regret was that it had taken her so long to see that ultimately this was where she belonged. She'd missed the final years of her parents' lives and that made her sad when she allowed herself to dwell on the thought.

The work was physically demanding but it was unexpectedly fulfilling. Now she understood what her mother loved so about the soil. While Naomi was growing up her dad had tried charming her with the planting of seeds and nurturing of the tiny sprouts. But she'd only had eyes for the stars. Back then she hadn't been afraid of anything. She'd wandered all over this farm alone, daydreaming.

There was little time for daydreaming these days.

The air was cool this morning. She shivered, wishing she'd pulled on her sweater. The rain had kept them out of the fields for the past four days. As soon as the soil had dried out enough it would be time to get back to work. There was a good bit to be done this time of year. They'd finished a second greenhouse for growing the salad mixes folks typically picked up at the supermarket this late in the year. In fact, the variety they offered was the envy of the local supermarkets. For now, they focused solely on selling to families who signed up for the program. In time, the goal was to open up a new revenue stream through local supermarkets. Keeping the product top-notch quality was the most important aspect of their forward momentum. Expansion and all else had to be secondary.

A cow lifted her head and watched as Naomi passed.

"Morning, Gertie." She couldn't help smiling. Naomi only had a few head of cattle so far. By spring she hoped to offer designer cheeses as part of their biweekly delivery. She passed the goat pen. As the herd grew that pen would need to be expanded. The goats and the cows kept her on her toes. But it was the chickens that soothed her soul. Honea Farm was very close to needing a second chicken house. One small local restaurant, the Good Earth, was already buying eggs from the farm.

The CSA subscribers loved the fresh eggs. She'd decided to move forward with the second chicken house over the winter when certain other work was slower. Sean Riley and Joe Jones, her only two year-round, full-time employees, would do much of the construction on the new chicken house. The concrete work and metal roofing would be subbed out.

By spring she hoped to be ready to add to the flock. She already had her eye on new Rhode Island Reds, leghorns and Sussex chickens. When she really thought about it, it was strange how she'd moved so far beyond the glitz and glitter of the west coast world. The best laying hens and spring planting were her primary obsessions now. She headed for the place she and Arlene called "the lab." It was where Arlene performed all her soil and plant testing with new foods and organic fertilizers.

Besides the lab, there were two barns, a hay shed and her dad's old workshop. She hadn't been in the workshop in ages. The last time she'd walked in she'd inhaled the scent of wood and oils, grease and gasoline. It had reminded her so much of him that it literally hurt. Her right boot suddenly sank into the mud.

"Well, hell." She made a face at the sucking sound as she pulled her boot free of the dirt. This is what she got for journeying into the past rather than paying attention to where she was stepping. She swiped her boot, one side, then the other, against the nearest fence post.

With the worst of the clumped soil gone, she unlocked the door and walked in. A flip of a switch had light filling the dark space. The smell of organic fertilizer concoctions and clean soil made her smile. Arlene was quite the chef when it came to creating organic enhancements for the crops. Naomi's mom had spoken of Arlene as if she were a goddess of science. Naomi's dad had, as well. The three of them had been more like a family than coworkers. The farm had gone through some rough times after Naomi's mother passed away. She wasn't sure of all the details as to how things went so far downhill, but Arlene had been instrumental in helping Naomi's dad pull it back together and into forward momentum once more.

In the lab, Arlene had a setup not unlike a high school chemistry lab. She gathered organic materials from all over the country—occasionally the world—to create the finest foods (aka fertilizer) for their plants. She also worked hand in hand with the veterinarian to ensure the animals received no hormones or other unnecessary substances. She truly was a bit of a magician in all things natural.

In truth Naomi felt a bit guilty for invading Arlene's territory without her this morning. This really was the older woman's domain and she was more than a little territorial, but Naomi needed the invoices for yesterday's delivery. Generally, Arlene dropped off the invoices on her way home each evening. But she hadn't last night and Naomi hadn't heard from her this morning. At any given time there was far too much going on to allow the paperwork to get behind. Naomi stayed on top of it. The others called her overly picky, but she had her way and they had theirs. Truth was, the lack of control she'd had over anything during her California days had kind of turned her into a bit of a control freak. She was working on relaxing and going with the flow. Easier said than done.

She surveyed the tabletops and file cabinets. No invoices.

As she circled the room once more the small flashing

red light on one of the freezers snagged her attention. She frowned as she moved closer and leaned down to check the temperature status on the control panel. Forty degrees Fahrenheit.

Her frown deepened. The temp was too high. Had Arlene somehow bumped the panel and caused the discrepancy? Naomi tapped the necessary keys until she'd lowered the desired temperature to a more appropriate setting. Since she couldn't be sure how long the temperature had been that way, she opted to open the lid and check the contents. Again, this was Arlene's territory and she hated to invade but this was necessary. If there were items already thawed, to refreeze them would not be a good thing.

One touch of the first package she encountered, and Naomi knew they were in trouble. It wasn't that the item was completely thawed but it was far softer than it should be.

Not good.

She needed to call Arlene and hurry her up. If there was anything in this freezer of particular importance there could be a serious issue. A bag, not a plastic garbage bag—something cloth—drew her attention deeper into the stack of frozen items. She tugged it from the mass, pressed one of the lumps in the bag and felt a little squish.

Definitely not good.

How in the world had this happened?

She opened the drawstring on the bag she now recognized as muslin and peered inside. What appeared to be the tip of a nose...definitely nostrils...dragged her attention to one package in particular.

She shook her head and looked again, expecting to find a mask left in the freezer to freak her out. Arlene was quite the prankster when the mood struck. Halloween was coming up. She probably had plans to give Sean or Joe a little payback for all the times they had pulled one on her.

"Arlene, you are one sneaky old lady."

In truth, the woman's sense of humor kept things from ever being boring around here. Winchester was a small, quiet town. Peaceful. Trouble rarely happened. Before Naomi came back there was a bit of a stir with the undertaker's daughter. Her dad had told her about Rowan DuPont Brannigan and the bizarre goings-on at the local funeral home. But that trouble was a rarity. Not much happened around Winchester. Weddings and funerals were the biggest social events besides church on Sundays.

Naomi reached for the package containing what appeared to be a nose. If this was Arlene's or maybe Sean's or Joe's idea of a joke, all she could say was payback was a devil.

Like the first package she touched, this one was slightly soft. She studied the fake nose that was actually part of a fake face. A mask. With Halloween coming up maybe Arlene was making something creepy for a friend. Seemed a little odd since Arlene was like Naomi. She didn't do a lot of socializing.

Naomi stilled. Damn. This mask certainly looked realistic. A shudder quaked through her and she sat the bag on the counter behind her to study it more closely under the light. Blood pounded in her ears as her pulse rate picked up. Naomi couldn't be sure what drove her at that point—perhaps some instinct hovering way down, deep inside. Whatever it was, it compelled her to turn back to the freezer. She dug beyond the packages scattered around the top of the pile.

Ear.

Her stomach clenched as her brain assimilated what her eyes saw. Ear. *Two* ears. Her hand shook as she reached for the clear plastic bag. The same sort of bag her mom might have placed ears of corn in for stocking the freezer. Only this was certainly not corn. Another poke into the pile of packages revealed a wad of dark…something. *Hair*, she realized as she clutched the clear plastic bag.

Wait. Wait. Wait.

Her heart pounded harder and the air seemed to trap inside her chest.

This wasn't some mask to be used for a prank. This was…

No. No. Impossible.

Even as she shook her head at her own thoughts and warned herself the idea was totally crazy, she started to dig once more. *Skin.*

Hand skin…it looked as if it had been peeled from the bone like a natural glove.

Fingers trembling, Naomi reached into her back pocket and tugged out her phone. Whatever this was, it was time to call the sheriff.

Sheriff Colton Tanner needed to see this…whatever it was.

"Arlene," she muttered, "if this is some sort of joke…"

Every instinct Naomi possessed warned that this was not a joke.

It was the start of a nightmare.

Chapter Two

Honea Farm, 11:00 a.m.

Sheriff Colt Tanner and several of his deputies were scattered over the farm. Two of Winchester's new forensics technicians were going through the farm's lab. The sheriff had confirmed Naomi's potential nightmare.

The remains were human. Real human. Not silicone masks. Not a Halloween prank.

Naomi reminded herself to breathe. She grabbed hold of the nearest fence post and steadied herself. There was a dead person in her freezer. Or at least part of a dead person.

Holy moly, as her dad would have said. How the devil did this happen? Arlene, Sean and Joe were the only people who had access to the lab. Besides Naomi, of course. There was no sign of a break-in. She shook off the silly thought. Who would break in and leave human remains?

Sheriff Tanner had asked her to wait outside the fenced area that surrounded the lab. She didn't mind. The more distance between her and the remains, the better. She'd called Arlene's cell phone three times, but the call had gone to voice mail on each attempt. Maybe Arlene was on her way and had forgotten her cell. She could have been in an accident. A heart attack? She was seventy-two or -three.

"Stop it," Naomi muttered. She was making herself crazy.

"Naomi."

She shifted her attention to the man striding her way. "Did you find anything else?"

Sheriff Tanner was the quintessential cowboy—boots, hat and all. He stopped a few feet away, propped his hands on his hips and glanced around as if he was unsure where to begin with what he had to say. Not a good sign.

"Any luck reaching Ms. Beck?" he asked.

"My calls keep going to voice mail. I'm hoping she'll show up anytime." This was so unlike her. Arlene was as dependable as the sun rising in the morning. Naomi's parents had always complimented the woman's loyalty and dependability. Not showing up or calling was very much out of character.

The sheriff's brow furrowed with concern. "How many employees you have this time of year?"

"Just two. Sean Riley and Joe Jones. They both have the day off today. The only person who was supposed to come in today was Arlene." Naomi stared pensively at the long drive that wound through the front fields connecting the road to the house. Having Arlene show up and explain everything away would be so good about now.

"Well, I'll send one of my deputies out to her house to see if she's had any trouble this morning. Maybe she broke down somewhere between her house and here. She drives that old VW Bus and the thing has been on its last legs for a while now."

"I appreciate that." Naomi had thought of going but she wasn't sure of the protocol. Was she supposed to stay put during this search? It was official police business. He was right: that old Bus of Arlene's was like something from the flower-child days. Although the era was right for Arlene's age, Naomi couldn't see her as the hippie flower-child type. Then again she had seen a photo of her mom and dad looking like hippies. Not so odd considering her dad was a farmer but a little strange given that her mother had been somewhat of an uptight physician. She'd operated a clinic in town until just before her death.

"Why don't you see if you can get Sean and Joe to come in? Don't mention the reason. If either one of them knows anything about those remains, I don't want him taking off or developing a cover story."

Naomi nodded, then shook her head. "I will, but I really can't imagine either of them doing something like this." It was totally over the top. She'd known these two men for years. They had worked for her dad.

"I agree," Sheriff Tanner said, "but one of them may have allowed someone not employed at the farm to use the freezer. Maybe one or the other stored something for a friend. Probably had no idea what was in the bags."

Made a sort of sense, she supposed. "Okay. I'll call them." She tugged her phone from her hip pocket.

"Meanwhile," Sheriff Tanner went on, "I've put in a call to Dr. Brannigan. She's coming by to help us out."

Dr. Brannigan was Rowan DuPont Brannigan. Everyone knew the undertaker's daughter. She was also the county coroner. "Thank you."

Naomi wasn't sure what she was supposed to say but "thank you" seemed adequate.

"You don't have to wait around out here," he offered. "If you have something else to do, feel free to do whatever it is. We'll be here for a while."

If she went to the house, she would only walk the floors. She might as well stand around and keep an eye on how this situation unfolded. The idea that she might still make it in Hollywood with a film about an organic farmer who skinned people and froze their body parts almost made her laugh out loud.

She was delirious. Obviously.

"I'm fine," she said, forcing a stiff smile. "I don't think I could wait inside knowing all this was going on out here."

He nodded. "I understand." The sound of a car engine drew his attention toward the long drive. "We'll see what Dr. Brannigan has to say."

Rowan DuPont Brannigan was a gorgeous woman. Tall, thin, with blond hair. She was also smart. A psychologist, she had worked with Nashville's Metro Police Department for years before returning to take over the family funeral home after her father's death. Nowadays someone else ran the funeral home and Rowan served as the county coroner. Made sense. She had quite the reputation in solving crime and she certainly had a firm grasp on the ins and outs of the dead. In addition, she was married to Chief of Police William "Billie" Brannigan. Even though he was more than a decade older than her, Naomi remembered him from her high school days. Billie was a local hero. Hometown boy made good. Everybody loved Billie Brannigan.

"Good morning, Sheriff," Rowan said as she approached. She turned to Naomi. "Ms. Honea."

Naomi nodded. "I hope you can figure out our mystery. I'm completely at a loss."

Dr. Brannigan smiled. "I can promise you this—if I cannot, I will call in someone who can."

The woman's confidence made Naomi feel far better.

Sheriff Tanner and Dr. Brannigan headed for the lab and Naomi made the calls to Sean and Joe. Keeping the events of the morning to herself wasn't easy. Both men liked their time off, and since they'd had to work all weekend, the call wasn't one either had wanted to receive. While Naomi waited for the guys to arrive, she watched the deputies move about the area, checking for any little thing out of place. Footprints, etc. They would find plenty of hers where she'd stepped in the mud.

Unable to wait any longer, she walked to the house and used the bathroom. Brushed her teeth to rid her mouth of the taste of stale coffee. It was lunchtime and food had been the last thing on her mind. A cold glass of water settled her stomach and helped her feel slightly more steady.

Human.

There were human remains in the freezer on her property.

How in the world had this happened?

She watched for Sean's and Joe's arrivals as she sipped her water. These were people she had known for years. Good grief, her parents had known Arlene for decades! There had to be some reasonable explanation. Human remains hadn't just appeared in that bag in the freezer. Someone had put them there and, unless Dr. Brannigan said differently, they were real.

Who was she kidding?

They were real. *This* was real.

Naomi tried Arlene's number again. Same as before. Voice mail. "Arlene, please call me as soon as you get this message. It's really important."

Sliding her phone back into her pocket she spotted Sean's blue pickup sailing down the drive. Joe's white truck followed close on his tail.

Maybe one of them would be able to provide some insight into this insanity. Naomi started for the door, but Sheriff Tanner was already approaching the guys. She might as well hang back and let him give the news. It wasn't something she was looking forward to doing herself.

She should probably make a fresh pot of coffee. Distracted by the stunning find on her property she hadn't thought to offer water or coffee to the sheriff and his deputies. She had to get her head back on straight. Preparing coffee was the least she could do.

Ten minutes later with the carafe in one hand and a stack of disposable coffee cups in the other, she walked outside and caught up with the deputies one at a time. She thanked each one and was just pouring the last cup when Sheriff Tanner waved her over to the lab.

"I just ran out of coffee," she said when she reached the door where the sheriff waited. "I can make another pot."

"That's a good idea," he said, to her surprise. "I'll give you a hand."

"Sure." He ushered her to the back door of her house rather than into the lab, which was yet another surprise. She wasn't sure whether to be worried about what he'd learned from Sean and Joe or if there was some other more horrifying update about this morning's find.

"Takes just a few minutes," she said as she prepared the grounds and refilled the water reservoir.

Sheriff Tanner removed his hat and sat down at her table. "Naomi, my deputy couldn't get anyone to the door at Arlene's house. Her vehicle is in the driveway so I gave him the go-ahead to use force to get inside. At this point we have to assume there's something wrong."

Naomi's chest tightened. No. No. No. She'd lost both her parents in the past few years. She didn't want to lose anyone else. In spite of the worry choking her she managed to give a nod. "Of course. I understand."

"Arlene was not at home, and based on what she's found so far, Dr. Brannigan believes we're looking at the remains of possibly three people."

The news slammed into Naomi like a load of bricks falling from the sky. "Three people?" She squeezed her eyes shut and shook her head. "How in the world?"

"Sean and Joe seem to be as surprised by all this as you." He shrugged. "For now, I'm reasonably confident they're telling the truth."

Of course they were. Which left Arlene.

"Why would Arlene do something like this?" The concept made no sense whatsoever. The woman was kind, caring. A little quirky. She wouldn't hurt a fly much less a person. It just wasn't possible.

"Both Sean and Joe said basically the same thing."

At least she wasn't the only one who hadn't noticed anything off. Surely one of them would have picked up on something off-kilter.

"Have you found…" How did she say this? "The rest of the parts?"

"No bones. No organs. Just…tissue."

"So the flesh and…muscle were literally filleted from the bone."

"It looks that way."

Deep breath. "I think the coffee's ready." She walked slowly to the coffeepot, struggling to maintain her composure. Someone had filleted three people and left the remains on her property.

Who were these people?

Who in the world—her world—would have done such a thing?

For the love of God, she was almost always here. Right here on the farm. How had this happened?

She managed to pour the sheriff a cup without spilling it. "Cream or sugar?"

"Black is fine."

She carried the mug to the table and placed it in front of him. "Can you use fingerprints or DNA to identify the…the victims?"

"We're going to try. Even if we're successful it might take some time."

Her head was swimming with possibilities. "Surely they've been reported missing?" With ubiquitous devices, people noticed when a friend or family member disappeared. Even those separated by geography stayed in touch via cell phone or social media.

But that wasn't always the case. There were people who had no family. Homeless folks. The ones society often ignored.

Her hand went to her stomach as acid burned there. "What else can I do?" She felt totally helpless under the circumstances.

"Right now," he said, "you're doing all you can, and we appreciate your cooperation." He sipped his coffee.

What she would give to have her dad here to work this out. He had never been one to operate on emotion. Sadly, Naomi seemed to have inherited the propensity for emotional unsteadiness. Her mom had been sure it was from her own mother's side of the family. On the other hand, her dad had insisted it was his only sibling, sister Trina—the one who left Naomi the car.

"What happens next?" She had an awful, awful feeling that this was not going away any time soon.

There were parts of no less than three people out there—of course it wasn't going away quickly.

"I've put in a call to the FBI office in Nashville. They're going to send a team to have a look around. Their crime scene investigators have far more experience and far more state-of-the-art equipment. If there's anything to be found they'll find it."

The FBI.

The ability to breathe escaped her for a moment.

The sheriff held up a hand. "Don't get unnerved by the federal authority becoming involved. I know the agent they're sending, Casey Duncan. He's a good guy and he knows his stuff. The case will be in good hands with him."

"But why the FBI? Why not the Tennessee Bureau of Investigations?" Seemed far more logical to her but then she knew little about police work beyond what she saw on television shows and in movies.

"Considering we have three victims," he explained, "there's a possibility we're looking at a repeat offender."

He didn't say the words, but she knew what he meant. *Serial* killer.

The queasiness returned with a second wind. "Serial killer?"

He gave a noncommittal nod. "Possibly. This is nothing we want going public, but we have to consider all possibilities. Whatever happened here, it happened more than once to more than one person."

She managed to swallow back the bile rising in her throat. "Should I be concerned for my safety?"

"I can't say for sure at this stage, but I'd feel better assigning a security detail. Just as a precaution."

She nodded, the movement so stiff she felt her neck would snap if she so much as tilted.

"We've focused our attention on the building where the remains were discovered and the immediate area surrounding it. The FBI will want to search your home. Your office. Basically, everything on the property. It would be best for all concerned if you agreed to all their requests. A warrant would be easy to obtain under the circumstances."

"Of course. Whatever they need to do." She had no reason not to cooperate. No reason at all.

"Good. I'll pass that along to Duncan."

Duncan. The name sounded familiar, but she couldn't place it. "He'll be here today?"

"He will. Might be three or four later this afternoon or early evening, but he will be here today."

"Thank you."

The sooner they figured out what in the world had happened, the sooner life could get back to normal.

She pushed away the idea that *normal* might just be wishful thinking.

How did you move on from something like this?

They were talking about *murder.*

Chapter Three

Honea Farm, 4:05 p.m.

From her kitchen window Naomi watched the man called Casey Duncan. There was something so familiar about him. About his name. She'd heard it before… maybe seen him before. And yet she couldn't place him.

Maybe she was mistaken.

He didn't look like she had imagined he would—for an FBI agent. No suit. No shiny black leather shoes. Nothing like the ones in the movies and crime shows. He wore jeans, a flannel shirt in blocks of tan and brown that matched his eyes. His blondish brown hair was a little longer than she'd expected, touching the collar of his lightweight leather jacket at the nape of his neck. The well-worn jacket covered the weapon she'd gotten a glimpse of strapped to his side via a shoulder holster.

The strangest part of all was the cowboy boots. The boots were the preferred footwear of locals, but he was FBI from Nashville. Judging by his Southern drawl he was definitely born and raised somewhere in the south.

Sheriff Tanner had introduced him, and Duncan had

given her a nod. Hardly anyone shook hands anymore with concerns of the virus after last year's pandemic making the moment whenever she met a new acquaintance feel awkward. Not following the urge to reach out in that familiar social exchange seemed wrong somehow. In this case, however, she was grateful for the societal change. Whatever it was about this man—and she couldn't quite pinpoint the origin of the feeling—it disquieted her on some level.

Two forensics technicians, also from the FBI, had arrived at the same time as Agent Duncan. Their vehicle, the expected black SUV, appeared to be loaded with the tools of their trade. She'd watched them go back and forth to and from the lab loaded with a number of cases.

Dr. Brannigan had left with a new arrival, who'd wheeled what looked like a massive cooler in and then out of the lab. Naomi suspected the remains were taken for further examination. To the coroner's office, probably. She was surprised the FBI hadn't wanted to take them to their own lab. She had no idea of the protocols. No one had updated her since Agent Duncan's arrival. The sheriff had his hands full so she didn't actually feel slighted, just anxious.

Sean and Joe had been allowed to go home. They hadn't come to her door and spoken with her. Just left with their heads hung as if they'd been given a stern talking-to. Probably a forceful interrogation. Completely unnecessary in her opinion.

Naomi wasn't sure when her crew could return to work. At this point she wasn't sure of anything. Still no word from Arlene. The deputy who'd dropped by her house hadn't gotten an answer, so he'd gone inside. Nothing appeared amiss. She simply wasn't there. But her VW was in the driveway, which was odd. Arlene preferred driving her vintage VW Bus to riding with anyone else. Naomi had racked her brain trying to think of someone Arlene might have needed to visit or some emergency contact who may have heard from her, but really there was no one. Sean and Joe hadn't heard from her and had no idea who to contact, either. Arlene was a bit of a loner as far as they knew. If she had any relatives, local or otherwise, Naomi certainly wasn't aware.

Naomi pressed her fisted fingers to her lips. This wasn't right. Arlene wouldn't just disappear like this. Naomi kept expecting to wake up from a nightmare. For the dozenth time she asked herself how this could have happened.

The answer was the same: she had no clue.

The fact that Arlene was MIA was surely a coincidence. Maybe Naomi should go to her house and have another look around. Knowing Arlene as she did, Naomi might notice something the deputy hadn't.

She grabbed her keys and was turning for the door when a light knock stopped her in her tracks.

She moved closer and peeked beyond the curtain.

Agent Duncan.

She drew back. Maybe there was news. She tossed her keys on the counter, unlocked the door and opened it. "Have you found something else?" Her breath stalled in her lungs as she waited for more bad news while mentally crossing her fingers in hopes that things couldn't possibly get worse.

The whole idea still felt utterly surreal.

There were human remains on her property. She had been so shocked by the discovery she hadn't actually taken the time to evaluate what this meant or how far-reaching the effects might be.

Who would want to buy from an organic farm where human remains had been found?

Good grief. She held more tightly to the door to keep herself steady. This was so, so bad.

"May I come in?"

His voice was the one trait that didn't seem familiar.

"Sure." She backed up and held the door open wider.

He walked inside—swaggered actually. He had the kind of saunter that spoke of a cockiness only found in the male species. She closed the door. "Have a seat." She gestured to the kitchen table. "I'm anxious to hear whatever news you have." She sighed. Gave her head a little shake. "No, what I'm anxious about is for some explanation of how this…" She searched for the right word, but it eluded her. "This…"

"Homicide," he provided.

She flinched. Couldn't help herself. "Yes. How this all happened." No point arguing or denying the reality. People were dead. What else could it be called other than homicide?

"I don't have any concrete answers for you just yet," he explained.

He stood at the table but hadn't taken a seat. She suddenly realized he was waiting for her to do so first.

She pulled out a chair and sat. He followed suit.

"What do you have?" she asked, cautiously hopeful

that there was at least some measure of forward movement. Some form of law enforcement had been combing the lab and the area around it all day. Surely they'd discovered some clue to explain how this…homicide happened.

She didn't know any killers.

Sean, Joe and Arlene were good people. Certainly not killers.

The niggling idea that Arlene remained out of touch tugged at her, but Naomi ignored the ridiculous possibility. Arlene wouldn't hurt anyone or anything.

"I ran background checks on Riley, Jones and Beck." Agent Duncan removed a pocket-size notepad and flipped over a page. "Jones and Riley are clean."

Naomi could have told him as much. "I wouldn't have expected otherwise."

"And Beck," he said, "how long have you known her?"

A frown tugged at Naomi's brow. "Are you suggesting you found something in Arlene's background?" The very notion was ludicrous.

When he didn't immediately respond, she said, "She has worked on this farm for more than three decades. My parents considered her part of the family."

"I understand," he said, not taken aback the slightest by her statement. "Do you know where she lived before moving to Winchester?"

He'd completely ignored her question and moved right on to another one of his own. This annoyed her far too much. What was it about this guy that got under her skin? "I don't recall, but I'm sure my parents or

Arlene spoke of her life before. I simply can't remember anything specific. Exactly what are you implying, Agent Duncan?"

He shook his head. "Nothing. I'm only wondering why we can't find anything on a seventy-something-year-old woman beyond the time she has lived here, working for your family."

"There must be some mistake. Maybe Beck is a married name." Arlene had spoken of a brother. Where was it she mentioned having grown up? The answer just wouldn't surface through the fog of confusion revolving around today's events. Or maybe she hadn't mentioned her past at all. Naomi just couldn't say.

"I thought you'd like to take a ride with me to her home. Have a look around and see if you notice anything out of the ordinary."

The offer startled her. She'd just been thinking of doing exactly that. Only she'd intended to go alone. "Sheriff Tanner said she's not home."

"She wasn't when his deputy called on her and most likely she's not now. Tanner assigned a surveillance detail to her house and no vehicles have stopped by. No sign of Ms. Beck."

Naomi got it now. "You want me to go into her home when she's not there?" Naomi wasn't sure how comfortable she was with invading Arlene's privacy. This felt completely wrong. All of it. Crazy wrong.

"Ms. Honea," Agent Duncan said as he rested his forearms on the table and leaned in, putting him a little closer to her. "If whoever did this is somehow connected to or watching Ms. Beck, she could be in trouble.

It's imperative that we do everything possible to find her and any connection she may have to this situation."

When he put it that way, Naomi couldn't exactly deny the logic.

"All right." Naomi stood, pushed in her chair. "But I warn you, you're barking up the wrong tree."

Beck Home, 5:20 p.m.

ARLENE'S HOME ON Pleasant Ridge was deep in the woods. A prepper's dream. The old cabin had a homey charm despite the No Trespassing and warning signs. The VW in the classic dove-blue color sat in the post-and-beam carport.

"Put these on."

Naomi turned to the driver, who offered her a pair of latex gloves. She'd kept her attention focused on the passing landscape on the drive over. He hadn't spoken and she hadn't, either. But the smell of his aftershave had made her very uncomfortable. It wasn't that the scent was overwhelming or unpleasant. In fact, it was so subtle she wondered if it was nothing more than him. Soap, maybe. Either way, it made her uneasy.

She took the gloves and tugged them on. He donned a pair, as well. When he opened his door, she did the same. Rather than go straight to the front door of the cabin, he stopped at the VW and tried the driver's side door. Locked.

He peered through the windows, moving from one to the next. Curiosity getting the better of her, Naomi mimicked his moves. Arlene's emergency bag was in the back floorboard. The older woman insisted that being prepared was the key to survival. In case of a breakdown of some sort, she carried bottled water, protein snacks, a blanket and some handy survival tools. Her shopping bags were in the back. She outright refused to touch a plastic or paper bag. Too wasteful, she insisted.

Naomi's mom had once said that Arlene was an old hippie. Until she was older, Naomi hadn't understood what her mom meant. Then she'd watched a documentary on Woodstock. Oh, yes, a hippie was right. Arlene wore the jeans and tees and had the long braided hair with the occasional flower tucked in when she felt the urge. Never mind that her hair had long since gone gray and that her weathered skin was now wrinkled, she wore the clothes and the confidence of her youth like a badge of honor.

"Anything jump out at you?"

Agent Duncan's voice made Naomi jump. She cursed herself and gave a shake of her head. "No."

She should pay closer attention rather than getting lost in thought.

"Let's have a look around inside her home and then we'll check the yard and outbuildings."

Naomi followed him up the steps and across the porch. Arlene's rocking chair sat empty save for the hand-crocheted throw and a cotton pillow that were always there. The flowers in the scattering of pots looked healthy. No sign of neglect. Obviously the thriving plants had been watered recently. Arlene couldn't have gone far or for long.

The door opened without the knob being turned. The wood around the knob and lock was split from the deputy having had to enter the property by force. Naomi would need to have the damage repaired or, at the very least, the door secured until Arlene was back. Her home couldn't be left in this condition. Before following Agent Duncan inside Naomi glanced over her shoulder at the Franklin County cruiser stationed in the driveway. She supposed as long as the house was being watched securing the door wasn't a pressing need.

Inside the home appeared to be in order. Arlene's taste ran toward the very rustic. The walls were sawmill-grade wood. The one other time Naomi had been here the older woman had explained that the cabin had been built using salvaged wood from old barns. Inside, the floors and walls were created from the same vintage wood. The ceilings were vintage tin, complete with a little rust here and there.

There were only four rooms. Living room and kitchen were one big space. Two bedrooms with a single bathroom tucked into the corner of the larger one. The second bedroom was set up as a home office. Agent Duncan lingered in that room sifting through the contents of drawers and file cabinets. Naomi wandered around the kitchen, checking inside cabinets and drawers. There was yogurt and cheese and a handful of grapes in the refrigerator. A mostly empty carton of almond milk. She moved on to the bedroom and looked around. Arlene wasn't one for fancy clothes or jewelry. Jeans, tees and sweatshirts were the mainstay of her wardrobe. Sneakers and rubber boots were her chosen footwear. There was one pair of well-worn sandals.

On the secondhand dresser was a single framed photograph. Arlene was much younger in the photo. Maybe late forties, early fifties. A man who appeared to be several years younger held her in an affectionate embrace.

Her brother?

Naomi took the photo from the frame and checked the back. As she'd expected there was a date but no name as she'd hoped. Since she hadn't found anything else unexpected or suspicious, she took the photo to Agent Duncan.

"This could be the brother I recall her mentioning."

He accepted the photo and studied it a moment.

"There's a date on the back but no name."

He turned over the photo and confirmed. Then he snapped a pic of both sides with his cell and passed the photo back to her.

"Thanks," he said.

Naomi stood in the home office for a moment. The notes on the bulletin board about different fertilizer methods for the farm made her gut clench. For the first time since she found those remains in the freezer the possibility that something bad had happened to Arlene started to seep into her, tying her belly into knots and making her chest ache with worry.

"I think I'll have a look around outside," she said, desperately needing to get out of this house. Arlene's home. Away from this man who seemed to already know what Naomi still wanted to deny.

People had been murdered…dissected like biology

specimens and stored on her farm—in the lab over which the missing Arlene ruled.

"I'll be right behind you."

Naomi managed a tight nod. She took the photo back to Arlene's room and placed it in the frame once more, hands shaking so hard she could barely accomplish the task.

Outside, she drew in a deep breath and reached for calm. What she needed more than anything was to keep her wits about her. This was not the time to come undone.

Arlene would be back soon and explain everything. Naomi was sure of it.

Pushing aside the fear that had her doubting that end, she took a peek in the well house. Nothing unexpected. There was an old smokehouse and a barn that had been a part of the original homeplace. Arlene had built her cabin on the same footprint as the previous home.

The smokehouse served as a toolshed. Naomi checked the bigger toolboxes. The sight of the chest-type freezer in the far back corner made her heart start to pound. She walked slowly in that direction. Naomi felt reasonably sure she would never be able to look at a chest-style freezer the same way ever again.

A strange laugh sputtered from her. This was exactly like being in one of those cheesy horror flicks she laughed at as a teenager. Then she'd ended up taking a part in one just for the movie credit. It was impossible to get a SAG card without those credits. Why in the world would she think of that at this bizarre moment?

Perhaps because of the sheer absurdity of this situation? Things like this didn't happen to her. She was a farmer now. In a small town where everyone knew everyone else.

"Where the hell are you, Arlene?"

Deep breath. She covered the final steps to the freezer. Arlene would show up and there would be a perfectly logical explanation for all of this.

For a long moment Naomi stood very still, one hand on the lid. This freezer was an old one. Much older than the one at the lab. Made complete sense that Arlene would keep specimens here, as well. There was most likely all sorts of experimental plants and fertilizers around here. The woman loved her work.

Naomi moistened her lips and swallowed.

"Just do it," she muttered.

"Why don't you let me do that?"

She barely suppressed a yelp as her hands fell away from the lid. Naomi turned to Agent Duncan. "Thank you. Yes."

He moved up next to her and reached for the lid.

Naomi held her breath.

As he hefted the lid open, her gaze settled on the contents of the vintage freezer.

Gray...skin and hair.

Arlene.

The woman was clad in a long white flannel gown and curled in the fetal position.

A scream shattered the still silence.

Chapter Four

Honea Farm, 9:00 p.m.

Naomi stared into the darkness beyond the living room window. The county cruiser sat in the driveway next to her vintage pickup. It had been her dad's truck. He'd had the Honea Farm logo painted on the doors. Naomi blinked. Arlene was dead.

Sheriff Tanner had insisted that a security detail was necessary just in case whoever murdered Arlene was still around and wasn't finished yet.

More murder. Body frozen. Naomi closed her eyes for a moment to block the horrible image. How could this be happening? Again she thought of that one horror flick in which she'd managed a small nonspeaking part. Only this was real.

Arlene had been murdered. At least three other people had been, as well.

Naomi shuddered and pulled the curtains together, then hugged her arms around herself. Based on Dr. Brannigan's preliminary exam, Arlene had been strangled and then stuffed into her own freezer. It must have been early when she was attacked since she had still been wearing her nightgown. If she'd been snatched from her bed, the killer had taken the time to make the bed.

What kind of killer made the bed?

Naomi had wanted to rush out of the house and wait in Agent Duncan's SUV until someone could take her home, but he'd insisted he needed her in the house with him. For her own protection. His request had made no sense at all. Primarily because she needed to be away from the horror of what she'd found. It wasn't until she'd collapsed in a kitchen chair at Arlene's small table for two that she'd grasped his reasoning for not allowing her to escape.

Whoever had murdered at least four people was out there somewhere. Maybe watching every step taken in the past twelve or so hours. Waiting for the opportunity to complete some other part of his demented plan. The idea felt surreal. Like a bad script that simply couldn't be salvaged.

Who would murder Arlene? It was true that she didn't have very many friends, but she had no enemies that Naomi knew of. She worked all the time. It was the story of farm life. You worked, you slept. If you were really lucky you made a living.

Eventually one of Sheriff Tanner's deputies had brought Naomi home. She didn't recall his name. He was older and said that he knew her father. Not surprising. Everyone in town and around the county had known her parents. The move to organic had made the Honea farm the first of its kind in the area. Her mom's medical clinic had been highly respected and always busy. The deputy had assured her he would stay parked outside her home until the next shift took over. Somehow, she'd dredged up a smile and thanked him.

After walking the floors for a while, she had forced down a few crackers and a little water. Eating had been the last thing on her mind today. She turned away from the window and started pacing again. She'd done a lot of that today. If she kept moving, she wouldn't have to dwell on the shocking things she'd seen today. No matter, the haunting thoughts hovered at the edges of her mind.

Going to bed wasn't an option. There was no way she could sleep. No way she could stop the bizarre images from flashing through her mind.

Somehow the discoveries had leaked to the media. Another deputy was stationed at the end of her driveway keeping reporters off the property. She felt like a rare animal caged at a zoo. Everyone wanted a glimpse of the near extinct species trapped in its new habitat. She needed something to do until she heard from the sheriff or Agent Duncan again. Anything to keep her mind occupied.

She went to the study that had served as her parents' office. Amid the books on the wall of shelves were the family photo albums. She piled the albums on the floor and settled next to them. One by one she sifted through the decades of memories. Arlene had always been there in the background for as long as Naomi could remember. A blurred image in the backdrop or the one behind the camera.

Naomi frowned as she moved from photo to photo. Surely a clear image of the woman was in at least one photograph. Naomi remembered her being present at every birthday party…every holiday. She really hadn't liked having her picture taken, but she was in a great many.

One by one she flipped through the photo albums and found nothing. Not a single image where Arlene was looking directly at the camera. She was in plenty but never looking at the camera or in focus. How odd was that?

Quite, she decided, and for the first time since she discovered those remains this morning, Naomi understood that this, whatever it was, wouldn't be a simple case of mistaken identity or wrong place. This had something to do with Arlene. Maybe with her distant past. Naomi certainly couldn't think of one thing in her present life that would have made Arlene a target.

With the last album shoved back onto the shelf, she searched the bedroom her parents had shared. The idea was a ridiculous one but at this point she was beyond merely desperate.

According to Agent Duncan there was no documented history of Arlene's existence before she came to work for Naomi's parents. There had to be a mistake or some explanation. Her parents would never have hired anyone with a suspicious background, much less drawn that person into the family.

The bedroom search yielded exactly what Naomi had expected. Nothing.

She moved back to the study and prowled through the old files. Sean's and Joe's employment records as well as those of numerous other part-timers were all there but nothing on Arlene. Why had she never noticed this?

Because there had never been any reason to suspect, much less look for an anomaly. Omission actually. The only documentation related to Arlene Beck was a W-2 form. Naomi stared at the social security number and then the name.

"Who the hell were you?" she muttered.

Naomi closed the final file drawer and stood. She surveyed the room, her gaze roving over framed business licenses and milestones depicting her parents' journey from the purchase of the land to the official designation as an organic farm. Her mom's medical diploma and awards from various civic and community organizations.

Knocking on the front door drew her from the study. She glanced at the grandfather clock in the hall. Half past ten. Dread filled her belly. She'd just about had her fill of bad news today. At this hour, what else could she expect?

She made her way to the front door, took a breath and opened it.

Not surprisingly Agent Duncan stood on her porch.

He executed one of those single nods that men use so often to acknowledge someone or something. "Ms. Honea, I'm sorry to bother you so late."

Why not? Today had been one big, long bad day. "Come in."

He followed her inside, closing the door behind himself.

"Can I offer you something? Water? Coffee?" she

asked. Personally, right about now she would prefer a stiff drink. And a vacation. She'd intended to take one this year. She'd been far too busy last year. But she and Arlene had gotten the books back in the black and the new aspects of the business in working order. The vacations would come later, she'd told herself.

She'd always wanted to go to Italy. Relax and enjoy for a couple of weeks. Nothing over the top. Just an out of the way villa in a quaint little town with lots of wine and books. Fat chance that would be happening anytime soon.

"No, thanks," he said, snatching her back from the fantasy that today's events had shattered. "Just a few moments of your time."

She nodded and gestured to the sofa. "All right. Sure."

They settled, her into the chair that had always been her mom's favorite and him on the sofa. She braced herself.

"Have you recalled anything else about Ms. Beck?"

"Nothing beyond what I've already told you." That wasn't entirely true, but she wasn't sure if what she'd noticed in the photo albums was relevant or just her imagination running away with her. It was late and she was mentally and physically exhausted.

He executed another of those nods that neither confirmed nor refuted his acceptance of her statement. Somehow this made her feel guilty of something. Maybe it was better to just tell him about the photographs whether it was relevant or not. She didn't like feeling deceptive on any level.

"I thought about how Arlene has always been a part of the family so I looked back through the family photo albums." She paused to gather her thoughts. "She's just always been there. I never stopped to consider or to wonder why or how. But as I looked through the albums, I couldn't find a single photo of her that fully showed her face. She's either not in the frame, or her image is blurry or she's looking away. It's probably nothing but it feels strange." Like this entire day. There was always the chance she was reading too much into the notion. Could be nothing more than a touch of paranoia.

"Do you mind if I have a look?"

"Please do." She stood and led the way. No one wanted this mystery solved more than her. Even if the ending shattered all that she had thought she knew about the person closest to her parents.

Naomi lingered in the doorway while Agent Duncan reviewed the family albums. Using his phone, he snapped pics of several photographs. When he'd prepared to take the first one, he'd glanced up and asked if she minded. Of course she'd said she didn't mind. Saying she did wasn't exactly an option. A shaky breath filled her lungs and suddenly she felt more tired than she had since those first few months after her return to the farm…after her dad's death.

When he'd finished, Agent Duncan put the last of the albums back on the shelf. "Again, I realize it's late, but do you mind answering a question or two?"

Yes, it was late and she was exhausted but in the interest of getting this done she nodded. "Sure."

He was walking toward the door before she had the

presence of mind to back out of the way. She headed for the living room and took her usual seat. She should have made coffee whether he wanted any or not. She had a feeling this was not going to be a one-and-done sort of Q and A session. Some part of her understood that simplicity had gone out the window hours ago. The situation happening here was complicated and sordid and way, way over her head.

He settled on the sofa, making the white slipcovered piece of furniture look far smaller. Naomi placed her hands on the arms of the chair to prevent clasping them in her lap in anticipation. She ordered herself to relax. After this she was going to run a very warm bath and soak while consuming the better part of a chilled bottle of white wine. She would sleep tonight, she decided, one way or the other.

"You don't recall ever seeing or overhearing anything regarding Ms. Beck that concerned you in any way? No comment by one of your parents that suggested some sort of concern?"

"No. Never." Hadn't she answered that question before? Whatever had happened, her parents had nothing to do with it. She needed to make that very clear right now. The sheriff knew Naomi's parents. This man did not. "My parents were above reproach, Agent Duncan. I have no idea how this happened or why, but I can guarantee you they were not involved in any way."

Absolutely not. No way. No how.

When he remained silent for five or so seconds, she asked, "Is it possible Arlene was in witness protection or something like that? Maybe that explains the missing information about her and her apparent need to avoid being photographed."

The idea certainly explained how she apparently appeared in their lives out of nowhere since the agent had already said she seemed to come into existence when she began working on the farm. There had to be a mistake or some explanation like witness protection—as far-fetched as that seemed. Arlene had been in her late thirties when she began at Honea Farm.

Still, he said nothing. But he did study her. Closely. This unnerved her completely. She shifted in her chair. Forced her hands to stay put and not start fidgeting. Told herself to relax. *Impossible.*

"I'm looking into the possibility," he finally said in answer to her question—the one it felt like she'd asked half an hour ago, though it had only been a minute, maybe two.

"Good." It was the only answer that came to mind.

"Tell me about your parents."

He stated this with such a casualness, almost as if he only wanted to fill the time and that the request was not even relevant. Deep down Naomi recognized this was no insouciant suggestion. This nontypical federal agent was feeling out scenarios. Searching for pieces that completed the puzzle he suspected as the most likely.

"My mother died five years ago. She was a medical doctor. The clinic closed after she became ill." Naomi smiled as she recalled how incredibly dedicated her mother had been to helping others. "In whatever spare time she had, she joined my father in his work on the farm. She felt strongly about what he was striving toward. She believed organic food is the best way to help the world take better care of itself. She started wellness sessions at her clinic and helped Arlene and my dad to develop the perfect crop plans for supporting the community with good, healthy foods. She was very passionate about helping others be healthier. She's the one who actually brought Arlene on board to help with the best ways to nurture the crops in a completely organic way. She firmly believed that totally organic was the way to go."

"And your father?"

"Bottom line? He wanted whatever made Mom happy. He wasn't quite so passionate about the organic path, but he would have done anything she wanted. He did feel strongly about not being wasteful and producing good food. He felt our throwaway, cancel culture goes against the natural order of things. He liked reusing and repurposing."

She couldn't help but smile as she thought of how her father would buy a certain candy bar whenever he was in town. If he and Naomi went to town together, there were always secret treats. *Don't tell Mommy*, he'd say. It was their little secret. He fully supported her mom's concept of healthy eating but he loved his Snickers bars.

Out of the blue a disturbing idea slid into her thoughts. *Was that the only secret her dad had kept?*

"Did your parents have out-of-town guests often?"

His question drew her from the worrisome thought. "No." She shook her head, then frowned. "When I was in high school there was an influx of visitors to the farm. I'm not sure where they came from or who they were. I probably wasn't interested enough to pay real attention. I think my dad mentioned something about the people being interested in how he and Mom had developed the farm. Something like that."

"Businessmen? Businesswomen? Suits? Casual wear?"

What in the world did it matter what the people wore? She shrugged. "I really don't recall."

"Casual wear, then," he suggested.

When her frown deepened, he added, "If there had been strangers visiting who wore suits or some other professional wear, you would have wondered about it. Maybe even asked. And you'd likely remember."

Made sense. "I guess so."

"Did you meet any of these people?"

She had to think about the answer for a moment. "I don't recall being introduced to any of them, but I did see some of the visitors. If it was the weekend or after school hours, I was generally here. I'm sure I met several."

"You may have heard one or more speak," he suggested.

She tried to recall an instance when she was home and overheard a conversation or walked into a meeting of some sort during that time. "I'm sure I did."

"But you don't recall," he pressed.

As if he'd given her a shake, a memory tumbled loose. "There was once when I overheard my dad talking about soil properties to this one man. I remember thinking that the way he talked reminded me of a friend from California I once knew. Not really an accent, more a nonaccent. TV talk. The nonspecific voice."

The usual nod. "California?"

Naomi couldn't pinpoint exactly what it was but something about Agent Duncan shifted just then. The way he looked at her…the sound of his voice. It was like a defense mechanism but not. Perhaps it was a guardedness that slipped into his bearing. She couldn't fathom why. Didn't try. She was way too tired.

"Yes, I met a boy on our annual vacation once. To Gulf Shores, on the coast in Alabama. He was from California. His mother was an actress." The memory relaxed some of her anxiety. Whoever Arlene Beck was and whatever had happened on this farm because of her, Naomi could truly say that her childhood had been a good one. A happy one.

Agent Duncan stood. "Thanks for your time. I'll keep you posted as we dig deeper into the case."

He was halfway to the door before she could make the transition from the past to the present. She shot to her feet and followed.

There were at least a dozen questions she wanted to ask but none would allow her to pull them out of the fog that suddenly swaddled her brain.

Door open, the man turned back to her and gave another of those nods. "Good night, Ms. Honea."

It was that moment, that single instant when his deep brown eyes collided with hers, that she felt the overwhelming sensation that she had met him or knew him somehow. Her mouth opened and, "Do I know you from somewhere?" popped out before her brain could override the reaction. Her cheeks turning warm with embarrassment, she stammered, “It—it feels like we’ve met before.”

“I don’t think so.”

And then he was gone.

He was probably right. It was likely just one of those odd and unexpected feelings of familiarity.

But it sure felt real.

Chapter Five

Franklin County Sheriff's Department
Wednesday, October 20, 9:30 a.m.

"We have nothing," Assistant Special Agent in Charge Preston Wagner of the Nashville field office stated unconditionally.

Casey hadn't expected anything else. He'd hoped possibly there was information about Arlene Beck in some top-secret file to which he had no access. But that wasn't the case. Beck simply didn't exist anywhere on paper prior to her arrival in Winchester.

"Thanks, sir. I'll be in touch when I have more." Casey ended the conference call and surveyed the other two men at the table. Chief of Police William Brannigan and Sheriff Colt Tanner. Both appeared to have something on their minds, and it didn't take a psychic to figure out what.

"When something like this happens involving a well-known family," he offered, "it can sometimes be more than a little surprising. We all form opinions and have certain expectations for the people we know, especially those we know well."

The two local lawmen exchanged a look. Now he'd annoyed them. There was nothing for it. He had a job to do whether they liked what they were hearing or not. Whatever happened on the Honea farm, it was not accidental. It was murder. Likely it was somehow tied into something bigger.

"I've known the Honea family my whole life," Brannigan said. "Fine people. Whatever happened on that farm, it wasn't their doing. I'm confident."

This was the response Casey had expected. "I appreciate your confidence, Chief, but things are not always what they seem. This, unfortunately, is one of those times."

Since Chief Brannigan had about a decade on Casey age-wise and far more experience, he understood he'd likely failed to articulate this adequately. Brannigan had no doubt been faced with circumstances like this more than once. To suggest otherwise would be seen as an insult. But these were the sorts of investigations Casey worked every day. He imagined the two men rarely ran into a situation like this one.

Before Brannigan could respond, Tanner piped up. "We both know this family. There is no way—no way—they were or are involved in criminal activity. You can take that to the bank."

"Agent Duncan," Brannigan said, his tone casual but his expression warned he didn't intend to budge on his stance. "I'm well aware that people can wear two faces, can be good and bad. But what you need to comprehend is the fact that Muriel and Nolan Honea were good people who supported their community. You'll be hard-pressed to find a soul in this county who didn't like them or have the utmost respect for them."

"We appreciate the need for us to keep open minds," Tanner offered to support what Brannigan was saying. "But understand that we expect you to tread lightly where Naomi is concerned. She's been through a lot the past year. You won't find a harder worker and more dedicated member of the community."

It was possible Tanner had a point. Casey didn't doubt his assessment. The question was whether either of these men could see beyond what they wanted to see. What they'd always seen. It was human nature. Think the best of those who've given you no reason to do otherwise. You see what your mind tells you to see.

"I want to share something with you." Casey opened the file folder lying on the desk in front of him and removed Honea Farm's bank statements for the past five years. "Have a look and tell me what you see."

While the two studied the statements, Casey considered Naomi Honea. He hadn't thought of her in years until he saw her in that offbeat horror flick. But it wasn't until the body lotion commercial that he was certain it was her. He'd spotted the half-moon-shaped birth mark on her left shoulder. Had to be her. How many blue-eyed redheads had a half-moon birthmark in exactly that spot on their left shoulder?

Not that many, he'd figured, so he'd done a little digging. This was early in his days with the Bureau. He'd just gone from flying a desk to fieldwork. Sure enough, he was right. The actress in the sexy body lotion commercial was Naomi Honea from Winchester, Tennessee.

Small world.

"Have you asked Naomi about these deposits?" Tanner asked.

Casey dragged his attention back to the present. "I intend to do that today."

"I can see how this looks suspicious," Brannigan admitted, "but there may be a perfectly reasonable explanation. He may have sold equipment or an acre of land here or there. Land prices have skyrocketed the past few years."

"Possibly," Casey agreed. Although in his experience, reasonable and logical weren't always the same thing. When a person was desperate, many things could be deemed reasonable. Logic rarely played into it. The survival instinct kicked in and all else was banished for the duration.

"I get the feeling," Tanner said, his gaze narrowing, "you're not being completely open with us. Seems like there may be more we should know."

Both were topnotch lawmen. He hadn't expected to pull anything over either man. "I've given you all I'm able to confirm." This was true. The rest of what he suspected was pure speculation. No need to stir that pot until something conclusive made it worth the trouble.

Brannigan leaned forward, braced his forearms on the conference table. "What parts have you not been able to confirm?"

This was where things got tricky. He really didn't want to go there just now but he might not have a choice. Tanner and Brannigan were accustomed to being in charge.

"I'm sure you've heard of the green burial concept." This wasn't really a question. Most people had at least heard of the method.

"My wife's father was an undertaker," Brannigan confirmed. "There's little in the field I haven't heard about."

"I'm vaguely aware of the concept," Tanner said.

"Green burials are an effort," Casey explained to ensure they were on the same page, "to eliminate as many chemicals as possible in the process of internment. Biodegradable products are used in the process. The end goal is to protect the environment. Bring life and death into balance, environmentally speaking."

"Last I checked," Brannigan said, "we don't have any cemeteries that meet the criteria in Franklin County."

"We have a *Green* cemetery," Tanner pointed out. "But not a green burial cemetery."

Casey had already checked and there were none in Franklin County. "Another method of dealing with the remains of the dead in a more environmentally friendly way is human composting."

He had their attention now. Both men sat a little straighter and peered a little more intently at him. "Also known as natural organic reductions. The first legal operations turn the remains of deceased loved ones into mulch or soil, to put it simply."

"I see where you're going with this," Brannigan said, his tone a warning. "I would encourage you to proceed with caution. I don't want this family's reputation damaged unnecessarily."

"You have my word, Chief," Casey assured him. "This is just one of my working theories based on what we've found so far."

"Maybe I'm not up to speed," Tanner said, "on the latest information but doesn't human composting include the bones? I haven't heard anything about the bones being separated from the rest of the body. Maybe I missed something."

No one appreciated a stranger coming to town and accusing a respected family of the latest craze in saving the earth. Casey got that but this scenario was at the top of his list. Maybe it was something else, but this was an option he intended to explore thoroughly.

"At this point, I have no working theory on that aspect of what we've found. The bones could be used in some other way or we just may not have found them yet. Whatever the case, the Bureau has tasked me with an in-depth search. Specialized equipment will be arriving later in the week. The Honea farm is a sizable one. Be aware this is going to take time."

"All right," Brannigan said, "we'll do all we can to support your efforts. Just keep in mind that we expect to be kept in the loop. *All* the way in."

Tanner offered a nod of agreement. "I'll keep one of my deputies on security detail at all times."

"I'll keep the media off your backs," Brannigan said.

"I appreciate the support, gentlemen." Casey gathered his file and stood. "We're good, then."

A few more minutes of conversation continued as

they moved along the corridor toward the stairwell. Tanner agreed to have his chief deputy start interviews with friends of the Honea family. Brannigan and his wife, the coroner, would check through records to ensure all deaths over the past years were accounted for in terms of final arrangements. If any bodies couldn't be accounted for, they would go on a list for further investigation.

The remains found at Honea Farm had to come from somewhere. Could be local, could be from anywhere. But they had to start the search somewhere.

Honea Farm, 12:00 p.m.

CASEY HAD CHECKED in with his folks on the ground. Nothing new so far in the search. A call from Dr. Brannigan had given him an update on cause of death for Arlene Beck. *Homicide.* Not that he'd anticipated otherwise, but he'd been waiting for confirmation before interviewing Naomi again.

He climbed the steps to her porch and knocked on the front door. It opened instantly as if she'd been waiting on the other side. If she'd seen him arrive, she probably had been. She looked from him to the file folder he held and back. Uncertainty sparked in her blue eyes.

"You have a few minutes?" he asked.

Those blue eyes seemed to burn a hole into him. Judging by the dark circles beneath them she'd barely slept last night. She looked tired and resigned. And gorgeous. She'd always been a looker. Thirty really did look good on her. Yesterday had been her birthday and he'd wanted to say something, but he'd thought better of it. Hell, she didn't even remember him. She'd likely think he was a little off in the head for remembering her for all this time. Like he could forget. She'd damned sure made an impression that stuck with him. He'd fantasized about her way too often, especially after that body lotion commercial.

Unable to help himself, his gaze wandered to her shoulder. *Back off*, he warned. This was not the time to go stumbling down memory lane. He should have forgotten those memories long ago.

"Yes, of course," she said.

He followed her inside. She sounded tired, too. Frustrated and tired. Who wouldn't be? Her world had been turned upside down. Prior to just over a year ago, she had been away from Winchester for the better part of a decade. A lot could have happened back home on the farm during that time. A lot she didn't know about. Particularly after her mother's death. Her mother had appeared to be the one spearheading the operation to some extent. It was after her death that all the anomalies had started to show up.

Naomi sat in the same chair she chose every time and he lowered onto the couch. Over and over today he'd thought of last night when she'd asked him if they'd met before. He'd almost said yes. But muddying the waters at this point would be a mistake. Then again, it was possible she might trust him more if he told her. He'd play it by ear and wait for the right opportunity. Anything that impacted the investigation had to be handled with kid gloves.

"The coroner has listed Ms. Beck's death as a homicide. Cause of death was manual strangulation. Of course, that's just a preliminary. There's toxicology and such still to be done."

He allowed the news to sink in a moment before going on.

"As you can imagine," he continued, "this means we're looking for an active killer. One who perhaps needed to cover up something. Maybe someone who worked with Beck in some capacity."

Naomi cleared her throat delicately. "It sounds as if you've made up your mind about Arlene." She shrugged. "Maybe even my family and me."

There was an edge of anger in her voice. Nothing he hadn't expected. A shocking insanity had descended on her life. Before this was over she would experience a range of intense emotions. The survivors always did.

She wasn't a suspect in his opinion. Maybe that was a mistake but so be it.

For now.

"I don't believe you have anything to do with the remains you found or with Ms. Beck's death. Obviously, you wouldn't have called the authorities if you were somehow involved with the find in your freezer."

She blinked. Nodded. "At least there's that."

The tinge of anger lingered.

He placed the file folder on the coffee table between them and opened it, then he passed the bank statements to her. "Have a glance over these and tell me if you notice anything unusual."

She accepted the pages and with visible reluctance began a half-hearted perusal.

These weren't the full statements but the annual summary sheets of deposits and the subsequent balance after each for every month over the past five years. The report for five years ago showed little or no deposits. The balance from the previous year diminished quickly after that point. By midspring four years ago, the balance in the farm account was nearly gone. Then suddenly large deposits started to appear. The largest in more than a decade. His forensics accounting specialist was still reviewing records but what she had found so far couldn't be called anything other than suspicious.

He watched Naomi's face closely. The changing expressions that danced across her face told him she hadn't looked back as far as five years. Probably not beyond the past two. She'd come back just over a year ago to a hell of a mess and pulling it together had been top priority.

"Five years ago is when my mom died." She looked up from the pages. "It was a very difficult time. Obviously, Dad allowed the work to fall behind."

"If the work fell behind for better than a year, would he have been able to recover so quickly?"

Naomi righted the pages and offered them back to him. "It depends."

He resisted the impulse to ask on what. A miracle? Donations? He didn't have to ask. He already knew the answer. Sean Riley and Joe Jones had been employed by Mr. Honea for more than five years. Both had talked at length about how difficult things were for the year and a half surrounding Mrs. Honea's illness and death. Some weeks they'd only received half their pay. Others they weren't paid at all, but they hung in there to help the Honeas. Mr. Honea had made it right after things got better. Neither one could explain how things got better. Only that they did. New equipment, new plants, all sorts of new and improved items were brought to the farm.

"Your employees can't explain how the financial situation recovered."

"I wasn't here," she admitted, her voice sounding hollow. "I'm sure there was insurance money."

"No insurance." He'd already checked. Jones had explained the circumstances as a part of his statement regarding the "lean" years. He'd overheard the conversation between Beck and Naomi's father. "Ms. Beck loaned your father the money for your mother's final arrangements."

Shock claimed Naomi's face. "That can't be right. He would have told me." She stared at the pages lying on the coffee table. "He never said a word about things being so…difficult." Her gaze lifted to his once more. "The truth is he didn't tell me she was dying until she was gone. He said she wanted it that way."

Pain. The memory was still very painful. The people she loved and trusted the most had shut her out of something that may have landed them in deep trouble.

"Did he give you a reason why she didn't want you to know? The two of you were on good terms?"

"We were." She swiped at her eyes. "I had no idea she was ill. We talked every Sunday. To tell you the truth, when he died I still hadn't forgiven him for keeping the truth from me. Now I wish I had."

And there it was. Proof that her father could and would keep secrets from her. Her mother, too.

"Is it possible there were other things that were kept from you?"

"My dad wasn't a murderer," she snapped. She blinked back more tears. "My mom wasn't, either. I don't know how any of this happened, but I know—knew my parents. They would never harm anyone or anything."

Jones and Riley had said the same thing. The Honeas were above reproach. Except that the evidence said someone on this farm wasn't.

"Ms. Honea," he said, "our forensics technicians have found evidence of other remains on the farm."

"What?" She shook her head. "No. That can't be right."

"They've checked random locations on the property as well as various specimens Ms. Beck was working with in the lab."

"What the hell are you saying?" Naomi shot to her feet. "That can't be true. There must be a mistake."

"There's no mistake, Naomi."

Her attention arrowed to him, showing him the confusion and surprise in her eyes before she banished the reactions. "I'd like you to leave now. I need to think."

He pushed to his feet. "I really need your help. I'm not accusing you or your family of anything. I'm only trying to determine what happened here and who is responsible. Your parents may not have known exactly what was going on." He doubted this but he felt compelled to offer an out. He needed her to trust him.

She considered his words for a moment. "I can assure you they had no idea." She folded her arms over her chest. "You can make all the allegations you like but I am certain you will never be able to prove a single one."

"I'm not trying to prove anything, ma'am. I'm attempting to find the truth."

She flashed a fake smile but even the intensity of it jarred him. "It doesn't feel that way from here."

"I can imagine it's not a comfortable place to be," he offered, "but you are the one person who can speak for your mother and father. There's no one else. If you don't help me—for them—no one can."

Her angry face vanished, and hope glimmered in her eyes. "Tell me what I need to do to help."

"Work with me. Help me find something that will tell us what really happened here and who was responsible. There's always evidence. Always. It's just the finding it that can be an issue sometimes."

"I'll help you," she said. "Whatever you need me to do. I want the truth."

Unfortunately, what he needed her to do and what he wanted her to do were two entirely different things.

That problem was one he would have to work on. He never allowed personal feelings to interfere with an investigation. He wasn't going to start now.

Then again, maybe he already had.

Chapter Six

Dogwood Apartments, 2:00 p.m.

Naomi couldn't remember the last time she'd talked to her uncle Donnie. He had this habit of popping in and out of their lives, more out than in. When he showed up, he always had lots of adventures to share. He was the spotlight on the rare occasions he bothered to visit. But his mind remained as sharp as a tack and he loved talking about the past—especially his past. But he knew Naomi's mother better than anyone else. He had even helped out at the farm now and then ages ago.

She rang the bell and waited, hoping against hope he was home. Knowing her uncle he was out gallivanting around. That was what her mother always said. Donnie loved women. The problem was he couldn't love just one. Her mom would say he had the same problem with jobs. He never loved even one long enough to call it a career. Instead, he had floated around from one to the next, using his social security check as his main source of income. And the occasional donation from her mom—who'd sworn if he didn't do better she wouldn't help him the next time.

But she always did. Isn't that what mothers or rather sisters did?

To Naomi's surprise the door opened. Donnie wore ragged cutoff denim shorts and a sweatshirt, hood up. He'd kept his summer tan with the help of the ancient tanning bed he had in the second bedroom of this dinky apartment. Her mom had told her about the tanning bed. She'd laughed and said he refused to be pale like her. The O'Connor Scottish roots had given the three of them red hair, blue eyes and creamy pale skin. She smiled. Except that Uncle Donnie had spent so much time in the tanning bed that he looked perpetually sunburned. Redheads never tanned that nice golden brown the way other people did.

"Naomi!" He grabbed her for a hug, then drew back. "What brings you to my humble abode?"

He ushered her inside, closed the door and dropped the hood from his tangle of red hair. He obviously hadn't combed the thick mop today. This was something else they shared, very thick hair. Like a horse's mane, her mom had always said. Today Donnie's looked a little more horsey than usual.

Naomi sat on the sofa. Donnie dropped into a recliner that had apparently been his favorite for most of his adult life judging by the wear to the fabric and the indention in the padding that seemed to cradle him perfectly.

"Did you hear about Arlene?"

He scrunched up his face in a frown. "Arlene? No.

I've been in a cleansing cycle. I'm not my best as you can see. I'm avoiding everyone and everything—except my favorite niece, of course—for two more days." His frown returned. "So what happened to Arlene? Don't tell me the old hag finally croaked."

Naomi winced. She knew he was kidding but he wouldn't find it funny when she told him. Donnie had loved sparring with Arlene. Naomi always thought he had a thing for her, but she always ignored him, which made him pretend to dislike her.

"She's dead. Murdered."

He leaned forward as if he wanted to ensure he was close enough to hear more clearly. "What did you say?"

"Dead. She's dead. Strangled and stuffed into her freezer."

He collapsed back into his chair. "Who in the world would want to kill Arlene?" He made a face, eyes shimmering with a new brightness. "Except for me on the rare occasion when she didn't tell Muriel or Nolan I'd called."

Her parents, Muriel and Nolan. Her chest ached. "There's more. The remains of three people were found in the lab freezer."

He held up his hands. "Okay, wait a minute. You're blowing my mind here." He took a big breath, met her gaze and said, "Come at me again."

"Arlene is dead. Murdered. And the remains of at least three other people were found in the freezer at the lab. The FBI as well as the sheriff and the chief of police are investigating the farm. Me." Her hands went to her chest. "Mom and Dad. Everything. It's crazy... but, sadly, real."

She struggled to hold back the tears. Even after twenty-four hours and having discussed the situation repeatedly, it still felt shocking. Surreal. Like a nightmare that refused to end after she awakened.

"That's just ridiculous. My sister took an oath to help people. She wouldn't have hurt a fly, much less a person. And she loved everyone." He waved his arms magnanimously. "God knows Nolan couldn't possibly have hurt anyone. He was too kind for his own good. Trust me, I know. I took advantage of him way too many times when Muriel turned me down."

Naomi opted not to respond to the latter remark. "Do you remember when Arlene first came to Winchester? Where she lived before? Anything about her past before her life here?"

"I just remember coming back from a trip to Cancun with one of my old college buddies and there she was. She never liked me and I never liked her." He made a face. "God rest her soul."

"Why didn't you like each other?" Naomi knew the answer, but she might as well hear his side of things. She doubted it would make a difference.

"I had a thing for older women, and I guess I came on a little too strong and she never forgave me." He shrugged. "What can I say? I'm human and Arlene was a looker in her day."

"Just how strong are we talking?" This part she hadn't heard. Knowing her uncle, he made a pass or two.

"Let's just say I kissed her, and she didn't want to be kissed."

"So, you assaulted her," Naomi offered, horrified. Why was it that some men could never understand that no meant no even if it was just a simple kiss?

"It wasn't like that, Naomi. It was just a sloppy, drunken kiss on New Year's Eve. She overreacted. Anyway, Muriel held it against me for, like, forever. I think Arlene was pleased she'd put that wedge between Muriel and me. She had a mean streak like that."

Interesting. Naomi had never heard anyone mention Arlene having a mean streak. She'd have to ask Sean and Joe if they'd ever noticed Arlene being anything other than bossy. This was the one negative the two always said about the older woman. Moving on, she asked her uncle, "You really have no idea where she lived before?"

He shook his head. "Sorry. Muriel always said I drank so much the first fifty years of my life that I killed a lot of brain cells. I guess they were mostly memory cells."

Just Naomi's luck. "Was there anyone else Arlene was close to? I mean, I know she basically knew everyone in town, but she was always kind of a loner as far as I could tell." Almost standoffish, if Naomi was completely honest. A very private person.

"She didn't let anyone close. If she had any friends, you would never have known it." His eyebrows shot upward. "But there was one guy she seemed to have a thing with for a while." He rolled his eyes. "I don't know why when she turned me down flat."

"Who?" Naomi had never known Arlene to have a boyfriend. She figured the older woman was widowed and never got past the loss or just chose not to have a partner in order to remain independent.

"You remember that old hermit, something Cotton is his name. He lives over in Shake Rag. Last I heard he's still alive. A real strange one, though."

"Strange how?" If she was going to show up at someone's door in the middle of nowhere, she needed to understand what kind of strange she would be facing. Just eccentric or a killer?

"He was some sort of space engineer with NASA. Big top-secret stuff. He, like, kept his briefcase handcuffed to him, the rumor was. Wore dark glasses all the time. A real peculiar guy."

As strange as it was, he sounded exactly like Arlene. She had always been secretive and sort of odd. But she'd been kind and loyal. Naomi's parents had relied on her. More than once she remembered her mom calling Arlene a genius. Maybe some measure of odd came with being a genius.

This was likely the best she was going to get from Donnie. It wasn't much, beyond his personal recollections, but she intended to follow through. "You have more specific directions to this Mr. Cotton's home?"

"I don't, but if you ask anyone in the area, they're bound to know him."

"Please call me if you think of anything else, Uncle Donnie. I need to find the truth about Arlene—otherwise, Mom and Dad are going to end up looking like the ones who did something wrong." Agent Duncan had helped her to see that she was the only one who could or would be their voices in this.

Naomi couldn't help feeling guilty about making Arlene seem like the bad guy in this unholy mess. But what else was she supposed to think and do? The lab was Arlene's domain.

Donnie gave her a hug and promised to call if anything came to mind. Which was code for she likely wouldn't hear from him again unless she knocked on his door or he ran into financial trouble.

The drive to the community of Shake Rag didn't take long. She took Highway 64 from Winchester to Huntland and made a couple extra turns, and there she was in the middle of nowhere. Maybe she should have asked Agent Duncan to go with her. No, she needed to do this on her own. His job was to solve the case—hers was to clear her family name. The first house where she stopped, the owner had no idea who she was looking for, but house number two proved her uncle hadn't been completely wrong. The owner had given her directions to the "nutty as a fruitcake old hermit's house." Folks could be judgmental. Especially about things they didn't understand.

She followed the directions and ended up at a ramshackle old cabin tucked deep into the woods next to a creek. The place looked deserted. At least three of the four vehicles had weeds and small trees growing up through their decaying frames.

She held her breath all the way to the door, hoping there wasn't an aggressive dog running loose. The first step up to the porch had her drawing in a lungful of air. So far so good. A couple more steps and then half a dozen feet across the porch. The wood creaked with her every move. She grimaced, mentally crossing her fingers that she didn't fall through the old floorboards.

A rap on the door, then another. The place looked and sounded deserted. The occasional burst of breeze whispering through the trees and the distant trickle of the creek were the only sounds. As if to prove her wrong, a bird cawed from amid nearby tree branches. She started. Ordered herself to calm.

"What do you want?"

The harsh voice made her jump again.

It originated right in front of her on the other side of the still closed door.

Okay. Deep breath. Just do this. "Mr. Cotton?"

"I said, what do you want?" roared through the rickety wood door.

"I'm here about Arlene Beck."

The door opened a crack. One pale silvery eye peeked out at her. "What about her?"

"May I come in, Mr. Cotton?" She really didn't want to tell him the news on his porch. Plus she really wanted to get as much info from him as possible. Inside, she might have more luck. Out here it would be too easy for him to tell her to go and not respond once she answered the question asked.

The door opened wider. "Well, come on, then."

She stepped inside and when the door closed behind her the room was nearly dark. Her pulse reacted to a rush of adrenaline searing through her veins. Before she lost her nerve completely, a light flickered on.

Fluorescent bulb, she decided. The lamp sat on a table next to a chair.

"Who are you?" he demanded.

"I'm Naomi Honea from Honea Farm."

"What's going on with Arlene?" His voice sounded rusty as if he rarely used it.

Rather than tell him, she asked, "You don't watch the news?"

The story had reached last evening's regional news. The Honea Farm sign over the front gate had flashed on the screen just before the headline: Murder in a Small Town. She worried that the headlines were only going to get worse and more targeted. The more sensationalized the news, the more viewers who tuned in.

God, she hated this sort of publicity.

"I don't watch the news," he said. "You can't trust anything they say. It's propaganda."

Deep breath. Just say it. "Sometime after she left work at the farm on Monday, Arlene was murdered."

On the drive here she had come up with a story to explain her questions. If Mr. Cotton was as strange as Donnie had suggested, he might have conspiracy issues, as well. For once she thought her uncle had been right. A quick glance around the room revealed boxes and boxes of what appeared to be files. They were stacked from floor to ceiling. The one part of the wall she could see was like a bulletin board with yellowed newspaper clippings pinned all over it. Most of the headlines appeared to be political in nature.

Very strange.

Maybe he was writing a book, she told herself. Some

of the writers she had known in Hollywood created story or inspiration boards.

The man abruptly burst into sobs. The unexpected reaction rattled her. Should she say something? Do something?

"I'm so sorry, Mr. Cotton. This is a terrible tragedy. Do you know if she had any family? I just want to be sure anyone who should know what's happened is contacted."

His sobs stopped as abruptly as they'd started. He wiped his eyes with the sleeves of his khaki shirt. She noticed then that he wore khaki trousers, as well. Khaki socks. Like a uniform of beige.

"She had no family." He reached into his pocket, retrieved a handkerchief and blew his nose. "The farm and the people there were her family. She loved that farm."

Emotion burned Naomi's eyes. "She was family to us, yes," Naomi agreed. "She was like an aunt." Arlene had always been there. She had been a tremendous support since Naomi's dad died. Moving forward would be difficult without her.

"Do you know where she lived before she moved to Winchester? I'm so worried there might be someone we don't know about. A distant relative or close friend."

He stared at her for a long moment, his silvery eyes seeming to narrow as if he were assessing her motive for asking about the possibility of next of kin.

"What do you know about me?"

Oh, no! He was a conspiracy theorist and already paranoid that she was here spying on him. If there was a way out of this cabin besides the front door that she would have to get past him to reach, it wasn't visible beyond all the boxes. "I'm sorry, Mr. Cotton, I only know that you knew Arlene. I wanted to make sure you heard about what happened."

He nodded. "Good. Knowing anything about me is dangerous. More dangerous than you could possibly comprehend."

She suddenly wondered if she had misjudged the innocuousness of this man. Paranoia might not be his only issue. He could indeed be dangerous. "Is there anything you can tell me about Arlene and where she came from?"

He chuckled, an out of practice and oddly out of place sound. "They're on to what she was up to, I take it, and they've sent you here. That didn't take long."

"I don't know what you mean."

He stared at her, evaluating her motives, she imagined. Was she lying? After something only he possessed? Paranoia did that to a person.

"If you don't know now," he countered, "you'll know soon enough."

The man was very good at answering without actually telling her anything.

"I'm afraid I have no idea, Mr. Cotton."

"They'll keep looking until they know all the answers, trust me. It's what they do."

Well, that was as clear as mud. "Do you know of anyone else in town who might have known her or had a connection to her?"

"I can tell you that Arlene learned everything she knew from the master."

Now she was really confused. "I'm sorry, who is the master?"

He stared at her for a long, uncomfortable moment. "You should know the answer to that one. Everyone who ever studied history, however briefly, should know."

But she didn't. Before she could say as much, he lifted his hunched shoulders and let them fall in a careless shrug. "You could have a look around that house of hers. Perhaps you'll find what you're looking for there."

"I've already been to her house on Pleasant Ridge. I didn't find anything useful." At least nothing had been found as far as she'd been told. Now she was getting paranoid.

He shook his head. "Not that house. The one on High Street." He grinned, showing his stained teeth. "The one no one knew about."

"Arlene had another house?" She was absolutely certain this was a mistake. At some point in all these years she would have heard about that.

"She did." He gave her a knowing look. "It was a secret, but I knew. She didn't know I knew, but I did. I'm smarter than she wanted to believe."

Naomi's heart rate kicked into a faster rhythm. "Do you know the house number?"

He frowned. "I never noticed the number."

Naomi rephrased her question. "How will I know which house?"

"Oh, that's easy." He nodded adamantly. "Look for the cats. She loved cats."

Cats? How on earth could Naomi have known the lady all those years and not have been aware that she loved cats?

High Street, 5:30 p.m.

SHE DROVE SLOWLY along the street, craning her neck to visually search each yard and porch for cats. Cats. Who knew? Naomi wondered if her mom had known Arlene liked cats. Or that she had some sort of odd relationship with an even odder hermit living at Shake Rag?

Maybe Naomi just never paid attention. From the time she hit puberty she had been focused on one thing—getting off the farm. She only had eyes for the stars on the west coast. There were probably lots of things she had missed.

She thought again of Casey Duncan. He was so familiar to her. She must have met him before or something. He'd said no. Maybe he only reminded her of someone she'd run into eons ago.

Something darted out in front of her. She slammed on her brakes. Her heart launched into her throat. A cat pounced across the yard to her left. Close. Too close. She had to pay better attention.

She glanced in her rearview mirror, grateful no one was behind her. Then she checked the houses on either side of the street. This was the first cat she'd spotted.

On the right, a dozen or more cats lounged on the porch of the old bungalow that had seen far better days. This had to be it. Naomi backed up a few feet and turned into the driveway. As she emerged from her car, felines bounced off the porch and romped out to the driveway to greet her. She leaned down and stroked the sleek back of one and then the next. Dark velvety bodies twined around her legs, rubbing and purring.

By the time she reached the porch she had counted seventeen cats of all types and colors. Besides a rocking chair and a rickety table, three boxes waited on the porch. She checked the labels, didn't recognize the senders' addresses. The boxes were addressed to "occupant."

The squalling cats drew her attention. She realized they were probably hungry. If this house did belong to Arlene, she hadn't been around to feed them. An ache bloomed in Naomi's chest. She checked the door… locked.

"Okay, kitties. I can go to the store and get food." One of the cats trotted over to a large plastic container tucked behind the rocking chair and rubbed against it. Naomi wandered in the same direction. She had a look at the container, white plastic. With little effort she popped off the lid. "Aha."

The scent of cat food had the many felines crowding up against her. Since she didn't see any bowls she dropped handfuls all around that end of the porch. When she estimated she'd distributed enough, she closed the lid and went back to the boxes. Why would Arlene have things delivered to this house instead of her own? If intended for her, why wasn't her name on the boxes?

She cupped her hands on either side of her face and stared through the windows. The house looked empty. No furniture. Dark inside save for the tree-shaded light that filtered in through the windows.

Naomi moved down the steps and from one side of the house to the next and peered into each window. Every room she could see was the same: empty. Mostly dark.

When she reached the front porch again, she knelt down to examine the boxes more closely. Three typical cardboard shipping boxes, three different senders from three different addresses. California, New York and Idaho. She picked at the packaging tape across the top until she'd peeled it back far enough to open the box flaps of the first one. Inside was a white Styrofoam object.

Cooler? She shuddered at the thought of what she'd found in not one but two freezers.

This was just a cooler, she reminded herself. Not big enough for a body. She tried to pull it out of the box, but the fit was too tight to lift the cooler free. She turned the box upside down and shook it. It was heavier than she'd expected. Slowly but surely, her arms burning with the effort, the white cooler slid out of the box. The cooler was taped across the top, as well. More picking and tearing with her nails. She kept them cut short, so it took some time. Finally, the stubborn tape was all peeled back, pulling white dots of Styrofoam with it.

Briefly she considered she should probably call Agent Duncan. He would want her to wear latex gloves for this. He would most likely want to check this out himself.

Too late. She'd already touched the packaging. She might as well finish what she started. Besides, her curiosity was killing her. She tugged at the lid until it came loose. A steamy fog rose from the container. She reared back.

Dry ice, she realized. Her mom had ordered holiday hams that came packed this way. The dry ice wasn't like regular ice. It was best not to touch it.

She waved away the fog and peered inside. She closed her eyes a second, shook her head and then looked again.

Eyes, wide open, peered back at her.

Face.

Dread expanded in her stomach.

A face. Female.

It was a face…a *head.*

A muffled cry tore from her throat. She fell back onto her butt, then scrambled away like a crab.

She clawed at her pocket for her cell phone.

She had to call Agent Duncan.

Chapter Seven

High Street, 9:30 p.m.

Casey tucked his cell phone back into his pocket and surveyed the ongoing work in the High Street house allegedly rented by Arlene Beck. The place had appeared vacant but had proven anything but empty.

As he watched, more of the paneling on the walls was removed. Two forensics techs had crawled around under the house checking between floor joists and in any other potential hiding place. So far, they'd found just under two million dollars. All in small bills and bundled neatly for storage in the wall cavities.

The call he'd just received had added another twist to this already bizarre case. Dental records had confirmed the identity of the woman whose head was in the box Naomi opened. The woman had been missing for more than a week. Her identity had changed everything.

This was no longer a mere homicide investigation. This thing had sprouted roots that went far and deep.

"Got more money in the back bedroom."

The words echoed through the house.

Casey walked through the rooms, each one lit like a photo studio with all the auxiliary lighting they'd brought in, until he reached the newest piece of evidence. More bundles of cash lined sporadic spaces in the wall cavities.

The tech glanced at Casey as he entered the room. "I'm guessing we have another million in here."

Earlier today Casey had decided on the most likely scenario for what Arlene Beck was up to. He'd suspected she was conducting illegal green burials. It was fairly easy to set up a professional-looking website and then to make the necessary arrangements. Once the body was turned over to Beck the family probably never inquired as to additional details or locations.

Beck was not simply burying the bodies free of chemicals and anything else that inhibited decomposition, she was using the bodies for her own purposes. Doubling her money so to speak.

With today's find he understood the business was far more sadistic.

Casey snapped more pics with his phone to use when he briefed Naomi. "Check them all," he said to the tech. "The attic, too. If there's anything else in this place I want to know about it."

Sheriff Tanner was outside briefing Brannigan, who'd already done a walk-through of the house. Casey joined them on the back porch. A crime scene perimeter had been set up around the yard, front and back. Already reporters had gathered on the street out front and shouted questions at any uniform or official-looking person who appeared. Brannigan had agreed to handle tonight's crowd at a ten o'clock press briefing. The three of them—Casey, Tanner and Brannigan—had put together a statement that really didn't state a lot. But it was all they were prepared to give at this time. Far too many unanswered questions remained at this point.

"The vic in the box has been ID'd," he told the chief and the sheriff as he approached their position on the porch. It was well past dark but the single bare bulb in the overhead light provided enough illumination for Casey to see the lines of worry on the other men's faces. No one wanted this kind of evil to visit their community.

But crime didn't pause at the borders of any town. It crossed lines of all kinds.

"Helen Radner. She vanished just over a week ago. Her abandoned car was only a few blocks from her home in Philadelphia. She had agreed to testify against Big Tom Richmond."

Brannigan gave a long, low whistle. "I heard something about that. The missing woman was the first witness who'd ever agreed to testify against him."

"She made the mistake of calling to say she was coming in. They were monitoring her phone and had her before she was out of her neighborhood." Casey shook his head. "I guess now we know where she ended up."

"Damn." Tanner pushed back his cowboy hat and rubbed at his forehead. "This will go national," he said, stating aloud what they all already knew. "I'll call in my reserve deputies. We'll have reporters from every major news outlet in the country descending on us."

"Good idea," Brannigan agreed. "I'll do the same."

To Casey he said, "The lab in Nashville picked up the other remains found at the farm. Rowan will be forwarding her final report to you tomorrow."

"Thanks." This was officially the Bureau's case now. Brannigan and Tanner would continue to assist as needed, which would be immensely helpful since this was their territory. They knew the place and the people. "I should go break the news to Ms. Honea."

Casey made his way toward his vehicle. A local shelter had called in volunteers from all over the county to pick up the cats for safekeeping until they could be rehomed. Photos of each one would be posted on the city website in case anyone in the neighborhood had a cat missing. Cats liked to roam. Casey had never been a cat person but his older-by-two-years sister and only sibling had loved them.

"Agent Duncan!"

"Agent Duncan!"

Reporters shouted his name but officers prevented them from following Casey to his SUV. There would be a second official press conference tomorrow or the next day that he would conduct. Tonight Brannigan and Tanner would inform the citizens of their community about the ongoing investigation and give assurances as to their safety and the steps local authorities planned to take.

Driving along the country road in the darkness Casey considered how often he'd thought of Naomi over the years. She had been his first real crush. Of course she had no idea. She'd basically ignored him, but he hadn't been able to ignore her. Once he'd learned what became of her with that glimpse into her Hollywood life, he'd made an effort to keep up with her. Looking back, he decided his walk down memory lane after seeing that commercial must have been the result of a breakup. His relationships never lasted very long. Even when he put in the extra effort.

The situation only grew worse after he *found* Naomi again. He ended up unconsciously comparing every woman he dated with Naomi. It was totally ridiculous, he recognized. When the right person came along, he'd forget all about Naomi and ancient history.

The front porch light at the end of the long driveway to the Honea farmhouse had his pulse skittering like a guy about to go on his first date.

"Idiot," he grumbled.

He parked next to her vintage pickup and got out. The conversation to come wasn't one he looked forward to, but it was necessary. At this time, he had no reason to suspect she was involved in whatever Beck had going. The concept that he wasn't completely objective where Naomi was concerned wasn't lost on him.

He glanced up at the full moon hanging low in the night sky. Halloween coming up and the full moon seemed somehow fitting with this increasingly strange case. He glanced around the place. The big old white barn in the distance and the towering dark trees crowded around the white farmhouse spoke of peace and quiet. Solitude and contentment. But there was a lie behind that picturesque facade. The real questions were how did that lie start and how deep did it go?

Equally important, who started it?

The door opened as he climbed the steps to the porch.

Naomi, her fiery red hair backlit by the light inside, waited for him to say something, he supposed. It wasn't unseasonably cool tonight, but she had the afghan that usually hung on the back of the sofa draped around her shoulders.

"I know it's late," he offered, "but I hoped we could talk."

Almost eleven by now, he guessed. He was tired and she probably was, as well. This had been a hell of a two days.

"Would you like coffee?" She turned into the house, leaving him to follow.

"Coffee would be good. Thanks." He closed the door behind him, locked it before joining her in the kitchen.

The scent of coffee grounds filled the air as she scooped generous heaps into the brew basket. When she'd added water to the reservoir and hit the brew button, she faced him and said, "I watched the press conference. Chief Brannigan was very vague."

"Vague is the best we can do right now," he explained, hesitated, then went on. "We've identified the woman."

She pulled the afghan tighter. Waited. Said nothing.

"She was to be a witness against the head of an organized-crime syndicate in Philadelphia. She disappeared about a week ago."

Naomi's eyes closed for a moment as she absorbed the impact of his words. This was not the kind of news one wanted to hear about a longtime employee—a member of the family, really.

"Why..." She drew in a sharp breath as if what she

had to say was almost too difficult to convey. "Why was her head mailed to Arlene?"

The brew process started its gurgling and hissing routine, ushering renewed smells of dark roast coffee into the air. "I can't answer that question with any measure of accuracy, but I can make an experienced guess based on the only other evidence found at the property."

She squared her shoulders, causing the afghan to drop from one side, revealing a pale length of skin between her shoulder and her throat. "I'm listening."

"Money. Bundles of cash hidden in the wall cavities. A lot of cash."

"But you can't be sure the money was Arlene's."

"We've confirmed the house was leased to her. The landlord stated she—Arlene—leased the property for immigrant workers at the farm." He knew this to be only a cover story. The employees of the farm were all locals who didn't need housing.

Naomi turned away, reached for a mug with a trembling hand. "Then you're telling me that Arlene was somehow connected to organized crime." She poured the mug full of steaming coffee and offered it to him.

He accepted, grateful for the caffeine-infused liquid. "I believe she was, yes." He sipped the coffee, winced at the burn of hot liquid, but at the moment he needed the fortification it promised.

She walked back to the living room and sat in her usual chair. After downing another swallow, he wandered back the same way. Took a seat on the sofa.

"You've decided my father was taking money from Arlene and most likely was helping her do..." She hesitated as if uncertain how to label the horrible thing lying cold and raw in front of her. "To cover up murders. Why would this Philadelphia mob bother sending a victim all the way to Tennessee? Why not just dispose of her there? Or someplace closer? This seems far-fetched at best."

"That is a piece of the puzzle I don't have yet. It doesn't add up strictly from a logistics standpoint. I can only assume there is—was—some sort of agreement between Arlene and the man in charge."

"This makes no sense at all. If she had an agreement, why is she dead?"

"Mob families have rules. They have territory. To cross the line is to make yourself a target. When a person makes the decision to go into business with these kinds of criminals, there is no going back and no room for error."

"Now you're saying she double-crossed the mob." Naomi held up a hand and the afghan fell to her elbows. "You've been here hardly more than twenty-four hours and already you've decided my family is involved with organized crime. What happened to innocent until proven guilty?"

Casey stared at the dark brew in his mug for a moment, took another swallow, a deeper one now that it had cooled. Then he sat the mug on the coffee table. "I'm speaking in general terms, ma'am. At this point, it's difficult to rule out Ms. Beck, with the mounting evidence that points to her involvement, but it's not my job to prove her guilt. My job is to find the evidence and solve the crime based on what I can actually prove, not on speculation. There are lawyers and judges who determine if the evidence I find is significant enough to prove the actors I allege to be involved are guilty."

NAOMI WATCHED THE movements of his hands, the way he inclined his head as he spoke. Somehow, she knew this man. "I'm sorry," she interrupted his monologue about the difference between what cops do and what lawyers do. "Are you certain we've never met? You said no before but I swear…" She shook her head. "There's something about you—maybe your eyes?—that seems so familiar."

Her timing was ridiculous, of course. There were far more pressing issues. But she needed to know or maybe she just needed a moment that wasn't about murder and bodies and mobsters.

He stared at her for so long she decided he wasn't going to respond. Then he finished off his coffee and leaned back on the sofa, his attention fully on her.

"I grew up in Mississippi. Meridian, Mississippi. Attended Ole Miss. My first assignment with the FBI was in Jackson. Then I ended up in Nashville."

"I don't recall ever having been to Meridian," she said. Why did he seem so intent on evading the real question? "I've been to Nashville a million times. Maybe we ran into each other there."

"Every summer my family spent a lot of time on the coast. Gulfport. Biloxi. But one summer we went to Mobile instead. Stayed at a resort in Gulf Shores."

Naomi's eyes locked with his and in that instant she

remembered. "I was eleven that summer. You were thirteen. You had a dog… Jefferson. A chocolate Lab."

A smile tugged at the corners of his mouth. "Loved that dog. He died while I was in college. I still miss him."

Her heart pounded so hard she could scarcely breathe. "We played all the time. The first few days I was there we were inseparable." How could she have forgotten? The boy had grown into a very handsome man. "Why didn't you say something?"

"I wasn't sure myself at first."

"Wow." The memories flooded her, making her feel light somehow. "It really is a small world."

He leaned forward, braced his forearms on his thighs. "Actually, I wasn't completely honest with you. I did remember you. I saw you in a commercial and I thought, wow, that looks like the girl from that summer in Mobile. Later on I spotted your name in the cast of characters in a movie and I knew it was you. I sort of kept up with you after that. Your career, I mean."

She made a face. "The career that wasn't really a career." A sigh burst from her. "I wasn't cut out for showbiz, as they say. I was lucky to land a few parts and a decent number of commercials but I'm fairly certain things were never going to take off. When my dad died, I came back here to settle his affairs and ended up staying. It felt a lot safer, career-wise, than Hollywood." She laughed at the irony. "Good grief, just look how that worked out."

"Hey, you made it a hell of a lot farther than most. You were actually in a movie."

"Two," she corrected with a sad laugh. "The other one never made it beyond the cutting room floor."

"Lots of commercials." He nodded. "The body lotion one is my all-time favorite."

"I was so embarrassed when my dad mentioned that he'd seen the commercial." It wasn't that she hadn't been fully covered or that it was even remotely related to anything pornographic, but it was definitely suggestive. It really hadn't fit with the daddy's little girl image she'd always felt described her dad's view of her. Surprisingly he'd told her it was great. She was all grown up and had every reason to be proud of how beautiful she was.

Of course, daddies were supposed to say things like that. She'd never considered herself beautiful. More unique with all the freckles and the wild red hair. A sort of Nicole Kidman. Maybe that was stretching it, but a director had once made the same comparison.

"When did you decide to join the FBI?" The different paths their lives had taken fascinated her. "I don't remember you talking about cops and robbers or anything related that summer."

He shrugged. "I was thirteen. The only thing on my mind was girls." He chuckled, looked away. "But going into law enforcement was no surprise to my family."

"I'll bet your father is a cop, too." God, it was such a relief to relax just a little. The past forty or so hours had been brutal. She could use the respite.

"No, my mom was the influence. Captain Irene Duncan of the Meridian Police Department. She's planning to retire next year."

"Wow. What does your dad do?"

"Believe it or not, he's a defense attorney. The best one in town, most people believe. The crookedest one, according to my mom."

Naomi's jaw dropped. "How do they manage?"

"They don't. That summer at Gulf Shores is the last time we were a real family. They divorced. Mom got primary custody of me and my sister. My father found a new wife who appreciated his talent and started a new family."

No wonder he remembered that summer so vividly. He'd lost his father that year. His whole life had changed. "I'm so sorry. I'm sure it was a difficult time for you."

"It was the best and the worst summer of my life all wrapped into one."

Wow. She couldn't imagine having to bounce back and forth between parents. It was so unfair to the children. The opposites-attract thing, however, she had experienced firsthand.

"My parents were like that, very different. My mom was a medical doctor. My dad always said she was so studious she ignored a social life entirely. He, on the other hand, dated every single girl in Franklin County before they married, I think. I can't tell you how many locals I have run into over the years who explained how they'd dated my father pre-Muriel. His father was a farmer. There were no siblings, so he inherited the farm. He had a little run-in with a chain saw, cut his leg and had to go to the ER. Until the day he died, he swore that Mom bewitched him that day. She was the physician on call and stitched him up. Forced him to have a tetanus shot and antibiotics, both of which he strongly insisted were unnecessary."

"How did they end up together?" Agent Duncan asked. "Did he break an arm for a return visit to the ER?"

Naomi laughed. Now there was something else she remembered about the handsome young boy from that summer—he had a wicked sense of humor. "No, he sent her flowers at her clinic. That same evening she showed up at the farm, the big vase of flowers in hand, and said she didn't accept gifts from patients. My father explained that he was not her patient. It wasn't his fault she was on call that day."

Casey laughed. *Casey.* How could she have forgotten his name? The idea that he had remembered hers and followed her career warmed her, maybe a little too much.

"Did she keep the flowers?" he asked, grinning.

"No. She left them on the porch. She did the same thing every day for a week. He kept sending flowers and she kept bringing them back. One night he had dinner prepared and suggested she join him. She was so exhausted from a long day at the ER she gave in and had dinner with him. There was no going back then. They were married a few months later but it was a while before I came along. I was a surprise. Mom thought she was too old to be having children. Not medically, of course, but just as a person. She was set in her ways. Had her routine. Dad insisted that he made her fall in love with me. After I was born, she started a clinic to better control her work hours. She didn't want to miss out on raising her child."

"I like your story way better than mine."

"Thanks, but it seems my story is all tangled up now." Reality rushed back in with a sharpness that almost took her breath.

"Sometimes great stories don't have a happy ending for reasons outside a person or persons' control."

Defeat kicked her in the stomach. "You're convinced my father was somehow involved."

"I can't ignore the sudden influx of large deposits. I know the farm started to thrive after you took over but that doesn't explain the years before. Show me where he sold property or other assets. Maybe there was an insurance policy of some sort you didn't know about." He turned his hands up. "Did your mother publish a paper that earned unexpected royalties? Find an explanation for the money and you have my word I will take him off the suspect list. Otherwise, I have to follow the evidence. There is a possibility that evidence will show that your father was completely innocent. We can't be sure what sort of private deals he made with Arlene. Did he or she mention his selling shares in the farm to her?"

Naomi hadn't considered that possibility. "No one mentioned any arrangements like that. There was nothing in the settling of the estate about any business shares belonging to anyone except my dad. Surely Arlene would have told me."

"It'll take time, but I will find the truth. With this latest development, there will be a whole team of agents working on this case. Between now and then, my primary job will be to ensure your safety."

She suddenly wondered who was supposed to ensure the safety of the woman from Philadelphia. Following that train of thought right now was not a good idea. She would only offend him if she verbalized her concerns, and she was too tired to deal with a deeper discussion on how federal agencies worked. She pushed aside the nightmare and forced a smile. Better to stick with something lighter. "I can't believe I didn't remember you. I remember that summer so well. It changed the course of my life."

"I think you only had eyes for one boy that summer."

"Slade," she said. "Slade Kenton. His mother was in Fair Hope filming a movie. He invited me to the set and from that day forward all I could think about was becoming an actress."

"A good old boy from Mississippi couldn't compete with what he offered."

As if the defeat in his tone had kicked a memory loose from her brain, she instantly remembered her first kiss. Her *real* first kiss. The one this man—the boy version of him—had given her.

"Ah," she said, "but he didn't get to be the first boy I kissed."

For a moment they stared at each other. The tension was thick.

Then he stood, picked up his mug. "I'd forgotten about that kiss."

"Me, t-too," she said, feeling offended somehow. "Completely. It only j-just occurred to me." If only she hadn't stuttered and stammered and sounded like a complete liar, her story might have been believable.

"I wonder whatever happened to him?" Casey asked. "I don't think his career took off the way his mother's did. I guess celebritydom isn't meant for everyone."

With that profound statement he took his mug to the kitchen. As he passed back through on his way to the front door, he gave her one of those nods and said, "Good night, ma'am."

Chapter Eight

Honea Farm, 11:20 p.m.

Ma'am.

For a few minutes Naomi had been certain the human part in Agent Casey Duncan had emerged. They'd had a personal connection that went back decades. On some level she had recognized him, but she hadn't been able to pull the memory from the gray matter that was so shaken by the events of the past two days.

Maybe if she'd run into him under different circumstances…

She stalked back to the kitchen. Glared at his cup, then tucked it away in the dishwasher. He'd acted almost annoyed that she had recalled how they first met. Was she not supposed to remember? Or was he somehow still miffed that she'd only had eyes for Slade instead of him, as he put it. She'd been eleven, for goodness' sake. She hadn't known what she wanted.

The notion that he would hold the actions of an eleven-year-old against her was ludicrous.

Her determined pace back into the living room

slowed and her gaze narrowed. Maybe the fact that they'd met before was just coincidence, but he'd used it to take her off guard. Certainly she'd opened up more than she would have otherwise. But nothing she'd said had confirmed his conclusions about her dad or Arlene.

Though it was difficult to justify in any way whatever Arlene had been doing.

How could such a seemingly nice woman have been making bodies disappear? Not just any bodies at that, the bodies of murder victims. She fully expected that when the remains discovered in the lab were identified they would be those of homicide victims, as well.

What did you call someone who made bodies disappear? Not exactly a cleaner since they typically cleaned up an entire scene or situation. This was only body disposal.

At least as far as Naomi knew.

What if there were notes or files about the bodies hidden somewhere on the farm? Surely Arlene kept business records. It was a business, wasn't it? Based on what Agent Duncan—she refused to call him Casey since he'd behaved so strangely before leaving—said it appeared that Arlene was paid vast sums of money to get rid of human remains. Add to this information the evidence found in the lab and in other areas on the farm, it made sense that Arlene, as an agronomist, would have taken her work to the next level.

Human composting.

Fear snaked around Naomi's chest. If Arlene had composted human remains on the farm, using it as some sort of fertilizer, there would be endless lawsuits. Whether Naomi or her dad knew about it or not, they owned the farm. They signed up the subscribers for the CSA.

Holy cow, she was in serious trouble. She needed a really good lawyer.

She hesitated, one hand on her hip, the other on her chin as she tapped her cheek in hopes of prodding forth some revelation that would provide an out. Could a lawyer actually help if the question of who did what still remained? Or did it matter? Was she and her dad as well as her mother still culpable simply because they owned the property? "Of course you are, dummy."

She'd gone over the house fairly well and found nothing unexpected, certainly nothing that suggested there was some illegal operation on the farm.

What she needed was the opportunity to go through the lab and office.

Hurrying to the kitchen, she found her jacket, tugged it and her boots on and found a flashlight. Before going out the door she confirmed that her keys and her cell were in her pocket.

Check.

Slipping out the back door she disappeared into the darkness, opting not to use the flashlight. She'd made the trip to the barn and lab a million times. She knew the way. Besides, in retrospect, if she turned on the flashlight her security detail would see. She needed some time alone in the lab to think and pick through the decades of papers documenting the work done on the farm.

The door to the lab was locked. Since the investigators would be returning tomorrow, they hadn't sealed the door with crime scene notices. No matter, she understood that what she was doing probably broke the law.

She entered the building, anyway. Now she would use the flashlight. If she turned on the overhead lights anyone outside would be able to see the glow cast through the skylights. Unless she directed the flashlight upward, that wasn't going to happen. First, she did a walk-around and assessed what the forensic investigators or technicians had been doing. Thankfully they put things back as they found them after completing their tasks on a given worktable. She'd expected lots of jumbling and fingerprint dust. Did they even use that stuff anymore?

The storage room was the same. The items on the shelves weren't exactly where she and Arlene had put them, but they were close. Arlene preferred everything in its exact place all the time. If you moved it, you'd better put it back precisely where you found it.

This was one of the traits her mom had loved about Arlene. Everything was always in its place. Her mom had been basically the same way. Even now Naomi found herself lining up the cereal boxes and cans in perfect order, arranged by product.

But Naomi was more like her dad. Not so picky about where things were. Perfection wasn't even an aspiration in her reality.

The familiar tables and small greenhouses were comforting somehow. Without the darkness to distract her she noted the humid scent of warm soil and rich green plants.

This was where Arlene tested her plant food. She never called it fertilizer. Food. Like humans, the plants needed food.

Naomi shuddered at the idea that the woman may have been feeding the plants humans.

Finally, she moved on to the office. The desk was hers, but she and Arlene had shared it, depending on who was doing what. No need to try cramming another desk into this little office. She sat down in the wheeled chair and began her search. The drawers first. Picking through each scrap of paper, business card and report, she moved from drawer to drawer. In the bottom right she found a piece of her favorite soft caramel candy. She peeled off the wrapper and popped it into her mouth.

"Hmm." Nice. On busy days those chewy delights were sometimes her lunch.

A thorough check of the credenza and she moved on to the row of file cabinets. These massive file cabinets were the primary reason there was no room for another desk in the room.

Not that she would need a second desk now.

She stilled. Arlene was dead. Her parents were dead. She was it now.

And everything had gone to hell.

Emotion burned in her eyes, but she blinked it away and focused on the task at hand. Now, finding the facts was the most important task she had to accomplish. Folder by folder she read the headings of each. Customer names. Each business from whom they purchased goods or sold goods had a file. Each individual who bought from the farm had one, as well. She knew them all personally.

She passed the Franklin County Lumber file but went back. Something stuck out of the folder. Arlene never left anything arranged in a sloppy manner. Maybe the forensics folks had bunched up some of the papers in this file.

Naomi removed it but it wasn't the lumber company's file that was the problem. It had gotten tucked into another folder. This one was unmarked.

Pulse thumping, she opened the file. Empty. Maybe it was just an extra file that stuck to the lumber company one. She scanned the front of the folder with her flashlight, then the back side.

The beam of light stilled midway across the back side of the brown folder.

Numbers.

She placed the folder down on the desk and went over it more carefully. There were dozens—no hundreds—of numbers written on it.

"What is this?" she muttered.

Holding her breath, she turned on the desk lamp and looked more closely. Numbers. Numbers. Lots and lots of numbers. She took a photo with her phone, then slid it back into her pocket.

Her first instinct was to call Agent Duncan.

"Nope."

She intended to look into this herself before handing it over to him. After turning off the desk light, she slipped the folder back into the drawer next to the one labeled Franklin County Lumber. Maybe the numbers were combinations to locks. But there were no locks with combinations that she knew of on the farm. They all had keys.

Something else she would need to look for.

Maybe it was time to take the UTV, a utility terrain vehicle, around the property. See if there was a building somewhere she had missed. She really couldn't say for sure that she had been over every acre of the property since she came back. Considering it wouldn't help to do it in the dark, tomorrow would have to be soon enough.

The air felt chillier as she left the lab or maybe it was just the idea that it was dark save for the moonlight. She paused and stared up at the low-slung full orb. There was no comparison when it came to country nights. It just wasn't the same in the city.

"You really shouldn't be out here in the dark."

Her scream came out more a squeak.

Fear slammed into Naomi like a fast-moving truck.

Casey. Agent Duncan.

When she could breathe again, she said, "You scared the hell out of me."

"Spotting something moving in the dark didn't do anything for my serenity, either. Imagine me picking up movement between two trees. I am armed, Ms. Honea, as is the deputy on duty. This is a bad idea for everyone."

No matter that she knew he was right, anger overrode her good sense. "What are you doing here? I thought you left."

"I decided to hang around awhile."

"Why?" Her anger and frustration amped up a notch.

"So you can come up with some other way to make me believe one or both of my parents was involved with whatever the hell is going on here?"

"Looks to me like you were the one searching for something. Maybe you could tell me what was so important that you had to go out in the middle of the night and enter an ongoing crime scene to find it?"

She didn't have to tell him anything. "I needed the latest invoices, but I couldn't find them. They must be in the house. I guess I overlooked them."

"Your invoices aren't on some app or software on your computer?"

"Good night, Agent Duncan."

She strode toward the house. The moonlight was plenty for her to see the way. Even if it hadn't been, she wouldn't have turned on the flashlight. Maybe he'd run into a tree. She rolled her eyes and mentally scolded herself for being petty.

At least she wasn't holding a nearly two-decade-old rejection against him. And it wasn't even really a rejection. It was nothing but two silly kids and hormones.

She stamped up onto the porch and still he followed right behind her. She wheeled around. "Why are you following me?"

"I intend to make sure your house is clear before you lock yourself in for the night."

She gestured to the county cruiser in the drive. "I have a security detail."

As she made the statement another car pulled up and the one that had been parked all evening backed up and drove away. Shift change, she supposed.

The driver's door opened and an older deputy, broad shouldered and round bellied, got out of the car and waved. "Evening. I'm Deputy Lawton. I'll be here for the night."

"Thank you," Naomi called back. "If you need anything please let me know."

He nodded and climbed back into his vehicle.

"Was there anything else you wanted to say?" she asked the man still towering over her. He looked almost as irritated as she felt.

"Whatever I said that ticked you off," he announced with an exaggerated sigh, "I apologize."

"You accused my dad of being a criminal. You even suggested I might be one. All because you have no idea who the criminal is in all this." Probably not entirely true but saying it felt good.

It gave her quite the bit of glee, in fact.

"You're right. I apologize for that, too."

Too. So, he did realize he'd been petty.

"Thank you." She turned to the door once more.

"Ms. Honea, I really need you to think long and hard about the difference between what you've always believed and what the evidence shows. This will go a whole lot more pleasantly and a lot more quickly if we work together."

He'd said she should help him prove her parents were innocent in all this. So maybe she was the one being petty. Maybe he was only doing his job and she was the one fighting the process.

"I looked through the files. There's an extra empty folder next to the Franklin County Lumber file. It's empty but it had numbers written all over it. Combinations or some other number sequences."

He nodded. "Thank you. I'll check it out."

He descended the steps, heading back to the lab.

She went after him. He glanced her way as she caught up with him. "It's late, Ms. Honea."

"I can't go in the house." She pressed onward, matching his long strides as closely as she could.

He cut a glance in her direction. "Why is that?"

"You said you had to make sure it was clear before I go in."

CASEY LAUGHED. "YOU'RE RIGHT. I did say that. I guess I owe you another apology."

She made a "who cares" sound and kept walking.

"You know you can't go back in the lab." Casey knew she would. That was something else he remembered about her. She was fearless. *Are you brave enough...?*

"Then I'll wait outside."

He unlocked the door and waited for her to go in before him.

This time she turned on the lights. He'd followed her here. He'd been doing a walk around her house when she'd exited through the back door. Years of experience weren't necessary to know where she was headed.

In the office he pulled the file she'd told him about. He propped against the desk and reviewed the numbers. Some were written in black ink, others in blue.

"Do you think the coloring of the ink is significant?"

A logical question. "Maybe." He glanced at her. "Maybe not."

She stared at the scribbled numbers. "There aren't any combination locks around here. We only use locks with keys."

"Passwords," he suggested.

She leaned closer and he stopped breathing.

"None of our computer passwords are number sequences. We use a combination of letters, numbers and special characters." She smiled up at him as if she fully understood he couldn't breathe. "The passwords are stronger that way."

When she drew back, he breathed again. "What about online accounts? Any of these resemble bank account numbers? Credit cards?"

Her brow lined as she studied the numbers again. "I don't think so, but I can check."

"We're here." He moved away from the desk. "Why not have a look now?"

Beyond the fact that it was the middle of the night and that she shouldn't be in here.

Naomi slid into the chair behind the desk and started clicking keys. Casey walked around the office, surveyed shelves and items he'd already inventoried two or three times. Never hurt to have another look. Mostly he just wanted to let her feel like she was accomplishing something. He'd played this all wrong. Bringing up the past and making her feel vulnerable was the incorrect tactic. He didn't usually make those kinds of elementary mistakes.

Maybe the truth was that he'd let that tiny slice of shared history rattle him just a little.

"Let me see the folder." She held out her hand and he placed the folder in her fingers.

He watched as she looked from the computer screen to the folder time and time again. Her pink lips were pursed, making him wish he could touch her there. A lock of red hair fell across her face and it took every ounce of strength he possessed not to reach out and tuck it aside.

Maybe that was why he'd asked for this case as soon as it came across the SAC's desk. He wanted to see her. To see if she remembered him. To help her find the truth. Or maybe to prove she was involved somehow.

But that third option was wrong. She wasn't involved. He knew this already. Could he clear her father's name? Maybe not. But he would find the truth and he would do what he could to prevent tearing her world any further apart.

"None of the accounts we have match any of those numbers." She logged out of the computer and shut it down. "Back to square one."

"It's late." Past midnight, he imagined. "We should call it a night and have a fresh look in the morning. I'll run it past our forensics accountant."

"At least we tried."

If having tried made her feel as if she were helping, he'd made the right choice. He really did need her cooperation.

He followed her out of the building, locked the door.

When they reached the house, he gave her a nod. "Good night, Ms. Honea."

"Why are you calling me that?"

He hesitated, looked at her. "It's your name."

"Let's get this part out of the way," she suggested. "You call me Naomi and I'll call you Casey. We can't pretend all this formality. Not after what we shared."

He stroked his chin as if considering her offer. "All right, Naomi."

"Drive safely."

She reached for her door.

"I'm not going anywhere."

Her attention swung back to him. "Why? I have a security detail. Is it really necessary to have two right outside my door?"

He considered the deputy in the cruiser, then turned back to her. "I don't really care for motels. I'm more at home in my SUV. I'll be fine."

He started down the steps.

"No."

He looked back. "No?"

She shook her head. "The deputies get to change up every eight hours. You don't have anyone to relieve you. You can stay on my couch. Get some sleep, like you said. If anyone tries to get to me, you'll be right there *on the couch*."

"As long as you're okay with the arrangement, ma'am."

"Naomi," she reminded as she unlocked and opened the door.

"Naomi," he amended.

She nodded to the open door. "I'll let you go first. Make sure it's safe for me to come inside."

He doubted she had anything to worry about in there

and most likely she knew it. She was using his own words against him. In reality, the problem was right here. With him. Maybe she didn't understand or maybe she did.

Guess he'd find out.

Chapter Nine

Honea Farm
Thursday, October 21

Casey's eyes opened to darkness.

He listened.

All quiet. But something woke him. He reached beneath the pillow Naomi had provided and found his cell. Checked the time: 3:00 a.m.

He tossed aside the blanket and sat up. The sofa, he had to admit, was far more comfortable than the bucket seat in his SUV. He pulled on his shirt as he stood, buttoned up while he searched for his boots. Tucked his weapon into his waistband. Then, running his fingers through his hair, he took a moment to allow his eyes to adjust to the darkness. Turning a light on would wake Naomi. No need for that.

Taking his time, he moved across the room to the stairs. The Honea home was a typical two-story farmhouse. Bedrooms were upstairs. As best he recalled from the search of the home on Tuesday, there were no squeaky steps on the staircase.

He moved up quickly, going straight to the room on the right at the far end of the narrow hall. He had known this was her room the moment he entered it. Celebrity posters still covered the walls from when she was a teenager living at home. The posters were the right era, so he had assumed as much, anyway. The walls were white, allowing the colorful posters and banners to stand out on a blank canvas. The bed had been unmade. He had her figured for a girl who didn't bother making the bed every morning. He, too, was firmly rooted in the what-difference-did-it-make camp. He was only going to climb back in that night.

She'd left her door open. Good. At this point his eyes had adjusted well to the lack of lighting. Her form was easy to make out in the soft white covers. He knew the covers were soft because he'd touched them. Hadn't been able to help himself. Her red hair was a dark cloud spread over the pillow. The sound of her soft, steady breathing confirmed his estimation that she was sleeping soundly.

Back downstairs, he pocketed the key she'd left on the table near the door and grabbed his jacket. He slipped out and stood for a moment on the porch assessing the county cruiser parked in the driveway. The best he could tell the vehicle was empty.

Where was the deputy?

Maybe he'd needed to take a leak and the car door was what Casey had heard.

Palming his weapon just in case, he made his way down the steps and toward the cruiser. No one in the car. Next he looked through the windows of his own

SUV, then looked under both vehicles. Naomi's truck was the same—empty.

From there he took a walk around the house. All quiet. No shadows moving through the moonlight.

Where the hell was that deputy?

Moving toward the lab a sound alerted his senses. Casey stilled. The snap of a twig, crunch of gravel. Then he spotted the movement. A dark form progressing through the night, only visible when it passed beneath a slip of moonlight that filtered between the branches of the trees.

The form moved closer to the house. Casey waited until he—presumably the deputy—was close enough to touch. He lifted his weapon to the form's head.

"Stop right there."

"Whoa!" Male voice. "I'm Deputy Lawton. Just had to do some private business, if you know what I mean."

Casey lowered his weapon. "Sorry about that, Lawton. Special Agent Casey Duncan. I thought I heard an intruder lurking about."

"You hear all sorts of sounds out here in the country, Agent Duncan. Owls, raccoons messing around the trash cans. It's not like in the city. Sometimes a sound we're not used to hearing will rouse us from a dead sleep."

"You're right." Casey tucked his weapon back into his waistband. "I'm more accustomed to the wail of sirens and the rush of moving vehicles."

"I had you figured for a city boy," Lawton said. "How long have you been in the Winchester area?"

Casey asked as they moved back toward the front of the house.

"Since I decided life in Birmingham was not for me. Every time I turned around it seemed one of my fellow officers was getting shot. I headed north, spent a night in Winchester and decided this was the place for me. Until I got on with the department, I used to help Mr. Honea out on the farm. Stayed on even after I was hired as an auxiliary deputy. Once I got on full-time, I had to give up the extra work. He was a good man. Always the first to help when the community needed him."

"Did you notice any changes in the way the farm operated or in Mr. Honea's personality over the past few years?"

"Not that I can say." He paused next to his vehicle, shook his head. "It was tough when his wife was sick and for a while after she passed. But that's understandable. You won't find a finer family than the Honeas. Good folk. Never any trouble out here. Like I said, always helpful to their neighbors. Always the first ones to pitch in during a crisis. This awful business is a real shame."

Casey had gotten pretty much the same statement from everyone he'd interviewed.

"What about Arlene Beck? How well did you know her?"

"Well, now." He adjusted his belt as if his trousers were having difficulty staying up on his round shape. "Arlene was a different kind of bird. Definitely an odd one. Friendly enough most of the time. She wasn't one to socialize. Not too many friends as far as I could tell.

There was that one old conspiracy fella she spent a good deal of time with."

"Conspiracy fella?" Casey asked.

"Elmer Cotton," Lawton said. "He used to work for the government. NASA, I think. Had to retire early. They say he lost his mind." He made a circling motion at the side of his head. "Went a little crazy. Anyway, he lives sort of off the grid over in Shake Rag."

"Shake Rag?"

"A little community near Huntland. I'd be happy to show you the way when the next deputy arrives if you'd like."

Casey skipped over the offer for now. "How was Beck involved with this Elmer Cotton?"

"Well, I can't say for sure. I just heard she spent a lot of time with him. Might've been just a rumor. But you know what they say, 'birds of a feather flock together,' and those two appeared to have a lot of *oddness* in common. Don't mean to speak ill of the dead, but she was a strange one."

"How well do you know Naomi?" Saying her name always caught Casey off guard. He'd thought about her plenty of times over the years, especially whenever he spotted her on television. But saying her name aloud was new.

Maybe at some point he had gone beyond curious about her. Maybe he was a little obsessed. Not a good look on an agent. Particularly under the circumstances.

"Not as well as I knew her daddy, Nolan," he admitted. "She was gone out to California for a good long while. After Nolan died, she came back and helped Arlene pull the farm back into shape. Things were pretty bad there for a while."

Strange, it certainly didn't look that way on paper. The farm dropped into the red after Naomi's mother died. But a year later it appeared—on paper—to have been thriving with more cash flow than ever before. The bank statements showed a drop-off the final year of Naomi's father's life. Another oddity. Why the drop in income with little or no drop in production? Jones and Riley had insisted that work had been steady for the past five years, and even an uptick since Naomi came home.

"Failing crops?" Casey asked. "Equipment issues?" Most of the farm equipment appeared to be fairly new.

"I can't say," Lawton confessed. "Nolan wasn't one to poor-mouth. I just know he looked like a man at his wit's end. There was this one time that he mentioned he just didn't know what he was going to do if things didn't turn around."

Naomi hadn't mentioned any discussions with her father about ongoing issues. "Did he ask Naomi for help?" Casey ventured. "Maybe she feels guilty for not coming home to help."

"I don't think he would have worried her with whatever problems he had. He wanted Naomi to be happy. Even if it meant her chasing after her dreams way out in California."

"Maybe he discussed his concerns with Arlene since they were partners."

Lawton chuckled. "I don't think he and Arlene got on so well after his wife, Muriel, died. She and Muriel were a team, but Nolan was kind of like a third wheel.

I think that might have been a sticking point for Nolan and Muriel. But now, I have to tell you that part is just gossip. Nolan never spoke ill of anyone, least of all his Muriel. Arlene was a part of this farm and always here. I guess it was the three's-a-crowd thing."

"Thanks, Lawton." Casey gave him a nod. "I appreciate the information. You need anything out here? Water? Coffee?"

The older man shook his head. "I'm good. Got a thermos still half full of coffee and a couple more bottles of water.

"How well do *you* know Naomi?" Lawton asked when Casey would have turned to go back into the house.

"I don't know her," Casey said, which was basically true.

"Oh." Lawton shrugged. "I just thought the two of you were close."

This was the man's roundabout way of pointing out that he was aware Casey had been in the house all night while he was out here in his county cruiser.

"It's my job to make sure Ms. Honea stays safe. If sleeping on her couch makes that possible, then I can handle it."

"We do what we have to," the older man said with a chuckle.

Casey considered saying more but decided against it as he watched the deputy slide back behind the wheel of his vehicle. A small-town thing, he decided as he headed back into the house. When everyone knew everyone else, it was human nature to be curious about a change or disruption to the norm.

As he unlocked the door a light came on inside. "It's me, Casey Duncan," he said as he opened the door.

For all he knew Naomi could have her dad's shotgun. He'd seen one propped behind the door in the man's bedroom. He felt confident Naomi knew it was there even if she hadn't bothered moving it—or anything else in her parents' bedroom for that matter. The room was like a shrine to the late Honeas.

It was a big enough house, he supposed, no need to be in a rush to clear out or pack up their things.

Standing at the bottom of the stairs, Naomi pressed a hand to her chest. "You scared the hell out of me. I heard voices outside and I worried that something else had happened." She closed her eyes, shook her head before meeting his gaze once more. "Anyway, is everything okay?"

"Everything's fine," he assured her. He closed the door and locked it. "The voices you heard were Deputy Lawton and me. We had a look around outside."

"Why?" She moved toward the sofa.

He raised his eyebrows in question. "Why what?"

"Why were you looking outside at this hour of the morning?"

He should have known that question would be coming. "I heard a noise and went to check it out." He explained the circumstances. "No worries. It's all good."

She pushed her hair back from her face, glanced around. "Okay, well, I'll be back down in a bit. Feel free to get some more sleep or make coffee or whatever."

He tried his best to keep the smile from his face. He got it now. She'd just realized she was standing there in a nightshirt and with her hair a wild mass of curls.

He loved it.

She hurried back upstairs.

He glanced at the couch. More sleep was out of the question. He'd log into the server via his cell and have a look at the latest reports from forensics.

Keeping his mind off the woman upstairs would be best for both of them.

Honea Farm, 8:00 a.m.

NAOMI NIBBLED A slice of buttery toast and contemplated how she could possibly answer the multitude of emails and text messages from concerned CSA subscribers. There was no way she would be making this week's delivery. Chances were she wouldn't be able to make the one after that. Sean and Joe were being allowed to come back to work tomorrow but how could she do anything until she understood the situation more fully?

Any second now she expected to receive notification that all deliveries were to be halted until a health and agriculture department investigation could be done. The farm's certification was unquestionably in jeopardy.

This was a major catastrophe. Thinking beyond the fact that people had died had been difficult until now. But at this point she had to face the reality that maybe she should have sold the farm last year.

And she'd been so certain she was doing the right thing for her parents' legacy. For her future.

She tossed the remainder of the toast into the trash. She needed more coffee.

Casey had left the house half an hour ago to meet his team in the lab. He hadn't mentioned any new developments. No news so far on the remains from the freezer. The identification could take months or years.

She'd spent some time searching the internet about human composting. Her stomach seized at the thought. It was a tricky business. Bodies used had to be tested for certain issues that might be passed along in the soil and onto plants. It wasn't an "anything goes" sort of concept. There were rules and laws and licenses. Not unlike the many, many hoops to jump through for an organic certification. If the remains found here were tested and any issues discovered, the situation would grow exponentially worse for her farm.

For the first time since Casey had shown her those bank statements, she asked herself if there was even the remotest possibility her dad could have known what Arlene was doing. This was assuming Arlene was the one responsible for this ungodly mess. Who else could it be?

There could be no other explanation in light of the money found in that house she leased. The box with the head inside had been addressed to that property. No question. Arlene's friend, Mr. Cotton, had said she used the house on High Street for deliveries.

There just wasn't any other explanation.

To pretend otherwise was beyond ridiculous at this point. She looked out the kitchen window at the lab. A swarm of federal agents had arrived and spread out over her farm. People were coming in and out of the lab. She felt like a rat watching the comings and goings and uncertain when the trap would snap, catching her in its lethal hammer.

She had to do something.

Naomi grabbed her jacket, tucked her phone into the pocket and walked out the back door. This was her property. She had agreed to whatever searches the authorities needed to do but she had a right to know what was happening.

She hadn't seen Sheriff Tanner or Chief Brannigan today. This was the FBI's case now so she wasn't sure when or if she would hear from them again. She felt confident they were being kept in the loop. At least, that was the way it worked in crime shows in the movies and on television.

The ground was drying up, which was a good thing. There was work that needed to be done. Until this week the rain hadn't let up. The only thing she knew to do was to carry on with the fall planting and winter prep. This farm was now her livelihood. If the farm went under, so did she.

The idea that Arlene could have more money hidden around the property crossed her mind. She really had to be losing it to think that way. And would the government seize the farm as a criminal venture?

More knots formed in her belly.

The lab door opened and an agent exited. This one was a woman. She smiled and nodded and hurried to a vehicle parked near the house. Naomi had no idea exactly how many agents were here or what they were all doing. Sometimes ignorance was bliss. Hopefully this was one of those times.

She opened the door and stepped into the lab, breathing in the familiar scents. She surveyed the faces she saw in search of Casey. Some of the agents looked familiar. She'd seen them around before. But others were strangers.

"Is there something you need, Ms. Honea?"

The voice behind her startled her. She turned to face the man who'd spoken. "I'm looking for Agent Duncan."

"He's in the office on a Zoom call with our forensics team leader back at headquarters. It shouldn't be much longer."

She glanced toward the office—her office—and spotted him immediately, seated behind her desk. Another agent sat in the chair Arlene always used. Both were in deep discussion with a face on the computer monitor. A briefing, she supposed. Or maybe news from another source.

"I'll wait."

The agent wandered away.

Naomi walked to the storeroom door, noted the two agents going through boxes and packages, canisters and jars. They appeared to be taking samples. Made sense. Everything was suspect now. She wandered to the greenhouse area and checked the plants. They were really only seedlings at this point but soon they would be ready to move to the larger greenhouse for growing winter greens. Once they were moved out, new seeds would be planted to start the spring plants.

No matter that winter brought dormancy to much

of the farm, there was always work to do in the greenhouses. Always a step that led into another on the land. An endless cycle that reaffirmed the beauty and endurance of nature.

As a little girl she'd loved playing in the dirt. Her mother had adored flowers and she'd planted all sorts around the house in pots and beds. But as the organic farm operation grew, the time to spend with her flowers had grown less and less. Naomi had intended to start growing a few of her mother's favorites again next spring. Just a pot here and there around the porch. The house needed some color. Starting with a few potted blooming plants seemed an easy enough place to start. She'd also considered getting a dog. Growing up there had always been a dog on the farm.

Just another of the things that had changed after she moved to California.

Not for the first time she wondered if she had stayed would she have been able to make life easier for her mom. Maybe her dad wouldn't have had that sudden heart attack. Why hadn't she come back after her mom died and stayed? Some part of her had recognized her dad likely needed her. But the part in that movie had just been offered. Even her dad had urged her to go back to her life. He and Arlene could take care of the farm.

She should have stayed. Whatever happened over the past years led to this.

Naomi scanned the comings and goings around her.

Murder.

Why hadn't he said anything?

She'd visited at least once a year. Called two or three times a month. He'd never said a word.

Guilt weighed down on her shoulders. Made her feel sick.

Drawing in a deep breath she kicked aside the self-pity. This was no time to worry about what-if. She couldn't fully depend on anyone else to clear her dad's name. It was up to her to make sure the authorities found the truth. Like Casey said, she was the only one who could advocate for her parents.

The office door opened, and Casey and the other agent emerged. As if he'd sensed her presence his gaze landed on hers. He said something to the other agent and then started in her direction.

Despite everything else that was going on, she couldn't help admiring the way he moved. The ease with which he pulled off that sexy, masculine swagger amazed her. *So not smart, Naomi.*

The instant he reached her, he asked, "Everything okay?"

She was fairly certain nothing would ever be okay again, but she didn't bother explaining the feeling. "As okay as it can be. Any news from your people?"

"We have a DNA match for one of the three victims in the freezer. The name likely won't mean anything to you. Jimmy Bagwell of Chicago. The word was his boss caught him skimming the weekly takes. He disappeared about a month ago."

"Are you serious? Another connection to organized crime?" What the hell had Arlene been doing? Running a disposal service for the mob?

"We should talk in your office."

Something in his voice warned that things were about to get worse. Defeat tugged at her as she followed him across the lab.

He closed the door of the office and waited for her to sit. She took her rolling chair and he settled into Arlene's. Except Arlene didn't need it anymore. She was dead. Never coming back. Arlene had been involved with bad people, doing very bad things. Getting rid of evidence—bodies. The realization jarred her. She pushed back the emotion and held on to her composure with both hands.

"It's becoming clearer and clearer that Beck was providing a disposal service."

"I actually just had that very thought." Her head was spinning now. It was one thing to consider an off-the-wall theory but to have an official confirm the possibility was mind-blowing.

"Whether it was disposal or whatever, she was working with very dangerous people. Considering she was murdered, we can safely assume something went wrong. She made a mistake. Crossed a line, ticked somebody off. Take your pick. The concern now is if there's another shoe going to drop. Did Arlene owe them something they didn't get?"

"Like maybe all that money in the walls on High Street?" But weren't they supposed to be paying her?

"Maybe it was about the money," Casey said, "but I'm guessing they knew about the address and would have torn the place apart if they were looking for money or something easily stored in a wall or under a floor."

Naomi felt ill. "But there's something. Something she did or didn't do."

"Most likely," he said. "You were going to talk to someone? An uncle, maybe? Were you able to find him?"

Oh, good grief. She had completely forgotten about her visit to Donnie and then the hermit over in Shake Rag. "Yes, I'm sorry. With all that's been going on I completely forgot to share what I'd learned with you."

"Anything significant?"

"I'm not sure. My uncle couldn't remember where Arlene lived before moving to Winchester. He did recall that she had a sort of thing, maybe only a friendship, with this man—Mr. Cotton, over in Shake Rag. I was able to catch him at home. It was a strange conversation. He said a good deal without saying anything that meant a thing as far as I could tell. When I told him Arlene was dead, he mentioned that they—whoever they is—were probably on to what she was involved in. He was very cryptic."

"He didn't explain what he meant?"

She shook her head. "He said I would know soon enough. And he mentioned that Arlene had learned from the master."

"Sounds like we need to talk to him again." Casey stood. "You free now?"

"Sure." She was surprised that he wanted her to go with him.

"He may speak more openly since you've talked to him before."

Made sense. "Okay."

"Besides—" he reached for his jacket "—you know the way, right?"

"Yes. I… I do." She hoped the man didn't shoot at them this time.

Most folks in Franklin County kept at least a shotgun or a rifle in the house. Then again, Casey had a weapon. She supposed that evened the odds. But a man like Cotton—already on the edge and obviously troubled—probably lived by the motto that he had nothing to lose.

Guess they would find out.

Chapter Ten

Shake Rag, 10:15 a.m.

"Did I mention this was a bit off the grid?"

Casey parked. "You mentioned it, yes." He glanced around the woods that marched right up to the narrow dirt road that stopped a good distance from the cabin barely visible in the distance. "You came out here alone?"

"I grew up here, so I'm used to this sort of thing." Naomi reached for her seat belt. "Mainly, I think I was running on adrenaline."

He grunted. The lady was definitely pretty fearless. The weight of the weapon nestled against his torso was reassuring. Off-the-grid types like the individual in this case could be a little sensitive to strangers.

"Let's see if he's accepting visitors." Casey emerged from the vehicle and adjusted his jacket. He really didn't want to get himself shot today. As he moved beyond the hood, he glanced at Naomi. He definitely did not want her to get hurt. "Stay behind me."

"Somehow it didn't look quite so ominous before."

"Desperation sometimes prevents us from seeing the danger before we make the leap."

"I've taken a few leaps like that in my time," she confessed.

"You were fearless even at eleven," he pointed out as they started moving toward the small ramshackle structure ahead.

She laughed, then covered her mouth and stared forward as if expecting the hermit to start calling out threats to halt or else.

God, she had the bluest eyes.

Focus, man.

He parked his attention back on the potential danger lying ahead. This was no time to go wandering off the task at hand.

"I have no idea what you mean, Agent Duncan," she said in a stage whisper. "I've never considered myself fearless."

"The rule was no diving off the pier."

She stalled, looked at him. "Oh my God. *I* jumped."

The words came out in a sort of awe as if she'd only just remembered that long ago day.

"You did. We had decided we were going to do it. Before either one of us had the good sense to stop, we were both standing on the railing. Someone shouted, *No diving.* The next thing we knew people, including security, were rushing toward us. We looked at each other and you just grinned and said, *Are you brave enough to jump?* Then you jumped. I didn't have the guts."

"My parents had a fit. I didn't understand all the fuss.

I was a great swimmer. It was amazing. Those moments in the air before I hit the water were incredible."

"I think it had to do with sharks, rough waters and pilings. You know, all that dangerous stuff."

The image of strands of her red hair in the breeze, those blue eyes sparkling with mischief. And that smile. He'd never forgotten that moment.

"I thought I was a mermaid in disguise. There was nothing to fear."

A *mermaid*. The perfect description.

"I almost gave my mom a heart attack." She shook her head. "It really was a foolish thing to do."

Now he felt guilty. "It may have been my fault."

She stared at him now, but he kept his eyes on the shack ahead. "How could it have been your fault? I'm the one who chose to jump."

"I recall there being a double dog dare involved."

She gasped. "You're right. I dared you to jump and the challenge escalated from there."

The great diving incident had been the last day they spent together without the cooler kid from Cali. He'd heard about Naomi's escapade and wanted to meet her. He and his mother were in the high-end condo community next door to the one Casey and Naomi were at. From that point on the west coast kid spent his every free moment on their side of the brick wall that separated the two communities.

"We were kids," he said, continuing on the path to the shack of a cabin. "Kids are reckless sometimes."

"I'm just glad to have survived."

Casey moved more fully in front of her as they

reached the narrow porch on the shack. At the door he raised a fist and knocked a couple of times. It was way too quiet. They'd made plenty of noise on the walk up. The last thing he wanted to do was surprise the old guy.

"Mr. Cotton," Naomi called. "Are you home? It's Naomi Honea. I brought a friend." She glanced at Casey. "I hope you don't mind."

"We're friends?"

She smiled. He forgot to breathe. He gave himself a mental shake and knocked on the door again.

No response. Not even the slightest sound.

An old truck sat next to the house. There were other vehicles, too, but none that would run without taking a sapling or two with them. "You know if that truck is his current ride?"

"No idea. It's the same one that was here before. The others, too."

Casey knocked again. Louder this time.

Still nothing.

He hitched his head to the right. "Move over there."

She did as he asked, and he reached for the door. The knob turned without any resistance. Unlocked.

"Stay put," he ordered as he drew his weapon.

He moved beyond the threshold. Exigent circumstances were questionable. He actually had no real reason to believe Cotton was in danger. But he wasn't answering the door. An operable vehicle sat in the yard. The resident was a hermit and the door was unlocked. Casey doubted he would go anywhere without locking the door.

"Mr. Cotton?"

The house was dark with only narrow slats of light slipping in through the closed shutters on the windows. He used the flashlight app on his phone to look around. No light switches, not even a pull string from an overhead fixture. Cotton was obviously a hoarder. Stacks and stacks of newspapers and magazines and boxes sat around the perimeter of the room. Otherwise, it was surprisingly clean and tidy.

A fireplace appeared to be his heat source. Beyond the living room area was a small kitchen as well as a bedroom. He checked the bedroom first. Narrow bed tucked against the wall. Small dresser with drawers. No closet. He walked back into the kitchen. A window over the sink drew his attention. He crossed the small room in three strides and looked out over the small clearing that comprised the backyard before disappearing into the dense woods.

Then he understood why Mr. Cotton wasn't answering.

"Naomi!"

She stepped in through the front door. "Did you find him?"

"I did." He turned to her. "I want you to stay here in the house. I'll be right back."

He exited the back door, which was also unlocked, before she could question him. The grass was knee-deep in the back. There was a small shed at the edge of the woods. An old-fashioned hand-operated well.

Elmer Cotton hung from an orange nylon rope. The ladder lying about three feet away appeared to be the way he'd reached the sturdy tree limb and tied the rope there. It would seem that he'd made a noose on the other end, put it around his neck and then jumped from the ladder. There was no question he was dead. The lividity in his bare feet was obvious.

"Oh my God."

Naomi stood at the back door, her hands over her mouth.

"Stay where you are," he ordered, "until I've had a look around." The unknown subject could still be in the area.

He moved all the way around the clearing. Scanned the ground for trampled grass. At the front of the house he found no indentation showing a vehicle had been in the yard other than his SUV. The killer likely parked on the road and slipped through the woods. Taking the elderly man completely by surprise. He moved back into the house then. Naomi waited in the kitchen near the back door just as he'd asked her to do.

"Don't touch anything," Casey warned. "This is now a crime scene."

It was possible the old man had taken his life. He'd been pretty upset when Naomi told him about Arlene's death. But Casey never liked a scenario that was too easy. Too convenient. Until he was certain, he wasn't taking any chances.

Casey was grateful for enough bars on his cell to call Sheriff Tanner and report the situation. Once the call was made, Naomi followed him back to his SUV where they donned gloves. They'd already been inside so no point in bothering with shoe covers.

"Let's have a look around." He glanced at her. "Let

me know if anything looks different than the way it was when you were here before."

She nodded. "Got it."

Fearless Naomi was a little shaken at the moment. Her lower lip had trembled when she spoke. Jumping off a pier and breaking the rules was vastly different from murder and so far she'd stumbled into several murder scenes. This may or may not be another but it involved a death nonetheless.

He surveyed the wall of articles and photos Cotton had collected and displayed. Definitely a conspiracy theorist. His focus appeared to have been primarily on politics from decades ago. More recently he'd gone off on a tangent about pesticides and food additives. A few articles were related to climate change. But most of the recent articles were about how humans were being poisoned in an effort to depopulate the earth.

"Hey! I think I found something!"

The shout came from the bedroom. Casey joined Naomi there. Above the small dresser was a painting. Maybe eleven by fourteen. The woman was nude, seated on the edge of a pool or fountain, looking back over her shoulder at the artist.

"I think this is Arlene," Naomi said. "She looks much younger, maybe thirtyish, but I think it's her."

Casey reached out and carefully lifted the unframed canvas from the wall. He turned it around and there was a large envelope tucked into the back.

"How about holding that for me while I put the canvas back?"

Naomi removed the envelope. He placed the canvas back on the wall and took the envelope from her. "Let's have a look."

With the top of the dresser clear, he opened the envelope and spread the contents there. More yellowed newspaper articles. A few pages cut from magazines. A couple of photos. *Old* photos.

"Some of these are in German," Naomi pointed out.

One article showed the date: 1958. November.

Casey carefully laid out the articles in German and snapped photos. "I'll send these in for translation."

"Here's one in English." Naomi pointed to another article. "This one is from 1964." She pointed to the photo next to the article. "This is the woman in the painting."

"Has to be." Casey quickly read the article. Naomi did the same, hovering close to see over his arm.

> Ursula Becker escaped East Berlin with her five-year-old daughter, Anna. Becker, a brilliant scientist, defected to the US and has been offered a position at the prestigious Johns Hopkins.

"Anna," Naomi said. "Becker. Beck. This must be Arlene and her mother, which would mean the painting is her mother, not Arlene."

"That would be my assessment, as well." Casey moved through the articles. The newest one was from 1975. "Ursula Becker was murdered in 1975."

Naomi took the article from him and read it. "The police believed her to be a victim of a so-called Nazi hunter for crimes against humanity during the Holocaust." She moved her head slowly side to side. "What in the world is all this?"

Dread thickened in Casey's gut. Were they looking at mob murders or something else altogether?

Honea Farm, 2:00 p.m.

NAOMI ENTERED DIFFERENT words into the search box. There had to be more about Ursula Becker. Naomi had come back to the farm an hour or so ago. A deputy had driven her home. Casey was still at Mr. Cotton's shack—the latest crime scene. She shuddered.

For her sanity's sake, she had stayed away from the news and social media. Reporters were all over town. She'd seen all sorts of different news vans on the drive back through town. They had descended on the Cotton property right behind the forensics team. Naomi had hunkered down in the rear floorboard of the county cruiser to escape without the reporters seeing her.

To occupy herself, she had been searching for information since she got back to the farm. If Arlene was Anna Becker, Naomi had never once heard her use a German accent or a German word, much less a phrase. But she'd been in the United States since she was five years old. It was possible she didn't remember living anywhere but the US. Her mother may have worked hard to avoid the use of her native tongue—even going so far as to erase her accent. Had her mother changed her name to Beck, as well? No, no. The article from 1975 had used the name Ursula Becker.

Ursula Becker came to this country as a renowned

geneticist. The accusations against her as cited by the words scrawled on the wall above her dead body all those years ago were for her crimes against humans at Auschwitz alongside Josef Mengele. A handful of survivors from Auschwitz insisted she had served as Mengele's closest assistant.

Naomi reminded herself to breathe. Had her parents known who Arlene really was? About her family history? If any of this was true—and Naomi was so blown away by the idea that she couldn't quite make the leap—how could they not have known? This was beyond the scope of anything she could have imagined when this nightmare began.

The portrait in Mr. Cotton's house and the photo in the newspaper article of the woman, Ursula Becker, certainly resembled Arlene. The likeness was uncanny. At this point there was no confirmation, but it couldn't be anything else.

Had Mr. Cotton discovered Arlene's true identity?

Naomi gave herself a mental shake. She had read about these horrors in history class. Watched the occasional documentary. A movie with her dad once. But this wasn't something that happened in small-town Tennessee. This was truly stranger than fiction.

Unquestionably more horrific than fiction.

If it was true that Ursula Becker was guilty, that didn't mean Arlene—her daughter—was guilty just because of the family connection. She left Germany when she was five. How could she have known or even remembered?

How on earth had Mr. Cotton gotten involved with

this? How had he figured it out? She thought of all the political articles she'd seen posted at his place. Maybe she should have read them instead of assuming what they were. No doubt Casey's people were combing each one thoroughly.

Mr. Cotton had asked her what she knew about him, then he'd said there were things about him that were dangerous.

Is this what he'd meant?

At least now she had some inkling as to why Arlene appeared not to have existed before coming to work on the farm nearly forty years ago.

Where had she been between 1975 and when she showed up here? In hiding? After her mother's murder, maybe she had been on the run. But why? At five years old when she fled Germany it was doubtful she had harmed anyone or knew things that could be helpful to anyone. Why would she have no choice but to hide? Why would anyone want to harm her?

Unless she'd followed in her mother's footsteps and had done some inhumane work here. On the farm. The remains she'd found…the body parts in the boxes—all of it made Naomi's chest constrict.

This was all too over the top. Like a bad movie. And if there was one thing Naomi knew it was bad movies.

She stared out the kitchen window toward the lab Arlene had loved so much. What kind of person kept human remains in their freezer? Had recently decapitated victims delivered on dry ice to their secret address? Terror, black and inky, slithered through Naomi.

Good grief, what had her parents gotten themselves

into? Her mom and dad had been very intelligent people—her mother was a physician, for God's sake. Surely they weren't fooled for all those years.

Naomi hoped they had been.

She really, really did.

A rap on the front door drew her to the living room. She peeked beyond the curtain and spotted Casey. She unlocked the door and welcomed him in. Her mind needed a break from this new level of her ongoing nightmare. Not that he likely had any good news but at least she would stop coming up with more terrifying theories if she were distracted.

She didn't even want to consider the rumors likely going around the community. Honea Horror Farm. She shuddered inwardly.

"Were you able to get the articles translated?" What was she saying? Of course he had. He was the FBI. They could make anything happen.

"Is that coffee I smell?"

"Yes. You want a cup?"

"I would love a cup."

Naomi hurried to the kitchen and filled a mug, then joined him in record time.

"Tell me," she urged. She lowered into her chair and waited.

He sat down on the sofa. Sipped his coffee and smiled. "That hits the spot."

Her nerves were jangling. She forced a smile. Silently she urged him to get on with it.

"The articles were lauding the brilliance of a young scholar, Ursula Becker. She was mentored by the top research scientists in Germany. There is no mention in her history about being at Auschwitz or any of the other places used by the Nazis. The trouble comes later, after the war, when her name showed up on a list put together by a group of survivors. Her murder was never solved, and no one openly took credit. Her daughter, who was a senior at Harvard no less, vanished. They kept their lives very private, so we haven't found a lot of background yet, but we've got people on it."

"How did Mr. Cotton play into this insanity?"

"We don't know. He was a research scientist at NASA. About twenty-five years ago he had what was referred to as a breakdown. No one has heard from him since. I guess that's when he went off the grid here."

"So, Arlene shows up here. Then Cotton. They had to know each other before. It's the only logical conclusion."

"We're leaning toward that scenario, but we have no proof just yet."

Naomi took a breath. "I need to know what conclusions your team has reached regarding the farm and all that's happened here." Right under her nose, she didn't add. Under her parents' noses!

"I can share with you what we have so far." He savored another slug of coffee. "The remains found in the freezer were filleted from the bones. There are no parts of organs present."

Her heart thumped harder with his every word. "The red market," she said, her words hardly more than a whisper.

His gaze narrowed. "What do you know about the red market?"

"Only what I found on my internet searches since finding what I did in that freezer. Sometimes the organs and bones are sold separately from the rest."

"We believe," he went on, "that is likely the case. The organs were obviously harvested before the rest ended up here. We're investigating the possibility that Beck was using the rest of the tissue in her work on your farm. The part we haven't been able to work into the scenario is the absence of the bones. Like you said, they were likely sold. Separately obviously. It just seems strange not to find a single one. Did she sell those first? Who knows? But we have some measure of evidence on the rest but nothing on the bones beyond the probability that they arrived here like the intact remains we found on her High Street porch. From there, we don't know yet."

The shaking started deep inside Naomi. This nightmare had reached new, unfathomable levels. "You have to believe me when I say my parents would never have gone along with something like this. She had to be doing this on her own. Maybe after my mom's death, during my father's grief."

His steady brown eyes held on to hers for a long moment. "You have my word that we are exploring every possibility, including that one."

Naomi wanted to feel relieved but honestly it was impossible. To ask this man—his team—to assume all of this happened right here on the farm where her parents lived and worked without their knowledge was a stretch. She was aware.

"I've worked with Arlene for over a year and I had no clue."

He nodded. "It's possible. Some people are very good at hiding the bad things they do."

Was that an agreement with what she'd just said or a warning to brace herself for learning what her parents may have been doing?

"What happens now?" she asked, her voice sounding hollow. She was so tired. More tired than she had ever been before.

"I'd like you to help me with the search. You grew up here. If I know you as well as I think I do, you probably explored every square inch of this farm."

A real smiled touched her lips then. "I did. I'd roam the woods and the fields daydreaming about my escape."

He chuckled. "I think we all did some daydreaming about escaping as kids."

An escape would really be nice about now. Except reality was not going to allow that to happen anytime soon.

"Let me grab my hiking boots and we'll get started."

"The temperature is dropping, and the wind is up, so you might need a hat of some sort."

"Good idea."

She hurried upstairs, used the bathroom, then located her most comfortable boots, a scarf and a beanie. As she passed her parents' room, she hesitated. "I hope you weren't keeping secrets from me."

Not these kinds of secrets, anyway.

She rushed back downstairs and found Casey waiting for her at the door.

"You ready?" he asked.

"As ready as I'll ever be."

But not nearly ready enough for what might be coming next.

Chapter Eleven

Honea Farm, 4:00 p.m.

Sheriff Tanner and his deputies had shown up with UTVs for roaming the farm. For the past going on two hours, they had covered the open fields and pastures. More deputies, federal agents and officers had taken the woods, moving on foot in a grid pattern to ensure nothing was missed.

So far Naomi had noticed nothing unusual. Nothing different than it had been when she was a child. Her hopes were dwindling.

Yet, she knew there had to be someplace Arlene carried on this evil part of her work. There was nothing in the lab—other than the remains found on Monday—that even hinted at an operation like Arlene appeared to have been running. Naomi wanted to feel guilty for thinking such bad things about the woman, but she was so far past that point now she felt nothing but anger.

Casey stared across the latest field they'd explored. "Think hard, Naomi. What we're looking for could as easily be underground as aboveground."

He'd reminded her of this about a dozen times already.

"I get that but..." She heaved a weary breath. "I haven't seen anything that jumps out at me."

"I'll check in with the other teams and see how they're coming along."

The disappointment in his voice made bad matters worse.

Surely there was something she was missing. She closed her eyes and thought of all those days she had roamed this farm, unafraid of running upon anything she couldn't handle.

"Idiot," she muttered.

Her mom had always scolded her for running off in the woods. She'd remind Naomi that there were sink-holes and caves around Franklin County that could swallow up little girls.

Caves.

"Casey!" She turned all the way around looking for him. Found him only a few feet away deep in conversation.

She waited, barely able to contain herself, until the phone call ended. "There's a place," she blurted. "In the woods near a spring that comes out of the hillside. I used to sneak over there all the time. There are lots of rocks and trees. It was like a grotto in the hillside. I didn't consider it as someplace Arlene might use until just a moment ago when I thought about all the caves in this part of the state. There was a narrow opening in the mouth of the hillside where the water came out. It might lead to a deeper cave."

"Show me."

They climbed into the UTV and headed toward the woods on the back side of the farm. The grotto wasn't in the woods but it was nearby. Casey spoke to Sheriff Tanner en route and had him and a couple of his deputies meet them at the location.

By the time Casey parked not so far from a cliffy side of the hill, she was ready to leap off the UTV and rush down the hill. How had she forgotten about this place? Maybe she'd erased more than she realized from her memory banks. When she'd gone to Hollywood, she'd worked hard to keep the memories of home at bay.

She'd been homesick but refused to admit it even to herself.

As they approached the spring-fed pool, she stalled. "This isn't how I remember."

There was no narrow opening next to the water. She recalled vividly having to wade through knee-deep water to reach the narrow opening and peer inside.

"You're certain it was here."

She nodded. "Positive."

Sheriff Tanner, hands on hips, surveyed the terrain. "We didn't run upon any other underground springs in our search."

Naomi was as certain as she could be and at the same time terrified that she might be wrong. Still, she insisted, "This has to be the place."

"Sometimes these hillside cave openings collapse," the sheriff suggested. "With the water coming out there, you can bet there's been an opening at one time."

"We need to get an excavator in here and start digging," Casey suggested.

"We'll likely run out of daylight before we can get set up," Sheriff Tanner warned.

"If you have the resources," Casey said, "let's get them in place so we can begin first thing in the morning."

"I'll make the call now," he assured.

Naomi walked closer to the small pool. The runoff from the pool traveled beyond her line of sight down the hillside. Even in the hottest part of summer there was water here. Sometimes in the winter ice would form on the pool. She remembered trying to skate on it and almost falling through.

She really had been too adventurous. Fearless, as Casey said.

She remembered all the times her father had to take her to the clinic and have her stitched up. Or to get a tetanus shot. Naomi was forever stepping on old rusty nails or ripping open a wound on some rock or what have you. The nurse who worked for her mother for as long as Naomi could recall would always say, "Uh-oh. Here comes trouble."

Nurse Sarah. Sarah Holland.

Naomi had forgotten about her. She always gave Naomi whatever shots she required. Sarah would whisper to Naomi that her mom couldn't bear to stick a needle into her little girl.

"Sheriff." She walked over to the man who'd just ended a call. "Do you know if Sarah Holland is still around?" Naomi hadn't heard anything about her or run into her since she'd been back in Winchester this past year.

"She is," Sheriff Tanner confirmed. "She's the administrator at the Happy Valley assisted living facility near the hospital."

"She was my mother's nurse when she had her clinic."

He smiled. "That's right. She came to the school on career day once when I was in high school."

Naomi walked over to where Casey was crouched by the pool. The way he studied the terrain she hoped he could see what she saw. Rocks and shrubs and secret places that ignited a child's imagination.

He pushed to his feet. "If there's anything here we'll find it."

She felt confident he only said this to make her feel better since the opening she recalled was nowhere to be seen. "There's a nurse who worked with my mom when she had her clinic. I'd like to go talk to her."

"We could go in the morning," he offered.

"You need to be here. My security detail can take me, right?"

"Sure. We can arrange that."

Anticipation fluttered in her belly. They could be getting closer to finding something useful in the search for answers. At least she hoped.

Happy Valley, 5:00 p.m.

HAPPY VALLEY ASSISTED living was one of the newer facilities in the Winchester area, Naomi learned as she waited to see Ms. Holland. According to the brochure on the lobby table, the facility was state of the art and the first of its kind in middle Tennessee. A very expensive and classy joint. Naomi was surprised. The rooms, if the photos in the brochure were any indication, were like high-end apartments only smaller. The shared dining room and kitchen were every bit as sleek and well-appointed as a five-star restaurant.

If a senior needed help with everyday living, this was the place to be.

"Ms. Honea."

Naomi looked up. "Yes."

The woman smiled. Her hair was gray, and she was now pleasantly plump, but Naomi recognized Sarah's face.

"Ms. Holland." She stood. "Thank you so much for making the time to see me."

"I'm sorry we haven't done this sooner. Let's go to my office."

Naomi followed her along the corridor to a large, airy office that overlooked the grand fountain out front.

"You've done a marvelous job of creating a sanctuary," Naomi said as she settled into the offered chair. "I'm amazed at how peaceful and lovely it is here. I'll bet you have a waiting list."

Smiling broadly, Ms. Holland nodded. "We do. We're very lucky that people have recognized and appreciated the priceless value of a place like this one."

Naomi figured the priceless part was the one sticking point.

Sarah's smile slipped into a frown. "I'm so sorry to hear about the horrors you're experiencing at the farm.

It truly is quite awful. Your mother would be beside herself. Is there anything I can do to help?"

"Actually, that's part of the reason I'm here. In all the years that you worked with my mom did she ever mention any issues at the farm? Maybe with any of the people who worked with my dad?"

Her mom had spent countless hours each evening after a long day at the clinic to help out on the farm. It hadn't seemed strange at the time. To a nine-year-old there was no difference between a doctor and a farmer. They were both jobs. But now she understood that what her mom did was above and beyond the call of duty.

Mrs. Holland pursed her lips. "You might not remember but one of the reasons your mother decided to work so hard with your father on the farm was because of Lanita Carlson. She was only four and she suddenly fell terribly ill. Your mother felt as though she didn't diagnose her in time to save her life. She never got past it. Every physician loses a patient eventually, but this one haunted her. She started to second-guess herself in everything she did. It was quite painful to watch. After you left for California, she actually spent more time on the farm than at the clinic. A nurse practitioner took care of the patients."

Naomi felt sick. "I had no idea."

"It wasn't something she wanted to talk about. Instead, she devoted herself more and more to the farm. Truth be told, your mother was the one who turned it around. Nolan, bless him, worked very hard to make a go of things. But he just wasn't as savvy as your mom. He had the vision but couldn't quite pull off the execution. Your mother really was a genius. To her way of thinking, the way to a healthy life stared with healthy eating."

"My dad seemed happy to have her with him in any capacity." Naomi didn't recall any tension between them, but she'd been a kid. She may not have noticed.

"He was thrilled. As I said, she was the brains behind the vision. With her help, he had the farm thriving in no time flat."

"Arlene Beck had been working for my dad for a good number of years already when my mother started pitching in. They seemed to work well together also."

"Arlene was another one who had cutting-edge ideas about how to elevate the farm to an organic farm. She and your mother became quite close, I think."

"I guess you heard she was murdered." It was ridiculous to think for a second she hadn't. The debacle at the farm was big news. National news.

Something flashed in Ms. Holland's expression. "It's all quite tragic. Your parents loved the farm. I know they would hate to see it torn apart this way."

On Naomi's watch at that. How had she allowed this to happen? Surely there were signs. Had she just not been paying attention?

"It's unsettling to say the least." Naomi considered how to best frame the next question. She'd already ventured into this territory but she needed to be sure. "When you were working together at the clinic, did Mom ever mention anything about Arlene? I don't recall there ever having been any issues at all."

"I can't think of a time when there was an issue. But

then, your mother was very private when it came to her personal life."

"Did you know Arlene very well? I haven't been able to figure out where she lived before Winchester. Or if she had any family I need to contact."

Ms. Holland frowned. "She was already here when I moved to Winchester. I suppose I've never thought of her as living anywhere else. I don't recall her ever saying."

"No accent that suggested a particular part of the country?"

Ms. Holland considered the question for a moment. "There was a bit of an accent. Nothing like ours down here. I assumed it had to do with where she'd been educated. These kids go off to college and come back talking like strangers."

Naomi could vouch for that scenario. She'd spent ages trying to conquer her Southern accent. "She never mentioned family or friends from somewhere else?"

"Not that I recall." She smiled, but the gesture was obviously forced. "I really didn't know Arlene well." She glanced at the clock. "Oh my, it's time for my next appointment. I hope we can chat again soon." She stood, broadening her plastic smile.

"Thank you for your time, Ms. Holland. Please let me know if you think of anything that might help us learn more about Arlene."

"Of course."

Naomi left with the strangest feeling that she'd said something that made the woman uncomfortable. She'd seemed fine until Naomi pushed the subject of Arlene. She hadn't wanted to go too deeply into that past.

Certainly it was possible she did have an appointment but no one had been waiting in the lobby as Naomi left. Or perhaps she simply didn't want to get involved in this bizarre case.

Maybe Donnie would have some insight into Ms. Holland's relationship with Naomi's mom and Arlene. Didn't hurt to ask.

Dogwood Apartments, 6:00 p.m.

DONNIE WAS SURPRISED to see Naomi again so soon. She was surprised herself. Her uncle wasn't one to keep in touch and Naomi hadn't really put forth the extra effort to try to change that reality. Frankly, she'd been a little busy.

"This is wild," Donnie said after listening to her rundown of the latest news. "You're saying Arlene's mother might have been some sort of war criminal?"

"I can't say for sure, but that's the way it looks so far. I'm having trouble accepting that Mom didn't know any of this. Dad might have overlooked it. You know he didn't like to get into people's business. But Mom was so keenly perceptive. I can't see her missing all this."

She thought of the story about the patient—the child—her mom had lost, and her heart ached. Why hadn't her mom ever talked about it? Had her dad known? What was worse, all these questions were making her doubt everything she thought she knew about her family. Naomi didn't like that feeling at all.

"I can't see it, either," he agreed. "Muriel was always the smart one. She was far too perceptive for anything to be happening around her and not recognize it. There's something off with all this, Naomi. I'm very concerned. Would you like me to come to the farm and stay with you for a while? It's not like I have anything pressing to do around here. The fresh air might even do me good."

"You're always welcome, Uncle Donnie." She thought of how Casey Duncan had slept on her couch and likely would tonight and instantly regretted having extended the invitation.

"Oh, snap," he muttered. "I did promise Heloise I'd look after Mr. Grumpy this weekend. She's going to visit her sister in Indiana. He's quite the feisty little pooch and her sister hates him. I'd have to come back and forth through the day and evening to take care of him."

"It's not necessary right now, Uncle Donnie. I have my own personal bodyguards."

"Just like a celebrity," he teased.

She rolled her eyes. "One more question," she ventured. "Do you know of anyone in the area who might have emigrated from Germany after the war? Anyone who might have known Arlene's mother?"

"You mean like a Holocaust survivor?"

"Yes, I suppose I do."

"There were a couple I remember reading about, but that was years ago. I can't recall their names."

"Maybe I could find something at the library?" If it was still open. Damn. She always seemed a day late and a dollar short.

"I'd call that lady who owns the newspaper, Audrey Tanner. She's the sheriff's wife. I'll bet she can tell you right off. I just remember that it was in the newspaper a while back."

Naomi started to go but decided she had another question or two.

"Do you think Arlene could have done something like this? I mean, really, was she so coldhearted?"

He stared at his clasped hands hanging between his knees. "You know, she was a little cold. Standoffish. Not with your folks, I don't think, but she rarely spoke to me." He chuckled. "Everyone likes me. But like I told you before, I sort of stepped on it where Arlene was concerned."

Naomi smiled. "You're just a likable kind of guy."

Her uncle gave her a half smile. "Try talking to Audrey over at the *Winchester Gazette*. She'll know if I'm recalling right."

Before leaving Naomi asked, "You remember that cave-like opening by the underground spring I used to talk about all the time? The one Mom told me time and time again to stay away from?"

"Sure do. I even went in it one time. I was hoping for lost treasure or hidden booty of some sort. But I didn't find anything at all."

"You could actually climb inside?"

"Yep. I saw it with my own eyes."

"There was only one on the farm, right?"

"As far as I know. Why do you ask?"

"We went out that way this afternoon and it must have fallen in or something."

"That's too bad. It was pretty cool once you got past the part that required you to belly crawl through it."

"Cool how?"

"It was a big room. Like a cavern. Seems weird that it would just fall in like that. But it happens. Usually something causes it."

Very weird, she agreed. She could only imagine what had caused it.

Something more to add to this horror story.

Tanner Home, 7:00 p.m.

THE *WINCHESTER GAZETTE* was closed so Naomi asked her driver, the deputy assigned to her security detail this evening, to drive her to the Tanner home. Casey had called to check on her—he was heading to the chief of police's office for a big conference call with all the entities involved with this ever-evolving case.

Just her luck to have the most bizarre criminal case to ever happen in Winchester. Her family would likely end up a part of some documentary.

Not at all the fame she'd hoped for when she ran off to Hollywood.

Naomi knocked on the front door of the Tanner home and waited. She was bone tired. When she got home she was having a long, hot shower to relax her muscles and her mind. Maybe some wine to take off the edge.

The door opened and a very pregnant blonde woman smiled at her. "Naomi Honea. Nice to finally meet you."

See, the sheriff's wife already knew her. "Likewise," Naomi offered.

She didn't know very much about Audrey except that her family had owned the local newspaper forever, it seemed. Like Naomi, Audrey had left Winchester to follow her own dreams but then returned to take over the family business.

They apparently had a good deal in common.

"Do you have a few minutes to talk?" Naomi asked, hoping her impromptu visit wouldn't be too much of an inconvenience.

"Sure. Come in. Colt is still at work but I'm on maternity leave and bored stiff."

Naomi hoped one day to have children of her own. That dream seemed a long way off these days.

"I'm sure Sheriff Tanner has filled you in on what's happening at the farm."

"To the degree that he can, yes. Please have a seat."

They settled into chairs facing each other near the fireplace.

"Has your paper in, say, the past thirty or so years done a story on Holocaust survivors living in the area?"

Audrey thought about the question for a bit. "We did. I think it was about ten years ago."

"Could you share names with me so that I might speak—?"

"I'm afraid they've both passed away since then. But I can round up next of kin for you if that would help."

"I'd appreciate it. I'm trying to make sense of all this and it's just not happening."

"Sometimes it doesn't until the final piece of the puzzle is discovered. I'll locate the information and text it to you."

They shared cell phone numbers and Audrey showed Naomi to the door. Back in the county cruiser she thought of how lonely life would be on the farm now. Her parents were gone. Arlene was gone.

If there was even a farm left when this was over.

Chapter Twelve

Honea Farm, 8:15 p.m.

Thirty-five minutes ago, Naomi had arrived home. Her first thought as she stood on the porch was, *What now?* All the official personnel and vehicles appeared to be gone for the day. Her surveillance detail had told her that Casey was still in the teleconference in town with the sheriff and the chief. A moment later as she entered the house, it occurred to her that it had been days since either of them had the opportunity for a decent meal. She had no idea why food even entered her mind. It certainly hadn't before now.

Even so, she rummaged through the fridge and the freezer to see what she had on hand. Stocking the shelves had been the last thing on her mind, but now, tonight, she was suddenly starving.

It was weird. Her emotions and senses had been in some sort of partial limbo and suddenly they were all roaring at once.

She was hungry. She was confused. She was alone. All of it swirled inside her like a cyclone.

Thankfully she dug up a box of frozen lasagna that was not out of date. Frozen rolls that only had to be browned and frozen green beans that could be steamed in the microwave. It wouldn't be five-star cuisine, but it would be edible.

She had forty-five minutes before the lasagna would need to come out of the oven. A shower was essential to her feeling human again. Sweats would be comfy. While the water in the shower heated up, she grabbed a comfy pair of sweats and fuzzy socks. The weather app on her phone alerted her to cooler than usual temps tonight. Since the rain set in, the weather had been unseasonably cool. Maybe she'd have her first fire of the season. One of the things she loved best about this old farmhouse was the big fireplace in the living room.

Wine, too. Definitely wine.

The water felt fantastic as she closed her eyes and allowed it to sluice over her body. For a long time she only stood there, allowing the heat to envelop and relax her. Her muscles loosened and the insanity of the day slowly started to drain away. She washed her hair, working her fingers over her scalp, massaging and kneading.

She continued on to her neck muscles, urging the tightness and the tension away. Before she could stop herself she imagined how it would feel to have Casey's long fingers and wide hands moving over her body this way. She sighed and smiled a secret smile.

Maybe it was the desperation she had felt for days now or the shock radiating through her again and again as each day brought some new harsh reality. Another stunning jolt…another murder. Somehow at this moment it coalesced into a need so strong she could hardly contain it.

She placed her hands against the cool shower walls and took slow deep breaths until control was hers once more. A few moments passed and she felt ready to face the world again. She refused to allow the events of this week to take her down. Her parents had worked too hard to make this farm what it was. She owed them her every effort to right things once more.

After drying her skin, she stood before the mirror and considered her hair. Wild and even redder when it was wet. She toweled it dry and applied the tiniest bit of product to stave off the frizzies. The sweats felt soft and warm and the fuzzy socks were the finishing touch.

Descending the stairs, the smell of lasagna filled the air. It wasn't homemade but it sure smelled good. Her stomach rumbled. She took the final step down and stalled.

A blast of cold air slipped around her, made her shiver. She walked to the front door and ensured it was fully closed. Then she headed for the kitchen. She froze in the doorway.

The back door stood open.

For three beats she couldn't move…couldn't even scream.

The timer sounded on the oven, shattering the eerie silence.

Naomi forced one foot in front of the other until she reached the door. She pushed it closed. Locked it.

Had she failed to shut it properly?

No. She had come through the front door. She hadn't touched the back door.

Someone had been in the house.

She reached into the pocket of her hoodie and closed her fingers around her phone. Then she went to the counter and pulled out the biggest knife in the block. The silver blade gleamed against the light.

With her back to the sink versus one or the other exits from the room, she moved to the stove and silenced the timer, then reached for the knob to turn off the oven.

It was already off.

She stared at the knob. Closed her eyes. Looked again. *Off.*

This was an old stove. Not one of the new ones that turned off the oven when the timer signaled. You had to manually turn off the stove. The timer was just a timer.

The blood pounding in her ears, she moved toward the front door. The deputy on duty was right outside. No more than a dozen yards from the porch. All she had to do was go outside and wave to him.

She backed across the living room, splitting her attention between the kitchen door, the hall and the stairs. Those were the only three usable routes to get to her… if someone was in the house.

Her back bumped the door. She reached behind her, flipped the lock. In one fast move she whirled around and pulled the door open. She was on the porch and moving forward. Didn't bother waving. She rushed down the steps and across the grass in nothing but her fuzzy socks. She didn't stop until she reached the deputy's car.

Where was he?

She moved closer. Peered through the window.

Empty.

She checked the back seat.

Nothing.

Fear pulsed in her veins.

Before she could consider another option, she got in behind the wheel and hit the lock button.

She called 911.

Honea Farm, 10:30 p.m.

CASEY BURST OUT of his SUV before it stopped rocking in the driveway. He rushed to the county cruiser. Naomi stared up at him, blue eyes wide with fear.

"Unlock the door," he said gently.

The click sounded and Casey pulled the door open. He grabbed her and pulled her out of the car.

Deputies and officers poured across the property to start the search for the missing deputy. The security detail who had apparently vanished.

"You okay?"

She nodded. Dropped the big knife she'd been clutching. It clattered on the ground. "I am now."

"Let's get you inside." He urged her forward, to the house.

By the time they reached the porch Tanner was coming through the door.

"House is clear."

"Thanks." Casey breathed a little easier.

Naomi looked from him to Tanner and back. "Where's the deputy who was here? The one who drove me home?"

Tanner gave her a nod. "Don't worry. We'll find him."

Inside the smell of marinara sauce reminded Casey that he hadn't eaten since before lunch. Didn't matter.

Naomi dropped into her chair and he sat down across from her. "Tell me what happened."

"I put food in the oven and went upstairs for a shower." She shivered. "When I came down the back door was open. I closed and locked it. Thought maybe I hadn't shut it properly. But the stove was turned off. I didn't turn it off. Then I realized I came in through the front door. I hadn't been near the back door since I came home. Someone was in the house while I was in the shower."

"Let's take a walk through and see if anything is missing."

"If something happened to the deputy or if he is dead…" A shudder quaked through her.

"Let's hope he's after whoever came into the house."

She nodded.

They moved from room to room, checking the closets, drawers, cabinets. In the downstairs study Naomi stopped.

"He was in here." She glanced around. "Assuming the intruder was a he."

"Can you determine if anything is missing or what he may have been looking for?"

"It'll take a minute."

"Take your time."

Tanner stuck his head in the door and Casey stepped into the hall to join him. "I hope we don't have another body." The count was already far too high, and they were no closer to finding the answers they needed.

"Almost. We found the missing deputy. He'll pull through but he took a hell of a blow to the back of the head. He spotted someone at the rear corner of the house and went after him. He didn't get a look at his face, just a general size. It was an ambush. Looks like it bought the perp some time to get into the house."

Damn it. "Keep me posted on the deputy's status."

Tanner assured him he would and headed back outside. Casey returned to the study to see if Naomi had discovered anything missing.

"The deputy's going to be okay?"

"Looks that way. He confirmed there was an intruder. Have you noticed anything missing?"

"I can't be certain, but it really looks like he only riffled through papers. Whatever he was looking for must not have been here."

"We'll check for prints," Casey said, "but chances are he protected his identity with gloves."

This was what they'd found throughout the lab and other areas of the property. No prints other than those of the people who worked there.

Within the hour the deputies and officers had cleared out for the night. Naomi had insisted on finishing the dinner and sitting down to a civilized meal. The bottle of wine surprised him.

"Would you like to share notes from our afternoons?" She tested a bite of lasagna.

"We found evidence to prove Cotton not only knew Arlene, but he had also been watching her for years. He left endless accountings of dates and codes. The final pages from the past month were all the same."

Naomi looked at him expectantly waiting for him to go on.

"'She has to die. She has to die. She has to die.' Every entry was exactly the same."

"Is it possible he killed her?" She lowered her fork back to the table. "He seemed so overwrought when I told him she was dead."

"Maybe he was upset because he felt we were on to him."

"But we weren't." She frowned. "So, if he was Arlene's killer, who broke into my house tonight?"

"A very good question to which I do not have an answer." He took a bite of lasagna and made a satisfied sound. "This is really good."

"Please. It came from a box in the freezer." She suddenly looked paler than usual. "I'll never be able to reach into the freezer and think nothing of it again."

He smiled reassuringly. "You seemed to have managed tonight."

"Maybe." She speared a green bean and brought it to her lips.

He watched with far too much interest. Caught himself and focused on his plate. "GPR picked up on some anomalies near your grotto so we're excavating a small location to have a look."

"GPR?"

"Ground-penetrating radar. It's a way of looking beneath the surface of a location without digging randomly."

"Wow." Emotions flickered across her face. "I'm beginning to wonder when this nightmare is going to end."

He understood this entire situation was incredibly overwhelming. Murder and puzzles like this were his work. Steps, routines and methods he went through with each case. For her, it was foreign, intrusive, more than a little scary.

"How about you?" he asked, moving on. "You learn anything useful today?"

"I talked to the nurse who worked closely with my mom when she had the clinic. She operates an assisted living facility now. She only had good things to say. She was unaware of any problems and didn't know Arlene very well. She did mention that Arlene had a bit of an accent in the beginning but not one she could readily identify."

"Sometimes you have to beat the bushes for a while before something pops out."

"No kidding." She sipped her wine. "I told my uncle what we had learned and suspected so far. He wasn't a lot of help, but he did mention that there were two Holocaust survivors in the Winchester area. I spoke to Audrey Tanner, the sheriff's wife. She owns the local newspaper. She confirmed what Uncle Donnie said, but unfortunately, the two had passed away. She's going to look up the names for me and get us the information."

"We should hear more from my sources in the Bureau tomorrow. I have my doubts as to whether this relates back to Beck's family history, but it's important that we thoroughly investigate every possibility."

"I guess the mob connection is more likely." She picked at her lasagna.

"You don't agree?" He sipped the wine. One glass was his limit.

"I'm not sure. It feels like this is bigger than the mob connection. Arlene is dead. Why keep coming back? Why murder Mr. Cotton?"

"If he was murdered," Casey countered.

"If," she agreed.

"The only reason for anyone to persist beyond her murder is if there's something more they need or want. Something she hid from them."

"So, we keep looking." She cradled her wineglass.

"We keep looking until we've done all we can to find answers. At this point we have at least six victims. I want to make sure it ends now."

From this point forward if he had to be away from her for any reason, he would have a second deputy or officer stand in his place. The risk was too great. Whoever was behind this business, he wasn't finished yet. He had come into this house with her here and alone and left without harming her. Casey would like to say that meant he had no intention of hurting her. But he wasn't fool enough to believe anything of the sort. Without a doubt, he was searching for something.

People who killed to accomplish a goal sometimes had rules, lines they didn't cross and even a modicum of honor. But those same people would typically do whatever necessary to protect themselves.

"I suppose when this case is over, you're off."

Casey watched her as she gingerly tasted another green bean. "Back to Nashville," he agreed.

"You have someone there?" She dared to look at him this time.

"My mom. My dad died a couple of years ago."

"I'm sorry to hear that."

"Thanks. And I have a sister—if you remember—who is bossy and nosy and better to me than I deserve."

A smile spread across Naomi's face. "I do remember her. Blonde? Very pretty? About sixteen that long ago summer?"

"That's the one. She's married, has four kids and thinks she knows everything. I cannot tell you the number of blind dates she has arranged for me. Generally, without my advance knowledge."

Naomi laughed out loud this time. "She sounds like a wonderful sister. She and your mother have probably got your wedding planned already. They just have to find the right bride."

"I'd lay odds on it."

They picked at their foot in silence. Casey imagined she was as exhausted as he was, but he wasn't ready to crash. He wanted to talk to her. To *be* with her.

"What about you?" he said. Turnabout was fair play, right?

"Me?" She shrugged. "I've been so busy with the farm I haven't had time to think about a personal life."

"You mean all the single guys in Winchester haven't been knocking on your door?"

"Are there single guys in Winchester? I'm pretty sure they're all taken. Not that I've been looking, mind you."

The pink blush that crept over her cheeks told him she wasn't entirely comfortable with the conversation.

Casey allowed another taste of his wine. "You just turned thirty, right?"

She made a face. "Is that supposed to mean something? Is my life over because I'm thirty and single?"

He held up his hands. "No, no. That's not what I meant at all."

"Good." She sipped her wine. "I can assure you I will never forget my thirtieth. I found human remains in my freezer."

"That's too bad. Definitely made for a memorable event."

"I'll get over it. As my father would say, just another day."

Except it wasn't just another day. It was a really bad day.

Casey stood, gathered his plate and glass and took them to the kitchen. Naomi trailed him. Without further conversation they cleaned up the kitchen and tossed the remains of dinner in the trash.

Naomi poured more wine and Casey wished he could indulge but he wouldn't take the risk. The sweatpants and hoodie sweatshirt made her look like a little girl.

"What are you smiling about?" She held up the bottle. "You want more?"

"I should pass."

She stared at him over the rim of her glass. "What's

the smile about? I swear, I can't think of a thing either of us has to smile about at the moment."

If he told her would she be flattered or annoyed? "I like the sweats. You look relaxed."

She tugged at the baggy top. "When I came home all I could think about was standing under the hot spray of water and getting into something utterly comfortable."

He had to remind himself to speak since his brain was still stuck on the image of her under that hot spray of water.

She set her glass aside. "Okay, I don't know if it's the wine or the insanity of the past few days driving me, but I have to do this. I cannot take it anymore."

He frowned. "What can't you take anymore?"

"Kiss me." She planted her hands on her hips. "I know you're feeling the attraction just like I am so let's get it over with. See if the real thing can stand up to the memory."

"You want me to kiss you?" he confirmed, his pulse already hammering.

"Only if you want to—if you're as curious as I am, then I'm certain you want to."

She had no idea.

He took her face in his hands, glided the pad of his thumb over her cheek. "I've dreamed of doing this again for a very, very long time."

He kissed her.

His lips melted into hers and the rush of sensations made it impossible to breathe.

He drew back just far enough to look into her eyes. "How's that?"

"I'm not sure. Can we do it again?"

A knock on the door sent them stumbling apart.

Grappling for his composure, he held out a hand for her to stay put. He walked to the window and checked the porch.

Deputy Lawton.

Breathing easier, he moved to the door and opened it just enough to hear what the man had to say.

"Just wanted you to know that I'm on for the night. You have any trouble you let me know."

"Keep your eyes open, Lawton," Casey warned. "I'm sure you heard what happened to the deputy earlier."

"Got it, Agent Duncan."

He turned on his heel and walked back to his car.

Casey closed the door and locked it.

When he turned back to Naomi she was standing at the bottom of the stairs.

"See you in the morning."

Then she was gone.

One thing was for sure. That long ago kiss didn't hold a candle to the one they'd shared just now.

The memory would haunt him for another twenty years.

Chapter Thirteen

Honea Farm
Friday, October 21, 6:00 a.m.

Casey had just poured his second cup of coffee when he got the word. He was needed at the excavation site. They'd found something.

He hadn't heard a sound from upstairs. He'd worried that when he showered she would wake up, but she hadn't stirred. It was late when she went to bed. Considering the recent events, he doubted she went to sleep immediately. Probably didn't sleep well, either. He'd wanted to follow her up those stairs last night something fierce. But she hadn't extended the invitation and he knew better.

At least they'd had that kiss. The memory warmed him.

Whatever happened when this investigation was done, he would think of that kiss for a very long time to come.

Casey found paper and pen in a drawer and left her a note to call when she was up. He pulled on his jacket and headed out the front door, locking it behind him. It was warmer this morning than last night. He hurried down the porch steps and to the cruiser parked next to his SUV.

The deputy powered down the window. "Morning, Agent Duncan."

Not Lawton. There must have been an early-morning shift change. Casey was surprised he hadn't knocked on the door to announce the change.

"Deputy." Casey gave him a nod. So far this week he'd met a different deputy for each shift. Except for Lawton. He'd showed up for the detail three or four times now. "I'm heading across the field to the excavation site. I'd like you to move to the front porch until Ms. Honea is up."

"Yes, sir."

While Casey loaded into his SUV, the deputy climbed the porch steps and took a seat in a rocking chair. Casey backed up, then turned toward the narrow dirt road that led deeper onto the property. He could drive most of the way. A ping warned he had a text message. He stopped and had a look.

Call me.

Casey put the SUV in Park and made the call to his ASAC. Assistant Special Agent in Charge Preston Wagner answered on the first ring.

"Duncan, this case just elevated to the highest priority."

Casey braced for whatever profound news he was about to receive. "I'm listening."

"Dental records and prints confirm your vic, Arlene Beck, was Anna Becker. Those numbers on the file jacket are showing up as foreign bank accounts that go back decades. There's a lot we don't know. But we were notified to stand down. I need you to wrap up and get back to Nashville."

"Wait—" Casey took a second to slow his frustration. "What does that mean, *stand down*?"

"You know what it means, Duncan."

"I know what it means," he growled. "I'm asking you in what capacity should I stand down on this one? We have multiple homicide victims and no confirmation that they're all related. If—"

"It means that whatever you find, it has nothing to do with Becker or that history. It means this is bigger than the Bureau and a task force will be taking over."

"Give me the day at least," Casey argued. "There are loose ends to tie up here."

"I can give you that," Wagner agreed, "but you cannot move forward on this investigation. It's above our pay grade."

"I can live with that," Casey relented. "But I want to know how did this Anna Becker end up in Franklin County, Tennessee, as Arlene Beck?"

"I don't know much," Wagner admitted, "but I know that after the death of her mother, Becker—Beck—disappeared. She was the one to turn her mother in to the authorities. I have no idea why and probably never will. Before the authorities could move in on her mother—Ursula Becker—she was murdered. The daughter was never heard from again. It was assumed that the daughter was dead, as well. Apparently, that was not the case."

"Thanks. I appreciate that much." He had a feeling this information explained a lot more than maybe Wagner understood.

"Duncan, I know this isn't what you want to hear, but the order came from above."

"Got it." Casey ended the call before more could be said. No need to give the man time to toss out any other restrictions.

Casey had never been one to break the rules. But this was different. He wasn't going to pretend he didn't know what he knew. He damned sure wasn't leaving Naomi in the dark when she deserved far more. This was her home. Her family.

When he reached the grotto, the excavator sat dormant, but judging by the amount of dirt and rock lying in a pile to one side, the digging had been going on for a while this morning. He was glad he hadn't gotten the call from Wagner before the excavation began. Maybe they'd uncovered more pieces of the puzzle Naomi would need to get on with her life.

Whatever was going on, he wanted the whole story. He wanted to protect Naomi from anything that might be coming. Hell, at this point they still had no idea who the bad guy was.

Casey parked and headed for the half a dozen people huddled around the open pit that had been unearthed just above the pool of water below. One of the team members, Ted Letson, glanced up at him and shook his head. When Casey reached the other agent and had a look into the pit for himself, he understood the reaction.

What the hell?

In the pit was a pickup and a car. Both were damned rusty and bent up from being dumped into the pit and then covered with dirt. The vehicles looked to be thirty or more years old.

“One of the Franklin County deputies who is licensed in cave rescues,” Letson explained, “is down there trying to locate a license plate on one or both vehicles. He had his gear in his truck, so we let him have at it.”

Casey snapped a pic. “You called Tanner or Brannigan?”

“On the way. Called them right after I called you.”

Casey opted not to mention his conversation with Wagner. He intended to push forward as far as possible before the new investigators arrived.

“Yo!” the deputy in the pit called out.

“What have you got?” Letson called back.

“We got bones in both vehicles. Like entire skeletons. One in each.”

More victims. At least two. Damn. Casey said, “We need a bigger forensics team.”

“I think you’re right,” Letson agreed. “I’ll call Wagner.”

“Don’t worry about Wagner. Call Jensen directly. He’ll get someone down here ASAP.”

Rule break number one. Wagner would not be happy when he found out.

Letson made the call. While he did, Casey removed

his jacket and donned the proper gear. He was going down there. Every minute they wasted put them closer to being shut down. He'd made a promise to Naomi that he'd find answers for her. He wasn't going to let her down.

Casey used the same ladder rope the deputy had put in place to make his way down to the vehicles. The car appeared to have been dumped on top of the pickup. The scent of disturbed soil rose up and filled his nostrils.

"Have a look," the deputy said as Casey found his footing atop the car.

The driver of the car was still strapped into the driver's seat. Like the deputy said, the skeleton remained intact. The clothes were mostly rotted away, but a pearl necklace hanging from the neck area suggested the remains were female.

"Can we get a good look into the cab of the truck?" Casey asked.

"It landed kind of canted to one side so there's a good slice of cracked window right beneath the right front tire of this car."

Casey slipped down lower to a crevice where dirt had not filled in around the truck.

"Be careful," the deputy said. "I don't think this car will move, but you never know."

"Got it." Casey eased closer to the blue truck's driver side window. It was necessary to force his head into the small area between the car and the truck to see inside. Another set of bones. Mostly intact. No seat belt this time. The bones lay against the passenger side door as if the victim had been slung there when the truck landed in the hole. Like the other victim, the clothes were mostly gone, but a good portion of a set of sneakers remained. He was only guessing, but judging by the length and width, this was likely a male victim.

His assessments would need to be confirmed but he was usually on the money.

"I can make out part of the car's license plate," the deputy called out to him.

Casey climbed back in that direction using the occasional rock protruding from the earth and parts of the vehicle's undercarriage.

"I can see the first number but nothing after that."

Casey looked around. "Let me climb over the quarter panel and see if I can get a shot with my cell phone."

The deputy pushed on the car. It rocked ever so slightly. "Better be careful, this thing is not as stable as it looks."

"With that in mind," Casey said, "you get back on the ladder while I do this."

"I'm not sure," the deputy began, "it—"

Casey shot him a look that warned this was not a debate. The deputy moved back to the ladder and climbed up a couple of rungs.

When the deputy was safely out of the way, Casey moved up onto the vehicle. The car rocked slightly, and he stilled to wait for it to settle. Then he started to move again. When he was lying facedown across the quarter panel over the rear tire, he slid just far enough to lower his arm between the rear end and the dirt wall. He took a couple of pics and checked the screen.

He got half the license plate, but he needed the whole thing.

He slid on his belly, moving closer to the bumper, and reached deeper this time. Angled his phone a little more.

The car moved.

This time it didn't stop.

Honea Farm, 7:00 a.m.

NAOMI SPREAD THE covers over her bed.

She'd smelled the coffee and roused half an hour ago, but she hadn't wanted to go down and face Casey just yet. It was silly, she knew, but she was a little embarrassed about having insisted he kiss her.

Sleep had eluded her last night. Between finding Mr. Cotton hanging from that tree and…

Good grief, how could this all be happening? Murders rarely happened in Franklin County. Suddenly the homicide rate had quadrupled and her farm was the primary crime scene. It was totally crazy. Beyond crazy.

She walked down the hall and paused at the door of her parents' room. Surely they had no idea all this was happening.

But how could they not? It wasn't just one thing, it was so many things. So many bodies. So many puzzling pieces. The hidden money. The strange strings of numbers. The remains in the freezer. A human head in a box!

Still, big questions remained. Where were the bones? Who did this? Why? Beyond the money obviously.

She thought of Arlene and all the years she had been

part of this family. Other than Sarah Holland, her mom's nurse, Arlene was the closest friend her mom had. Between the farm and her mom's medical clinic, her parents basically knew everyone in town, but they were busy people. Always working either at the clinic or on the farm. There was the occasional community function to which her parents felt obligated to attend but there wasn't a lot of socializing. Hellos and updates were provided in passing at the Piggly Wiggly or the Farmer's Co-op.

Naomi wondered if the lack of close friends was related to all this somehow.

No. No, her parents had nothing to do with any of this. The idea was ludicrous.

She moved away from their door and headed downstairs. The coffeepot was calling her name. She hoped Casey had received an update that answered questions rather than piled on more.

The final step down, she called out, "Good morning."

Footsteps in the kitchen drew her in that direction. At the door she almost bumped into a deputy.

"Morning, ma'am."

She blinked. Scrambled to recall his name. "Good morning, Deputy Lawton. Sorry, I was expecting Agent Duncan."

"He got a call to go out to the excavation site, ma'am," Lawton explained. "He asked me to stay in the house since you were still asleep. He's a little worried after last evening's scare."

So was she. She pushed a smile into place. "Well, all right, then. I am dying for a cup of coffee."

"Just made a fresh pot. The other was a little stale."

"Thanks." Casey had likely made coffee before daylight. A fresh pot was a good thing.

She poured a cup and savored a long, warm swallow before moving back into questioning mode. She leaned against the counter and turned her attention to the deputy. "Have they found something near the pool?"

"I'm afraid I haven't heard anything specific, only that they needed Agent Duncan there." He, too, leaned against the counter on the opposite side of the kitchen.

Naomi enjoyed more of her coffee. Lawton's cell phone made a sound and he pulled it from his belt and checked the screen. News, she hoped.

"Looks like they have found something, ma'am." He put his phone away. "Sheriff Tanner says the two of us should have a look around here. See if we find any old keys. They found an old car and old truck buried out there by that underground spring."

Naomi's breath caught. "Oh my God. How is that possible?"

"I don't know, ma'am." He shrugged. "Sometimes our folks don't tell us all they know. They keep secrets. I suppose they think it's for the best, but it usually turns out to be not good at all."

No kidding. Naomi set her cup aside. "It's the craziest thing I've ever seen. I always considered my parents very honest people. I can't believe they were keeping secrets like this. And Arlene." She shook her head. "It's just stunning that she did the things it appears she did. I still can't fully believe it. Did you know her?"

Lawton shook his head. "Not really. I mean, I've

seen her around, but I didn't know her. One of the other deputies told me she was cutting people off the bone. Wonder what happened to all those bones?" His eyes bugged out a little. "And I heard about that box with the head in it. You're right. That's pretty dang crazy."

"I've tried to think of where she might have hidden the bones, but it's possible she sold the bones to a buyer on the red market. I'm sure you've heard of the red market."

"I've heard talk about it," he said, "but I don't know much. It's not something you like to think about. And we don't get a lot of that kind of thing around here. There was that one time Chief Brannigan discovered an employee at the funeral home was taking things—pieces—from folks they prepared for burial."

Naomi had almost forgotten the incident. She supposed it was possible there was a connection. She straightened away from the counter. "Shall we start the search? Keys, you say?"

"He said keys and I guess it wouldn't hurt for us to look for any kind of hiding place we can find. Like you say, those bones have to be somewhere."

She would certainly rather be doing something than standing around waiting for more bad news. "Sure. You're probably more of an expert than me. Where would you suggest we start?" She had checked all the places in the house she could think to look already. But then she was so close emotionally to this, it was hard to know if she had been thorough enough.

"We can start at the top and work our way down.

I've found that's usually the best. Could be a trap door or a hidden room."

Naomi managed a smile. "See, I knew you would have better ideas. I didn't really consider a secret door *or* room."

She shook herself as she trudged up the stairs. These were her parents they were talking about. Would her parents really have a secret room of some sort they hadn't told her about?

At this point she wasn't sure of anything anymore.

What if she never knew the whole truth?

The thought shuddered through her like a mini earthquake. She didn't want to feel this uncertainty about her parents for a minute longer than necessary.

She stopped at the door to their room, couldn't help the guilt that sheared through her. "This is their room."

"First we check behind anything hanging on the walls and under anything in the room."

"No need to go through the drawers?" She was surprised he didn't want to start there.

"You probably already looked through those."

She nodded. "I did."

"Well, there you go. You check under the bed and under chairs and side tables. I'll take the closet."

"Got it." Naomi got down on all fours and started with a visual search under the bed.

Once she had moved aside shoeboxes and dust bunnies she confirmed there was nothing under the bed but dusty hardwood floor. One by one she dragged the bedside tables away. Nothing on the floor or the wall where they had stood. With that in mind, she went to the footboard and tugged until she slid the headboard a few inches from the wall. She inspected that area as well and found nothing but plaster. Pulling the narrow rugs on either side of the bed aside, she found nothing there, either.

There was a chair on each side of the bed. Her parents each had their own chair for reading or taking off shoes at night. Just in case, she removed the cushions and found nothing. Then she also pulled the covers back on the bed and checked there, then under the mattress all the way around. It was fairly easy to lift each side as she moved around the bed.

Back to the chairs. She turned them over, checked the floor beneath them and the bottoms of the chairs.

Since Deputy Lawton was still in the closet, she decided to remove the drawers in the night tables and check under them. After that she did the same with the dresser drawers. She had looked in all the drawers, but she hadn't pulled them out or looked at their bottoms.

By the time she'd finished she had drawers scattered on the floor all over the room. She'd even pulled the dresser from the wall and checked behind it.

Deputy Lawton came out of the closet. He glanced around. "I think we can call this room clear."

Naomi nodded. "What's next?"

He lifted his eyebrows. "Your room?"

"This way." Naomi led the way to her room and started the same process.

"You sure you don't mind me digging around in your closet?" The deputy looked a little skeptical.

"Have at it." At this point Naomi had nothing to hide and doubted anything would embarrass her.

While he started on her closet, she took the same steps with her bed and the rest of the furniture in the room as she had in her parents' room. Like before, she found nothing. The deputy found nothing. They moved on to the guest room and the two bathrooms.

With no luck on the second floor, they moved downstairs.

Naomi checked her phone repeatedly. Nothing from Casey. She'd sent him a couple of text messages to see how it was going. It hadn't been that long, maybe an hour since she and the deputy had started searching. Hopefully, she would hear something soon. One of his fellow agents, Letson, had called to check in with her a little bit ago and he'd assured her Casey would be in touch soon.

The bathroom and hall closet downstairs were the same as upstairs. Dusty but little else that wasn't expected. Nothing in the study, either.

The living room took only ten minutes since there was no closet and only a few drawers in the side tables.

Naomi sat her hands on her hips and surveyed the disarray. "Should we move into the kitchen or take a break?"

Deputy Lawton's face was red and he seemed to struggle for a breath. "No, no, I'm good. Let's keep going." He checked his phone.

"News?" She sure hadn't gotten a word from anyone.

"Just checking the time. Does the house have a basement? A lot of these old houses do."

Basement? She shook her head. "If there's a basement I've never seen it or heard my parents mention it. As many storms as we spent time hunkering in this downstairs closet, I feel like if there was a basement we would have been there instead."

No basement for sure.

He nodded thoughtfully. "How about in the barn? Any hiding places you remember as a child?"

"We can check." She wanted to be cooperative. "I remember climbing around in the loft, horsing around in the stalls. But not much else."

"Your daddy had a workshop."

"I'm sure the forensics technicians went through the shop and the barn, but we can have a look if you'd like." Even a trained specialist could overlook something.

"I think that's a good idea. Do we need keys for the shop?"

"Yes." She crossed the kitchen and reached into a cabinet for the old stoneware saltbox. It was empty save for a few keys. It was also an antique.

"Well, I'll be," Lawton said, pushing his cap up a little off his sweaty forehead. "Who would have thought of looking for a key in an old saltbox?"

"Dad said there was no use making things easy for thieves."

"Your daddy was a smart man."

The deputy followed Naomi out the kitchen door and toward the workshop. She glanced across the fields, wishing she'd hear something from Casey. He usually stayed in touch.

Usually.

That was a stretch. They'd only met on Tuesday and this was Friday. Their meeting nineteen years ago didn't actually count. Well, maybe a little.

Once the shop was unlocked, she and Deputy Lawton spread out and started the search. The place smelled of grease and tools. Her father had one of most anything one might need to work on the old farm equipment and the buildings. He never threw anything away.

They checked all the shelves—the wall lockers, Deputy Lawton called them. They looked like metal cabinets with doors to Naomi, but she would take his word for that.

"What about that?" Lawton asked. "Has it always been there?"

He pointed to the ancient hydraulic lift. When she was a kid, her dad would drive his truck or her mom's car onto the lift and send it up into the air for changing the oil and any other maintenance that required going under the car. Her dad had always been a little claustrophobic. She couldn't help smiling at the thought. He had gotten trapped in a closet when he was a child and he never could stand to be shut up in a small space again. It was his one fear. Otherwise, her daddy had always been the bravest man she knew.

"It has." She shrugged. "At least as long as I can remember."

"You don't mind if we check it out?"

She shrugged. "Go ahead. It might not even work. Dad hasn't done his own maintenance like that in years." Age changes everything.

Deputy Lawton crossed to the little door on the wall.

Her dad had put the control in a sort of electrical breaker box that could be locked. He didn't want Naomi or any of her friends messing around with it.

He picked through the keys they'd taken from the saltbox and unlocked the panel. He pressed the necessary button and with a low growl the lift started to rise.

When it was about halfway up, four or so feet off the floor, Naomi blinked, stared at the concrete floor again.

What in the world?

Instead of just two tracks that car tires usually sat on, a portion of the concrete went up with the two tracks.

Now, with that section up in the air, there were stairs going down.

"Has that always been that way?"

Naomi shook her head. "I have no idea. I've never seen it before."

"Come on." He pulled a flashlight from his utility belt. "Let's have a look."

Chapter Fourteen

Excavation Site, 10:00 a.m.

Casey held stone-still while the crane struggled with the weight of the car.

He was trapped.

When the car moved, he had slid down between the truck and the bottom of the pit. The car had tipped and then wedged over him. He had no idea where his phone had landed.

More than an hour had been spent trying ways to dig him out, but the consensus was any additional dislodging of dirt would only send the car further off balance. Now a crane had been brought in to extract the car from the pit.

Letson had checked on Naomi half an hour ago and she and the deputy on detail were searching the house again.

She was fine. Safe. Keeping herself occupied.

The problem was, Casey was between a rock and a hard place.

Metal whined and the crane strained as the car

started to move. Casey eased deeper against the dirt wall. The smaller he made himself, the less of a target he would be if something went wrong.

The noise ceased.

Casey braced for bad news.

"You still okay down there, Duncan?"

"I'm good."

"All right, then. The car is a few inches above the truck so we're going for it."

"Let's do it!" Casey called back.

The whining and groaning began again. Casey steeled himself and waited it out.

Another few inches of space appeared between the car and the truck. Casey relaxed just a little. Another foot, then a second one. Now they were getting somewhere.

The sound of metal shearing jerked his attention upward. The car was a good four feet above the truck now, but something had torn.

Rusty metal ripped.

The car dropped.

Casey covered his head with his arms.

Shouting above.

Silence.

Casey looked up. The car had stopped. They'd only lost about fifteen inches, but could they go any farther?

"Duncan!"

"Yeah?"

"The guys up here are worried the metal is going to tear even more if we keep pulling the car upward. We're thinking you should try to get out of there. Fast, man. Really fast."

"I'm coming."

Casey scrambled up from the ground and over the hood of the truck. He'd made it to the other side of the pit where the ladder hung when one end of the car dropped, slamming into the hood of the truck.

Damn. That was close.

"Get outta there." Letson was at the top of the ladder waving him up.

Metal screaming, Casey propelled himself up the ladder and out of the pit. He sat on the ground and watched as the car dropped completely onto the truck.

Letson clapped him on the back. "The good news is while the car was in the air I got a shot of the license plate. The numbers were readable. Alabama tag, thirty-one years old. Hopefully we'll have the owner's name soon."

Casey stood, dusted himself off. "I should get back to the house, check on Naomi."

"Naomi?" Letson echoed, his eyebrows raised.

"Ms. Honea," Casey amended, not appreciating the man's pointed question.

"Duncan!"

He turned to Tanner, who was jogging in his direction. Damn. He hoped there hadn't been another body found.

Worse, Wagner may have called Tanner and informed him they were to back off and wait for whoever the Bureau was sending to continue this complicated investigation.

"I just received some interesting news from Rowan," Tanner said as Casey met him a few yards from the pit.

Rowan was Chief Brannigan's wife, the coroner. Casey said, "Something I hope will fill in some of the missing pieces on this one." The case had just taken another complicated turn with the find in the pit. Two more victims who had been missing for at least three decades.

"When I was bringing Rowan up to speed on this business with Beck/Becker and Cotton yesterday, she got a hunch and had some lab work done. You know, she used to work with Nashville Metro. She made a lot of invaluable contacts. Anyway, she got one of her friends at a private lab to run DNA comparison for us on Cotton and Beck."

Judging by the excitement in Tanner's voice, Casey figured this was big news. He needed a turning point. He was running out of time.

"Elmer Cotton," Tanner went on, "and Arlene Beck are siblings."

"That is an interesting turn of events. Considering the age difference, if Ursula Becker is the mother, then she had another child after arriving in this country."

"Makes me wonder if Cotton decided his sister was too evil to live. Maybe he killed her and then himself to end the line."

"A definite possibility," Casey agreed.

Now the question on Casey's mind was how did Arlene Beck entwine herself so deeply in the Honea family? Were she and Naomi's mother related somehow? Of like mind? Or maybe it was the dad, Nolan. It was becoming more and more difficult to believe they had nothing to do with all that was happening on their farm.

Casey stared at the pit. Digging that pit, transporting the vehicles with the bodies inside, had taken teamwork. Careful organization. And complete trust.

Based on the age of the vehicles and the time frame they were buried, Naomi either hadn't been born or was a little baby. A hell of a lot had been hidden from her all these years.

The need to talk to Naomi was stronger now. "I should go back to the house and give Naomi an update."

The distant *whomp whomp* filled the air. The sound drew Casey's and Tanner's gazes to the sky. A helicopter came into view, lowering as it neared their location.

"Friends of yours?" Tanner shouted over the din.

Casey spotted Wagner in the passenger seat as the helicopter sat down in the middle of the field. He decided not to mention it was probably trouble. Instead, he nodded. "Yeah, the assistant special agent in charge."

Tanner looked from Casey to the helicopter. "I guess he has something important to say since he made such a grand entrance."

Casey made a sound of agreement. No doubt. He strode toward the helicopter as it powered down. Wagner jumped out and hunkered down as he rushed to meet Casey. This was probably not going to be pleasant.

The engine shut down and silence fell over the field. Deputies and agents watched, waiting for whatever orders the brass was about to relay.

"Duncan," he said when they came to a stop a few feet apart.

Casey gave him a nod. "Wagner."

"I couldn't reach you by phone and this was too important to wait. Between the State Department and various other agencies, we've been ordered to turn over all evidence ASAP. I need your team to pull out now. Locals, as well. I believe I mentioned this in our previous conversation. I had a feeling—" he glanced at the excavator "—you might have some difficulty extracting yourself from the scene. I thought I'd give you a hand."

"This was already happening when we had our previous conversation." Casey gestured to the crowd gathered. "There was a bit of a glitch and I haven't had a chance to pass along your order."

Wagner appeared to let that go. "We should sit down with the locals and debrief."

"You can say whatever it is you've got to say now, sir." Tanner moved up next to Casey. "I'm Franklin County sheriff Colton Tanner." Rather than extend his hand, he planted both on his hips. "Coming there—" he nodded to the cowboy striding toward them like a character out of an old Western movie "—is Chief of Police William Brannigan. We're more than happy to hear what you've got to say, but this is our town, our case. We won't be shutting anything down."

Wagner looked to Casey and he shrugged. He wasn't about to give an assist on this one. Whatever had happened here, Tanner and Brannigan had a right to have the full story. Their community deserved the full story.

While Brannigan and Wagner were discussing how they could all proceed together, Casey intended to slip away and check on Naomi. "Can you give me a ride back to the house?"

"Sure thing," Tanner said. "We should bring Naomi up to speed."

They loaded into the sheriff's truck and headed back across the field.

"It's wild how you can know someone your whole life and never suspect what they might be hiding," Tanner commented. "I guess even being a lawman doesn't make you immune to deception."

"Being a lawman just makes it harder when you discover you've been deceived," Casey commented. "You feel like you should have seen it when no one else did. But we are only human."

Casey relaxed when he saw the county cruiser parked in the drive next to Naomi's pickup. But he wouldn't be satisfied until he laid eyes on her. She was the biggest victim of all in this mess. She had been deceived by everyone around her.

Inside, the house was empty. Casey's guard went up. "She said she and the deputy on detail were searching the house again." Though this looked a little intense, maybe she'd reached her limit on patience. Naomi wanted answers more than anyone.

"Let me give my guy a call and find out where they are."

Casey would breathe easier when he knew where she was. He waited while Tanner made the call. When he frowned and ended the call, he said, "No answer."

They walked back outside and to the cruiser. Tanner looked it over, glanced inside. "I thought Higgins had detail this morning, but this is Lawton's vehicle."

Worry niggled at Casey. "I was going to ask—there's been a different deputy on detail every shift except for

Lawton. He's covered several shifts this week. Is he one of your most trusted deputies?"

"They're all trusted," Tanner said as he put through another call on his cell. "Lawton volunteered for extra shifts because his sister is a longtime friend of the Honea family. She was Dr. Honea's nurse for years."

"Is that right? He never mentioned it." Casey thought about all Naomi had said about her mom's clinic. "As a matter of fact, Naomi didn't, either. She mentioned the nurse but not the connection to Lawton."

An uneasy feeling welled in his chest. Casey had to force himself to hold still while Tanner did what he had to do.

Tanner ended the call he'd made. "Lawton's not picking up, either." The sheriff made a third call then, ordering someone on the other end to find Deputy Higgins. He surveyed the parked vehicles in the driveway before turning his attention back to Casey. "Naomi's vehicle is here. So is Lawton's. Let's operate under the assumption they're both on the grounds somewhere."

"I'll get my people over here searching." Casey reached for his phone, realized he didn't have it.

Tanner nodded. "I'll have my people bring your people." He made another call. "While I'm at it, I'm having Lawton's sister picked up and brought over here. I think we need to talk to her. Clear up this confusion."

Casey was fairly convinced there was no confusion. Only desperation.

"I CAN'T BELIEVE THIS."

Naomi had been pouring through ledgers for the past half hour or more. Arlene kept precise notes on every incoming "product" and each sale. Naomi was equally stunned and horrified.

She looked up, surveyed the rows and rows of glass containers. Each held carefully stored bones. Every imaginable human bone. All carefully cleaned, from the looks of them, and stored. The room—basement, whatever it was—was climate controlled. It wasn't that large, maybe twelve feet by twenty feet. Spotless, immaculate. The floors, the walls and the ceiling were white. Boxes of gloves sat on a table, she suspected for handling the bones.

"It's pretty incredible," Deputy Lawton said. "Can you imagine how long it took to build a collection like this?"

Naomi stood from the desk and moved toward the wall of bones. "I can't even imagine."

"The prep area is state of the art," he pointed out.

She turned to the opposite side of the room. He was right. Stainless-steel tables and sinks. Refrigerator, supply shelves. How on earth had this room gotten here without her parents' knowledge? It just didn't make sense.

"I don't understand," she murmured. "How is this possible?"

"I'll bet it took lots of money."

Naomi glanced at the deputy. He seemed astonished, as well. Who wouldn't be?

"My parents couldn't have been part of this. It's impossible. They would never do this."

"You're right," Deputy Lawton agreed. "It takes a certain kind of person." He tapped his temple. "A certain genius, too."

Naomi wasn't sure she would call it genius, but she understood what he meant. Maybe. She walked back to the desk and opened more of the drawers. Arlene had been meticulous in her record keeping. The buyers were recorded as numbers. Now all Naomi needed was the key to the numbers. The buyers should go down for their heinous parts in this, too. She thought of the numbers on that file folder. There had to be a connection. Now that she thought about it, the patterns were similar.

"What you looking for?"

She glanced up. "There should be a key or a legend somewhere that tells us who the buyers are or what these numbers mean. I'm certain the FBI will want to round up the buyers, too."

"I can't let you do that, Naomi."

She looked up from the middle drawer. "What?" She must have misheard him.

"You see." He sat his hand on his service weapon and started toward her. "My sister and I have worked a very long time to help build this business. We started a very long time ago, but it wasn't until we met Arlene that everything clicked. She truly was a genius. It's a shame her disturbed brother thought he had to save the world from her. We told her to get rid of him a long time ago, but she wouldn't." He laughed, a deep one that shook his round belly. "Can you image, she couldn't bear the idea of killing her brother when she did all this." He waved his free hand around the room. "Oh, and far more. You have no idea all the things she did."

Naomi backed away from the desk.

He continued coming toward her.

As much as she wanted to charge him and try to get past him, the gun be damned, she desperately needed him to keep talking. She needed to know the truth.

"How did she hide it from my parents? I can't believe they missed all of this." She looked around the room. "It's too much." He only grinned. So, she took a different tactic. "Maybe I'm wrong. It must have been my mother. She was a *true* genius. I'll bet she's the one who arranged everything. The mastermind. Arlene probably took orders from her."

Fury tightened his face. "Oh, no. Poor Muriel was like you, she believed the best in everyone. But then she let herself get in the way." He shrugged. "She may have gotten a little suspicious, but Sarah took care of that. Did you know there are certain chemicals you can add to a person's food and drink that will cause cancer? Really fast, fatal cancer."

Pain followed immediately by outrage roared through Naomi. "Are you saying she poisoned my mother?"

He shook his head, grinning like a fool. "I said no such thing. But while she was sick and with you so far away, it was easy to set all this up. To expand the business. We took every opportunity to construct the things we needed but after you moved to California your parents just didn't take vacations the way they used to. A couple of days here or there but nothing extended. Your father wouldn't leave her side in those last months. We accomplished a lot during that time."

Ice slid through her veins. "What about my dad?" Every fiber of her being screamed in pain at the idea of what this man—this monster—was telling her.

"For a long while he only muddled through, allowing Arlene to do as she pleased, but then he started to get a little nosy. Maybe it was all those extra deposits she made for him. He started to wonder where she was getting all that extra cash."

Her heart seemed to rip apart in her chest.

"Exchanging his heart medication for something stronger was simple. Took no time at all. He didn't suffer. Not the way your mother did. It was too bad, but it was the best way to do it, my sister said. No one is ever suspicious of cancer and, you know, heart attacks happen all the time."

For the first time in her life, Naomi wanted to hurt someone. No, rage exploded in her chest—she wanted to…

What she wanted didn't matter. She had to find a way to escape. Casey and Sheriff Tanner needed to know what had happened here. They needed to stop these people. Otherwise, her parents would end up being blamed in the end.

She would not allow their reputations to be destroyed.

She held up her hands to stop his advancement. "Just tell me what you want. The farm? What? They're probably going to blame my parents, anyway. I'll just go back to California and never look back. We all get what we want."

Another of those deep rumbling laughs burst from his throat. "Don't try pulling that on me. I've got your number, lady. My only job was to find this place. You see, Arlene didn't trust us completely. She liked hiding certain things like the records." He nodded to the desk. "And the money. She doled it out like she was the only one in control. All I have to do now is set this place on fire and leave you to burn up with the evidence of our buyers."

She had to get out of here. "But what about the money? Don't you want it? I know where she hid the money."

His gaze narrowed. "Don't lie to me."

Obviously Sheriff Tanner and Chief Brannigan had not briefed all their deputies and officers about the find at High Street. Thank God.

"You remember where I found that head in the box?" She held her breath. Prayed he would believe her.

"'Course. I heard about that. I'm a deputy, after all."

"Well, what I didn't tell anyone was that I found money, too." She shrugged. "I didn't know what was going to happen with all this and I thought I might need to run away if the police tried to blame me. So I hid the money. It's a lot of money. A whole lot of money."

He studied her a moment. "I don't believe you."

"It's in bundles. All small denominations. A whole lot of money." She emphasized the last part.

"Where did you put it?" His fingers tightened around the butt of his weapon.

"I'll show you, but I'm not telling you. And you already know it's not in my house. I'll bet you've checked the barn and the lab."

His lips pursed with anger. "Tell me or I'll kill you now." He drew his weapon.

She shrugged. "Then I guess you'll never get your

hands on the money because you will never find where I hid it. Never in a million years."

For a moment she was certain he wasn't going to go for it, then he motioned with his gun. "Let's go. You do anything I don't like, and you'll regret it."

She nodded.

"First, take out your cell phone. Turn it off and leave it on the desk."

She hated to give up her cell but if it got her out of here, she would have a far better chance of survival. She took it from her pocket and turned it off as requested and then placed it on the desk.

"This way." He motioned with his gun again.

She moved in front of him. She should have known something was wrong when he lowered the hydraulic lift after they came down the stairs. But the sight of all those bones had thrown her off balance.

No problem. He had to raise it again for them to get out. When he did and they got to the top of the stairs she was running, gun or no.

Rather than go to the stairs and press the button behind the locked glass panel, he went to the cabinet next to the sink. He opened the doors and checked inside, then moved around the wall on that end of the room, sliding his hand over the white surface. What the hell was he doing?

"There it is." He stood back and watched as a panel opened in the wall.

Okay, this was too much.

"I thought you didn't know where this place was." What a liar!

"I didn't, but my sister said Arlene talked about it all the time and the escape tunnel she installed." He hitched his head toward the wall of bones. "I figured it probably wasn't there or behind the desk where all the files are. This was just a guess." He gestured to the small opening. "Ladies first."

"Why don't we just go out the way we came in?" This is not how she had planned this happening.

"Your FBI friend is probably back at the house by now. For all we know, the place could be crawling with feds and cops."

Exactly what she'd hoped for.

"Let's go," he repeated.

She ducked into the opening, grateful for the dim lighting, and walked two steps before she could straighten to her full height. About every ten feet there was a small dim light overhead. Like emergency lighting in a stairwell. He came in right behind her.

"Let's go," he ordered.

"I thought you were burning the place." If he set a fire, surely smoke would set off an alarm in her dad's workshop. There had to be ventilation.

"I'll do it after I have the money."

She got it now. He didn't care about destroying the evidence. He had just assumed the money would be here with the bones and ledgers, but it wasn't. He had searched the place while she studied the ledgers. The money is all he wanted.

"Fine."

She started forward. "Do you have any idea where this goes?"

"Nope, but I'll go back the way we came if you run into a booby trap."

Her heart skipped a beat. She hadn't even thought of that.

They walked onward. The tunnel was narrow and she was surprised his broad body didn't scrape the sides. The floor and walls looked like concrete, but she couldn't be sure. Finally, the tunnel ended at an iron ladder that led upward.

"Start climbing," he ordered. "When you get outside, if you run, I'll shoot you in the back. I'm not going to prison."

He was if she could do anything about it. "Okay."

Naomi steadied her breathing and reached for the ladder. She was halfway up when he said, "Don't forget I'm right behind you."

She reached the top of the ladder and the exit appeared to be one of those round hatch openings like the ones in submarines—at least in the movies. She had to grab hold with both hands and twist with all her might to open it. When the lock released, she pushed the hatch upward as she climbed the last few rungs.

The opening was narrow. If she was lucky, he'd get stuck.

Looking around, she took her time climbing out. She needed to get her bearings before his head was out of the opening.

Woods. Had to be only a short distance from the house. They hadn't walked that far. She climbed out, pulled herself up onto the ground.

All she had to do was run.

A strong hand clamped around her ankle and jerked.

She hit the ground face-first.

Lawton was out of the hole and towering over her with his gun before she could scramble up. "If you scream, I will shoot. If you run, I will shoot," he growled as if he'd been reading her mind all along.

She eased into a sitting position and stared up at him. "So, shoot."

He grabbed her by the arm.

She grabbed the weapon with both hands.

Chapter Fifteen

Tanner's missing deputy had been slugged from behind, secured in the trunk of his cruiser and left on a side road less than a mile from the Honea farm.

Casey found no relief in his statement of events. Lawton had arrived and told him there was a problem at the barn. Halfway around the house Lawton had attacked. When Higgins had awakened he had been secured in the trunk of his own cruiser. Naomi had still been in the house at the time Lawton showed up, only minutes after Casey had left. Naomi had likely still been asleep.

Fury whipped through Casey. He and the others, including Wagner, had fanned out around the farmhouse and started the search. The barn, the lab and workshop, and the woods around the perimeter of the front and back yard had yielded nothing so far. Brannigan had ordered a team with dogs but it would be a bit before they arrived.

The cell phone Casey had borrowed from a deputy vibrated. *Tanner.* "Is the nurse here?" he asked the sheriff.

"My deputies just arrived with her. Two others stayed back to search her property. You want to question her, or do you want me to do it?"

Casey considered going back to the house, but he needed to be on the ground. "See what you can find out. I'll stick with the search."

With all the vehicles accounted for, unless someone picked Lawton and Naomi up, they had to be out here somewhere. If the sister had picked them up, hopefully they would soon know.

"I'll call you back as soon as I know anything."

Casey put the phone away and started walking again, deeper into the woods.

"Agent Duncan!"

The shout came from his left. Good distance away. He shouted a response and started in that direction.

"We've got something over here."

Casey found the two officers from Brannigan's department maybe a hundred yards from the workshop. They were huddled around something on the ground.

His gut clenched and his heart slammed against his sternum.

"It leads down a ladder into a tunnel," one of the officers said. "You want me to check it out."

"Call for backup first," Casey said. To the other officer, he ordered, "You come with me."

They started forward as the officer left at the tunnel opening called for backup.

"Which direction is the road?" Casey asked. If that was an emergency egress, there was no doubt a way to get away from the farm. A vehicle or something stashed nearby.

"This way, sir."

The urge to call out to Naomi was so strong he barely held it back. They couldn't take the risk. The element of surprise might be their only leverage at this point.

Casey and the deputy covered a good distance when a sound…a whisper or wheeze…stopped Casey in his tracks.

He held up his hand, then motioned with a finger to his mouth for the other man to stay quiet. The sound came again. A gasp or wheeze.

Fear, icy cold, rushed through Casey's veins.

Was Naomi injured?

He moved silently toward the sound. Gasp…whoosh… gasp.

The sound grew more frantic and louder as he neared a patch of thick undergrowth between two trees.

His weapon at the ready, he rounded the first of the two trees.

Lawton sat on the ground, leaning against the tree, service weapon in his hand. Red painted the front of his shirt, originating at a hole mid chest.

His shuddered with the violent gasps sawing in and out of his sagging mouth.

"Where is she?" Casey demanded as he took a step closer, his bead on the man's head.

Lawton stared wordlessly at him while attempting to raise his weapon.

Casey tensed. His finger curled around the trigger.

The hand grasping the weapon fell back to his thigh. The weapon slipped free of his grasp.

Casey collected the weapon and pitched it aside.

The officer who'd come with Casey rounded the clump of trees and underbrush.

"Call Tanner," Casey ordered. "Then, if this bastard tells us where Naomi is, call an ambulance. If he doesn't, just leave him here to die."

While the officer called Tanner, Casey started walking away.

A frantic attempt at a howl echoed behind him. He turned around and Lawton managed to raise his left arm and point into the woods on his right.

Casey nodded at the officer to call for an ambulance, then he lunged in the direction Lawton had pointed. He called Naomi's name. He raced through the woods, dodging trees, shouting her name at the top of his lungs.

His own name echoed back to him. It was a distant cry. An anguished cry. But it was her and she was alive.

He rushed toward her voice.

She raced right up to him and threw her arms around him. "He was going to kill me."

"You're okay now." He set her back. "Are you injured?"

She shook her head. "I'm okay." She glanced beyond him. "Is he still alive?"

"Barely."

"We struggled. The gun went off, he staggered back and I ran." She blinked repeatedly to staunch the flow of tears, her words coming in a rush. "I just kept running even after I realized he wasn't chasing me anymore. I was so hysterical I couldn't remember the way to the road. I think I've been running in circles."

He hugged her close to his chest. "It's over now."

She drew back, stared up at him. "His sister. She poisoned my mom and caused my dad's heart attack." The tears turned to a river now.

"Come on." He pulled her close and started back toward the house. "We'll make sure they don't get away with what they've done."

"My parents never knew," she said. "They didn't do anything wrong."

He tightened his arm around her shoulders. "I don't think anyone ever believed they did."

"I know where the bones are now," she mumbled against his chest. "There's a bone room. Under my dad's workshop."

This was going to take a long time to sort out.

Casey wasn't leaving until it was done.

"NAOMI."

She was pretty sure she was dreaming. In this dream she could hear his voice. Casey's voice. It was about the sexiest voice she'd ever heard.

"Naomi."

A hand touched her shoulder, gave it a little shake.

Her eyes opened and she sat straight up.

It took a moment for her mind to orient itself. Sheriff Tanner's office. Sofa. She'd fallen asleep in the sheriff's office.

Casey smiled and sat down beside her. "Hey."

She leaned into his warm body. "Hey."

The case was solved, and he would be leaving. Maybe tonight. She wasn't ready. At all.

She looked around the room for a clock. "What time is it?"

Where was her cell phone? Oh, yeah, in that underground bunker bone room. She shivered.

"Midnight," he told her. "I came to tell you it's okay to leave now."

She could leave? It really was done. She could not go back to the farm. Not right now. Maybe not ever. The idea of what those people had done to her family…the reality that if she had been there instead of chasing a dream in California…

"I can't go to the farm." She barely got the words out without bursting into tears again. She'd cried so much already her eyes were raw from it.

"I was thinking about a place where you'd feel more comfortable and where the reporters won't think to look."

She stared up at him then. Even as exhausted as she knew he was—not to mention his near-death experience in that pit—he looked amazing. "Where?"

"I'll be able to confirm that any minute now."

"Okay." God, she was confused. "This is way too crazy for a movie or a book. No one would ever believe it."

"I think you might be right." His arm went around her.

She snuggled into his side. Arlene—Anna, whatever—killed her own mother. Of course she hadn't thought twice about killing Naomi's parents.

Sarah Holland—aka Juanita Tripp—claimed in her statement that Arlene had bragged about learning everything her mother knew and then getting rid of her. Her only mistake, she'd said later, was in not killing her little brother at the time. He'd only been a kid. She hadn't expected him to remember that Nazi hunters hadn't been the ones to kill their mother. She certainly hadn't expected that he would one day find her again and try to get close. Once he confirmed that she was doing the same heinous things their mother had done, he'd killed her and then himself.

If that wasn't weird enough, there was Deputy Lawton and his sister—who was really his wife. The people in the pit—the ones whose identities Lawton and Holland had stolen—were just innocent victims who fit the profile of what the depraved couple were looking for.

Tripp had needed a nurse identity in order to get close to Naomi's mom so she picked Sarah Holland. Holland had no children. No husband and no close family. She was easy to become. Lawton was a little more complicated. He was a cop in Mobile, Alabama. But like Holland, he had no close family or friends. A loner. Easy for Richard Tripp to become him. Claim he had to suddenly move up to Tennessee for a sick relative, eventually getting a position with the sheriff's department. His background checked out. It was easier back then to change personnel files. Not like now in this electronic-driven world.

"But this is your story to tell," he offered. "You might be surprised and end up with a book deal and a movie deal."

Could she? "This is Winchester, Tennessee," she argued. "How does something like this happen in such a small town?"

"It's the perfect place to disappear," Casey said. "It's small, quiet. Not much happens in the way of crime. So, nobody looks too closely."

He reached into his pocket and retrieved his cell. "We are confirmed."

"Confirmed?"

He stood and offered his hand. "We are the guests of Sheriff Tanner and Chief Brannigan at the Falls Mill Bed and Breakfast."

"Really?" She'd only been there once on a tour. Years ago. But she remembered that it was charming and tucked away from the world.

"You game?"

She accepted his hand and moved up beside him. "Are you my bodyguard for the night?" She really, really wanted to believe this part was not about work. The investigation was done for the most part. But that only meant that he would be going back to Nashville. Her chest hurt just thinking about it.

"I was considering making an offer to guard your body for the foreseeable future." He shrugged. "As long as you need or want me. Especially if you end up starring in your movie."

A smile stretched across her mouth. "I guess that kiss sealed our fate. The one the other night, I mean."

He cupped her cheek and smiled back at her. "I'm fairly certain the one from when we were kids did the trick. I've never wanted anyone the way I want you."

"Well, Agent Duncan—" she tucked her arm in his and turned him toward the door "—I think we should explore these wanton desires you have and see where they take us." She paused at the door and looked straight into his eyes. "All we have to do is be brave enough to jump."

* * * * *

Available at

weloveromance.com